The Reckoning

A Tom Keeler Thriller

Jack Lively

Chapter One

TUESDAY

Laura's hand rested on the horse's neck. The muscle beneath pulsated with blood and power. The autumn air was crisp against her skin. She loved it. The animal surged forward up the slight incline, like an engine. They'd ridden together fifteen times within a couple of months. It wasn't her horse, but they had a genuine bond.

She leaned forward, running her hand over the horse's neck, feeling her fingers enter the mane and gently tugging. Laura put her cheek against the warm animal flesh, enraptured by the connection. She felt the beast respond. The horse's eye, light and glossy, was alive.

Laura said, "Good girl. You're a good girl."

They came over the rise. A rail fence line was on the right. The wood beyond broke into residential houses and agricultural buildings. She'd seen no one actually outside. Beyond the fence, near a large farm building, figures appeared.

The horse veered right. Laura tightened her legs, guiding the animal to center. She saw the people, and what was happening. A shockwave traveled her body, from pelvis to head. It was a young woman, with long black hair askew. A powerfully built man stood behind, his hand deep in her hair. The man was dragging her away from the fence, pulling her by the hair. The woman had her hands up, desperately grabbing onto his wrist, trying to mitigate the damage.

The woman shrieked.

Laura sat deeper into the saddle. She pressed her weight down and closed her fingers on the reins, applying a steady backward pressure. She leaned down again, squeezed her thighs and relaxed her lower legs.

"Whoa. Easy."

She pulled gently on the right rein.

It wasn't just the woman being dragged by this guy. The others by the building just stood and watched. The woman screamed again and flailed. She was facing Laura and they made eye contact.

Laura brought the horse up to the fence.

She said, "Let her go."

The man pulled the woman tight toward him. He looked at Laura with great indifference, then back at the young woman he abused. He was holding her against his chest and doing some kind of whispered shout into her ear. The girl was helpless in his grip. She had Hispanic features and was very pregnant.

"What the fuck?" Laura raised her voice. "Let her go. Now!"

The man pushed the pregnant woman down, releasing her. She fell to her knees, the long straight black hair cascading over a flushed face.

The man said, "Get back inside."

Laura dismounted, releasing the reins.

The man had a massive build. He was also Hispanic upon closer inspection. He glanced at Laura.

"This is private property." He spoke with a clear American accent.

Laura said, "What the hell is going on here?"

The big man was at the fence. "Move along, lady. This isn't your business."

Two more men stood near the building. They were both corralling the onlooking women inside. The weird thing too, those women had their eyes cast downwards. Laura watched, mesmerized, as the women turned uniformly, heads bowed and submitting to single word commands. They entered the building. Each of these women, like the first, was Hispanic.

The man had his forearms resting on the wooden fence rail, leaning his weight on it with a cocked hip, like a cowboy. He gave Laura the most indifferent and surly look she'd ever seen on a man. The face was a blank slab of masculinity, wispy beard and mustache. Like he was sizing her up as some kind of bestial property. It filled her with a rush of anger.

For a moment, Laura stalled. She felt suddenly alone and clueless. What she'd just seen demanded attention. But then again, what do you do? The women were all inside now. She found herself alone with the man. What the fuck was going on in that place? Two things happened simultaneously at that point. The man realized Laura was armed, and Laura decided to change the situation.

His eyes drifted to the pistol holstered at her hip. The event Laura had witnessed raised questions. That solidified her resolve.

She pulled the pistol from its holster and aimed it at the ground between them.

Laura said, "I'm coming over the fence. Move back."

The man recoiled, raising his hands.

He said, "Don't come over the fence, lady. I just had an argument with my girl, is all."

Laura switched the pistol to her left hand, placing her right hand atop the fence. She stepped up, then swung her leg over the middle rail.

"Move the fuck back, asshole. I'm going to talk to her."

The man took a small step back. When she came over the fence, he scooted closer and Laura found herself only about eight feet away from him. With the fence behind her, she couldn't create more distance, instantly feeling in danger. She got both hands on her gun and aimed it at him below the waist. She was a skilled shot, sure she could hit his thigh if needed—but she'd never drawn on a person before.

"If you don't move back, I'm going to have to shoot you."

Laura's brother had convinced her that if you're going to carry, do so with a round chambered. She practiced and maintained good trigger discipline. Right then, she was simply glad that she'd followed his advice.

The man said, "This is private property. You're trespassing, lady." His face exuded aggression. "You're in danger."

Then Laura spotted them—the two other men from before, circling from opposite sides. She backed into the fence.

One man called out to her. "Whoa there. Stay where you are."

The man in front of her said, "Where do you think you're going, lady?"

The horse whinnied behind her.

He used that as a distraction and took a fast step toward her, hand up and grabbing at her weapon. Laura wasn't taken by the move. She anticipated just in time, sidestepping his lunge and kicking the man's knee with a riding boot. The guy stumbled, giving her enough time to duck back through the fence.

But it wasn't quite enough time to reach the other side. His hand closed around her right wrist, tugging hard at her and almost wrenching the arm out of its socket. The violent movement made Laura's head bang against the top fence rail. She felt a sudden weakness, knowing in that moment that the guy would disarm her within the next few seconds.

The other two were closer now. She saw them as a blurry image. Men moved steadily towards her. Their facial expressions appeared to Laura as a sort of spinning composite.

Her vision cleared. She shook off the blow to the head.

The man was on her again, grabbing at her. Laura brought the gun around and pushed it into his chest. She fired point blank. He fell back, releasing the grip, and Laura pulled herself out of the fence. The others stopped in their tracks. She saw them hesitating, looking at their friend and thinking about what to do. The friend wasn't doing well. In fact, he wasn't doing much of anything at all. The man lay motionless in the grass.

Laura turned for the horse. She pushed the gun into the open saddle bag and swung up into the saddle. Taking the reins, she squeezed her calves and clicked her tongue. In ten seconds, she was galloping over the hill. Riding hard toward the woods and a way out.

* * *

Back at the stables, Laura dismounted, feeling woozy. Her hands were shaking. It occurred to her she might faint, so she sunk into a shallow squat and started breathing carefully. This helped to get her head straight. It hadn't been an especially muddy or dusty ride, but she felt dirty and sweaty herself.

She hosed the animal down and got out the soapy water and pail. She scrubbed the horse enthusiastically, taking extra care to get into the hidden folds of animal flesh. She went at it with the hoof pick, prying out dirt that had hardened with time.

Later, she rested on a stool, leaning against the barn. The shakes were gone. The sun sank low. The glare was sharp. The man's face ghosted in her sight. She saw him over the fence, dragging that pregnant woman across the dirt. The way she struggled and the guy's expression...Simply mean determination and something worse, like he was dealing with an animal, not a fellow person.

Then Laura got a hit of his smell, like an olfactory hallucination. The man was up close and aggressive. Then, the feeling of putting the gun into him and pulling the trigger for real. So, what was going to happen next?

Laura brought out her phone and started composing an email to her brother.

Chapter Two

FRIDAY

Tom Keeler hadn't eaten in three days. He'd been walking through mountainous desert for two of them. Then he'd caught a bus and had slept for 24 hours straight. Now, he'd made it to a diner.

Breakfast came sliding across the counter. Two eggs over easy with a side of bacon. Hash browns well done, two slices of buttered rye toast. He looked briefly at the grill man, watching him in the stainless steel backsplash. Keeler gave a curt nod, receiving a return nod as the grill man settled into his next project. Keeler put his head down and went in with the knife and fork. The game was over within a few minutes. The plate was clean, just like his French mother had liked it.

At which point he looked at the reflection in the backsplash again, checking on anomalies he'd noticed walking in. The out-of-place couple in the corner booth, and the solo eater at a deuce by the window.

The well-dressed couple in the corner were engaged with

handheld devices. Both had a coffee cup in front of them. Keeler ticked them off like a checklist. Done.

The solo eater wasn't alone anymore. A waitress hovered over him—though not like a waitress should. Keeler couldn't hear the conversation because she was whispering, but it was a shouty kind of whisper, not the gentle kind. And it wasn't a conversation, because she was the only one speaking. It was more of a scolding.

The man still hadn't touched the once steaming pile of eggs and sausage on his plate. The waitress moved away and with it, the man's attention shifted to the window, his gaze fixed at some point toward the parking lot in front of the diner. Beyond that was Route 60. Two double lanes divided by a median strip. Motels, stores, and franchise restaurants on either side.

The solo eater was in his early sixties. A stringy guy with no apparent body fat, wearing a baseball cap with a fabric front and mesh back. An old and well-worn cap, with a Purina Chow logo on the badge. The man looked like a farmer, and this was Ohio.

That turned Keeler's attention to the parking lot. He swiveled on the stool to see. A dozen regular cars, two expensive cars, and a Ford F-150 from yonder years. A good-looking truck, cream with sky blue and brown stripes.

"Refill?"

Keeler swiveled back. The waitress stood on the other side of the counter holding a glass coffeepot. He racked focus to his own mug and saw that it was empty.

"Don't mind if I do."

She filled the mug. Tall and maybe thirty-five years old. Red lipstick, subtle eye liner, and natural red hair in twin braids running down her shoulders. The uniform was green and white checkers, and hers fit well. She didn't seem exactly afraid of him, but there was some kind of edge there. She was alert to him, put it that way. Like he was to her.

Keeler broke the ice. "You do those braids yourself?"

"No sir, my daughter's the expert in the house."

A clear message, received.

Keeler felt the waitress's assessing gaze, a silent judgment.

He said, "What?"

"What, what?"

"You were thinking about something."

She said, "A mind reader, huh?"

"If you say so."

She pointed at his clean plate. "I just saw you totally inhale breakfast in maybe thirty seconds. I'm assuming your uh, situational awareness keeps ticking even while feeding. Right?"

Keeler said, "It does."

The waitress looked past Keeler to the seating area.

She said, "Tell me what sticks out here. What's the situation?"

He said, "Besides you scolding that guy behind me?"

"Yeah, besides that."

"Besides that, it's another Friday morning in Trace Junction, Ohio. Except for the couple in the corner. They don't look very Ohio to me. More like Chicago, LA, or New York. And if I were to choose, I'd say New York."

She raised her eyebrows. "And what makes you say that?"

"Couple of things. Clothes, the hair."

The waitress examined the couple, looking over Keeler's shoulder. "The haircut. What about it specifically?"

"The fade up from the back of the neck. It's a thing up in New York."

The waitress said, "What else?"

"His wife, obviously. The way she uses her phone. She's not doomscrolling, she's working."

"What's her profession?"

"Lawyer."

The waitress giggled. "Not bad, mister. We get those kinds of people pretty often and we have a term for them. *Thoroughbreds*. Those are two classic Thoroughbreds waiting for Donald's Donuts to open. Which is why they haven't ordered a full breakfast yet." She chin pointed out the window to the side parking lot. "Check out their limo driver. It's always the same. Got a fleet of maybe three cars."

Keeler swiveled on the stool and took in the side parking lot, visible past the couple in the corner seat. Indeed, a suited man leaning back against the hood of his car smoking a cigarette. He spun back to the waitress.

Keeler said, "Thoroughbreds, huh? Like the horses."

"That's what they're in town for, yes." She smiled again. "So, if your guy's from New York, I'd guess they've got a place up in the Catskills or whatnot, just for the horses." Her eyes moved up and past him. Her expression hardened. "Excuse me."

Keeler tracked the waitress in the mirrored steel. She returned to the solo eater. He watched as they engaged in another furiously whispered argument. The waitress was bent over the man in the Purina Chow hat, doing the furious whispering again, while the poor old guy simply had his head down in supplication. She picked up the man's plate, still full of an untouched breakfast.

The man said nothing in return. He watched her take it.

Keeler now saw the waitress walking calmly back. She deposited the plate into the bussing bin by the kitchen entrance and stood there, wiping her hands with a cloth. She caught Keeler's eye and held it momentarily before briefly closing her eyes and then sort of resetting.

When she backed through the double doors to the kitchen, the man at the deuce was already walking out. Keeler swiveled on the stool and watched through the big window, expecting him to go right to the truck, but that didn't happen.

The man walked past the truck and ran a hand along the edge of the pickup's bed. He stepped over the curb and began to dodge and weave his way across the busy road. For a moment Keeler thought it was a suicidal move, but it wasn't. The man reached a low building opposite. The sign out front was at the wrong angle and Keeler couldn't read it.

He swiveled back to the counter. The waitress was there again, organizing the pots of jelly and honey.

He said, "What's across the street?"

She looked up. "Right opposite us?"

"Yeah."

She said, "That's Donald's Delicious Donuts."

"Good?"

She pointed at Keeler's empty plate, literally clean. Her lips parted, showing small white teeth. "Healthy appetite."

"Mmm hmm."

"Wanna settle up?"

"Yes please."

Chapter Three

Donald's Delicious Donuts. A mug of hot coffee was already in front of the man with the Purina Chow hat. Keeler sat three stools from a man reading a newspaper, holding what appeared to be a French cruller. A fluted and fried pastry shaped into a rough ring, coated with something sticky and sweet.

The donut man approached. White apron over a white t-shirt and white pants. The baker's hat set back on a shock of white hair. A professional.

"Coffee?"

Keeler nodded. "I'll take one of those French crullers, plus another of whatever's freshest back there." Indicating the wall of baskets where donuts cooled and waited to be selected for consumption.

The donut man said, "We've got forty varieties of donut, my friend. Why don't you take a little gander and let me know what strikes your fancy?"

Keeler faced the man wearing a Purina Chow hat. "What do you recommend, buddy? I'm lost here."

Watery blue eyes looked upward. He registered Keeler and

the question. His lips made a smacking sound as they parted. "I'm always partial to a Maple Long John. If you opt for a French cruller and seek a companion, consider a classic choice such as a chocolate frosted."

The donut man inclined his head with lifted eyebrows, like he approved.

Keeler said, "Chocolate frosted please."

The man in the Purina Chow hat was nodding to himself idly, watching Keeler now. He apparently hadn't noticed Keeler in the diner, presumably preoccupied with his own problems.

The donut man slid a small white plate laden with a single French cruller across the counter, joining the coffee mug that Keeler had already taken down by half. The donut had a well-defined shape, almost bronze, with a sheen from its sugary glaze. Keeler lifted it and bit. Teeth crunched through an exterior shell. His tongue made contact with a texture like sponge cake.

Outstanding.

Keeler looked up. The donut maker and the man wearing a Purina Chow hat observed him. He nodded. "Unbelievable."

The man wearing a Purina Chow hat looked from the donut shop to the parking lot, seen through the window. His features had crumpled and the ruddy coloring had turned pale. Keeler followed his gaze.

A red pickup truck was nosing in to park facing them, just outside the window. Two men were visible to him in the cab. Both wore sunglasses. The reflection on the windshield made it tough to see more.

Keeler said, "Friends of yours?"

The man in the Purina Chow hat said, "Not exactly."

The donut man said, "You want me to call Cheryl?"

The man in the Purina Chow hat stood up, lifting a remaining corner of his French cruller and popping it into his mouth. He chewed five times and took a final slug of coffee before swallowing. He lifted a napkin to his mouth and took a single swipe across the lips. Looking up at the donut man. "That's ok Pete, thanks."

Keeler studied the chocolate frosted donut on his plate. A classic shape, with a thick smudge of chocolate covering roughly half the surface area. The man in the Purina Chow hat moved to the door in a gallows walk. The donut man, Pete, watched him open the door and exit the establishment.

Keeler said, "What's going on here, Pete?"

Pete kept his eyes on the man outside, moving now towards the waiting pickup truck. He said, "Earl's got issues with those people. I guess it's a debt that he owes is all."

Pete seemed unsure.

Keeler bit off a quarter of the chocolate frosted donut. "Maybe Earl needs backup, Pete."

"Bad idea. That'd only make it worse for him, believe me." Pete was watching Earl. He said, "Bad for him and bad for us too." Glancing back at Keeler. "A guy pays you a vig you'd be foolish to kill him. So, I guess Earl will come out alright. Know what I mean, pal?"

Keeler said, "Sure, you kill the guy who owes you interest, there goes your income stream. Unless the guy can't pay you any more. Then you kill him as an example to the others who owe you the vig."

"Earl's just behind is all. Nobody's getting killed today."

Keeler said, "Who's Cheryl?"

"The Sheriff." Pete was leaning back against the counter. Sipping from a Donald's Donuts mug.

Keeler said, "And would Cheryl just show up and intervene if you called her?"

Pete sipped coffee. It wasn't a question requiring an answer. There was no reason to involve the law.

Keeler understood it then. The question, *do you want me to call Cheryl,* was a token show of support. Like asking a drowning guy if he needed a glass of water.

* * *

They watched as Earl arrived at the pickup truck. His body language was submissive, approaching the truck and speaking. The picture window prevented them from hearing what he said, but the lips moved. One of Earl's hands had secured a white envelope from the inside of his jacket. A hand fluttered the envelope, as though conjuring a magic trick. A thick hand at the end of a muscled arm emerged from the passenger window, beckoning. Earl took a few hesitant steps. The arm beckoned further and Keeler was thinking, *don't do it Earl.* The arm retreated into the truck as Earl came closer. Earl speaking and the man in the passenger seat nodding at him. Earl moved closer; Keeler judged him within striking distance.

The arm lashed out, a fist taking hold of Earl's ear and wrenching his head in through the window.

Keeler looked at Pete, who stood rooted in place, agog at the violent spectacle.

Earl had a hand pressed against the pickup truck's door frame, trying to remove himself from the trap. It was hard to say exactly what was going on with Earl's head in the cab. Hopefully, nothing too damaging.

Pete said, "Scumbags."

The passenger door of the pickup truck opened and a bearded man stepped out. He wore sunglasses, but his gaze was directed through the large window at Keeler and Pete, the donut man.

Keeler said, "Oh hello."

Pete said, "Say nothing. Shit. Maybe they heard me just now."

Pete's comment seemed odd. Paranoia was often justified. Believing that the walls had ears was stretching it a bit too much.

There was a flurry of activity inside the cab. Earl's body twitching and struggling. Keeler took another bite of the chocolate frosted donut, reminding himself to pay attention. The frosting was milk chocolate. The donut itself was soft and chewy inside, unlike the cake-like consistency of the French cruller. Earl had been right. Chocolate frosted was a good choice.

The sunglass-wearing man approached the window, peering inside. Keeler sipped coffee, watching Pete look terrified. The donut man busied himself cleaning a mug with a rag.

The door opened. The man stood there at the threshold, not actually entering.

He said, "How you doing, Pete?"

Pete said, "Oh yeah, can't complain."

"Yeah then don't. I need a half dozen chocolate frosted with the sprinkles."

"Chocolate sprinkles, or the multi-colors?"

"Let's do half half."

Pete got busy. Keeler watched the man. Earl's head was being abused inside of the truck. His thin body shivering with tension. Keeler was on the fence about intervention. He didn't want to make a bad situation worse. If Earl had gotten himself into debt, that was one thing. You can't fix the entire world. And what Pete had said made sense. Intervention could end up worse for Earl.

Pete extended a bag of donuts to the man at the door, who didn't even deign to enter, forcing the donut man to come all the way around and give it to him where he stood. There was no money exchanged. The guy was looking at Keeler.

He said, "What're you looking at?"

Keeler said, "You."

"Excuse me?" The guy standing there staring at him.

The donuts were served on a white plate with a folded paper napkin and a fork. The fingers of Keeler's right hand manipulated the fork so that it was palmed. He stood up, left hand holding the coffee cup.

Keeler approached the man at the door. "I was looking at you is all." He smiled. "Why, you don't think you're good looking enough?"

The man remained motionless. He just looked directly at Keeler. Pete was mouth breathing, almost huffing like an emphysema patient. Keeler had to glance at him to make sure he was alright. They made eye contact, and Keeler winked.

He looked back at the bully with his sack of donuts.

The man said, "Fucking faggot," and turned away.

Keeler stood, tracking him as he slowly sauntered to the truck, past the struggling older man and back to his place on the passenger side. He was thinking about the fork in his hand. Keeler realized that he really would have put it into the guy's eye if he hadn't gone back to the truck.

Pete said, "Shit man, you nearly gave me a heart attack. They might actually burn my place down now. You think of that before you got up off that stool?"

Keeler said, "No."

"You're new in town."

"Just got in."

Pete let out a long exhalation. "So, you can't have known. It's a kind of systemic problem we've had here for the last couple of years."

Earl's head came free of the pickup truck's window, now hatless. His thinning gray hair was stringy and disheveled from the roughing up he'd had. The white envelope, now empty and crumpled, hit him in the chest.

The truck reversed. Keeler examined the passenger. Aviator sunglasses set into an enormous head. A dark goatee was stuck on the man's face. He flipped Earl's Purina Chow hat out the window, the thing sailing in a spinning arc to the asphalt, dirt, and gravel.

Earl bent to pick up his hat and dusted it off. Although humiliated, he was alive and had full use of his limbs. Keeler went back to his seat at the counter. He popped the remaining wedge of donut into his mouth.

Chapter Four

As Earl returned through the front door of Donald's Delicious Donuts, both Keeler and Pete studiously ignored him, allowing the man a little space after his ordeal. Pete was back by the donut rack, picking out another donut and putting it on another small white plate. He came over to Keeler.

"Apple fritter. Fresh and hot. On the house. You'll like this one, champ."

Keeler was still chewing the remnants of the chocolate frosted. He was ready for more and mumbled in appreciation. Earl took his seat and set the Purina Chow cap back on his head.

Pete fetched the coffee pot and poured refills all around.

Keeler waited for the ritual to end and lifted his mug. The ceramic receptacle had heft and weight, white with a Donald's Donuts logo in red lettering. He took a sip of the hot brew. Earl was quiet, delivering a final piece of donut to his mouth with a thumb and forefinger.

Keeler said, "You alright there, buddy?"

Earl nodded without making eye contact. He sipped at his coffee and put the forefinger to the empty white plate in front of him, snagging a donut crumb and lifting it to his mouth. Keeler studied him surreptitiously. Earl had missed a couple of spots shaving, beneath the lower lip and up on his cheekbone. The man's face was splotched with red marks where he'd been abused by the guys in the truck who had literally captured his head and had their way with it.

Keeler recalled what Pete had said. Something curious, when the passenger had come down from the truck and approached the restaurant. He'd been looking in the window and Pete had been scared, saying something like, *maybe they heard me just now.*

What had they potentially heard and how could they possibly hear it?

Pete had called them scumbags. That was what he'd said.

Keeler lifted the apple fritter from its position on the new white plate. The new object was heavy with promise, literally. It was a fried donut like the cruller, but much larger and presumably contained apple. He bit into it, letting the teeth sink in. There was the now familiar crunch, followed by the smooth plunge into a doughy center. Pieces of soft apple hit the tongue, cool and sweet. A great donut.

Earl said, "Well, I'm alive, and they didn't break no arms or legs." He looked up then and made eye contact. "So yeah, all good. Thanks."

Keeler looked into Earl's pale blue eyes. Had they broken an arm or a leg previously? He saw a core of strength in Earl's gaze, but the man was clearly overwhelmed and over-matched. Guy his age, up against a couple of young guns with more natural physical strength and less fear.

Pete was coming out from the back now, carrying a new tray of fresh donuts. "Why did the scarecrow win an award?"

Earl said, "Because he was outstanding in his field." He

dropped his eyes to the counter. His plate had been cleared away while he'd taken the beating.

Pete laughed. "Heard that one before I guess."

"Only about half a million times, Pete."

Pete nodded. "Yeah." He examined Keeler. "Well, you don't look like either a farmer or an insurance broker, nor a salesman, at least not a good salesman. But you were ready and willing to assist young Earl here, so that's a good thing in my book."

Earl said, "I don't need assistance, thanks."

Pete said, "So what's your story friend?" Chin pointing at Keeler.

Keeler had taken a substantial chunk of the apple fritter. He held up a hand while chewing on it.

Pete said, "Take your time. We don't want you choking out here."

Keeler nodded, finishing the bite. "Thanks." He said, "I'm here to see my sister." He pulled out a folded piece of paper from his jeans pocket. "Maybe you guys can help me find her place. I don't have a *whatchamacallit*, a smart phone." He read the hastily penciled address from the slip of paper. "6315 Wildsong way."

"Wildsong way. Never heard of it." Pete's face had formed into a question mark, eyebrows knitted together with his mouth pursed.

Earl said, "It's Windsong, not Wildsong. Out by Licking Township. You might have made an error in writing the address down."

Keeler looked at his scrawl. "Yeah, that's highly likely. I guess I can get a bus out there."

Earl said, "You come into town on a Greyhound?"

"That's right."

"Bus is across the road." Pointing towards the diner.

"Number 57. You can catch it every half hour or so. Schedule's up on the bus stop."

Pete said, "Lakeland Hills area." He said, "She lives out there you'd maybe expect her to come pick you up at the bus station."

Keeler said, "Well, I didn't coordinate my arrival with her. Wasn't sure when I'd get in." He looked up for comprehension. "Know what I mean?"

Pete said, "Means she don't know you're coming."

Keeler shrugged. "Correct. No promises, no regrets."

Earl said, "Yeah, I get that, high plains drifter with no schedule type of shit. You start farming boy and you'll be put on a schedule by Mother Earth pretty quick."

Keeler said, "Exactly why I'm not a farmer."

Pete was looking past both Earl and Keeler now, distracted. He said, "Shit."

Earl looked up at him, then turned around on his stool. "Here they come."

Keeler swiveled and saw the couple who had been in the corner booth at the diner. Picking their way across the road.

Pete said, "Last time I had a couple of thoroughbreds in here they told me I oughta do a mail service to Santa Fe, New Mexico."

Earl said, "You oughta talk to the people over at the airport. My cousin's working on the refurb. He says it's looking swank. You never know Pete, just might find a delivery service for them donuts."

Pete said, "Well, I've heard worse ideas. It's enough work running what I got here. You ever want to look into expanding my donut business to San Francisco, or New York Earl, you be my guest."

Earl chuckled. He said, "Well I'm out of here anyway.

Thanks for the donuts, Pete." He turned to Keeler. "Good to meet you."

Keeler said, "I'm leaving too."

* * *

The two New York thoroughbreds had to step through a wood chipped obstacle on their way over to the donut place. Neither of them looked as if the experience was enjoyable. Keeler and Earl were at the roadside, watching them come over. The woman picked high heels out of the dirt. Her husband had to deal with her leaning on him.

Keeler had an intuitive understanding for why they'd come over the road instead of driving around and parking at Donald's Donuts. Still, it didn't seem like a thing that outsiders would intuitively understand. Particularly if they had a limo driver waiting.

Keeler said, "Why do they walk over the road, Earl?"

Earl said, "Well, it's a double lane with that center island. U-turn's about a half mile down. So, if you're already at the diner, you just walk over. Saves you time."

"But how would they know that, if they're thoroughbreds?"

Earl eyed him. "You already heard about the phenomenon?"

"The waitress told me at the diner."

"Uh huh." Earl adjusted his cap. "Well, they do that because it's what they're told to do in the little guide book given to them when they come out here for their special horse."

"Gotcha."

"Plus, you see that limo there?" Pointing at the buff looking SUV Keeler had seen earlier, with the driver leaning against it smoking.

"Yeah."

"Well, that guy gets to go into the diner and have his breakfast, while the two thoroughbreds get donuts." Earl grinned. "That's what you call a smooth system."

Keeler said, "Well, I'll take your word for it, Earl."

Earl was eyeing him, face was still splotchy from the beating he'd taken.

He said, "I doubt it's true thoroughbred horses attracting these people to Trace Junction. More like Warmbloods or Andalusians I'd imagine. Expensive enough of course. Never did hear of no Amish breeding actual thoroughbreds."

Keeler didn't know the first thing about horses. He followed Earl over the road. The bus stop wasn't exactly in front of the diner. It was maybe 50 yards to the left, a direction that Keeler registered intuitively as northeast.

Keeler said, "You okay Earl?"

The watery blue eyes looked back at him, red rimmed. Earl's eyebrows were ginger and white.

"Yeah, I'm alright, thanks."

"You in trouble with those people?"

Pete had said it was a debt, but Keeler would let Earl dictate the information he was comfortable divulging.

Earl said, "It's a relationship." He went for a smile. "Not ideal, but it's the one I've got."

Which meant he didn't want to talk about it.

Keeler nodded. "Thanks for the donut recommendations, Earl, they were right on target."

Earl chin pointed behind Keeler. "That bus'll take you right on up to Licking Township. Tell the driver where you're going to and he'll let you off at the right stop."

"Will do."

Earl nodded and turned, walking back over the grassy divider, stepping up on the curb and coming down to the blacktop parking lot. The F-150 truck was clean and tidy. Just looking at it you'd know that the engine would be equally well maintained.

But, Earl walked right past the truck and unlocked the driver's side door of a dilapidated white Honda Accord. The vehicle started with a puff of exhaust, engine whining loudly. Keeler watched Earl drive that thing out of the lot and make a left onto route 60, disappearing into the stream of morning traffic.

Chapter Five

The bus was scheduled to come every half hour, like Earl had said. Keeler didn't have a watch or a phone on him, but he did have a very good sense of time. Probably only ten minutes to wait. He'd come into town at around five in the morning. The walk up to the diner, the wait, the food, the donuts. All of that had most likely consumed a few hours.

Which meant that the time would be coming up on seven a.m.

The bus stop had no shelter, but it did have a bench. Keeler didn't feel like sitting down though. The breakfast and donut experience had been a little too static. He bounced on his toes and examined the world around him.

Cars came by on Route Sixty. Some kind of office building stood just behind the bus stop. The diner was to the southwest. Donald's Donuts lay across the road, with other buildings on either side of it. A barbecue joint had a huge sign advertising beer.

The waitress exited the diner. She had a jacket on now, presumably getting off the night shift. She had her head down, fishing in her purse for the keys no doubt. The bus came just then and Keeler got on. He had words with the driver. When he'd mentioned Windsong Way, the driver licked his lips. "What number?"

"6315."

"Up in the six thousands." A nod of recognition. "That should be Lakeland Hills. I'll let you know."

As Keeler walked back to find a seat, he saw the waitress through the rear window, unlocking the driver's side door of that beautiful Ford F-150. He had to stoop to see her through the bus's rear window. She climbed into the cab and closed the door. Sunlight glinted off her thickly braided red hair. The bus turned a corner, and that was it, she was gone.

A bus in a place like Trace Junction, Ohio, wasn't any kind of rich person's transport. It was populated with people who either couldn't drive or couldn't afford a car. Which meant laborers from south of the border mostly, both male and female.

Going to work.

With exceptions of course, like the large African American woman in front wearing sunglasses and staring straight ahead. Possibly blind. Where would she be going?

Work, possibly, or church.

And the cluster of teenagers, barely into their adolescence and too young to drive.

School.

A half hour later they weren't in Trace Junction anymore. The bus avoided the highway and stuck to smaller roads, looping around the hills north of town. Eventually the driver pulled it over to a remote stop at the foot of a closely cropped grassy hillside.

He was looking at Keeler in the big mirror. "This is you buddy."

Six minutes later, Keeler was hiking up Windsong Way. Number 6315 was like every other dwelling in the neighborhood, a single-story ranch house set back in a huge lawn. The density of residential structures here was sparse, more than comfortable. It was definitely not city living. The scent of two-stroke fuel and freshly cut grass was strong, accompanied by the noise of a motor.

Currently coming from out back, behind the house.

In the driveway sat a newish KIA, painted in muted green. Keeler brushed a hand over the engine hood, as a matter of habit. The KIA's chassis was cool to the touch. Which didn't mean much, Keeler had to remind himself. It could be a hybrid vehicle which hadn't needed to burn any petroleum product if the battery was charged.

The garage door was open, revealing a vehicular-sized cavity occupied by the shape of a low-slung car, currently covered by a beige tarp. That would be Laura's Corvette Stingray, a model from the mid 1960s. The car was old enough that it often required maintenance. It had been an inheritance from their father.

Keeler hadn't seen his younger sister Laura in three years. Seeing her car there under the tarp triggered something that he usually kept far to the back of his mind. A rush of emotion went through him like a wave and he missed her. Three years was long. Laura was only two years younger, so they'd been both siblings and friends. For most of their adolescence he and Laura had been a tight unit. The family had moved around constantly, following their mother from one geo-physics project to another, all across the regions of America where oil and gas could be found.

Then, Keeler had joined the military, and the bond had been broken.

He'd become a professional soldier, while Laura moved into the humanitarian field. In a way, he knew that she'd sort of followed him. Not directly, because the humanitarian work and military work were supposed to be completely different. Some people probably thought that they were opposite in nature, but Keeler knew that was bullshit.

He and Laura had ended up seeing each other in Iraq. She was working for a British-based humanitarian NGO in the south of the country, providing prosthetic limbs for kids who'd gotten too close to a mine or a cluster bomb. Keeler had been deployed at that time and it hadn't been easy to get down there and meet up with her.

In the end the reunion had only lasted a couple of hours.

That had been at Shaibah Logistics Base, a sprawling camp outside of Basra run by the British. Keeler remembered sitting outside at a round table, sweating in a hundred and twenty degrees over pizza and non-alcoholic beer served by middle-aged Bangladeshi men.

His sister didn't care about the weather. She was happy and tanned, gesticulating and talking about the job. At that time she'd believed in the mission more than him. Keeler was there doing it for the guys, motivated by a sense of responsibility to his brothers in arms more than anything else. He figured, someone was going to be there, and better him than somebody else.

He hadn't said anything like that to Laura though, she was still in the optimistic thrall of the war.

* * *

Keeler walked around back where the mowing noises were being produced. Laura's husband Josh was riding the machine, wearing dark sunglasses and ear protection. He wasn't noticing Keeler, who took the opportunity to observe his brother-in-law, a man he didn't know all that well.

Josh looked in decent shape, for a guy who chooses to buy a ride-along lawn mower. Keeler had to curb his criticism. What was the alternative, hand cutting that enormous lawn? Josh steered the mower up an incline, carving around a good-looking old oak. The guy had been with Laura for almost five years now, ever since she'd come back from working overseas. Josh was some kind of lawyer, specializing in human rights, if Keeler recalled correctly.

He and Laura were do-gooders.

Josh had ended up getting a job in Ohio, doing some kind of social justice work. What Laura was doing here for herself, Keeler had no idea. Josh hit a rock with the mower, making a terrible scraping sound. He backed off and turned the machine around the obstacle.

Josh had been born and raised in New York City, so his outdoor skills were most likely newly attained. At that point, Josh spotted him and stopped the motor. Keeler put a smile on his face, but Josh, walking over, wasn't matching it. Josh's face was a mixture of confusion and something worse, a negative emotion.

Like he wasn't happy to see him.

Josh removed the ear protection, letting the muffs fall around his neck.

Keeler walked over to meet him on the lawn. "Hey, Josh."

The brother-in-law took his sunglasses off and wiped the dust out of his eyes. "What are you doing here?"

Keeler said, "Laura didn't tell you I was coming?"

A shaking of the head. "Uh, no, she didn't say."

Josh was now standing just in front of him, a mixture of agitation and concern written on his face, tension actually visible in his body.

Keeler said, "How you doing?"

Josh averted his gaze and looked past him, at the house. His restless eyes came back to meet Keeler's. Josh said, "Did she contact you?"

Keeler said, "Yes, but it was cryptic. What's going on?"

Josh's face was now bright red with emotion. He was tearing up, eyes red-rimmed and now brimming. He wiped a forearm across his face.

"Okay, so you have no idea?"

"No."

Josh was nodding to himself, shaking his head like it was all very weird. He said, "Laura's in the county jail. They denied bail at her arraignment yesterday."

Keeler said, "What's the charge?"

"Right now they're going for Voluntary Manslaughter."

Keeler let that wash over him. Seven syllables, all of them bad. The first four were better than the last three.

He said, "So what happened."

Josh was staring at him. "She killed someone."

Keeler thought about that for a moment. "What did Laura say about it?"

"Well, she's the one who turned herself in."

That was surprising.

"She turned herself in, huh?"

"Yeah."

Josh was tearing up, snot beginning to run from his nose to his upper lip. Keeler watched him cough and blubber. He went to his brother-in-law and put a hand on his shoulder.

"Let's go inside Josh. Get some coffee going."

Josh nodded. "Okay."

Chapter Six

It wasn't lunch time, but it's always coffee time. Josh had a decent machine. Brushed steel around a glass cylinder with temperature control. Keeler set that magic in motion and came to the kitchen table where Josh was sitting, staring out the window.

Keeler said, "So, who is Laura supposed to have killed?"

Josh shook his head like that didn't matter. "So far a Juan Doe. Gang tattoos suggest he's from El-Salvador." Looking up at Keeler, the blue eyes wet with tears. "She won't talk to me about it."

"Why not?"

"I don't know. All I know is she turned herself in without talking to me, and now she won't discuss it with me when I visit."

Keeler said, "You two were arguing or something?"

Josh said, "Not at all. She's not speaking about it to anyone, not even to the lawyer I got her."

"I see."

Josh laughed. "You do? I don't know what the fuck you mean by that, because I don't see anything."

What Keeler saw was his sister, in jail, avoiding conversations about her situation. Laura would have a reason for that. Particularly if she was the one who approached the police.

He said, "Just to clarify Josh, Laura's speaking to you, but she's avoiding talking about the shooting, or whatever. Right?"

"She's happy to talk about banal shit. I feel like she's locked up in there, not only in the jail, but inside herself. You know what I mean? I can't communicate with her. I have no idea what actually happened. It's like talking to a fucking zombie."

Keeler didn't know what to say. He had no opinion on the matter. There wasn't enough available information to form one. So, he nodded at Josh. "Yeah, mmmm hmmm."

Josh was tearing up again. "What the hell is wrong with you? You're acting like this is all normal."

Keeler said, "Normal is relative Josh."

Josh started coughing uncontrollably. "Jesus. You and Laura. Like talking to twin psychopaths."

Keeler retrieved the coffee pot from the machine's clutches and poured a couple of mugs. The brew was hot and dark. What Josh might not know was that Laura had sent her brother a message about three weeks prior. The email had been just a couple of lines. It had been a cryptic message, which is what had piqued Keeler's interest.

The text came swimming to the front of his mind.

November's the best month here in Central Ohio. You should come, if only for the Mexican food. Which isn't Mexican anymore, maybe Salvadoran or Guatemalan or something. Anyway, I'll expect you for dinner soon. We can catch fire flies.

A weird message, maybe, but not completely out of character. Josh was calmer now, sipping at the hot coffee.

Keeler said, "I'm going to visit her. How does it work, I just go down there or something?"

Josh shook his head. "Not that simple. You need to book it in advance." He coughed a sort of half laugh. "I've got an account with their website. I'll do it right now. The whole thing's a nightmare." He held up his phone. "I had to download an app for that, plus another app just to put money on her commissary account, which isn't the same as the visitation account. Privatization gone insane."

Keeler watched Josh tap and swipe and stretch and pinch things on his phone.

Josh said, "You want to go there now?"

"Yes."

"You'll have to go without me, they only allow one visitor at a time."

"Fine."

"Alright." Josh finished booking the visitation and put his phone down on the table. "I'm sorry for losing it before. This is really stressful. I can only guess how you must feel now, finding her in this situation."

Josh used a torn paper towel sheet to wipe the snot and tears.

Keeler said, "Laura said that you got a job out here with some humanitarian outfit."

Josh nodded. "Ohio Immigrant Justice Coalition. It's based in Columbus, but one of the perks was that I get to work remotely. Just need to go over there once a week. It's an hour drive."

"Gotcha." Keeler said, "What about Laura, what was she doing here?"

Josh said, "Well, the reason that she agreed to me taking the job was so that she could live out here in the sticks. She got back into riding recently. Far as I can tell she was really happy here until this."

Riding horses, Laura's adolescent passion.

Keeler said, "She wasn't working?"

"Laura didn't tell you that she's in the middle of a master's degree at Ohio State? She was teaching there too. Now that's all..." Josh let out a puffing sound, his hand gesturing like something solid turning to dust. "Gone."

"Master's in what?"

Josh said, "Public Policy and Management."

Keeler said, "Which does what exactly, once you're done with the degree?"

"You can work in policy, government work, non-governmental work." He looked up at Keeler, the blue eyes pure and innocent as always. "It's a logical next step for her. With the overseas experience, a PPM master's puts her in line for executive level work in a bunch of institutions."

"Uh, huh."

Keeler excused himself to the bathroom upstairs and, following an impulse, started looking in the mirror cabinets for prescription medications. Josh was on an anti-depressant called Zoloft. Laura wasn't taking any prescription medicine, at least nothing that she kept in the bathroom.

Keeler had retired a few years earlier as an Air Force Pararescue operator. As a combat medic he was aware of medications like Zoloft, basically stimulating serotonin in the brain. Increasing the supply of feel-good chemicals. While he didn't really know Josh that well, it made sense that he'd be on a thing like that, since he was a New Yorker. Keeler liked that city, but living there could drive anyone to Zoloft.

Thinking about what Josh had said. What Laura was getting into here in Ohio. The upshot seemed to be that she was doing alright, at least according to her husband. Keeler was feeling some clarity. The mission was shaping up. Get Laura out.

Completing the mission might prove complicated, even complex, but the direction of travel was obvious. Laura could handle herself in a prison situation. He wasn't worried about that. A corporate run county jail in the United States of America was going to be downright luxurious compared to the penal institutions in almost any other place on earth.

Some people go to prison on purpose, particularly older men who are either homeless or have no family. Jail is three square meals a day with a television, plus heating, air conditioning, buddies with time on their hands, and recreation facilities. They even have libraries and educational programs.

Keeler looked at it in a binary way, because sometimes complicated things can be broken down into their constituent parts. If Laura had killed a man, it would have been for a good reason.

* * *

Josh said, "I'm going up to Columbus. Back around five. I'll pick up dinner on the way back. There's a barbecue place that Laura and I like."

He dipped into a tray by the front door and sent a set of keys looping through the air. Keeler caught them and did an initial examination. Front door plus a Chevy ignition key. Not the original. He looked at Josh.

Josh shrugged. "Use her car, it's available."

Keeler went first through the door. Standing outside in the fresh air, waiting for Josh to lock up. A small drone whined overhead. The thing was around fifty feet up, hovering over the house.

Josh had to raise his voice over the rotor whine. "Looks like the neighbor's kid got a birthday present a couple of days ago."

They stood together, looking up at the drone. Hard to see since it was so small. Commercial drones like this were better than ever. Camera probably had some insane resolution. 8K or 16K, or whatever K they were up to now. The drone pulled away and up, rising quickly to an impressive height, pretty much disappearing into the sky.

Like it was gone, but it wasn't. The thing would still be up there. Keeler imagined the neighbor's kid, maybe just sitting on the edge of his bed with a set of First-Person View goggles on his little head. Maybe still in pajamas.

A weird world, that was for damned sure.

Chapter Seven

The Muskingum County jail was a modern building that looked a little like a spaceship made out of beige stone. The few windows were mirrored, and the facade was smooth, as if designed to repel any attempts at climbing either in, or out. Keeler stood looking up at it. The thing was a fortress.

Cameras were built into the design, set into recessed folds in the stone structure.

Keeler entered through a revolving door punctuating a tall glass cylinder of windows. The entrance gave onto a well-lit atrium, at which point the place started to look more like a conventional prison. Surveillance cameras, bureaucratic furniture and installations, plus an abundance of desperate friends and relatives of the incarcerated.

The methodology here involved computerized machines and facial recognition, plus the scanning of his identity documents, followed by the technology failing and a uniformed facilitator ushering him over to a counter for a direct human-to-human experience.

The man on the other side of the thick glass divider managed to process Keeler's documents without the slightest facial expression, eyes hidden behind wraparound sunglasses, mouth sealed shut in a straight pink line in his face. Keeler was buzzed through an opaque set of double doors and found himself in a waiting room with a couple dozen others. Synthetic music was piped in through overhead speakers. A kid had pissed his pants, the mother agitated and angry.

Ten minutes later, Keeler was sitting on a shiny stool in a booth, the seventh in a long row of twenty such cubicles in the visitation hall. In front of him was a short steel desk and a thick piece of glass, through which he could see an identical cubicle on the other side.

Keeler waited for three minutes. Looking through the visitation glass at the wall on the other side, a white portal set into it with a small window square of steel-reinforced glass. A loud clicking sound reverberated through the facility, as all of the visitation doors unlocked simultaneously. The door was opened and Laura walked in wearing a set of orange jail clothes two sizes too large.

Keeler looked at his sister, thinking that she looked really good.

Laura had always been the better-looking one. He was generally more asymmetrical than she was, in terms of facial features. An observer, looking at Keeler, could change angle and almost see a different person. He'd tried it in mirrors. It meant that he wasn't photogenic. Laura's face was symmetrical and even. You could change angles and see the same good-looking person, as if her face had been crafted by a very precise sculptor.

He picked up the phone, waiting for her to get settled. She sat down and smoothed her hair before picking up her handset and setting it snug between shoulder and ear. Leaning back in the chair and examining her brother.

Keeler said, "You look good."

She laughed. "Where've you been?"

He said, "I was down in Texas."

"Hot as shit down there. What were you doing?"

Keeler said, "Started off on a hike but then it got complicated."

"You went to Texas just for the hike?"

"Not exactly, but I took a hike. It's a long story. What do we have here, fifteen minutes?"

"Twenty."

"Yeah, so maybe you want to tell me your story instead." He made a circling gesture with his free hand. Indicating their interesting surroundings.

Laura said, "No, I want to hear your story. I'm not interested in my own story bro, I already know it. I think about it all the time and what I need from you is distraction."

"Fair enough."

Keeler launched into a pretty complicated account of his time in Texas. Which was mostly a true story, with embellishments and redactions. As he spoke, he began to notice Laura's hands.

Free from the task of holding the handset, she had her hands directly in front of her on the little desk. Keeler had already scouted the surveillance cameras, which were set up on both sides of the visitation divider. The cameras could see his face, and hers presumably, but they weren't able to surveil the space between their bodies. So Laura's hands were masked. One hand was held open, palm up. The other hand was active, fingers touching the palm in combinations, with slight variations in gesture.

She was using *gobbledygook*, the secret language that they had made up, back when they were kids. It took him a second even to recognize what Laura was doing, but the sense of it came back fast.

At first she was repeating the same phrase over and over again.

Laura: *Do you remember this? Keep speaking and blink once for yes, twice for no.*

Keeler blinked once. He didn't stop talking, speaking about his friend in Texas and her dad making pancakes. He got the idea of what Laura wanted, keep talking about some bullshit, while the real conversation was going to be in gobbledygook.

Laura smiled at him beatifically. Her fingers jotted and scraped at her palm, making the intricate movements and gestures that they'd invented together. The language was based on a couple of simple principles. Each finger was assigned a series of alphanumeric symbols, and the palm was divided into a grid.

For example, the thumb got A, B, C, D, E, and the numbers 0, and 1. The index finger got F, G, H, I, J and the numbers 2, and 3. The palm was divided into a grid of five squares. So, depending upon which square the thumb was tapped into, an observer would be able to read the code.

Of course, since Keeler and Laura had used that code for years, they'd grown fluent in it, recognizing word patterns easily. It had been more than twenty years since those bad old days. Still, it did come back.

Laura: *I was afraid you wouldn't remember. Sorry that I won't be listening to your story about Texas.*

Laura: *Don't stop talking.*

Laura: *You won't be able to remember everything that I tell you here. You'll have to come back and visit again. I have a lot to tell you.*

Keeler set his handset between shoulder and ear. He tried using gobbledygook and found that it came back fast. It was a little hard to talk with his mouth and say something completely different with his hands, but he relaxed, managing to find a good rhythm.

Keeler: *Don't worry about my memory. Let's focus on getting you out of here. Give me the lowdown. I'll come back tomorrow or the next day.*

Laura: *They won't let you come back tomorrow. It's one visit per week.*

Keeler: *It's Friday, the week starts on Monday?*

Laura: *You're right.* She nodded once, as if to ready herself. Her fingers flew in minute patterns across the palm. *I got into a situation while riding. This is out past Hollow Hills up in the Amish country. Some guy was literally dragging a pregnant woman by her hair. So, I got involved. The situation developed in the wrong way and I shot him.*

Keeler: *Josh told me. Salvadoran guy with gang tattoos.*

Laura: *Yeah. Ended up having to defend myself from this maniac. Him, plus a bunch of other guys. I shot him in the chest at point blank range. Right there.* She tapped her chest close to the sternum. *Got back to the stables and calmed down and called the cops. First thing they wanted to do was come back to the scene of the crime right?*

Keeler nodded.

Laura: *Well, that's when it got even weirder.*

Chapter Eight

Two police cruisers rolled up to the stables, coming in the back way. Which indicated that they had some familiarity with the place. Laura stood up from the stool to greet them, unsure of what was about to happen. She wasn't shaking like before. Things felt steady, under control.

The cops came out nonchalant. Mirrored shades and dick head uniforms, basically. The lead guy was a large white male with a pink face and fuzzy crew cut blonde hair. The cop was chewing on a toothpick, like a caricature of himself.

"Evening ma'am. You the one called the Sheriff's office?"

Laura said that she had. She told them the story. The lead guy and his female partner chewing gum and watching her talk. The cops in the other vehicle just wandering. One just leaning against the cruiser. His partner poking around the stables.

Meantime, Laura was talking. The two cops impenetrable behind sunglasses. Standing there chewing gum and watching her with their poker faces. Exactly what Laura had hated about the troops in Iraq. Hiding their souls behind wraparound Oakley shades. What was up with that? When she'd finished talking there was a beat during which nobody said anything. She wondered if they were still alive.

"Hello." She said, "You guys still with me or what?"

Laura had expected an arrest and some form of hysteria. What she got was nothing very much. At least at first.

The lead cop said, "Maybe you should take us out to the site, where you say this thing happened."

Like they didn't believe her.

The female cop spoke then, a smoker's voice. "Thing is ma'am, we haven't gotten a call out. Since you say there were multiple witnesses to this incident. You'd think it'd be reported. Right?"

Laura said, "Yeah, let's go there."

She showed them where it had happened, using her phone and Google Maps on satellite mode.

The male cop said, "What about the weapon? The gun you used. We'll have to take it from you."

At which point Laura surprised herself by lying. "I left it there. Dropped it when I ran."

They looked at her blankly. The male cop grunted something unintelligible.

The female cop drove, Laura in the backseat. The farm facility was in a town called Belleville. Not exactly a town, or a village. Belleville appeared to be a farm facility more than a residential community. Driving in they'd passed through areas with animal pens and several large buildings. The female cop pulled up on the other side of the long building where the incident had gone down.

Laura said, "It happened on the other side of the building."

The male cop said, "We'll go knock on the door. After that we can take a look around back."

Both cops exited the vehicle, leaving her in there alone. Laura watched them walk out to the building. The female cop knocked on the door. Nobody opened it. The female cop used her hand to reduce glare, looking in through the little square of glass in the door. The male cop came back and opened the cruiser's rear door.

"Come on out, ma'am. Let's go and take a look around back."

Laura shook out the stiffness from her limbs.

They walked through the long grass. Around the side of the building and then, squeezing through the brush to the back. Laura was behind the two police officers. Watching them struggle with equipment belts and bulky vests. Pushing through the branches to the back. The woman was in front. She stopped after three steps. Laura caught up and saw the guy. Exactly where he'd dropped after that one gunshot. The cops both moved closer, looking down from on high.

The male cop turned to Laura. "This is the guy you shot?"

Laura looked at the man's face. Now a little gray. Lifeless, the eyes staring into grass. Fingers curled slightly.

She said, "That's him."

There had been others with him, and they just left him there.

The female cop looked at her partner. "Better call it in."

* * *

The paramedics showed up, along with two detectives from the Trace Junction town police force. The detectives came in all bellies and blazers, looking like twins, mustachioed, with mirror image bald craniums. One of them had a birthmark like Gorbachev. He must have been the senior partner. Gorbachev took one look at the scene and started getting pissy with the uniformed cops.

He pointed to Laura. "Get her out of here. You got a GSR kit in the vehicle?"

The female cop said, "Yeah, we do."

"Good. Swab her and then get her downtown to county and stick her in a room."

"Gotcha."

The two uniformed cops got out the gunshot residue kit and swabbed Laura right out there by the cruiser. The portable GSR test came out negative. Laura had cleaned up while washing the horse, but a real test would have found gunshot residue. The other thing she'd done back at the stables was change out of her riding clothes. That had been a good idea.

At that point, neither of the cops remembered about the gun. Which didn't strike Laura as weird because there was a lot of pressure with the detectives getting all hot and heavy like they did.

Later on, the prosecutor decided to charge her. She'd called Josh from the county jail and told him to go pick up her car from the stables. He'd freaked out, but they hadn't had much time on the phone.

The other thing was the farm facility. She hadn't been able to have a look around, but she'd asked the cops if they'd checked it out. She did tell them about the women and the other men who'd been there at the time of the incident. The police looked around and found nothing suspicious. It was some kind of animal husbandry facility run by a farm cooperative. That's all they'd said. No women.

Chapter Nine

Keeler: *Did they ever come back at you about the gun?*
Laura: *The detectives did, during that initial interview in the room. I said nothing, just lawyered up. Once I saw that guy lying there all abandoned, I knew that there was just trouble here.*

Keeler: *So what are you thinking?*

Laura: *Don't know exactly. Obviously there was something going on with those people. Made them just leave the dead guy like that. They still haven't identified the body. Apparently the tattoos mean he's from El-Salvador, and part of a gang. That's all we know. What I saw was the Juan Doe dead guy, dragging some sorry looking pregnant woman by the hair. Other people kind of looking on as if they didn't mind.*

Keeler: *They probably have something to hide. The dead guy's an illegal, with no identification and no record here in the USA. Untraceable unless they get lucky with cooperation down in El-Salvador.*

Laura: *That will take some time I guess.*

Keeler: *Yeah. What's the deal here. Safe?*

Laura: *Nothing's happened yet, but the guards are very uncool. To say the least.*

Keeler: *So, what's my first move Laura?*

Laura: *Go out there and find Beachy's farm. It's the horse place out by Hollow Hills. He's expecting you. Beachy doesn't know anything, but he'll point you in the right direction.*

Keeler: *Roger that.*

Laura: *I'm concerned about what they'd do if outsiders came sniffing around. You can handle yourself. I'm worried about Josh. Everything I do here is watched and surveilled. I haven't been able to talk to him about it.*

Keeler: *I get it. I'll talk to him.*

Laura said, "I like burritos, but tacos are always a more authentic option. *Al Pastor* is my favorite."

Keeler: *Who's the lawyer you got?*

Laura: *Josh hired some guy. I fired him this morning. Worse than useless to use a guy from here. Josh might not know yet. The asshole wasn't even able to get me bail without a single prior.*

Keeler: *What happened?*

Laura: *The prosecution's argument was that I fled the scene, making me a flight risk.*

Keeler: *Even though you turned yourself in.*

Laura: *Yes. He didn't insist that the reason for me leaving was the risk of staying at the scene. The shooting was self-defense. And then he had nothing to say when the prosecution argued that I had no community ties.*

Keeler: *Because you moved here recently?*

Laura: *They made a meal out of it. Me leaving the scene was framed as an 'attempt to evade law enforcement'. Then the community ties thing and I'm stuck in here.*

Using gobbledygook while speaking was almost like an out-of-body experience. Keeler could actually hear himself talk about the Mexican border with Texas, but managing to have his cognition shifted into the gobbledygook register. Very strange.

Keeler: *Why didn't you turn the gun in?*

Laura: *I'm not sure, I just didn't. Told them I dropped it at the site, like I was clumsy and scared and freaking out.*

Keeler needed to stop talking in both verbal and gobbledygook for a second to think things through.

Laura gets in a situation and uses her carry to extract herself safely. Turns herself in, but not the gun.

Keeler: *What vibes are you getting from the police?*

Laura: *I'm getting terrible vibes. I don't trust them or anyone in here. I think the police are colluding with those people up at the farm. Seriously.*

Keeler: *Josh is a lawyer. What about getting him to defend you?*

Laura: *The more clueless he is, the safer he is. Josh stays at home and goes up to Columbus for work once a week. Maybe he goes to the supermarket or the barbecue joint. He's uninvolved. You need to assume surveillance. Might want to check the house. I have no idea. Don't underestimate these people.*

Keeler: *Got it. How long can they hold you here?*

Laura: *Couple of weeks until the preliminary hearing. Then we can request bail again.*

A couple of weeks was a long time. Keeler felt himself growing hot with anger.

Keeler: *If I'm out there causing a ruckus you might get heat in here. You ready for that?*

Laura: *What doesn't kill you makes you stronger bro.*

Keeler: *Easy to say when you're not locked up.*

Laura: *I guess if I start getting shit I'll know you're out there doing what you do.*

Keeler looked at her long and hard. It was a tough call, but he wasn't a precision instrument for delicate negotiations, and

Laura knew that. He was a finely made tool for violent confrontation.

If anyone had been surveilling their conversation, they would have heard him winding up his account of the visit to Texas. His mouth was currently engaged in a story about a diner down there, burgers and breakfast were always topics he was capable of speaking eloquently about with no thought necessary. He shifted gears. That particular diner situation had turned a little wobbly and he didn't want to talk about it since their conversation was being recorded, and apparently analyzed by a hostile party.

He figured that the lawyer was something they could discuss openly. "I'll go and see your ex-lawyer now. He'll have the case files at least."

Laura said, "Yes. Good idea. His name is Finnegan. The firm's called Finnegan, Coldfield, and Thompson. Offices here in downtown but you'll usually find him out by Weasel Boy."

Keeler said, "Weasel Boy?"

She cracked a very winning smile. "I'll let you figure it out for yourself. Get the dossier from him. List of charges and whatever. They'll have information on the guy I'm supposed to have shot."

Keeler said, "Anyway, the Texas situation ended up just fine. Beautiful place. You ever get there?"

Laura said, "I think so, a time or two."

Keeler's eyes were roaming, finding the surveillance cameras and noting the guards and fellow prisoners. Making himself aware of the surroundings, unlocking from the intense dialogue. An announcement was broadcast over the public address system and the visit was over. As his sister rose from her seat, she made a final gesture in gobbledygook.

Stay strong brother.

Keeler: *Stronger together.*

Chapter Ten

Keeler watched the door close behind his sister. He glimpsed a corridor on the other side, prisoners being lined up by uniformed guards. Looked like they were attaching ankle chains as well as the handcuffs. He sat there a moment letting the fact that Laura was going through this sink in.

Everyone adjusts, but it'd be hard to imagine someone living a good life in prison. It's one thing to resign yourself to reality, but then there's what people call *the good life*, which is a step above baseline reality. Prison's baseline. How the saying goes, *three squares and a bed*. Keeler wasn't going to be happy with Laura living a baseline existence. He stood up from the stool and stepped away from the visiting booth.

Men, women, and children were moving towards the exit. A line was forming. Up at the doors it looked as if the visitors were being processed by guards. Some kind of formality before they could be released out to the atrium, and the civilian world beyond the building's entrance.

Keeler was slotting into the line. The process was slow, but at least there was movement. Two guards up front were taking people aside at random. A third and fourth guard were over to the side, conducting body searches. Which seemed strange. It was virtually impossible for any contraband to have been exchanged with a prisoner on the other side of that thick glass and steel separation.

The guards weren't being cool either, rudely pointing and demanding.

His turn came. The two guards looking at him now, four eyeballs turned in his direction in some way that made him instinctively realize they'd been waiting on him. One of those feelings. The guard on the left was a large specimen with a tightly controlled afro in corn rows running straight back over his head. He wore a gold earring and was chewing gum. The guy's face had a slight sheen of sweat, the bad lighting kicking glare off damp skin. The other guard was an opposite profile. Female, skinny, and pale, with one of the plainest faces that Keeler had ever seen.

The guard with the shine said, "Get out your I.D. and visitation letter."

Keeler had it out already. A driver's license and a copy of the visit email confirmation that Josh had printed. He offered the documents and the female guard took them. She took a quick look at the documents and raised her head, nodding at a third guard over to the side. The guard approached, and the plain faced one handed him Keeler's papers.

She said, "He's got a five-thirty-two."

Keeler said, "What's a five-thirty-two?"

She ignored him. The third guard had some kind of dermatological condition that wasn't being taken care of.

The guard said, "Come with me, sir."

Keeler said nothing. He kept his hands where everyone could see them. The female guard cleared her throat.

The dermatologically challenged guard led Keeler to a door. He put his thumb to a scanner, and the lock clicked open, revealing a small room with three rows of six chairs in front of a large counter separated from the waiting area by a plexiglass barrier. There were no human beings either behind the counter or sitting in the plastic bucket seat chairs.

The guard said, "Just take a seat in there."

"Why?"

"Just take a seat in there please, sir."

* * *

Keeler sat in the front row. The counter was sealed off by the plexiglass barrier. It took up the whole front of the room. Keeler let his mind wander, kind of going over all that had happened since his arrival a short time ago. The problem with Earl at the donut place. The way that Josh had appeared unstable. His medication. Laura's issue.

And now this.

What some people might call an escalating situation.

Obviously, it wasn't only his sister's problem anymore. Which suited Keeler just fine. Like he'd tapped into his palm in gobbledygook, *stronger together*. This thing here was harassment, regardless of any outcome. He hadn't done anything to merit being taken into a special room in the county jail. A five-thirty-two was just some bullshit code for *let him sit in the room*.

So he'd sit in the room.

And let his mind fantasize about what he could do.

Come in here all ninja. Kill every living thing in his path and spring her out. Then what?

Call that *Plan B*.

Could stage a diversion, assassinate the mayor, or blow up

the municipal building. Come in dressed as a guard. Prison guards don't carry weapons. It might take a while for the reaction force to activate. That window of opportunity could be extended in a couple of ways. Keeler ended the fantasy, reminding himself that it wasn't an actual war zone, and that the principle of innocence applied. Innocent until proven guilty.

Maybe.

An hour later a side door opened and an older guard stepped through and closed it behind him. He came to the middle of the desk holding Keeler's documents.

"Step up here."

The guy's appearance was a disappointment, since Keeler had been enjoying his time in the room.

If these idiots thought that putting him in the room was intimidating, they were wrong.

Keeler rose and felt the joints crackle and pop, a pleasant sensation. He took his time approaching the counter. Examining the new guard. Not much to look at. Thinning hair in a comb-over somehow glued to an oblong skull. Liver-spotted forehead grown large. Gray mustache over a thin-lipped mouth. Bad teeth and eyes that were colorless.

The kind of guy who'd be highly susceptible to a nighttime visitation if anything went wrong in here for Laura. Same as his colleagues. Highly susceptible. Keeler wasn't writing anything off. Hijackings, home invasions, assassinations, blackmail. Maybe even kidnapping of loved ones, why not? Whatever got the job done was plausible at this point.

He laughed to himself at the thoughts coming through his mind. Realizing how quickly he was able to go from zero to a hundred and twenty. Keeler wasn't jumpy with a short fuse, but he was certainly more than ready to rock and knew it.

And liked it. And was happy about himself.

This guard wasn't looking happy though. He said, "Something funny?"

Keeler observed him, almost ready to break through the plexiglass and kill him.

This asshole was part of the problem. They had his sister in there, cuffed and stuffed.

The guard looked down at his nail bitten fingers, tapping on Keeler's driver's license.

He said, "Military man, huh?"

Keeler said nothing.

The door opened behind him. A second man entered. He was dressed for the executive suite in a two-piece suit with a pink tie. The man's face was red below a fresh haircut.

He made eye contact with Keeler and stood behind the guard.

"Don't mind me."

The guard ignored the man.

He said, "What'd you do in military, drive a truck or mop floors?"

Keeler figured he might be on the street a fraction sooner if he just cooperated.

He said, "I served my country, officer. Whatever they said, I did. That's about it."

The guard looked at him, probably not entirely sure what to say in return.

Keeler said, "You want to let me go now?"

The man standing behind the guard coughed. He said, "Nobody's keeping you, son. We just needed to verify your identification is all, seeing as it's your first visit."

Keeler said, "Right. And you are?"

"I'm the warden."

The guard said, "You planning to stay in town some?"

"No plans as yet."

"Problem is, we haven't been able to verify an address for you."

Keeler said, "6315 Windsong way."

"Is that your address?"

"My sister and her husband."

"Uh huh. Seeing as your sister's in here. I'm going to have to verify with your brother-in-law. I hope he's got a copy of the marriage certificate and a homeowner's deed up there, cause we got vagrancy laws."

Keeler said, "You're kidding right?"

The guard looked at him for a long moment, trying his best for hard. Keeler shifted his gaze to the warden. He saw nothing in either man's face, just pure emptiness, a vacancy of soul. The guard smiled then, his bad teeth exposed and rotten.

He said, "Nah, you know what, I'm not fucking with you. This is what it is. You go on now, but take care. Next time you come in here you might be checking in for a longer stay than you'd like. You hear what I'm saying?"

Keeler said, "I hear." What he heard was a warning not to visit Laura again. A clear threat.

The warden said, "You take care of yourself now."

The guard nodded and stacked the documents in a pile, holding a palm over them.

He gave Keeler a look and held it for a significant moment. The prison guards wore steel gray uniforms with badges and a name tag. Earlier, Keeler had memorized two of the names. *Williams* was the guy with the muscles. *Slopes* was the female. This guy's name was *Richards*.

Richards slid the documents through a hole in the plexiglass.

"You go on, get the fuck out now while you can, boy."

Keeler took the documents and turned away. He was clicked out through a third door leading from a narrow corridor directly into the atrium. Now he was free and easy, but they'd made their point.

Walking out through the swiveling glass entrance, Keeler felt a rush of blood to the head, in a good way. A single word with only one syllable was looping slowly through his mind. *War*.

Chapter Eleven

Getting out of there was like exiting a space shuttle through a sealed hatch. The air was different outside, and not only because it was fresh. Spaces of incarceration were always going to feel more confined. Time to see that lawyer, Finnegan and get Laura's file. What she had said. The guy worked out of some place called *Weasel Boy*.

Keeler had parked a couple of blocks away from the county jail. He looked up at the traffic before crossing and saw the waitress's Ford F-150 pickup truck. Maybe fifty yards away and closing. She didn't see him, her eyes focused on the road. Beside her in the passenger seat was a young girl with mousy hair, maybe eight years old. The girl made eye contact with Keeler and stuck out her tongue. Keeler winked, and the truck went by.

Funny. He crossed the road and stopped a man in his thirties walking some kind of sheep herding dog. "I'm looking for a place named Weasel Boy?"

"Yeah, brewery down by the river."

The man struggled with the hyperactive canine as he made hand gestures, tilting his head south.

* * *

Laura's Corvette wasn't exactly the kind of car that allowed you to stay anonymous. The Stingray was a beautiful thing, glowing with polished silver radiance. It looked like the Batmobile and the engine rumbled and roared. The ride was enjoyable, the manual gear box well-tuned. Laura had upgraded the steering system. Something more modern had been fitted in there to replace the old manual steering. Whatever it was, the upgrade had been a good addition.

That upgrade made him think back to the gobbledygook.

It'd been more than twenty years since he and Laura had needed to use a secret language to hide their communications from an abusive father. When you grow up in fear, there's a moment when you realize that it isn't normal. Before that moment you simply live in the only reality available to you.

Keeler remembered that moment of realization, the awakening.

He'd been maybe ten years old already, Laura two years younger. Their father did his little evil routines whenever mom was away, which unfortunately was often. It always happened around dinner time. As usual, Keeler had been left to do the cleaning up. His dad had slunk off in shame to his bottle of scotch in what he called "the office," while Laura was crying in her room.

They'd been living in Colorado then, a new house, a new life, new school, and new friends. The difference this time was that Keeler had hit it off immediately with one of the neighbors, a girl named Sally who was a year older than him. What Keeler remembered of that evening: Sally knocking at the door. Him wiping his hands on the kitchen towel and opening the door, trying to get her to go away. He was feeling all confused and awkward and there was Laura crying in the background. Their father just an empty silence beyond the locked door to his office.

Sally had recognized immediately that something was wrong in the Keeler house. Wrong in a different way than a normally shitty family situation. Maybe it was the fact that she was older, and a girl. Maybe the way that the kitchen was trashed. Keeler had no idea why, but he'd just started bawling then and there, right in front of the neighbor, a pretty girl who he already had a crush on.

He remembered Sally's expression hardening and a look of recognition filling her young eyes. She'd hugged him tight, speaking at the same time into his ear. *It's your dad right? Is it your dad?* Remembering the way he'd nodded. The flood of relief as he unloaded to Sally. She'd taken his shoulders and looked hard at him.

You need to know that's not normal.

That was it. Sally's words woke Keeler from his hypnotic daze. There were some things that were neither normal, nor right. And it didn't matter that it was your dad who was doing it. You needed to know that it's not normal. That was when Young Tom Keeler woke up to the hard world. The rebellion had begun the day after, and part of it developed into their secret language, *gobbledygook.*

Eventually, after a long and messy war that Keeler and his sister clumsily waged, they'd gotten rid of the bastard. The secret language had stopped almost immediately after. Something that neither Keeler nor Laura had ever discussed. But now gobbledygook was back, and he remembered everything just like it had happened yesterday.

Thinking about that brought back the unpleasant past. Keeler wasn't the kind of guy who lingered on bygones. He was more of a present tense kind of person. And presently, the

Corvette's rear-view mirror was revealing an older model Ford Explorer that had been hanging back for a while.

The Explorer had been two cars back when it first caught his attention, while pulling up a curving ramp from city center to one of the feeder roads. That recognition hadn't triggered much more than the creation of a note in Keeler's mental filing system. Ford Explorer, silver and maroon model, maybe a decade old. The note had been deposited somewhere towards the mid section of his brain, along with a trace record of every other vehicle he'd noticed.

Now the Explorer had reappeared four cars back on another highway.

No such thing as a coincidence. The note was retrieved from the filing system of his brain and brought out to the front, hanging there like some heads-up display data feed. Details about the Corvette were coming back to him now. Dad bragging about the vehicle, back in the day. They'd move to a new town and Dad'd be out in the driveway with his fancy car, showing it off to other dads. Mister Keeler, all tall and handsome.

All for show.

But the vehicle was real. One of the hard things about their father was his competence. He'd been an abusive asshole, but he was also, and at the same time, coldly competent in everything he did, even the abuse. A cool competence that both Keeler and his sister had inherited.

The Corvette Stingray had an upgraded V8 engine with the standard fuel injection. So well tuned that the car sang like an instrument. The bucket seat didn't so much vibrate as hum, transferring the music into Keeler's body. Dad always said that his Corvette was tuned to a B flat. Keeler wasn't sure about that, but the thing was going strong and smooth. Pushing his boot down on the accelerator provided a precision flow of the sun's ancient gift.

The throttle was responsive and satisfying.

Keeler did nothing abrupt, simply let the weight of his foot gently increase the acceleration. Watching for the follow car in the rear view. Twenty seconds later he was doing a hundred and twenty miles per hour. The Ford had no choice but to expose itself, pulling out into the left lane while still attempting a deniable distance.

Keeler kept up the pressure. A few minutes later, the distance had widened. Problem was, you couldn't just keep going at 120 miles per hour without drawing the law. It was time to get off the road.

The next exit was indicated a quarter of a mile in advance. Keeler let his foot go hard on the pedal now, counting one Mississippi, two Mississippi. Approximately six seconds later the ramp loomed large. Three vehicles in the immediate vicinity, plus the Explorer, smaller in the rearview, but still coming on.

Keeler took the Stingray speeding past a Toyota minivan. Kids in the back seat staring as he zipped by. Moon-like faces, one of them sucking on a juice box straw, wide eyes in ruddy cheeks. The mother driving, blonde bob sprayed in place above well groomed eyebrows. Two hands on the wheel at 10 and 2 o'clock.

Keeler gesticulated at her, trying to catch mom's attention. He got a worried glance, a tense focus upon the steering wheel, and then another look of concern. Keeler gesticulated to his right, pointing a finger at her lane. He didn't wait for a response. Keeler nosed past her vehicle and got two car lengths in front. The ramp was there, looming fast. He pulled the steering wheel hard right. Saying in his mind, *stay cool mom*. The Corvette cut across the Toyota minivan into the right lane with a snarl and a squeal. The idea was to use mom's Toyota as a screen.

The Corvette shuddered, cutting across the lane. No antilock brakes on the car so he had to maintain the speed. The recirculating ball steering meant he'd rely more on strength than on mechanical aids. He had to hold the turn, moving now across the right lane and into the exit lane. Cutting hard right lifted the two left side wheels of the Corvette slightly.

The tires returned to the asphalt, gripping and swerving dangerously. The steering wheel threatened to rip out of his grasp, like an angry python. Keeler held fast, gritting teeth and breathing evenly. He shot through onto the exit ramp and down-shifted twice in rapid succession.

The Corvette straightened out and the immediate danger was gone.

The surveillance team in the Explorer would have seen Keeler moving into the right lane. They were in the left, which meant that by the time they arrived at the spot where Keeler had cut across it'd be too late. He was already on the exit ramp and moving off the highway, in a different direction, on a different road.

Unless they spotted the Corvette exiting. In which case they'd be too late anyway and would miss the exit.

Keeler stopped the vehicle at the bottom of the ramp. Listening to the engine idle, feeling it out, if the maneuver had been tough on the old beast. The motor hummed as before, a little creaky maybe on the suspension, but indefatigable. Laura had kept this thing in great condition.

He was looking in the rearview mirror. Waiting a moment to see if the Explorer would make it, knowing of course that it wouldn't. There hadn't been any terrible ripping sound of a crash, so he was assuming that mom and her kids were safe.

Keeler got the vehicle into gear. The clutch was smooth, the shift easy and fluid. He'd driven out of town and needed to circle back on smaller roads if he wanted to end up at the Weasel Boy Brewery. By his measure, Trace Junction was roughly south east of the current position. The landscape here was rolling hills, all farmland and perfect little farmhouses. Coming up through a tightly wooded valley the view opened. He had to slow down to pass a horse and carriage. Keeler glanced at the driver, a bearded Amish man with a whip and reins.

A sign up ahead caught Keeler's attention. Hollow Hills.

What Laura had told him. *I got into a situation while riding. This is out past Hollow Hills up in the Amish country. Go out there and find Beachy.* Beachy. Sounded like a surfer dude. Keeler took the right turn for Hollow Hills. The plan had been to see the lawyer first, but plans change.

Chapter Twelve

A single lane country road wound into the hills. Two Amish men on bicycles appeared ahead, grinding up a steep incline. They merged into a single file so Keeler could pass. Old ten speed bikes with steel frames. Both men sported chin beards without mustaches. That's a thing, Keeler figured, keep that lip clean shaved, let the fuzz below run free.

The guys were raw-boned, wearing collared shirts with rolled-up sleeves over tanned arms, corded with muscle.

Keeler hadn't been in Amish country since he was a kid and had a fuzzy memory of barns decorated with some kind of Dutch influenced patterns. The men looked to be in good physical condition. Which made sense given that they didn't use mechanized transport.

There was no specific sign for a farm, and Keeler had to double back a couple of times. He parked the Corvette at a turnout, maybe twenty yards from a muddy track leading to what looked like chicken coops. That counted as a farm, in Keeler's mind.

Which turned out to be correct.

Beachy was a man in his mid-fifties, solid and gray bearded

wearing a red baseball hat. He had the Amish chin beard but wasn't wearing the Amish clothes. Keeler found him in the chicken coop. The stink of ammonia was overwhelming. Giant fans roared, keeping the air moving. Beneath it all was a carpet of yellow chicks, thousands of individual chirps somehow manifesting as a massively high pitched shrieking drone.

Keeler had to scream over the noise. "You're Beachy."

"Yes sir."

"Tom Keeler, Laura's brother."

Beachy held out a big hand. Shouting over the noise. "You look like your sister."

Which wasn't true, but Keeler took the hand anyway.

The chin beard bobbed. The head tilted.

"Let's get out of here." The voice hoarse from screaming above the noise.

Outside was much better than inside, that was for damned sure.

Keeler sucked in fresh air, clearing out his respiratory system after the stifling stench of the coop. Beachy was brushing off dust from his overalls.

Beachy wasn't Amish, but he wasn't exactly *not* Amish. Beachy was Mennonite.

He said, "We use machines and electricity, and everything else, like hospitals, heart surgeons, and computers."

Keeler said, "Beach's your first or last name?"

"First name's Isaac, but they just call me Beachy. That's also my father's name. We got about a hundred Beachys up here. The kids get called by whatever first name they got and the elders like me just go by Beachy."

Keeler said, "How do you tell each other apart, if you're all having dinner or something?"

Beachy said, "It's easy. You don't need to call someone by name. It's not a requirement of communication. You just say the thing you got to say and if Beachy doesn't know it's him being addressed then it ain't worth saying nothing anyway."

Keeler imagined quite a lot of stoic silence among the Mennonite elders.

He said, "I guess it does help to have a unique name in some situations."

"That's true, I won't deny it. *A good name is more desirable than great riches* Proverbs 22:1." Beachy cleared his throat "But I do believe the interpretation is about having a good character or reputation, not any kind of special first name."

Beachy's teeth shone bright white. He pointed back at the massive chicken coop. "Sorry for the noise. Hatched the bunch of em just recently and the little ones sure do make a ruckus."

"How long until you take them to market?"

"These are broilers. Takes about six or seven weeks until they're ready for sale."

Which seemed pretty fast to Keeler.

"Laura said this was a horse farm."

Beachy jerked a thumb behind him. "Come on out back to the stables."

Keeler followed the older man through a narrow forest path. Sunlight came in shafts through the broad-leafed canopy. The autumn colors were very pretty. Beachy swiveled his head back to speak while walking.

"Got another entrance up at the stables. Just in case you're wondering. Farm backs onto the lane so we can get the horses in and out."

Keeler wasn't any kind of cowboy, barely knowledgeable in equestrian basics. But, he was capable of identifying a horse from a cow, and he'd been in the saddle once or twice. As far as he could tell you just let the horse go where it wants. Like riding a large dog. The stables were a wood structure out by a big barn, everything painted red, like an American fairytale. The place was idyllic, if that was your thing.

That was certainly Laura's thing, riding horses in a beautiful farm setting like this. Keeler wondered how she'd found the place.

Beachy said, "She showed up one day and asked if she could ride. So I let her ride my Ginny and they got along so good that I just kept on letting her ride." The big man shrugged. "You don't get between a girl and her horse once they find each other. I think she was hiking through maybe. Saw the stables. You get some hikers once in a while. Mostly families from one of the communities out for a Sunday walk."

Keeler understood the lingo. Community here meant Amish or Mennonite.

"Laura said you'd be expecting me."

"Sure am. I've got something for you."

Beachy disappeared into the barn without inviting Keeler inside. The Mennonite came out a minute later holding a white plastic bag by its handles. The bag was heavy with something dense for its size.

Keeler said, "What's that?"

Beachy said, "Uh, I believe that this is a gun, sir. I haven't touched it, nor will I touch it. I haven't even opened this bag. Laura left it for me with a note asking that I pass it on to her brother." He inclined his head towards Keeler. "And I'm doing exactly what she asked."

He made eye contact. The guy stood there looking like Benjamin Franklin's lost twin. The gaze was even from his brown eyes, neither evaluating, judging, or concluding. A man of God.

Keeler said, "You didn't think it'd be a good idea to give this to the police."

"Well, if the police had come around and asked, I would

have given it to them, and I would have told them everything I knew about it. A half-truth is a whole lie."

"Sounds like you trust my sister."

Beachy raised his thick eyebrows twice. "Only an idiot would disagree with the judgement of a horse." He hefted the bag. "That might be the devil's tool that she used to shoot at a man, but it wasn't any kind of murder. Your sister shot a man to defend herself."

Keeler said, "What do you know about it?"

"Just what I know about her is all. Murder is against God. Self-defense is a different story."

Keeler took the bag from Beachy. He opened it to look inside. The gun had just been thrown in there without ceremony. A Heckler and Koch VP9 with a handful of 9mm bullets thrown in after it and a slim inside-the-waistband holster made of leather and a Kydex shell. Keeler lifted the bag to his nose and sniffed. Gun oil and burnt powder. The weapon had been fired since it was last cleaned.

Keeler said, "Thanks for holding on to this. I appreciate it."

Beachy nodded. "My pleasure. You need anything at all and I'll do what I can to help out."

Keeler said, "I'd like to see where it happened. Can you point me in the right direction?"

"Ya. She'd go riding up there into the fields. I guess she got into the tussle up at Belleville, or thereabouts." Beachy had a pained look, as if his head hurt. He said, "I didn't get to talk to her, mind. But if she was out riding, it'd be Belleville. They got the Amish auction up there. A bunch of other stuff owned by the cooperative."

Keeler said, "Sounds promising."

Beachy pointed. "Just follow around past the barn. There's a path takes you out to the horse track. That'll bring you right down into the woods and up into Belleville. Laura would have followed the back trails into the hills and maybe came back around to end up there. You're on foot so just take the shortcut to town. Maybe a ten-minute hike for a guy like you. It's an Amish community up there." Beachy said, "You might find a couple of Mexicans hanging around. They're up here working for the community as farmhands, helping out with the animals coming to auction."

Keeler said, "The auction house is up there?"

"Yes, sir. Belleville's got an auction house and stables and holding barns and everything to do with that. Always something going on up there."

"Guess I'll walk. As long as you don't mind me coming back through here for the car."

Beachy said, "No problem friend. If you need me again, I'll be working in the coop for a couple hours. You get in touch any time you need something."

Keeler walked back to the Corvette holding on to the plastic bag. Last thing he wanted was to be walking around with a weapon that was involved in a criminal investigation. No upside. The Corvette didn't have a conventional trunk, only a shallow storage compartment behind the seats. As expected, Laura kept a canvas tool roll back there. He got down under the rear of the Stingray and loosened the bolts on the spare tire carrier cover, swinging it away.

There wasn't much room in the carrier tub, with the tire in it, but he managed to squeeze Laura's gun into free space and get the cover back on and the bolts tightened sufficiently.

Chapter Thirteen

The path around Beachy's barn led along a wooded ridge line, breaking out into pastureland. He found the horse trail, figuring it was what the Amish used to get around the fields, since they wouldn't be riding on tractors or ATVs or any kind of motorized vehicle for that matter.

He followed the bridle path as it wound down to a creek, crossed an old wooden bridge, and worked his way through heavy forest to the other side of the valley. The woods gave way to pasture again, and the incline leveled off as a small settlement came into view.

A half dozen Amish men were putting up a fence. Four young guys worked the post hole diggers, while a couple of middle-aged graybeards handled a spool of wire. Keeler guessed it was livestock fencing—not that he knew anything about farming.

"Howdy." Keeler put a hand up in some imaginary Amish greeting.

He got grunts and nods in return.

He said, "I'm looking for the auction house."

One of the graybeards stood up and wiped his hands on his

thighs. He had sleeves rolled up, revealing thick forearms covered in blonde down.

"Follow the bridle path into town. You'll see a bunch of stock barns."

Keeler said, "How do I recognize a stock barn?"

One of the younger guys was amused. He said, "You got the stock pens out front, then the barns. You can't miss it 'cause it don't look like anything else. Auction house is right there."

"Thanks."

The auction house turned out to be something resembling an outdoor theater, or maybe a rodeo arena. An area for the animals to be displayed, surrounded by bleachers for the buyers and onlookers. Stock pens and barns were where they kept the animals while they were prepared and waiting to be sold.

Well, that was Keeler's operational assumption.

Presently it was all empty, save a couple of goats penned out back.

Keeler noted security cameras installed at the proper locations.

A small girl, maybe ten years old, stood staring at Keeler. It took him a moment to peel his eyes from her. The girl wore a black cape and hood, looking otherworldly with her big eyes all staring at him. There was a sound behind him and he turned to see a large man in a one-piece work suit, red-bearded and wearing a beanie hat.

The little Amish girl scampered off.

The big guy held a broom and just stood looking at Keeler. There was neither kindness nor malice in his gaze; it was simply flat.

Keeler said, "I'm looking for the meeting house."

The man didn't respond. He simply turned and walked away.

Not so friendly, these Amish people. Keeler exited the

auction arena and walked toward what he assumed was the center of the little town. Not actually a town, since there were no stores or anything remotely like that. The place was a cluster of immaculate houses. Like the young guy had said, the meeting house was obvious. The building was white-painted oak with a pitched gable roof, surrounded by a picket fence and a well-tended garden.

Laura had described the building as long—like some kind of farm facility, in her words. It'd be on the edge of the town, or whatever this place was. She'd come at it from the fields, over a wood fence.

Besides the man and the little girl at the auction house, Keeler hadn't seen a soul. Maybe the men were all out working in the fields, like the guys building that fence. And maybe the women were all out doing something else, like driving a horse-drawn carriage or something.

Whatever the reason, Keeler had the feeling that he was in a ghost town. He got the lay of the land. The auction house was on the southwest side of Belleville. The fields were on the north-western side. He walked up a lane bordering two small and perfect houses. A white lace curtain twitched as he passed. Keeler got the briefest glimpse of an elderly woman's paper-pale face move back into shadow.

It felt weird.

That led out to a two-story building. Not exactly a house—something bigger and less homey. Keeler guessed that it was a dormitory for the farmhands. A large grassy area in front was dominated by a mature tree, denuded of leaves. A young woman in jeans and a fleece hoody leaned against the trunk, looking at a phone. Certainly not Amish.

She looked up at Keeler.

He said, "Hi there. I'm looking for someone in charge."

She was in her twenties, or younger. Looking at Keeler like

she had no clue what he'd just said. She spoke in Spanish. "*No hablo inglé, disculpe.*"

Keeler used the rudimentary Spanish that he had somewhere locked into his brain. "Looking for the jefe. Where's the boss?"

She pointed back at the building behind her. "*La oficina.*"

He took a wild guess and figured that word had something to do with an office.

Which turned out to be correct. An office on the ground floor of the dormitory building, occupied by a largish lady wearing glasses and doing Sudoku in a booklet with a pencil. She did not look either Amish or from south of the border.

Keeler knocked on the open door and the woman looked up at him. She put the pencil down, eyes magnified behind the lenses.

"Yes?"

Keeler said, "I'm a legal investigator. I wanted to ask you a few questions if you've got a minute."

The woman said, "I don't know anything about any legal case. Sorry."

Keeler said, "Understood. If you don't have answers, you just tell me that."

"Okay."

He said, "I understand that this is a dormitory site for migrant farmhands?"

She swiveled her chair to properly face him. "We call them newcomers, not migrants."

"Girls from Mexico?"

The woman said, "They aren't all girls, and none of them are from Mexico. The majority come from El Salvador, and we get some Hondurans and Ecuadorians. We work with partners in Latin America who supply farm workers as needed. It changes seasonally. Everything's run via the H-2A visa program."

"Gotcha. And what do they do when they're here?"

The woman said, "They work either at the auction facility or at other facilities owned by the cooperative." She had a sort of defiant look about her. "I'm not going to give you a list of our current farmhands or anything."

Keeler said, "How long have you been working here?"

The woman laughed. "Forever. I'm the OG here."

The only other detail he managed to squeeze out of her was that the animal auctions were held every Saturday, as that's considered a regular workday by the Amish.

He found the long building a few hundred yards further west. It was clad in white aluminum siding, with a gravel parking area and a glass front door. Keeler hung back and observed. He was looking for the subtle things. There were currently four vehicles parked out front. The gravel was not maintained and had run thin. Security cameras were installed at the building's two visible corners, plus another two aimed at the door from either side. He decided to come at it from the fields.

To that end, Keeler walked south, and then west, cutting through someone's yard and hopping the wood fence. Once out in the open field, he turned north again, seeing it as Laura must have—albeit without the drama. From that angle he was approaching at a slight uphill, stopping at the fence to observe.

The building was visible from that angle as a large white object with a back door. No windows. Keeler grid searched the area surrounding the fence. The grass had been cut, which was interesting. There were no traces of blood, as far as he was able to see.

Laura had described the event in detail. How she'd been caught up in the fence with the guy tugging at her. How she'd held the pistol and pushed it into him before firing. He took his time, checking the area.

Keeler came back to the fence and got on his knees. He dropped to his back, looking up at the underside of the heavy wood fence cross rails. Underneath the top rail he saw dark stains—possibly blood splatter, although it wasn't possible to make a determination. Plus, he had nothing to collect a sample with. He could come back and do so.

Keeler climbed back through the fence and walked up the hill. The building had a concrete foundation that clearly served as a patio for smokers, judging from the scattered butts. The back door was locked and windowless. Keeler looked up at the camera and smiled.

Coming around the building, he had to squeeze through a prickly bush, emerging onto the road and brushing off the detritus. The reception desk had a woman sitting behind it, typing into a keyboard, eyes up looking into a large old screen.

"May I help you?"

"You might, ma'am. I hear that there was a bit of a ruckus up here a couple days ago. I'm a legal investigator for the defendant."

She looked at him blankly. "How may I assist you, sir?"

"What is this place, if you don't mind me asking? What do you do here?"

She looked at him, surprised. "We're a veterinary research facility."

"Like an animal hospital," Keeler said.

The woman shifted in her chair. She actually laughed. "No. We specialize in large-animal reproductive research. Cows and goats and stuff." She pointed through the wall. "In there, you've got a whole lot of valuable specimens being monitored for viability."

"Connected to the auction facility?"

She said, "The facility used to supply animals for auction. That ended…" She looked at the ceiling. "Maybe five years ago."

Keeler was thinking about the thoroughbreds. He said, "Do you do horses?"

"We've worked with horse breeds before, sure. Mostly though it's cows, to be honest. Good old cows."

"Any chance that I could take a look at the place?"

"I can't let you go in there because it's a controlled environment. But there's an observation window. Would you like to see it?"

Keeler followed her down the corridor. Halfway down was a large window like you might see in a hospital. On the other side was a very big room with high ceilings. Keeler had expected something resembling a dairy plant, a series of stalls or pens with cows wagging tails. This was different. Through the double-glazed window, he might as well have been looking at an assembly line. Massive steel chambers painted an industrial gray lined the walls. He could make out some kind of bovine life. Looked like one animal per chamber.

He said, "What kind of machinery is hooked up to those stalls?"

She said, "Each stall is fitted with monitoring stations and intake hatches for feeding and whatever else they need. They're in what's called a critical evaluation phase. That's about as much as I know."

Keeler said, "Evaluating what exactly?"

The woman nodded. "Baseline testing, metabolic response, and other viability markers."

"What happens when they're cleared?"

"Oh, they don't stay here past evaluation. This is just the preliminary stage." She gestured down the corridor. "After this, they're sent over to the conditioning facility. That's where they're monitored for hormonal responses, metabolic stability, and long-term viability of livestock breeding subjects."

What Keeler was realizing, of course, was that the corridor split the place in two.

"Sounds complicated."

"You betcha. This isn't ma and pa's old farm anymore."

Keeler said, "And I guess it's not an Amish-run facility."

She said, "Well, you'd be surprised. The co-op is a hundred percent Amish-owned, but it's the community that owns it, not any individual farmers. Most of the experts here are not Amish, no."

"I see. How long do the cows stay here?"

"Depends. Usually a couple of weeks. We have to monitor for rejection rates, adaptability scores, and overall stability."

"How many do you handle at a time?"

She said, "We process a few dozen per cycle. This is a small facility. The larger ones handle hundreds."

"Excuse my ignorance, but each of these specimens comes from standard breeding stock?"

The woman looked surprised again. "Oh, no, there isn't any actual natural breeding involved. We rely on controlled methods. Artificial insemination. It's better all-around for consistency."

Chapter Fourteen

The walk back to Beachy's farm took another ten minutes.

Keeler navigated the muddy track past the chicken coops, emerging onto the single lane road where he'd parked the Corvette. The car was exactly where he'd left it in the turnout, maybe thirty yards away from the farm entrance. Walking to the vehicle, Keeler was thinking about the Amish community with the auction house and the program for migrant farmhands. The situation that Laura had been caught up in. Sounded like those people might have been farmhands.

Laura had mentioned a pregnant woman, but there's no reason that farmhands don't get just as pregnant as anyone else.

Maybe this migrant program wasn't a hundred percent above board. Maybe they weren't actually paying strict attention to the H-2A visa program. In which case, an illegal migrant's dead body might draw attention from law enforcement. This could account for what Laura was claiming, that the man she'd shot had been abandoned by his friends.

A pretty drastic solution to the problem, but it did make sense if they were all illegals.

A flicker of movement caught his eye, coming from the shadowed areas on the other side of the Corvette. The narrow road was tree lined. Keeler shifted his focus to a boxy vehicle parked maybe twenty yards beyond Laura's car. He had enough time to recognize that it was the same vehicle that had been following him, the Ford Explorer. Two men were out of the car with weapons pointed at him.

But the realization came too late for him to do anything about it.

Keeler had time to clock a muzzle flash. There was no time for his brain to successfully transfer this knowledge to his muscles, because the ordnance crossed the distance in a fifth of a second and hit him directly in the chest.

The shot knocked Keeler off his feet. A moment of blurry reality and then the hard fact of the back of his head hitting asphalt. Nobody is immune from the disorienting effects of impact. He was unable to breathe. The diaphragm had shut down, restricting air flow. Keeler's training kicked in at that point, several seconds after impact, telling him to relax. He'd been shot in the chest with a non-lethal round.

Some kind of rubber bullet.

The physiological reaction bypassed his conscious control and all Keeler could do was ride out the spasms. The involuntary expulsion of breath had caused his brain to go into an automatic panic mode that he suppressed effectively. He could hear the men standing by the Ford Explorer.

One of them was whooping like a cowboy. "Dialed in bro. Right on target!"

The other guy's voice was more of a low growl and came from closer. Keeler looked up, finding the bore of a high-powered rifle aimed at his head.

The man said, "This is your fair warning pal. From here on out, whatever you touch turns to stone. This shit is going to get fucking biblical if you do not desist. Take that pretty Stingray of yours out of state and stay there. No other warnings will be given."

The guy turned and walked away. Keeler focused on breathing. Ten seconds later the Ford Explorer moved out, the motor growling as it drove past. The driver sent a large globule of spit out the window, landing a couple of feet shy. Keeler sat up and looked for the round that had knocked him down. A black rubber slug was just under him. He examined the thing, 40mm standard range sponge round supposedly developed for riot control.

Pretty powerful for a rubber bullet.

On the ride down to town, Keeler considered the position.

What exactly did it mean that those two men had physically attacked him? What new possibilities were now available? It wasn't as if they'd made an attempt on his life. Still, the attack had opened up a legitimate path to ultra-violence. Keeler wasn't exactly a detective, or a legal investigator for that matter. He was much better at escalation dominance than the art of gentle negotiation.

Now that he had targets, it might not even be necessary to go through the grind of uncovering whatever misfortune had befallen the town of Trace Junction. He could simply go right at the guys in the Ford Explorer, who had done him the courtesy of revealing themselves.

Keeler changed gears and found himself enjoying the drive. He glanced in the rear-view mirror and caught the reflection of himself grinning with bared teeth. Which made him laugh. Shot with a rubber bullet. He pulled his shirt up and glanced at the impact point. A large bruise was welling up, the skin blue and red.

What kind of people would be messing with a riot control gun like that? Who buys a 40mm Multi-Shot Launcher? Law enforcement, military contractors, corrections facilities. Or just idiots who like to shoot things and have extra cash to spend. He mentally placed the two men in the idiot category until further notice.

He'd been navigating without thinking and found himself coming out of the rolling countryside to a suburban stretch of strip malls and intersections. A sign said Trace Junction with an arrow pointing up to a highway overpass. Keeler turned onto the ramp and joined the quickly moving flow of vehicles headed to town.

Chapter Fifteen

Weasel Boy was a two-story barn-like structure by a river just the other side of Trace Junction. The upper level of the building was surrounded by wide decking. The lower part looked to be a dedicated facility for fabricating artisanal Weasel Boy beer. Keeler gleaned all of this while swinging the Corvette in a wide curve around the spacious parking area, piloting the vehicle so that it faced the exit.

He sat in the car for a minute listening to the motor idle. The maneuver earlier hadn't done anything harmful to the engine. A vehicle that age might be susceptible, but not Laura's Vette.

Weather was good. A mid-autumn day with blue skies and warming sunshine.

Looking up at the brewery, he was thinking about Finnegan, a lawyer who liked to work out of the office. Keeler was wondering why. Maybe he didn't like offices. Maybe, Finnegan was a big fan of pizza and beer. Or, maybe Finnegan was an investor in the Weasel Boy brewery and liked to keep close to his money.

Maybe.

In any case, it wasn't hard to find him.

Finnegan sat in the back of the loft-like upper level, at a large farmhouse table by a big picture window. He had a laptop computer plugged into an AC outlet. The table piled with documents organized into neat sections of paper in and out of color-coded folders. The lawyer was a large man in his sixties with an impressive silver and black afro. As Keeler approached the table, he could see the blue reflection of Finnegan's computer screen in his wire-framed glasses.

Keeler said, "Finnegan."

The lawyer looked up at him through bifocal lenses, without moving his head. "Yeah."

"Keeler."

Finnegan's expression adjusted, but not in a good way. He wasn't happy to see Keeler. "The brother, huh?" The lawyer's eyes shifted over Keeler's shoulder to the bar area, then back again to Keeler. He had that thing with his glasses, needing to look over them at far away objects.

Keeler said, "Mind if I sit down?"

"Go ahead, I guess." The lawyer pushed the spectacles into place with a forefinger.

Keeler took a seat.

Finnegan lifted a smart phone from the table and fooled with it, returning it face down. He bent to the computer and continued typing. "One second, I gotta finish this sentence or I'm going to forget it."

Keeler let him finish, glancing back to the bar and seeing a man in his thirties, cleaning shaker style pint glasses with a cloth. There was eye contact and Keeler turned back to the lawyer, stretching and yawning and feeling a little impatient.

It took Finnegan a full minute to close the laptop and straighten up, pushing the bifocals up on his forehead. The gaze was even and steady, not exactly closed but certainly unrevealing.

He said, "Yeah." Looking expectantly but warily at Keeler. "What can I do for you? Your sister just fired me."

Keeler said, "I'm here to pick up the case file. Whatever you've got from the police and the prosecutor."

Finnegan shrugged. "Anyway, she wouldn't even discuss the case with me so how'm I supposed to represent her?"

Keeler said nothing.

Finnegan reached into a worn leather briefcase at his feet and retrieved a manila folder. He pushed it across the table to Keeler.

"Take a look while you're here. I'll answer any questions you have at this point." He said, "You got to know that I keep office hours, and it's by appointment only."

Keeler said nothing.

Finnegan said, "I'll consider this a one off, since I'm passing over the case."

Keeler squared the folder on the table in front of him and put a hand on it.

He said, "What did she plead?"

"At the arraignment? We pled not guilty. Self-defense." Finnegan was watching him. "Any idea who you're going to get to replace me?"

Keeler said, "No."

The lawyer said, "Might want to get someone from out of town if I were you. Not that it'll help but might be better."

Keeler eyeballed him. Sweat had been building up at his hairline. Finnegan had already glanced twice over Keeler's shoulder toward the bar. Keeler turned back and saw the guy still cleaning glasses.

Keeler reached across the table and pulled Finnegan's notebook and pen to himself. The lawyer twitched but restrained himself. He wrote on a fresh sheet. *You're sweating and a bad liar. Is this conversation being recorded? Answer truthfully or I'll sink this pen into your left eye and then kill everyone in here and burn the place to the ground.*

The lawyer's face went tense and a drop of sweat actually ran in a trickle from his hairline to his nose. He wiped it off and nodded. Chin pointing to the smart phone on the table by a stack of papers.

Keeler wrote. *Who's the recording for?*

Finnegan took the notebook and pen. *You want your sister out, I recommend that you get her to make a plea deal. Knocking the charges down from Voluntary to Involuntary Manslaughter would be the first step. You might get lucky and get a deal on Aggravated Assault. They won't accept anything else than a guilty plea. Which means she'd be looking at time served in the best-case scenario.*

Keeler stabbed a finger at the original question. *Who's the recording for?*

Finnegan avoided eye contact. He wrote, *I'm more scared of them than I am of you. Sorry.* He wrote more. *They know about you being here. Laura's big brother isn't making them shake in their boots.*

Keeler looked at the man and had a momentary feeling of pity for him. It passed quickly, and he thought, *whatever. This is unacceptable.* He rose from the chair and picked up Finnegan's iPhone, stabbing a finger at the lawyer. "You stay put."

Keeler walked to the bar, where the man was still shining the same pint glass he'd been working on a few minutes earlier. He stopped shining, a smirk frozen in place as Keeler approached.

A second man sat in a nook behind the bartender, fingering the keys of a laptop computer. This one was around the same age, wearing a baseball cap backwards and a black t-shirt with some heavy metal band's logo. Both of them looking at Keeler now.

The bartender said, "You lost?"

Keeler leaned over the counter. A tub of soapy water contained beer glasses.

He held up the lawyer's phone. "Buddy, do you mind holding on to this for me while I have a confidential conversation over there with my lawyer?"

The bartender smirked. "I doubt that's your lawyer, boy."

The other man with the backwards baseball hat said, "That phone is private property, go give it back."

Keeler extended the phone to the bartender, who reached for it. Looking straight into the bartender's eyes, Keeler dropped the phone into the soapy tub. The man froze, eyes tracked to the now submerged phone, invisible within the soapy sink.

The bartender was close, face flushing pink with anger. He said, "You little bitch."

Keeler got a fistful of his shirt and pulled him easily into a medium paced head butt. The superciliary ridge above the eyebrows connected with the bartender's nose.

It all happened fast but slow. Fast for him, slow for Keeler.

The impact was controlled, and he pulled back without doing serious damage. Leaving the bartender standing, but with a bloody nose that had ruined what looked like a new shirt.

Keeler said, "Looks like your shirt needs cleaning."

The guy with the backwards baseball hat was standing now, looking at Keeler.

Keeler said, "Can I help you?"

The guy had a flat gaze, nodding with a little smile. He had his right hand up, making a pistol shape with an extended forefinger. The man pointed the simulated gun at Keeler. "You can't even save yourself now pal, it's over." Pulling the trigger and fake shooting at Keeler. The smirk turned into a wicked grin.

Mouth caught in an *O* shape as he mimicked the gunshot. "*Pchhhhhh.*"

Keeler turned and walked back to where Finnegan sat. He put himself in the chair again.

The lawyer said nothing, now looking at him with a kind of dead eyed stare.

Keeler said, "Where were we?"

Finnegan said, "Look over the documents and then get the hell out."

Keeler said, "I'll leave when I'm ready."

He lifted the folder open with a finger and skimmed through the documents without actually seeing them. He felt his mind occupied with other things, visualizing Laura's hands speaking gobbledygook, tapping her response to his question. Keeler closed the folder and stood up. He didn't need to say any goodbyes, just turned and left.

Chapter Sixteen

Walking down off the deck to the parking lot, a glimmer of sunlight winked at him from the Corvette's perfect paint job. Like a sign of some kind. This had been Dad's car, back in the day. Until they'd gotten rid of their father. Laura had taken the Corvette not so much as an inheritance, than as a trophy.

Something cathartic about sitting in the low backed bucket seat, revving the engine.

He was feeling in his body exactly what their father had liked about this vehicle and, in some way, enjoying the same attributes. The cold facts of a powerful machine, the unapologetic styling. Something brutally honest about that. Dad had his issues and in the end they'd needed him gone. But, *nothing feels better than blood on blood*, is what Laura would have said.

Cruising out of there in the Stingray, feeling the motor, Keeler couldn't help wondering about that connection. What Laura must be thinking, each time she drove the vehicle. The constant reminder of their father. He figured that if it had been him who'd taken the Corvette, it would have been sold at the first opportunity. There were plenty of buyers for a classic car like that.

Keeler would have probably given it away free rather than keep it.

The other thing was that the Corvette was too visible.

He drove fast along a narrow S shaped strip of blacktop driveway, shooting out of the Weasel Boy estate between thick hedges near the riverbank. The driveway became a two-lane road and Keeler gunned it straight ahead towards a tangle of highway ramps and overpasses. He'd take the on-ramp north and get back to Laura and Josh's house to ruminate on next steps.

From the darkly shadowed underpass came the blink of a muzzle flash. Keeler recognized immediately what was happening. The Ford Explorer from earlier was now tucked back into a shady area under the highway ramp, waiting for him. The bullet struck the hood of the Corvette, just in front of him, ricocheting instantaneously to glance off the upper passenger side of the windshield, making a small spiderweb in the shatter proof glass.

The Explorer was pointed out for an easy exit, about a hundred yards away. Keeler could see the activity in the cab, as he sped towards them, closing the distance. The shooter was in the passenger seat. He'd had his rifle resting on the window. Now the weapon was being raised. A second shot wasn't planned.

More intimidation? Like they were playing a game. For a split second he considered ramming them with the Corvette, but the urge passed.

Moving past the Explorer now, glancing curiously at the two men in the cab. Who were these people? It's like he'd entered another world entirely. In Keeler's world firing a weapon at a person is a declaration of war, period. The fact that they hadn't been aiming to kill was not relevant. Period.

Keeler saw the vehicle pulling out behind him in the rear-view mirror.

He could hardly believe how the entire situation had moved from mystery to clarity, now, that the shooting had begun.

* * *

Keeler took the on-ramp and merged into thin traffic moving north. He kept to the speed limit, observing the Explorer in his rearview mirror. This time he wasn't going to try and get away from them. In fact, he was planning the opposite. An enemy with stupid confidence was a good thing.

Draw them in, take them out of circulation. Keeler saw it as a transformative process. Turn these two from an asset to their organization, into a liability. The only question was where. He wasn't sure, but he'd know it when he saw it. The gas tank was three quarters full, and this was America. Which meant that there would be a mall.

Forty minutes later, the wooded hills broke open revealing a large shopping center in the valley below. A cluster of buildings in what looked from above like a kind of campus. Other side of the road were adjacent parking lots about the same size as the campus. The signs said Buckeye Factory Outlets, so maybe it wasn't technically a mall.

Whatever it was, it looked good and right. The kind of place you could get lost and then found again. Keeler steered the Corvette through an arcing descent, liking what he was seeing.

The entrance to the Factory Outlets was choked with traffic, eager people trying to get in on the dream. The Explorer kept several cars back, the driver patiently dogging Keeler as he navigated to one of the parking lots.

Presumptuous, that was the five-dollar word for what they were. Keeler spelled it out to himself, four syllables. Presumptuous to assume that since most people were lemmings, that everyone was a lemming. They had met his sister already, and she had blown a hole in one their friends. Why assume that the brother would be so different?

According to a movie he'd seen on the bus up to Ohio, lemmings don't commit suicide. When the lemming group reaches a certain population density, some kind of collective impulse kicks in and they all set off on a migration. That's when thousands of them die. But, according to the documentary it's not suicide, it's just an accident.

Keeler didn't completely agree with the film maker's interpretation, since he wasn't a believer in coincidences or accidents.

If the group instinctively commits a mass migration, that has the effect of killing a high percentage of them, it's still a kind of suicide. Or, maybe suicide requires a desire to die, which makes the lemming thing coercive homicide, or just plain stupid.

Looking at the Explorer back there, Keeler caught himself comparing them to lemmings and couldn't help himself laughing out loud. He rolled the window down and whistled happily into the crisp autumn air, a sudden burst of enthusiasm.

By the time he'd parked the Corvette a seriously steady calm had come over him, from the head down to his toes. He was nodding to himself in a kind of confirmation of existence, being alive and feeling good. Pre-mission stuff, the accumulation of confidence that you get from serious experience. Like nobody can even remotely fuck with you. Tuned in.

The Explorer had disappeared, and he didn't actually care where it had gone. If the shooter had wanted to kill him he'd have taken a second shot, back there at the overpass. The fact that he hadn't wasn't Keeler's fault.

This place had the scent of America. Cut grass, hot asphalt from the crew filling potholes, and the faint odor of gasoline fumes, mixed with real fresh air from the woods. The best smells in the world. If they would package that as an after shave Keeler would take it. Until then, *au naturel*.

The Explorer was positioned by the exit, a couple of rows away. Keeler was actually impressed that these people possessed the sense to maneuver themselves in a way that allowed a clear view of him on foot, as well as being able to move out after him with the vehicle.

He walked out of the parking lot just like any other person would. Sticking to the pedestrian lane and moving carefully to avoid being crushed by some soccer mom's oversized family wagon.

The outlet buildings were straight ahead, all darkly stained wood and country styling. The outdoor speaker system was playing canned country and western music. Keeler crossed the road and came to the entrance arch. An LCD screen mall directory was placed prominently, and he examined the options.

Pretty much everything you could imagine was available at the outlet. From ice cream to kitchen wares, with a lot of fashion in between. Keeler was a big fan of ice cream, but that's not what he was looking for. Hunt & Hustle Sporting Goods was exactly what he wanted. It was over in zone three of the mall, just behind the food court.

The directory screen was conveniently reflective. Keeler could examine the people behind him, while seeming to study the available information. People coming in from the parking lot were grouped predominantly in twos and threes. The Buckeye Factory Outlets was an event, not a chore. Which is why the solitary hulking figure of a man, moving slowly, stood out from the crowd.

Keeler considered the options. Go at the guy right then and there and break his neck? There were civilians around. Plus the second man somewhere. It'd be better to go at them and the vehicle at the same time, group them back together and isolate them from civilians to the extent possible.

Plus, there was now the option of shopping for something nice to attack them with. He got moving, glancing into an oncoming store window to see the big dude coming after him.

Chapter Seventeen

Keeler made straight for the food court, a huge hall of picnic benches surrounded by fast-food franchises in an oval the size of a football field. Lunch of all kinds was happening, the action was intense.

The majority of franchise restaurants here were simply counters from which customers placed orders and waited for pickup, before moving out to the main area to consume their purchases while safely seated at the cluster of tables. There were two exceptions on each end of the oval, fancy restaurants with interior seating.

Keeler didn't want to turn around, so he just kept going to the restaurant on the far side of the food court, *Osteria Bella Vista*. The hostess began her greeting, but he put up a hand to stop her.

"My friends are inside, I'll just join them."

"No problem, sir."

He kept on moving. Feeling the heat of the big man's eyes on his back.

Osteria Bella Vista was a crowded restaurant with dark wood furnishings and painted murals of a Tuscan landscape, punctuated by clay cisterns of wine and framed by painted grape vines and angels with trumpets. The music was another flavor of American country pop that'd be more at home in a Cracker Barrel.

The toilets were to the right, behind a set of Venetian screens in dark brown. Over to the left was the kitchen and the wide double doors that he was looking for. Keeler estimated that the people following him would pause before entering the restaurant. Maybe they'd think he was meeting someone. Maybe that would get them excited.

He went straight through the double doors into the kitchen. The center-piece of the large space was a steel worktable. Three men were busy preparing identical tomato based plates, laying down basil garnish and olive oil, spooning pre-grated parmesan cheese, and squeezing some kind of white and green paste onto a steaming slab of grilled chicken breast.

He walked by, without garnering either comment or a glance. A mustachioed dishwasher made eye contact and Keeler winked at him. The back door was already open, and he went through it, happy to find himself in a fenced off area. Nice to be in a shopping mall, they'd always try and hide the unseemly things, like kitchen workers and garbage cans.

He joined the regular flow of happy shoppers behind the food court, satisfied to find himself without a tail now.

Ohio is a well-known hunting destination, with the seasonal openings in autumn and early winter. Looking into the display window, Keeler had the impression that Hunt & Hustle Sporting Goods wasn't going to disappoint, with a heavy focus on killing deer, and only a minor nod to golf and jogging.

He entered the store without a plan, merely hoping for a short term, tactical weapon. But, once he saw the breadth of possibilities he began to think more strategically. Thinking, *we're in it for the long haul.* There was no way of knowing what this was going to take, in terms of commitment and activity. He started with a medium-sized backpack, the base requirement of a weapon system.

The saleswoman was helpful, leading him around as piece by piece he accumulated the necessary components. All of it high quality and built to last. He avoided the blaze orange colors, opting for muted olive green and camouflage. They even had olive green duct tape. The basics were quickly acquired, duct tape, tactical light, a Buck knife and a small multi-tool Leatherman. He found a range finding scope for medium distance and a long distance spotting scope.

The saleswoman got excited about the spotting scope.

She said, "For the money, that's the best one out there. Can even take pictures if you want it to."

"Does it come with a memory card?"

"I'll throw it in for you at a fifty percent discount sir, given the circumstances."

Keeler's story wasn't complicated. He was in Ohio on a hunting trip and his luggage had been lost. Which justified the necessity of a full re-up. And, secretly, he was feeling lucky that he'd made decent money working for a friend out by the Vancouver coast a couple of weeks earlier.

Keeler was calculating the cost so far, coming up on a thousand bucks. The saleswoman looked happy.

She said, "Well I suppose what's left is the bow."

Which was a little surprising, since he hadn't figured on the bow, or a rifle. But if she was so convinced that it was a bow he needed, this could only be because gun season hadn't yet opened up. So that's what it would be, like fate, or destiny. Keeler nodded.

"Yep. Take me to the bow section and sell me something that's going to work in mud or rain or whatever."

"What are you hunting deer or turkey?"

"Deer."

She said, "We get award winning bucks out here, but you already know that."

He said, "It's why you're the Buckeye state I guess."

She stood off from him then, curious. "Well, you do know that we're the Buckeye state because of the buckeye tree. But, you might not know that the buckeye tree garnered its name because of how the buckeye nut resembles the eye of a deer. So, in a way you are correct sir."

Keeler hadn't known, but now he did.

The bow section was vast, and he wasn't an expert archer, just a guy with a problem to solve. But, the saleswoman was an expert, and she knew exactly what he needed, given his size, and strength, and the kind of thing he was looking to put down. She also knew what arrows, and arrowheads were best for a clean kill. And while she selected all the appropriate items that he would need for the hunt, Keeler visualized the razor-sharp broad-head arrow piercing the flesh of Laura's enemies.

On the way to the cash register, Keeler spotted another tasty item for his pack, a shrink-wrapped spool of Mil-Spec Type III Paracord.

Chapter Eighteen

There was no specific plan, only the hint of an idea, forming in his head the way a cloud shaped like a dog might form in the sky. Keeler called it *ambient thinking*. You have to trust that the back of your mind is working stuff out, while the front of your mind is concentrating on other things, like walking straight.

He was a high trust guy until he wasn't.

The idea forming in his head involved coming up on his new friends from behind. He spent a little time at Hunt & Hustle's glass door, looking left, looking right. Making sure that the men from the Ford Explorer hadn't figured out where he was. Making sure that they hadn't set up on him again, waiting.

If they hadn't been able to find him, they might be scouring the place. Another possibility was that they'd reconvene back at the parking lot. The thing about operating in a team was the people involved sometimes felt better together. It made them weaker because they sought the comfort of togetherness. Whereas Keeler had an implicit advantage, as he was comfortable either way.

Another consideration was that these people might be operating under strict conditional orders. Like, if you lose him, wait a certain amount of time. Reconvene at the vehicle within ten minutes. That kind of thing. Whatever, he couldn't guess.

Keeler moved out, walking toward the outlet's perimeter. He avoided the regular walkway to the parking lot, treading over some landscaped parts instead. This brought him over the road to wooded hills that bordered the northern side of the lot.

He got into the cover of trees and mounted the hill. Halfway up, he set down his pack.

The spotting scope had come in a box that was impossible to open without doing serious damage to the packaging with the knife. After a short wrangle, Keeler sat cross-legged with the pack on his lap. He rested elbows on it and stabilized the device.

The Ford Explorer came into focus, visible thanks to the elevation. Two bearded men standing by the rear of the sports utility vehicle, eating sandwiches out of wrappers. Someone had taken advantage of the food court. Two bottles of soda were set up on the roof. They were having lunch, waiting for him. Neither of them seemed prepared for an attack on their rear.

Unbelievable. It was almost unfair, but only almost. After all, does a hunter have guilty feelings when the buck approaches his blind? Not even remotely, he just gets excited at the prospect of putting an arrow down range. The ethical failing was theirs entirely.

The backpack was purpose-built. He was able to fix the bow to the rear and set up the side of the pack as a quiver for five of the arrows he'd bought. The razored broad heads attached to inserts glued into the shafts. Keeler had opted against a special wrench the saleswoman had tried to sell him, figuring it wasn't necessary. He only slightly regretted that decision.

Gear is good, but too much gear is an encumbrance.

Pack on his back, Keeler came down the hill onto the asphalt lot. He slipped between parked vehicles, planning on getting closer to the enemy before deciding exactly what to do. He had a few options, hunting knife, compound bow, fists, boots, and combinations of the above.

Getting closer now, he was able to see the men more clearly. Keeler stopped at the back of a fancy Dodge pickup truck. He had the long distance spotting scope in the left side jacket pocket and the medium rangefinder in his right pocket. One of the men wore a baseball cap and a fleece hoodie, the one who'd followed him on foot. The other guy had short, cropped hair and wore sunglasses. The first guy had been the rubber bullet shooter, while his buddy had put the scratch into Laura's Corvette.

Keeler watched the man with short hair, sitting on the open hatch back of the Explorer, finishing his sandwich. What looked like a chicken burger. Like some kind of parking lot picnic. His buddy paced and ate, one hand filled with a regular burger, the other clutching a bottle of sprite. This one took a bite and a sip, like that. Bite and sip, one after the other. Like a methodology.

Keeler took his pack down and removed the bow from where it was clipped into the frame. He put the pack back on, not yet entirely comfortable with how the system worked. He practiced taking an arrow from the quiver with the pack on his back and the bow in his left hand. It worked. Not totally fluid, but one at a time was alright.

In movies he'd seen people take two arrows at a time and quick fire them, like a semi-automatic, but he figured he'd do better operating the bow in single shot mode. The buck knife had come in a sheath, now attached to his belt. Things were looking good.

The parking lot wasn't empty, but there weren't too many people moving around in it. The existing pedestrians seemed focused upon car-based activities involving shopping. Either getting in the car, or getting out of a car, putting things into the car, or struggling to get close to the car. Currently there was only a multi-generational group of wide hipped women traveling slowly across the asphalt, maybe fifty yards off and two rows away.

Keeler moved in a crouch, out of sight behind parked vehicles. He got within forty yards of the Ford Explorer. He wasn't any kind of archer, but he'd shot arrows before and had more than enough strength to control the bow. Twenty yards was going to be a no brainer, unless the bow system was seriously off. The saleswoman at Hunt & Hustle had said that these days the bows were pretty much dialed in at the factory.

He nocked an arrow to the string, using a finger to keep the assemblage steady. Crouching and moving until he was one car row back, hidden behind a Subaru SUV. This was it, do or die. Another slow glance around revealed no obvious onlookers, either in or out of their vehicles.

Keeler stepped out from behind the Subaru and raised the compound bow. The saleswoman had said it had a fifty-pound draw, enough power to put down a medium-sized animal, like a deer or a wolf. But maybe not enough for an Elk or a bear. These guys looked softer than an elk or a moose, more like orangutans, if you were going to stick with the animal comparison.

Keeler pulled, steadily engaging the cams. The draw felt moderate, synthetic fibers smoothly rolling over, reducing let-off. The string anchored at full draw compressing the limbs, storing energy. Aiming was where it could get tricky. Looking through the riser and the multi-pin sight, Keeler wasn't any kind of expert. He decided to just eyeball it.

The two men were right there in front of him. The guy in the baseball hat had become aware of his presence, now staring at him with an open mouth, sandwich in there half chewed. His hands were entirely occupied by lunch. Keeler shifted his gaze to the other one, sitting on the explorer's open tailgate. The guy hadn't noticed him yet, so Keeler kept the sights on the standing one.

The release was crisp, making a satisfying *thwap*. The man was lurching off to the side, but Keeler had anticipated the movement, leading him. The arrow flew true along a flat trajectory and buried itself into the tall man's belly. Keeler set the bow down and sprinted the intervening distance. His right hand loosened the buck knife from its sheath. Within a second he was at the Explorer. The man with the cropped hair had dropped his chicken burger, fumbling now behind him. Looking for his weapon no doubt.

Keeler sank the six-inch blade into the man's denim clad thigh, pinning him to the tailgate. He reached around to where the guy had been scrabbling with his hands and retrieved a pistol tucked into the man's waistband.

The tall man was writhing on the ground. Hat knocked off by the sudden flurry of violence, one hand clutching the arrow shaft protruding from his abdomen. The razor broad-head would have caused all kinds of mayhem in there. The saleswoman had gotten positively romantic about the model, something Keeler wasn't completely understanding about a single beveled blade configuration being all the rage.

What he did know, seeing the guy on the ground, was that he'd be looking at serious surgical expenses, unless he simply died.

The chicken burger eater was sucking air and making a strange sound. The weapon stuck in his waistband was a Smith and Wesson M&P9. Keeler slid the pistol into his left pocket. He used a hand on the man's leg for leverage and pulled at the knife. It seemed to have stuck into the guy's femur and required a sharp tug. The man's eyes rolled up in their sockets as he passed out.

Keeler fished a leather wallet out of the guy's back pocket. Put it into the jacket with the man's weapon.

He turned to the other one. Observing him impaled by the arrow, booted feet kicking at the asphalt, spinning him in a twitchy kind of circle, the ground now slick with blood. The man seemed to be attempting now to gain access to a pistol, likewise tucked stupidly behind him and therefore hard to get at.

Which is why someone invented the holster. A better way of carrying a gun.

Keeler took a couple of steps, crouching over the injured man. "I need that arrow back."

He put down his pack, leaning it against the Explorer's wheel. The man was hyperventilating, bugged eyes staring. Specks of froth were collecting at the corners of his lips.

The guy had exactly the same pistol as his friend. Now, Keeler had two of them weighing down his pockets.

Keeler turned the man over. The single beveled broad arrow head had gone clean through. The blades were slick with blood. There wasn't enough shaft on that side for him to grab, so Keeler had to spend almost five seconds unscrewing the arrowhead. He put the deadly thing down and rolled the man over again. The guy was in shock now, pale and bleeding. Keeler grasped the carbon fiber shaft and pulled it out.

He looked at the man, lying there looking bad.

"What's the deal, why all the aggression, brother?"

The man's shirt tails were still dry and clean. Keeler wiped the arrow shaft. He began screwing the bladed head back on.

The man was having trouble opening his mouth. His pupils were dilated. He said, "We were told to scare you off."

"Who told you to scare me off?"

The guy licked his lips and stammered. "Gus said to give you a warning is all I know."

He said, "Do I look warned?"

"It wasn't my idea. After you went to Weasel Boy, we got the call to take the second shot. We told you to just walk away."

The guy flinched, pain diverting his attention. He looked close to losing consciousness.

Keeler raised his eyebrows. "Just because you tell someone to do something, it doesn't mean that it's going to happen. If you live, maybe you'll learn." He stood up. "You'll make it if the paramedics get here quick. You have a phone?"

"Thanks." The word came out, weak and soft. The guy got busy looking for his phone.

The one Keeler had shot with the bow had his phone out, gasping air and trying to operate the device. Keeler put their guns in his backpack, stashed in the main compartment. He came back across the alley to retrieve his bow, crouching to snap it back into the clips and replace the used arrow in the quiver.

The two wounded men were out of commission. The chicken burger man conscious now, dealing with a wounded leg. But that was it. No other activity. No witnesses in sight and no further problems. These two would now cease their surveillance and become liabilities to their employer. Keeler calculated the way through parked cars to the Corvette.

He stood and turned, making three strides around the large mini van parked to his left. A female voice spoke slowly and clearly from just behind him. "Stop right there or I'll blow your fucking head off."

Keeler stopped.

The voice was tense, the speaker was holding her breath. "Show me your hands."

Keeler put his hands in the air.

The voice gulped air and said, "Take two steps backwards."

Keeler took two steps backwards, realizing why. He was now stuck between parked vehicles, which constrained his ability to move.

"Turn around."

Keeler turned around to come face to face with the bore of a large nickel-plated revolver. Behind the weapon, the red-headed waitress from the diner crouched in a solid Weaver stance. One foot forward, toe pointed straight ahead. Her other foot was back, toe pointed out at forty-five degrees. Nice.

"Shit. It's you." Her eyes widened as she recognized him. "There I was thinking you were cute, when you're just another psychopath like all the men in my life."

Keeler shrugged. "Sorry about that."

The waitress held a revolver on him, crouched wide eyed.

She said, "At least you know how to apologize."

Chapter Nineteen

The Ford pickup was parked behind the waitress. The truck looking just as good, cream with that sky blue and brown stripe. The girl with the mousy hair sat in the cab. Eyes wide in a pale face. Keeler winked, and she smiled.

The waitress said, "Don't you even think about moving. I'll put you down, man."

Keeler's eyes shifted to her. She'd finished a night shift and had taken her daughter shopping. She looked tired.

He said, "Quit it with the gun. I'm not going to move and I won't do anything to you."

She laughed somewhat hysterically. "Yeah, right. I just watched you do..." The waitress blinked twice, as if recalling what she'd just witnessed. "Whatever the fuck that was," head pointing at the Ford Explorer. "You're like some ninja or something."

She might have gone without sleep for a little too long, but the hands were absolutely steady on that heavy gun.

Keeler shrugged. "I get it. If all you saw was me going at those two, it looks bad. I understand. But there's a whole bunch of other stuff that you didn't see."

She gave a short laugh. "What they always say, right? Context matters."

"They say nothing happens in a vacuum."

The waitress's brow was furrowed as she listened.

Keeler shrugged and sort of laughed. "Put it this way, I didn't initiate. Nice town you've got here." He chin pointed at the two wounded men. "I don't think it's just those two. There's more where that came from."

"Uh huh. Yes, we've got issues here, that's true. But here's the deal mister out of towner, we need to live here, you don't."

He said, "If I'd known you were watching I might have gone at it differently."

"Like how?"

"What I mean is, I understand how it looks to you, and what the stakes are here."

She said, "Okay, and what would you have done differently?"

Keeler said, "Maybe taken it somewhere else is all."

The waitress said, "Looks like at least one of them might bleed out and die."

The taller man in the baseball hat did seem to be floundering in his own blood.

Keeler said, "They started it with a rifle, I used what I had. The guy's bleeding. I told him to call 911 already."

The waitress had both of her hands wrapped around the grip of a powerful beast of a handgun. She seemed expert enough, standing there in her Weaver stance like someone who'd spent time at the range.

He said, "What do you want to do?"

She said, "I should call the police but my hands are occupied."

"They're already calling 911."

"Bullshit. Those people don't call the cops. They call their friends." She waved the big gun at Keeler. "This town might be FUBAR but we've got one or two honest people left in the department. You can't just get all vigilante the moment you run into some friction with people you don't like. Get out your phone and call the cops on yourself."

"Or what?"

"Or I put a round into your leg."

"You're not aiming for my leg."

"Shut up and get your phone out."

"I don't have a phone."

She rolled her eyes. "You can use mine." The waitress took one hand off the revolver and used it to pull a large phone from her jacket pocket. This was the moment when Keeler could have disarmed her, but he didn't. Watching instead as she managed the operation. The waitress tossed her phone to him. He caught it one handed.

He looked at the device, password protected.

"What's the password?"

"1234."

The Lock Screen snapped open to reveal a photograph of the waitress and her daughter, looking about the same age. An older man had his arm around the kid. Keeler recognized Earl, from Donald's Delicious Donuts. He recalled the waitress in a whispered argument with Earl at the diner.

"Who's this, your dad? Earl's your father?"

"Yeah, he's my dad." Her forehead wrinkled. "Shit, you went over the road to Donald's after eating that huge breakfast. What'd you do, have coffee and donuts with him?"

"I noticed that Earl's got his own problems. Maybe you should lend him that fat gun of yours."

"Murder isn't the solution, plus there are too many of them to kill."

Keeler shrugged. "That's often debatable."

She said something, but her words were drowned out by a loud tire squeal accompanied by engine growl. Keeler glanced to his left. A pickup truck roared into the parking lane and slowed as it approached the Ford Explorer.

Keeler said, "What were you saying?"

She was also looking at the newcomers through intervening car windows. Protected from view where she stood. The waitress said, "I don't remember."

He head tilted to the new arrivals. "Doesn't look like he called 911."

"No."

It was the same truck that had pulled up outside of Donald's Delicious Donuts. With the same men who had roughed up Earl that morning.

Keeler said, "You know them?"

She squinted at them through window glass. "Unfortunately."

"Walk back to your truck and leave, before you get involved."

Her weapon was down at her side now. "I'm already involved."

The truck was maybe twenty yards away, and now beginning to roll in their direction. They'd seen Keeler, but not the waitress, hidden from view by the parked mini-van. Keeler still held her phone.

Keeler said, "They haven't seen you yet, so leave."

She said, "Give me my phone."

He said nothing. The pickup truck was now too close, moving very slowly toward them. He took a step out from behind the parked cars. The two men in the cab, turned to him. Their faces made uniform and blanked by wraparound sun glasses.

Keeler turned to fully face them, mouth now curved into a

smile. In his peripheral vision the waitress retreated to her truck.

She said, "I'm on the night shift. I want that phone back."

The vehicle was now close. Would these people have any idea who he was? How could they? The pack on his back and the hunting bow wouldn't be visible to them yet. Plus, it'd be normal to see a man dressed for the hunt in Ohio, at that time of year.

He waved the phone in his hand and spoke to the men. "How you doing? I called 911. Police should be here soon with the paramedics."

The driver was closest to him. An angry looking bearded man wearing the sunglasses and a baseball hat.

The man said, "Alright. Just stay right there."

The passenger opened his door on the other side of the truck, leaping down from the cab. Evidently planning to come and narrow the distance. Which would put Keeler at a tactical disadvantage. Not to mention the interaction he'd already had with this passenger, back at Donald's Delicious Donuts.

Keeler moved. Not very fast, but fast enough. The waitresses phone went into his pocket. He took two steps past the driver's side window, putting himself in a place where the driver would be able to see only in the side mirror.

The driver said, "Hey!"

But the passenger had already committed to passing around the front of the truck. Keeler vaulted into the pickup's bed. One step across and he was dropping out the other side. By that time, the passenger had come around to the driver's side, so Keeler now had the truck between himself and the two men. Neither of whom had eyes on him.

Which enabled Keeler to get into a low crouch and hustle between parked cars, invisible now. He stopped moving when he was three alleys away, putting a parked vehicle between him and the truck and raising his head to peer at them through the intervening windshields.

He set the pack down and retrieved one of the pistols requisitioned from the two hunting casualties back there. Then he got down into a push up position so that he could see underneath the parked vehicles. Keeler waited like that for five minutes.

And nothing happened.

So, he flipped to a crouching position and looked through the various windshields again. Looking for anything moving, anything trawling for him. Any armed enemies that needed to be dealt with.

The stench of burning plastic hit him. A column of smoke becoming visible as he jogged towards where he'd parked Laura's Corvette. Coming around another parking alley the situation became clear, what he already knew instinctively. The Corvette was on fire. The passenger side window had been smashed in. So far, it was the interior upholstery that was burning.

And Laura's case file the lawyer had given him.

Keeler had just enough time to get under the vehicle and remove the plastic bag containing his sister's pistol from where he'd hidden it in the spare tire tub. By the time he was a hundred yards away, the car was fully engulfed in flames, the smoke black and billowing skywards.

Later, up in the woods on the ridge line, Keeler had the spotting scope steadied, examining the scene. Civilians were gawking at the burning vehicle. Two overfed security guards from the Buckeye Factory Outlets were establishing a perimeter, pushing back the shoppers.

The Ford Explorer was gone, along with the men he'd incapacitated. Only a large blood stain remained. Keeler was doubtful whether the incoming law enforcement would even notice.

The wailing of fire trucks approached. The squeal of police sirens had joined in. Having Laura's Corvette on fire was going to draw attention. He'd get Josh to call it in as stolen.

He watched the vehicle burn. Thinking now about symbolism and how sometimes an event like this can be a kind of marker in a life. That vehicle had meaning for her. The unspoken fact of it was that Laura kept the Corvette as a reminder of her resilience and the way that she'd constructed her own path out of trouble. Their father's fancy old car had been an emblem of this, and now it was gone forever.

Keeler removed Laura's gun from the pack and spent some time wiping it down. Then, he buried the weapon right there on the wooded hillside. Making the deepest hole he could manage with his hands and the buck knife. He didn't see any good reason to hold on to the gun, and in fact, many good reasons not to.

Chapter Twenty

Laura Keeler was in the county prison's canteen, sitting alone looking into the compartments of a lunch tray. The roasted turkey drumstick took up most of the space. The compartment next to it contained mashed potatoes made out of freeze-dried ingredients. The third compartment had a limp pile of iceberg lettuce with a squirt of thousand island dressing. A square wedge of green jello jiggled in the fourth and final section.

Laura was currently examining the interior of the jello, inspecting what looked like pieces of canned pear.

She had no favorite guards, since they were all enemies. But the one she liked least now took a seat on the stool facing her. This guard was a very skinny woman whose name was Slopes. At least, that's what was written in yellow letters on her shirt tag.

The fact that Slopes had approached and sat across from Laura was unusual. Which meant to her that other unusual things might happen. So, she got busy eating. Because, when unusual things happen you never know when you'll get another chance at nutrition. She lifted the turkey drumstick and took a large bite, finally making eye contact with the guard while chewing carefully.

Slopes was ugly in a shrunken, skinny kind of way. She was in her thirties and had stringy brown hair tied back in a pony tail. Laura stared at her, counting twenty chews before swallowing and starting again.

Slopes said, "We burned your Corvette. That was a nice car."

Laura said nothing. The hackles on the back of her neck raised, and she understood, from this, that someone was approaching her from behind. She didn't look though, preferring to maintain the outward appearance of equanimity. She took third bite of the drumstick and chewed steadily.

Slopes said, "Plus they killed your brother. I don't know if the state requires anyone to inform you of that, officially. But he got shot in the head by a gangbanger out of Cleveland. I heard he did it for a hundred and fifty bucks."

Laura kept the laughter inside. Her brother was indestructible, at least that's how she saw it. Maybe he'd succumb to a mob of jihadist zombies one day, torn limb for limb by a thousand sharpened fingernails. But until that day came he certainly wasn't going to be shot in the head by some gangbanger out of Cleveland.

Slopes said, "You don't care about your own blood, bitch?"

Laura took a final bite of the turkey and worked it with her teeth. Keeping eye contact with Slopes and wondering when the next thing was going to happen. The feeling of presence behind her increased. She lowered her head slightly and saw them in her peripheral vision. At least two guards right behind her.

She swallowed the turkey.

Laura lifted the plastic spork from its place by the tray and used it to spoon mashed potato into her mouth. She got a second spoon in before they moved on her. The guard behind and to the right slammed a fist onto her elbow, making the spork flip up and along with it the third spoon of mashed potato. Which went flying in an arc to land in a splatter on the adjacent table.

Slopes said, "That's anti-social behavior. Get her up and cuff her."

Hands dug into Laura's armpits from behind, wrenching her off the stool. Laura allowed it, keeping her mouth closed and chewing the remainder of her food, anticipating blows that would make it hard to swallow. Every molecule of nutrition counts.

Laura managed to put down the mashed potato just in time. A baton from behind came slamming into her kidneys, taking her breath away and reducing her to a gasping bundle of pain for a couple of seconds. By the time she was able to breathe again they'd kicked out her legs and had her face pushed into the floor.

Her tongue verified that the teeth were okay. A boot was stepping on her head though and she could hardly breathe. Another boot kicked at her ribs and Laura did her best to get into an embryonic position. Wondering, would someone come and intervene, or was this just going to go on and on?

She narrowly avoided a steel-toed boot to her eye, tucking the chin just in time and taking the hit on her forehead. That was it for the moment. They pulled her arms back and locked zip ties around her wrists. Laura got her breath back. Inhaling through nostrils and maintaining her mental balance.

Inside she was smiling, knowing that none of this would be happening if her brother wasn't gaining traction on the outside. Clearly, he'd pissed someone off.

Thinking about what had happened over the last four months, Laura figured that even if her brother massacred the lot of them and burned the town to the ground, it wouldn't be enough. Her only regret was that she might not get to participate. That, and a feeling of trepidation for Josh, who was a quiet introspective man, not built for combat the way the Keelers were.

But Tom could protect Josh. And if it ended up the other way, the wrong way, there wouldn't have been any good means of avoiding it. It wasn't like she'd gone out looking for trouble. She'd just happened to stumble into it.

The two guards got her up on her feet, facing Slopes. The other prisoners only glanced at her, keeping to their own business. Most of them knew better than to so much as cough, since the guards came down heavy here. Slopes wasn't the worst of them, just one petty enforcer out of many. Decisions were made at a higher level.

Slopes said, "Take her to the hole and make it hurt. Five days."

Laura kept her mouth shut, her lips making a straight line across her face. She maintained eye contact with the guard, not even thinking about head butting her in the face. The time would come for satisfaction. She was pretty sure now that total war was inevitable. It's a conclusion that her brother was going to come to soon, if he hadn't already.

When the reckoning came, solitary confinement three floors down from the main holding cells might actually be beneficial. At least in the hole she'd be protected from whatever destructive ordnance her brother might bring to bear.

Chapter Twenty-One

The guard unlocked the wrist and ankle cuffs, taking in the slack on the chains and letting Laura walk into the cell. Looking at the stainless steel sink toilet combo and the stark lighting scheme. Laura found herself contemplating the fact that someone had actually designed this. An architect.

That had to have been one cold son of a bitch.

Whatever.

The steel door clanged behind her. Laura walked the two paces it took to get to the cot and lie down on it. Now, looking at the ceiling and a ventilation grill, she felt her mind wandering to the past. Taking a stroll down memory lane. As it did so, a small section of her brain was aware that it might have been the Corvette which had triggered this nostalgic yearning.

Smell of smoke.

She closed her eyes. Darkness, flames appearing far off in the night. Feeling like she was drifting closer, smelling wood burning.

What Slopes had said, they'd torched Dad's Corvette.

Weirdly, Laura found herself hoping that this was true.

* * *

Night of the bonfire up in some wilderness outside of Portland, Oregon.

Dad claimed Tlingit heritage, got himself accepted, so the family got dragged up to the Pacific Northwest every couple years for some potlatch fire ceremony. Not that he looked remotely indigenous. Looked Irish is what mom used to say. When he was in a good mood that was funny, when he was brooding it wasn't.

What Laura saw: the fire far off in the night, maybe a quarter mile away. Walking hand in hand with another girl her age, who actually looked like a Tlingit and dressed like one. The long grass caressing bare legs, moonlight behind them casting shadows. The night warm and breezy, bonfire whipping up sparks and the friendly happy sounds made by people dancing around it.

She must have been like eleven or twelve years old by then.

Seeing mom cross legged with the other women. All of them clearly indigenous and mom looking more than French, auburn hair among the black tresses. But, mom didn't give a shit, never gave a shit about that kind of thing. Just diving right in on the situation and embracing it. No fear in that woman, all love and curiosity.

Her brother was doing something dumb with the other boys. Down by the river, something involving knives and rocks and fighting maybe. Or else he'd be hanging around with the girls, a young teenager now. Not that Laura knew about any of that back then, it was just occurring to her as she remembered it.

And as she always did when dredging up this particular memory, feeling guilty. Blaming herself for not having clocked the fact that dad wasn't there around the fire. Guilty because

119

she hadn't been keeping track of that bastard like she should have done. Like her and Tom had agreed to do.

Back at the cabin it was all darkness and peaceful. Everyone either sleeping or back at the main grounds around the fire. So strangely peaceful that Laura hadn't put on the light. Just gone about her business in the ambient moonlight. Brushing her teeth, getting changed for bed into a pair of jogging shorts and the Penn State t-shirt.

Swishing cold water around her mouth, spitting it out into the sink and running the faucet. Something glinting in the chrome reflection then, a movement. Turning and feeling the cold water dribbling down her chin. Dad sitting there watching her. Realizing he'd been there the whole time. Looking at her with no expression on his face. Eyes glinting in the moonlight, like he was assessing her coldly in some fashion. Like someone dealing in livestock. The way he got.

The cabin was an open plan with kitchen area and bunk beds against the opposite wall. Wood-burning stove for the winter and a rudimentary sofa covered in old blankets. Laura calculated the steps it would take to reach the bunk bed and haul herself up the ladder to safety on top.

Her father lit up a half smoked hand-rolled cigarette. How he always did it, one hand palming a lighter at all times. The other managing the smoke. She moved out. Padding across the wood floor boards, plotting a route that kept a chair between herself and her father.

Getting just past the table when he was up and onto her. The man's movements precise and economical. He'd never been into sports but he'd been a natural born killer, what he'd always said. *If they'd have wanted me for the war, I'd have notched a lotta kills.* But they hadn't wanted Dad for the war because he only had one working eye, so he hadn't gone.

Putting a large fist around the upper arm of a twelve-year-old girl wasn't tough. And that grip was hard. Remembering the bruise there afterwards. Dad, pulling her towards him. *C'mon Laura, just a good night hug for your dad.*

Knowing that resistance led to violence. Allowing the tug, her face pressed into his chest, the t-shirt moist and redolent of sweat and tobacco and whiskey. The hand containing the lighter up now in her hair, fingers in there and the actual lighter pushed against Laura's crown. Her eyes wide open looking into his shoulder. Thinking, *what the fuck do I do now?*

Then it was over. Maybe three seconds of something happening, which she wasn't able to see. Click of the door as it opened. The spring tension released with a boing and a squeak. A dull thud and Dad was on the floor. Laura turned, saw Tom standing there in jeans with no shirt on, hair all wet and wild from the river.

He said, "Got him on his blind side. Let's go."

Looking down at their father on the floor. Tom had hit him in the jaw, knocking him unconscious, just like Dad had taught him to do.

Her brother laughed shortly. "Fucking guy probably doesn't even know it was me."

"Oh." She got it now. The blind side. Dad's right eye was glass, so he hadn't seen Tom coming. Which meant there wouldn't be blowback.

Then, with Tom, running again through the long grass. Him yelling at her and hooting and howling. And down at the river with all the kids. She and her brother in the water laughing and crying and acting insane. None of it weird anymore because that's how everyone was behaving at the ceremony.

Chapter Twenty-Two

The car rental guy made Keeler wait.

Sitting in a blue plastic bucket chair in the sun soaked office looking at the colorful leaf display outside. He'd hiked back over the hill through the woods. Getting away from the general area where the mayhem had occurred. He'd remembered how useful a smart phone could be and used the waitress's device to find this place. An hour's walk through the woods, and then navigating a tangle of highway overpasses, feeder roads, off and on ramps and the final stretch alongside a tree lined irrigation canal.

Sitting now in the rental office, Keeler opened the phone again and actively prevented himself from looking at the waitress's photo album. He closed it and put it away. The car rental guy came out of the back office.

"Okay sir."

Keeler stood and approached. The man logging into a computer terminal. Looking up at him with recessed blue eyes and a light beard in a rounded face topped with a careful hair style. "Sorry about that. I had to deal with some..."

Keeler said, "Some bullshit."

Smiling and showing very white teeth. "Yes, excuse your French."

Keeler said nothing. The man got busy on the computer, making the keyboard clatter for a while before looking up again.

"Alright. So what's going on?"

Keeler said, "I'd like to rent a car."

"Absolutely."

"Give me something normal sized and not white."

"Okay." Looking into the screen as if it contained mysteries. "Got an espresso colored Durango." Swiveling the display so that Keeler could see.

The vehicle was a large boxy looking thing, kind of presidential. Below it were thumbnails for other cars, including a Dodge Challenger in black. Cheaper than the Durango and pretty wicked looking.

Keeler pointed at the Challenger. "I'll take that one if you've got it."

The man nodded. "Not a problem." Clicking into the system and making it happen.

Keeler had an idea. The wallet that he'd taken from the chicken burger guy had an Ohio driver's license and a credit card. The guy was bearded and not too far from Keeler's age. He pushed the license and credit card across the counter to the rental car man.

Keeler, feeling a sense of well being flooding through his system once again. Thinking, *do the good times ever end?*

* * *

An hour later he pulled into Windsong way and already knew that the good times were over. At least as far as Josh and Laura's house was concerned. The zone was flooded with firetrucks, cops, and nosy neighbors. The house already a smoking ruin, a smudge of black and gray with a little of color left where the fire had petered out.

Keeler sat in the car, watching the activity. Josh was up in Columbus, working. He used the waitress's phone to dial the memorized number.

Josh answered after three rings. "Yes?"

Keeler said, "Anyone tell you yet that your house is on fire?"

Hesitation and an intake of breath. "What do you mean?"

"Your house is on fire Josh. Stay in Columbus."

"The house is on fire?"

Keeler held the phone away from him for a second. Trying to figure out the best way to manage his brother-in-law.

"Yes. Anything here you absolutely need? I can try and fish it out." Looking at the firemen enthusiastically hosing the place down. "It's not looking good though. Fire and water in equal measure. Anything not burned is going to be soggy."

Josh said, "Jesus."

Keeler said, "Not going to help you this time, bud."

"You think it's because of Laura?"

"Seems related, yes."

"What should we do?"

Keeler said, "We should stop speaking on the phone. You should get a hotel where you are. Don't text or phone the details to me. I'll find you."

"When?"

"Maybe tomorrow."

Josh said, "How?"

Keeler said, "Just do what I'm telling you Josh. If you need clothes, buy them. You're a lawyer with a job. I assume you've got money. Capisce?"

Josh was from New York, he'd understand.

Josh said, "Capisce."

Keeler killed the call and watched two police vehicles pull in fast. A black unmarked cruiser led, the hideaway light flashing blue from the rear window. The second vehicle was Muskingum County and had the word Sheriff on the side. The front right fender was crushed in, the push bar bent where the impact had occurred.

The place was wet from firehose leakage. Two civilians got splashed by the incoming police, jumping back and hemming and hawing about wet trousers. Keeler couldn't hear them from where he sat, watching with detached amusement.

Two men emerged from the unmarked police vehicle. Big guys in unassuming workman's clothing. Eyes up, immediately scanning the area for threats. Coming out of the car combat ready. Keeler was spotted by one of the men, a sheriff's office baseball hat pulled low over hooded eyes, a lock of brown hair sweat plastered to his forehead.

Keeler maintained eye contact, gave a brief nod. The cop looked away, continuing the threat assessment.

These two beefcakes, behaving like bodyguards, keeping hands close to holstered weapons. The second man said something and the one who'd spotted Keeler thumped the back of the Sheriff's car a couple times. A code for all clear.

A uniformed policewoman emerged from the Sheriff's cruiser. She was short and wide with a face like a waffle iron, getting out of the vehicle with some difficulty. A graying blonde ponytail stuck out of a baseball hat. Keeler figured she'd be in her forties maybe. Was this the *Cheryl* whom the donut man Pete had been referring to earlier on?

The plainclothes cops flanking her, the Sheriff made her way over to a cluster of uniformed police standing around looking lost. One of the bodyguards limped badly with his left leg.

Keeler got out of the vehicle and leaned against the hood. The sheriff moved well for her size, athletic and light on her feet. Keeler watched her interact with the local police. Pointing, and gesticulating and listening.

A few minutes later, the sheriff had finalized whatever business she had at the scene. Walking back to her car and multitasking on a smart phone. The bodyguards moving with her, one of them holding a smart phone to his ear.

Keeler approached. "Sheriff."

The man with the phone stepped into the line between him and this woman. Essentially eclipsing her form with his heft. Looking right at Keeler with a cop's dead eyed gaze.

"Step back."

Keeler stayed where he was, showing hands.

"Just want to have a word with the sheriff."

The man wasn't playing, hair cropped tight to a massive head. Looked like Mike Tyson if Iron Mike had been 6 foot 4 instead of 5 foot 10. The cop with the hat was covering the rear, walking backwards. These cops were clearly operating in hostile territory.

For her part, the sheriff seemed used to this. She stayed behind her man though, looking at Keeler curiously, immediately assessing and analyzing.

She said, "Yeah, what can I do for you?"

He said, "I'm Laura Keeler's brother."

Now, she stopped walking. Phone hanging in her hand as the eyes assessed further. "Mmmm hmm."

The Mike Tyson look alike was now less interested in Keeler, scanning the surroundings.

Keeler focused on the sheriff. "That's my sister's house."

"Yes, I know." The sheriff nudged the bodyguard aside. "It's alright." She took three steps to Keeler and held out a hand. "Cheryl Valdez. Your sister just dropped that shit head Finnegan. It's what I told her she should do. You and me should talk, but not here."

Keeler said, "You want me to come down to the station?"

Valdez laughed. "What are you, a comedian? No. You got a phone number?"

Keeler had the waitress's phone, which had a phone number. Since Keeler didn't know that number, he had to call the sheriff's phone, who called him back. It took a minute, but they were connected.

She said, "I'll text you the details. Maybe an hour or two. We gotta keep operational security." Looking at the plainclothes man who'd been on his phone. "You know what time we'll be back at the place?"

"Yeah, maybe an hour."

Valdez nodded at Keeler, chin pointing to her man. "We'll get in touch." She jerked a thumb toward the house. "Nobody home, no vehicle in the driveway or the garage."

Keeler said, "My brother-in-law's out of town, and you know where my sister is."

Valdez didn't look like she knew how to smile. The face registered nothing. "We got a report about a fancy car registered in her name. Seems that the vehicle, like the house, has found its way to maximum entropy."

"What's that?"

"Second law of thermodynamics. Didn't you go to high school Keeler?"

"I wasn't a good student."

Valdez said, "I got a BA in chemistry. I know how things burn."

It was Keeler's turn to keep the poker face. "So what happened?"

"Well, let's see. I don't know you from Adam, but here you are." She stuck a hard finger into Keeler's chest. Then, swung it to the house. "And there that is. What do the French say, *Voila!*"

Keeler said, "What's that supposed to mean?"

Valdez nodded at him. "Means that you seem to have made an impression."

Keeler said nothing.

The Sheriff said, "Which is possibly a good thing. But I don't want you dead yet. So do me a favor. Go find a motel out of town and stay in it until I call. You hear what I'm saying?"

Keeler said, "Roger that."

Valdez returned her attention to the phone, and whatever business she was doing in there. The kid's drone was up again, whining above the area. Which didn't please the sheriff's bodyguard.

The Mike Tyson guy was looking at it with a critical eye. He said, "looks like a regular drone."

The guy with baseball hat looked up as well. "No payload."

Keeler managed to locate the tiny thing, up maybe a hundred feet up in the air.

Mike Tyson kept an eye in the sky and put a hand on Valdez's shoulder. A deep voice. "Let's move."

The sheriff got into her cruiser and moved out. Thick engine snarl and a blip bleeping of police vehicle yelp and whoop of the hi-lo tones. The two vehicles moved in unison. A civilian couple jumping out of the way as the unmarked car pulled a U-turn and sprayed a modest amount of wet gravel in its wake.

The little drone hummed again. Keeler, searching for the speck and finding it. Thinking about the way the bodyguard had reacted to the sight, and Josh's suggestion that this was some kid sitting in his bedroom messing around with a birthday gift.

He let his gaze move slowly around the neighborhood. Five

houses with line of sight to Laura and Josh's place. Keeler was seeking an open window and not finding one. Examining the horizon line, and finally coming to rest on a hilltop far to the north with a single large oak tree silhouetted against the sky. Though it was far away and very small, he thought he could make out the contours of a vehicle parked beneath the tree.

Chapter Twenty-Three

Keeler returned to the rental car and got behind the wheel. Thinking about this little drone, and how the sheriff had been behaving with her two paranoid bodyguards. Here was a FUBAR situation that just kept getting worse. He'd been in town half a day and he could already smell world war three coming.

And now some drone up there surveilling. Recalling the donut place. That thing the donut maker Pete had said was a whisper in the back left corner of Keeler's mind, growing to a murmur. The donut maker had said, *Maybe they heard me just now.*

A very weird thing to have said, given that there were just three of them having coffee and donuts early in the morning. But congruous with Laura's insistence on communicating with gobbledygook. If his sister believed that they were being surveilled, they were being surveilled.

The drone had gone out of sight somewhere. Not even a speck or a buzz now.

Keeler got the Challenger going and pulled away from his sister's smoldering house, back towards the highway. But that was for the benefit of surveillance. He pulled a left into one of the side streets of the development, finding his way up the hill to a cul-de-sac. He parked the vehicle in a turnout below the residential cluster.

Keeler hiked up the hill to the cul-de-sac and slipped through a backyard. The residential area ended at a livestock fence. He stepped the barbed wire down with a hiking boot and ducked through. A water trough loomed on the hill's crest.

Keeler settled behind it, letting the trench conceal him from the houses. He sat in wet grass, back against corrugated iron, using a bent knee to steady the spotting scope. The eyepiece was large and bright, a good piece of equipment. The view from up there was expansive. Keeler swept the optics slowly across the horizon line, finding the oak tree and that pickup truck, still silhouetted against the sky, this time at a slightly different angle.

The pickup's cab was empty, nobody there. The back was filled with some kind of agricultural stuff. A big plastic tank for pesticide or whatever, some other gear.

Well, maybe it *was* a kid's drone.

Keeler inched the scope to the tree. Not even a squirrel running up the trunk. He brought the optics back to the pickup and saw a dark flicker of movement. Someone was on the other side of the vehicle. Keeler kept the scope on the area around the front wheel, watching as once every few seconds something moved. He realized what it was, a guy sitting on the grass, back against the pickup truck's big wheel.

Keeler put the scope down and plotted a route that would keep him out of sight. He'd have to get over the rise and follow a ridge-line to a wooded section. From there he could make an oblique approach.

It took around ten minutes to get to the tree line. Keeler kept inside the narrow band of woods, not bothering to keep an eye on his target until a few minutes later when he thought it was about the right time. Staying inside the treeline, he used the scope again, holding it tight against a birch trunk.

The exposed oak tree and the pickup truck were up on a hill about a hundred yards away. The man there was leaned back, looking into a screen as he piloted the drone. Keeler could see him perfectly now, the visuals crisp and clear. A guy in his late teens or early twenties. The face was slack jawed and wide eyed as the guy mobilized both hands either side of a drone controller with a small tablet screen attached.

Keeler skirted the edge of the field and came out of the trees with only about twenty yards of open field to cross before the truck hid him from view. A minute later he was treading carefully towards the vehicle, hearing the guy's open mouthed breathing.

He came around the truck, the man looking up from the screen, seeing him too late. Keeler moved fast, watching dispassionately as this young guy tried to stand. The kid's face was perfectly exposed to Keeler's hiking boot, which whipped into the side of his jaw, sending the drone operator's head back into the truck's wheel well with a heavy thud, snapping forwards again into drooling unconsciousness.

Keeler said, "That was easy."

The controller had fallen from the man's hands into his lap. The tablet part of it now detached.

Keeler bent to pick up the gear. He reattached the tablet to the pincer devices connecting the screen to the controller. Looking now at an overhead view of the burning house scene. He wasn't a stranger to drone control software, and found the home icon, which usually just brought the drone back to its starting position.

The operator returned to consciousness. Opening his eyes and looking peaceful, as if he'd been enjoying a deeply satisfying sleep. Keeler was crouched to meet him when he came to. Looking into the man's eyes.

He said, "You feeling alright?"

"Yeah. What happened?"

"I kicked you in the face. You don't remember?"

"No."

Keeler said, "Even better that you don't remember me kicking you in the face. Do you know who I am?"

The guy said, "No." And blinked twice.

"What is it I need to hear from you?"

The guy looked lost. "You want me to say *sorry*?"

"For what?"

Confusion spread over his face. "I don't know. You know..."

The small drone was now descending, rotors whining as it parked itself fifteen feet away from the pickup truck and shut down.

Keeler said, "Did you set the house on fire yourself?"

"Uh, no."

The young guy was nervous, now properly awake. Maybe wondering how he'd be able to get out of this situation.

Keeler said, "Elaborate on that for me."

The guy said, "On what exactly?"

Keeler hadn't paid any attention to the truck, focused in on the human element. The outline of something boxy and bulky in the back caught his eye. He stood up, peering into the truck's bed. Having no agricultural experience, it took Keeler a few seconds to understand what he was looking at. A large quad copter drone, maybe the size of a big dog. The propeller arms were tightly packed away. A decently sized gas powered generator occupied the space behind a large tank of bright yellow liquid. All of it fitting perfectly into the back of the truck, some kind of crop spraying rig.

He looked down at the man, looking up at him with an attempted innocent expression.

The drone had a reservoir of its own, presumably used for spraying fertilizer or pesticides. Keeler moved to the back and released the tail gate. He leaned in and unscrewed the drone's reservoir tank. Put his nose in there and got a heavy whiff of something greasy and mineral.

The guy stood up on wobbly legs. Keeler walked over and kicked his feet out from under him. Catching the man by the collar and pushing his face into the side of the pickup truck.

"What'd you do, just spray the house from above and light it up?"

He released his grip, and the guy collapsed, clutching his ankle.

He said, "That's just Garlon Ultra man, it's an herbicide my company uses."

"You have a contract to spray up here?"

"Yes, I've been spraying all day. Just ran out of product."

"So, why are you checking out the house?"

"That's the drone we use to scout a job."

"Why the house?"

The guy shrugged. "I was curious is all."

"Curious about what?"

The young man exhaled. "Okay, okay. I was up here a week ago scouting the job and there was a lady there at the house. I was just seeing if she was alright."

The kid was talking about his sister, Laura.

Keeler said, "You mean an attractive woman caught your eye, and you wanted to peep some more."

"Just wanted to see if she was alright, given the fire."

Keeler watched this guy, sprawled out there with a messed up ankle. Not wanting to buy the story, but the tale was selling itself.

He said, "Well, why didn't you say so in the beginning."

The guy said, "You didn't give me a chance to say anything."

The smaller drone was parked out in the grass.

Keeler walked over to the thing. He said, "True." Not exactly ready to apologize but feeling a little bad.

The drone was a little Chinese made DJI model with a good camera on it. Keeler bent to retrieve it from the grass. Light as a feather. Walking back to the guy.

"Where do you want me to put this thing?"

"Anywhere, it doesn't matter."

Keeler turned the drone over to look at the camera.

Which is when he saw the thing that they'd attached to the underside. A windproof butane lighter locked into what looked to be a 3D-printed rig mounted to the device. The lighter's mechanism was up against a small battery-operated servo motor, presumably controlled remotely by the operator.

Keeler tested it with his hand, the motor pushing in the trigger to produce flame.

He looked back down at the man, silent now and watching sullenly.

Keeler said, "Busted."

Chapter Twenty-Four

The drone operator's name was Carlos Reygadas. He was twenty-two years old and a resident of Texas, according to his driver's license. Keeler drew the buck knife and crouched in front of Reygadas, fixing him with a stare.

"You do a lot of this kind of thing?"

"What kind of thing?"

"Arson. Burning people's houses down kind of thing."

Reygadas said nothing and looked away.

Keeler said, "I'm not going to be patient. That was my sister's house you burned down. And my sister who you were peeping at."

Reygadas's mouth closed in an unhappy line. He glanced at Keeler and looked away.

Keeler said, "I want you looking at me and giving simple and direct answers to the questions I'm about to ask."

Reygadas said, "I'm a dead man now, so it doesn't matter, right?" The guy's voice was shaking.

Keeler said, "You got involved. You've become..." He paused to find the words. Chin pointing at the man. "You're now this thing. That's you. Maybe you thought that every scum bag on earth thinks he's a scum bag. Is that what you thought?" Reygadas didn't respond, immediately. Keeler said, "That was a question."

"I don't know what you mean."

The guy looked directly at him again, confusion and fear clouding his cognitive abilities. Not guilt though, denial. Nobody thinks they're bad.

Keeler said, "Let's start with the work that you do. Where you do it, and who you do it with."

Reygadas was freaking out now. Shivering, literally. He said, "I'm afraid that they'll kill me if I talk man, you don't fucking understand who you're dealing with."

Looking at this guy, thinking about how he'd gotten involved with *these people*. Now becoming one of the people he was so afraid of. Keeler decided that there wasn't time to have an endless discussion with Carlos Reygadas.

He took a hold of the man's left arm and twisted it so that Reygadas was face down in the dirt. Keeler put a boot on his forearm, hearing the guy mumble something desperate. The buck knife sank into the knuckle joint of the drone operator's left pinky. The brand new blade was factory sharp, cutting through tendon, muscle, cartilage and bone like carving a roasted chicken.

Reygadas let out a scream. Keeler stood up and pushed his face into the dirt with a boot, examining the severed finger and letting the man express himself for a minute. Wind had picked up, blowing smoke from Laura's burning house over the fields. It didn't smell like burning wood or anything, more like burning plastic.

Reygadas went silent. Keeler pulled him up by his hair and propped him against the truck again. The guy stared at the bloody stub where his finger had been. Keeler lifted the small drone from beside him.

"Did you modify this yourself, Carlos?"

Reygadas was very close to becoming a useless blubbering pile, but was managing to hold it together, barely. When he spoke there was a hysterical edge to his voice.

"No. I just do what they tell me to do. If I have a problem or need something they've got a shop and a bunch of guys who do the modding."

He cursed, raising his hand higher.

Keeler flicked the modified lighter mechanism. "What's your role besides lighting up the occasional house?"

"Surveillance normally."

"On who?"

"Anyone the bosses want."

Keeler said, "So, what happens, you get a text message or something?"

"Exactly."

"You ever kill people with your drones?" Reygadas was silent. Which Keeler took for a yes. He said, "How do you do it?"

Reygadas let his head hang down to his chest, mumbling something quietly.

Keeler pulled him up by the hair. "You want me to take another finger?"

The drone man looked up at Keeler. "We got drones can shoot a guy. Just like a pistol."

Keeler had seen that kind of thing in videos. Drones modded with pistol or a shotgun, a remote control trigger. Thing wouldn't be able to self-reload, unless they did a heavy duty modification, but a fifteen round magazine can still take out fifteen targets. So why not? It was pretty sick to know that this was happening in the United States.

He indicated the truck. "You really do crop spraying, or is that just cover?"

Reygadas said, "That's the burn kit man. I got different setups depending on the job. There's no crop spraying."

Keeler said, "So what's this outfit called, that you're working for. They got a name?"

Reygadas looked at him, confused, frightened, hurt, hesitant.

Keeler laughed. "I'm worse than them, believe me."

Reygadas was holding that thousand-yard stare, something dawning on him. A change in the climate, a shift, a turning point.

He spoke quietly, not taking his eyes off Keeler. "Uh, they call themselves *Los Quebrados*."

"My Spanish is rusty. What's that supposed to mean?"

"The Broken Ones."

Keeler said, "Elegant. Are you a broken one?"

"Not technically no."

"Where do these broken ones come from?"

Reygadas said, "What I heard is they took two MS 13 chapters, from Cleveland and Cincinnati. Grouped up I guess. I'm from Texas. They sent me up here to help out with this shit." A jerked thumb indicated the truck and his drone setup.

MS 13, a Salvadoran crime gang originally from Los Angeles, but now with autonomous cell structures spread out all over the USA. The Broken Ones, *Los Quebrados*, a faction splintered out of the original group.

He looked at the guy, hand wet with his own blood. Keeler wiped the buck knife on Reygadas's shirt.

"So what, you tool up by yourself?" Indicating the drone equipment with his head. Keeler said, "Got your own workshop somewhere?"

Reygadas said, "Nah, I'm not the only one does this. They got a facility in town."

"Very good. That's where we're going." Keeler said, "You got a first aid kit in the truck?"

"Yeah."

"I don't want blood in the car. Go get yourself cleaned up."

Chapter Twenty-Five

The facility was a one story building set behind a Verizon outlet in a strip mall development. Out front was the row of street facing shops. Verizon, plus a nail salon and a Chinese food place. Behind that were three buildings separated from the strip mall by a two row parking lot. Keeler had a good view of it all from the driver's seat of the Dodge, parked at the edge of a garden center's lot a couple hundred yards away. The vantage point was up on a rise.

Keeler panned the long range scope across the front of the building. A regular front door and a roll up entrance beside it. Two windows just by the front door. Venetian blinds were shut.

Keeler said, "The roll up entrance is for deliveries or what?"

Reygadas said, "Yeah, they got two vans parked in there."

"Back entrance?"

"Not that I've ever seen."

Reygadas was in the passenger side foot well, curled into a fetal position. Keeler didn't know yet exactly what he was going to do with him. He'd used the duct tape roll to bind the guy's hands behind him.

On the way over Keeler had said, "How many people will I find in there?"

"Half dozen or so usually, I guess."

What Reygadas had told Keeler was pretty crazy. A repair and modification shop for drone tech and other devices. If the guy could be believed, *Los Quebrados* operated on an entrepreneurial model. Operatives were expected to figure out their own means and ways of getting the job done. Reygadas had said that the town was like occupied enemy territory, but in an under-the-table, gray market kind of way. He'd called the regular citizens *normies*.

Keeler had clarified. "So, you've got real members of *Los Quebrados*, connected freelancers like yourself, and normies. Have I got it right?"

"Yeah. Normies don't know shit anyway." Reygadas had laughed. "There's no difference for them man, they just get to live their little lives. As long as they don't make some dumb mistake or get too curious or anything."

"And if they do?"

"Someone gives a guy like me a call."

"Oh, so you're not the only one?"

"Everyone's got their niche." Reygadas laughed again, sounding like a hyena.

Keeler hadn't liked the laugh. He'd considered taking another finger. Problem was getting blood all over the rental. Plus, Reygadas was doing a good job now, loosened up and talkative. Probably the shock and adrenaline had made him giddy.

He said, "Better to bleed a live animal than a dead one, right?"

Keeler had understood. "Right. And every cartel chief pays in to the main bosses."

"Exactly."

A pyramid scheme, or an entrepreneurial opportunity for hard men. Hard to know how to call it.

The building looked calm, even empty. Nobody had come in or out and they'd been there a half hour already, watching. Five vehicles parked outside. Reygadas had said up to a dozen people in there.

Keeler said, "Are those people armed?"

"I've never seen weapons there, but I'd figure on at least the boss carrying. He's a fucking nut anyway."

"Good." The word coming out before Keeler could consciously think it.

Reygadas didn't respond to that.

Keeler took his eye off the scope and watched Reygadas, unmoving in the foot well. He still wasn't entirely sure what to do with him. Probably best to use him as a human shield. The people in that facility would know him, so he could go first, getting them inside.

After that, whatever.

He said, "Reygadas, think you can handle yourself going in there? Wouldn't want you to start bleeding all over their carpet."

The guy said, "What? What do you mean?" The guy almost choking on the words, in a sudden panic.

Keeler said, "Chill. You just walk in with me like we're friends. Like I'm one of the guys."

"I don't know if I can do that man. I just had my fucking finger amputated, you psychopath."

Keeler grinned. "Look who's calling me a psycho. Just get us in there without anyone having a fit. You can do it. I believe in you." He patted the guy on the head. "It's either that or I shoot you in the back of the head right now. You get to choose."

Reygadas made a muffled sound.

"What was that?"

The guy's mouth came off the floor. "I said, okay."

Keeler nodded to himself. Okay.

Chapter Twenty-Six

Keeler pulled the Smith and Wesson M&P9 pistols from the pack. Checked the guns and how they were set up for ammunition. These were the short four-inch barrel versions, standard sights with fifteen round magazines. Keeler removed the mags from one of the guns and let it drop back into the pack. He liked the compact version, how it sat in the hand, the weight and balance of it.

He cut Reygadas's wrists free with the knife. "Get up out of there."

The guy extracted himself from the foot well as Keeler pulled the Challenger out of the parking lot. Reygadas falling all over the place, trying to settle. Keeler steered the vehicle in a severe arc down the ramp, spiraling back to the main drag from which they turned off into the Verizon strip mall. By the time they were coming around the back of the line of stores, Reygadas had made it to the passenger seat, rubbing circulation into his hands.

Keeler glanced at the bandaged wound with a critical eye. White bandage with a dark blood splotch. Not like he could do anything about that. He parked out front. Still nothing going on with this building. Keeler was beginning to think there might be nothing there, that Reygadas was inventing the entire story.

Reygadas was hyperventilating, sort of choking on himself. Stressed out.

Keeler said, "Breathing helps. Maybe you should try it."

Walking across the lot, letting Reygadas lead the way. Keeler having his doubts, but feeling heightened anyway, a kind of elevation of spirit. Ohio, sun and clear air now. Keeler didn't know how to call it. This gambit. The guy was staggering across the parking lot, as if approaching his own funeral. Hunched over and having trouble keeping steady.

Up close, Keeler could see cameras set up on the building's corners and outside both sets of doors. Tiny things that he hadn't seen in the spotting scope. They were certainly being filmed.

Reygadas hesitated before the front door.

Keeler said, "Move." He pushed the man forward.

Reygadas had straight brown hair, now slightly greasy with sweat. Keeler smelled his fear up close and began having his doubts. Perhaps the man was just a coward. You didn't need to be brave in order to set someone's house on fire and surveil them. Maybe it was just a job like any other. Young guy like that didn't give a shit.

Reygadas went through the door. Twin bells tinkling as it opened. Keeler saw past him, a darkened lobby with an empty receptionist desk and a plasterboard wall behind it. The wall unpainted, with a dart board mounted up above.

Reygadas had given Keeler the lay of the land. This little entrance was just a front. Drop ceiling and the desk. He said sometimes they even had a guy working there doing clerical stuff. Behind the wall was the real deal, basically a large open hangar with work benches, racks of tools, storage areas, computer terminals, and according to the drone operator a very good coffee machine that made Italian espresso.

Keeler could smell the open space. He could hear it in the way their footsteps echoed. What Reygadas had said was, the guy who ran the facility had an actual office in the corner of the building that faced the parking lot. That office was straight across from the door out of reception.

Keeler said, "Go." He had the compact pistol in his jacket pocket. One hand on the gun, ready to rock.

Reygadas grunted and moved, taking a left, walking parallel to the reception desk towards a cheap wood door set in another unfinished plasterboard wall. Above the door was a small camera, its cable running loose up and through a rough hole in the wall. Keeler looked at it with distaste. If someone was watching and taking care then they were cooked.

Reygadas hesitated again in front of the door. Keeler used his foot to nudge his butt rudely forwards. Reygadas turned the knob. The door opened towards him, a pull. Keeler could see the space beyond this threshold. Larger, higher ceilings. Reygadas took two steps into the main space and paused. Across the way was another door, presumably the manager's office.

Keeler said, "Let's go see the boss."

Reygadas sniffed, an involuntary inhalation. He turned slightly to his right. Keeler got a glimpse of his right eye. Something glinting in its convex reflection. And then his head was blown off. A shotgun load coming from the right, jettisoning Reygadas's brains and bone and blood into the space to the left.

The shotgun cracked, a rolling boom reverberating off thin walls and roof. The body slumped and tumbled. Keeler took two large steps back and swiveled. He put three quick rounds through the plasterboard wall. Got into a crouch and sprinted through the doorway into danger.

A man stood to his right, holding a tactical shotgun in one

hand and touching his belly with the other, looking surprised that he'd been shot through the wall. Keeler had the Smith & Wesson up and put two rounds into the man's chest, knocking him on his ass. The guy around forty years old and balding, wearing a plaid shirt and jeans over a clean pair of Timberland work boots.

Keeler stepped over Reygadas's corpse, moving fast into the space. Four rows of work benches, racks and other stuff against the walls. There were two quick shots and Keeler felt the air move right in front of his face. He pitched forward in a dive to cover behind a tool chest. A stainless steel cabinet on wheels. Three rounds thudded into the cabinet, pushing the thing into him.

He rolled away, coming up in a shooting position. The guy there in front of him unprepared. Keeler pulled once, opening up a blossom in the center of the shooter's forehead. A door in the back was wide open. Keeler watched three men dash through it.

He called out. "Anybody here wants to live, you just stand up with your hands in the air. Nothing's going to happen to you."

There was only silence.

Keeler said, "You've got ten seconds."

A tall thin man stood up at the end of the hanger. He had his hands up. Blonde guy with glasses, maybe thirty-five years old.

He said, "I'm unarmed."

"Come towards me. Anybody else here?"

The man said, "No, sir. Everyone ran away when Ronny got the shotgun out."

Funnily enough, Ronny was still alive, even with three bullets in him. He was making terrible sounds, like a wounded animal. Keeler ignored the distraction.

The tall guy was close now. Eyes wide staring at the dying manager.

Keeler said, "I thought there were more people working here."

"It's lunch time. I was just eating."

The man actually holding a sandwich.

"What do you have there?"

"What?"

"The sandwich."

"Oh." He held it up, like a demonstration. "Ham and cheese. Mustard. Simple."

Keeler said, "Good to keep things simple. When does everyone get back from lunch?"

"It's Friday. We get a half day on Friday." He shrugged. "It's just me and the guys who just ran out the door."

A skeleton crew for the weekend. Looking around at the place now, seeing the details. Work benches setup with soldering stations. A 3D printer over by the wall. Buckets and trays with carbon fiber sheeting and LiPo batteries. Looked like something from a video out of Ukraine, not exactly Ohio.

Keeler said, "Why the half day?"

The guy shrugged. "The sabbath, I guess." He pointed at the manager. "Ronny's a man of faith. Uh sorry, was a man of faith."

Keeler walked back to the manager. The man of faith wasn't doing well, wasn't going to make it. Keeler knew that it could go two ways. Either they'd let Ronny bleed out and die, which could take a half hour. Or, he could put him away now.

Ronny was having internal struggles, mumbling in a language that wasn't English. He and Keeler had a small moment there, with eye contact and what felt like a full understanding.

Keeler said, "You could have been cool, Ronny."

Ronny's mumbling picked up in speed and vigor. Keeler raised the Smith & Wesson and put a round into his head. The man went slack, eyes rolling back. The skinny guy with glasses sucked in a shocked breath. Keeler glanced at him, hopeful that he wasn't about to choke on his sandwich.

Keeler said, "It's going to smell bad in here, bud. If you have to puke do it in the bathroom."

"Nah, I'm alright."

Keeler fixed the guy with a stare. What kind of person was so nonchalant at a time like that?

He said, "What's your name?"

"I'm Dwight. Who are you?"

"I'm the guy who just killed the boss, Dwight. You don't look too unhappy about that."

Dwight said, "I'm not. This is my place, or at least it was my place. Before these people came in and took over the shop. I might have signed the business away, but I'm sure that's not legally binding."

Keeler said, "What was the shop before they came?"

"Before they turned it into a killer drone shop? I'm in Robotics. This was my startup they took."

"Dwight, I need you to give me a tour of whatever this is."

"No problem." Dwight picked up his sandwich from where he'd left it on the counter top. "I can do that."

The waitress' phone began to vibrate in his pocket. Keeler pulled it. The sheriff was on the line.

Chapter Twenty-Seven

Valdez stood looking at the corpses. She was sucking on a Wendy's milkshake, trying to get the stuff out of the cup through the straw. Which wasn't working for her. Reygadas was the worst, essentially headless. The entire scene was beginning to smell bad. Ronny the manager, was a little more palatable to look at. His corpse face peaceful. The third dead man was curled up in an ungainly position under a workbench. The sheriff was with the two cops from earlier. The guy who looked like a tall version of Mike Tyson, and the other one.

The Mike Tyson cop was with her now, and the other cop had gone straight into the manager's office to check out the computer system. Valdez put the milkshake down on the closest work bench.

She said, "I don't want this anymore."

The Mike Tyson look alike took one look at the death scene and walked over to Keeler with a hand outstretched.

"I'm Carver. Good to meet you."

Keeler took the hand, and the two men made a hardened connection of muscled flesh and bone.

Carver was nodding his head in confirmation. Looking

around the place. He said, "I knew they had some place to fix up their drones, but I didn't think it'd be like this man."

Valdez said, "Smells like shit in here. It's truly disgusting."

Carver pointed at the manager's body. "That guy did that guy with the shotgun." He turned back to Reygadas's corpse, tracing the sequence of violent events. "And then you did that guy." Looking at the wall. "You plug him through the wall first?"

Keeler nodded. "I guess so."

Carver whistled. Turning in the direction of the manager again. "Then you popped him another time. I guess he fucked up huh?" Keeler was about to say something, but Carver stopped him with a raised hand. "One second. I'm on a roll." Excited, like a detective. He moved out into the open work space. "Then *that* guy took a pop at you and what, you put him down too?"

Keeler said, "Something like that."

Valdez said, "Fucking Sherlock Holmes over here."

Carver said, "I'm just putting it together boss."

Valdez looked at Keeler, her face a blank. The image that had come to him before, of her face resembling a waffle iron. It came back again, a little unfair but weirdly true. Some people just looked the way they did. Some looked like supermodels, others like squirrels, still others could resemble kitchen appliances. Keeler didn't make the rules.

She said, "Carver was gunning for detective before this all started happening. He's just practicing. Don't mind him."

The skinny tall guy named Dwight was still there, now sitting at the closest work bench.

Carver chin pointed at him. "What's up with that guy. The lone survivor."

Keeler said, "This was his place before. His name's Dwight."

Valdez looked at him. "Oh yeah?"

Carver said, "What kind of place was that?"

Dwight said, "It was my business. Robotics. We had some funding." He shrugged. "I had equipment they wanted I guess, plus the computer skills. One day Ronny showed up with a couple of guys." He pointed at the dead manager. "They didn't give me a choice. I have a family."

Carver said, "How long ago was that?"

"Just about a year now."

Valdez looked at Carver. "Check that out, what he just said." She saw that Keeler was looking at her. She said, "Sorry friend, we're officially paranoid now." Nodding her head to Dwight. "You understand."

Dwight said, "No problem. I understand."

None of the cops said anything witty. Seemed as if this was a common story in Trace Junction.

Carver had a laptop out, logging in and tapping keys. "What's the address here?"

Dwight said, "1458 Maple, Unit 3."

Carver tapped and swiped.

Valdez said, "You got I.D.?" Dwight opened his wallet and showed her a driver's license. She read it out to Carver. "Name is Dwight C. Larkin."

Carver grunted. Valdez gave the license back.

Keeler said, "Dwight's been giving me a tour of the facility."

Valdez said, "And?"

"And it's a full-on drone war system. Modification and repair shop, plus launch capability for a fleet of these things."

Valdez said, "You're talking over my head Keeler. What are you some kind of military guy, is that the deal here?"

Keeler said, "Something like that, yeah."

Carver said, "Figures. Arbel Systems." Looking at Dwight. "Still registered in your name."

Dwight nodded. "That's right."

"What's an Arbel?"

"It's my wife's name."

Valdez said, "Cute."

Keeler indicated an area over near the back door. "Come take a look at this Sheriff."

He opened a stainless steel tool cabinet. The interior resembled a rack of computer hard drives in a data center, except they weren't hard drives, they were mini drones. Each of them set into a docking station that supplied electricity and probably a connection to download footage from the internal memory. The drones were the size of a regular man's palm. Each of them a quadcopter with a high-quality miniature camera.

Keeler said, "So, what do you want to do here, Sheriff?"

Valdez put a boot up and began re-tying her shoelace. She coughed up a little laugh. "What do I want to do? What is it you want to do, Keeler? Now that you've decided to precipitate world war three." She finished the knot, standing up and putting her thumbs in her gun belt.

Valdez passed her hands over the dead bodies in the place. "I mean, some folks might see all this and use the word *murder*."

Carver said, "Not us."

Valdez said, "No, not us anymore. Lucky you didn't call the TJ police though, you'd either be dead now or sharing an address with your sister."

Keeler said, "TJ?"

"Trace Junction."

The other cop came out of the manager's office.

"You got to check this out, boss."

Valdez turned. "Check what out?" She turned to Keeler and pointed at the second cop. "That's Bobby Kennedy by the way. It's really his name."

Kennedy said, "I got into the computer. They've got facial recognition systems." Pointed at Keeler. "They clocked this guy coming in from the parking lot and nailed him with a full profile." He pointed at the dead manager. "Probably why this one started shooting." He laughed, looking at Keeler. "If I had read Mr *Keeler*'s bio and knew he was coming for me, I wouldn't be shooting, I'd be running out the back as fast as I could."

Keeler said nothing. Thinking that if true, his ID and profile wouldn't have come in so quickly. It was likely to have arrived while Ronny was already knocking on heaven's door.

Carver said, "Oh shit."

Keeler said, "How did you get into the computer?"

Kennedy said, "Password was taped under the keyboard."

Keeler and Dwight exchanged a look. They'd made a brief attempt to get into the computer, but there had been other priorities and only a couple of minutes were devoted to that problem. So, the enemy was connected up. Networked into systems that nobody was supposed to have easy access to.

Federal even. Certainly beyond Trace Junction and Muskingum county.

Valdez said, "You guys meet yet?" She pointed to Kennedy. "Bobby Kennedy meet Keeler."

Valdez said, "How long do you think we've got, Bobby K? Before they start coming back at us."

Kennedy said, "Not long. I shut down the system, but until I did, it's possible they've been watching us. I can't verify that, but it's a possibility. I think we need to get out of here sheriff. We don't have the resources to defend if they come in blazing."

Keeler said, "You have a secure location?"

Kennedy said, "Yeah."

Valdez turned to Keeler. She looked embarrassed, "For the time being, we're operating out of a civilian facility. It's been a few months now."

"You mean, not the county sheriff's office."

"Correct. I'll explain later."

"Sure." Keeler said, "But, we can't leave this place as is. Need to either defend or destroy. Believe me, I've seen the gear. Dwight gave me a tour."

Valdez said, "You mean the drones?"

Keeler explained to her that it wasn't just drones, even though it was certainly about drones. He told her about the other equipment Dwight had shown him. The parking bay had two vans. Each of the vehicles was a mobile drone launch facility, with a rack of several dozen UAVs along with the capabilities to control, power, and maintain them. And the drones weren't only for surveillance. A DynaLock explosive storage magazine in the corner of the warehouse here, contained bricks of C4 plastic explosives along with remote detonators. The drones in the van were modified to handle the ordnance.

Keeler said, "Tell you what. You guys get out of here and tell me where to meet up. I'm going to set up a little situation for our incoming friends."

Valdez said, "What kind of situation?"

Keeler said, "The unpleasant kind."

Carver laughed.

Valdez said, "Fine. I'll stay with you." She cast a hand over the others. "The rest of you meet back at the fort. Carver, you take my vehicle." Pointing at Dwight. "What's the deal with you? You on our side now?"

Dwight said, "I was never on their side, sheriff." He looked at Keeler, then back at Valdez. "But you guys need to take them down now, you understand that. I've still got a family."

Kennedy said, "You didn't move your family away, Dwight?"

"I did but these people know how to find them."

Kennedy said, "Yeah. They're no slouches."

Keeler and Valdez made eye contact. Something new

brewing up, a kind of understanding that a line had been crossed.

Keeler said, "We're going to take them down, Dwight."

Valdez looked away. Carver, standing there with his mouth open.

Bobby Kennedy said, "Well alright, folks. Let's get this show on the road."

Dwight said, "I can take one of the vans. That could be useful, believe me."

Keeler said, "How long will it take to get it ready?"

"Not long. Ronny had us prep a go kit just in case one of the cartel teams asked for it."

Keeler said, "I guess nobody wants to disappoint a request like that."

"Exactly." Dwight said, "Probably do it in five minutes."

"Take an extra two minutes and set me up with a drone pack," said Keeler. "I want to conduct a damage assessment after blowing this place." He pointed at Carver and Kennedy. "It'd be helpful if you two got the bodies out of sight. Just in case."

Carver said, "Roger that."

Dwight seemed to be a serious person. He said, "You'll want a pack with a UAV plus controller. I'll set up an iPad instead of goggles. You can record the footage anyway."

Keeler nodded. "Let's do that."

Dwight moved out. Keeler and Valdez exchanged glances. Keeler knew that she knew that he was going to ask some questions. Her face told him she was ready for that.

She said, "What are you looking at Keeler?"

He said, "You know you've got a special face. I bet I'm not the only one to look at you like that."

Valdez grunted. "Yeah, I know. Looks like a goddamned waffle iron, what my ex-husband told me." She laughed.

Keeler said nothing but couldn't keep from smiling.

Chapter Twenty-Eight

Valdez didn't know the first thing about explosives. She watched quietly from the center of the workshop, sipping again at her milkshake.

Keeler removed C4 bricks from the storage magazine. Setting four of them down on the counter. He got to work shaping the charges, using a soup bowl from the kitchen and patiently working the C4 into a cup-like shape. Into those he poured handfuls of screws and bolts, plentiful here in the workshop.

Valdez said, "Looks like you've done this before."

Keeler said, "Oh yeah."

There was enough det-cord to link the bricks, even fifteen yards apart. Enabling him to set up a kill zone in the reception area. Two bricks in there, divided into four parts. Another two bricks placed at load bearing parts of the structure. He wanted to bring the entire place down. All of it hooked up to a single detonator powered by a 9 volt battery.

Dwight had given him a key fob controller that would blow the entire thing.

Keeler didn't bother too much with disguising the charges.

He walked the entry route, seeing what an intruder would see, designing the trap accordingly. Walk in through the front door. See nothing. What you don't realize is that the calendar on the wall to your right covers a brick of C4 that's going to shred you into unrecognizable pieces. Basically, you're going to become a form of chunky soup, alongside your friends.

It took twenty minutes to set up. The gear was military grade. Top-notch stuff that wasn't easy for civilians to acquire, implying a military source. Scary.

Keeler and Valdez got into the Challenger and drove up to the garden center where he'd been earlier with Reygadas. The vantage spot that he'd found earlier was a perfect observation post, a good two hundred yards from the target. Which was important, since the kill zone would be rather large, given the amount of C4 he'd laid on.

Plus the secondary explosions he expected from left over ordnance in the DynaLock magazine, plus the van in the parking bay had some C4. Now it was just a question of waiting. Keeler had the detonator fob up on the dashboard. The spotting scope was out and ready.

Valdez said, "I'm getting hungry again."

"You just ate Wendy's."

"Nah, I had a shake is all."

He said, "While we wait for the A-team to show up, why don't you start telling me the story of your life, Valdez. Maybe we've got time for a full version of *what the fuck is going on here*."

Valdez chuckled. "I can do that."

* * *

Valdez was elected sheriff twice. Her second four-year term had only just begun when the normally deranged criminal behaviors in the county strangely began to diminish.

She said, "We'd go out into the county and even the crack heads were behaving themselves. That's when I started to realize that something was wrong in town."

Keeler said, "You didn't realize it earlier."

"No."

In hindsight, she could have noticed the signs. Attempted bribery, for one thing.

Valdez said, "They never came at me directly. It was always through someone on the force. Someone I already had a history with, you know what I mean?"

Keeler said, "Someone you trusted."

"Correct."

"And the approach was always oblique. Never once was it spelled out. First guy to come at me wasn't even my deputy. It was my boss, one of the county commissioners. Not officially my boss, but the guy who controls my budget."

"Which makes him your boss."

"Yeah."

"How'd he come at you?"

Valdez was slumped in the passenger seat looking through the scope at the target down below. Nothing doing there, just an empty lot with a closed down building. The neighboring structures were equally dead.

She said, "Invited me for lunch at his country club. Not the first time I'd been there. Actually, I remember now. Wasn't just me. He invited the family out for the day. Kids got to use the pool and my husband loves a sauna when he can get it. Guy's got luxury tastes. Anyhoo. Me and the commissioner eating crab if you can believe it. He says to me, Cheryl, how'd you like to come in with me on a little entrepreneurial thing I've got going here?"

Valdez shook her head, like the memory was fresh.

"And I'm like, what kind of thing is that, Gary?"

"Gary goes, it's a consulting gig sheriff. Me and some friends are thinking 'bout starting up a business down in Kentucky and we've got security concerns. He was smiling then, like a little pig. Dipping crab meat in melted butter. Didn't even have to crack it open himself, they do it for you up at the club. I'm eating a chicken sandwich."

"He said, 'You don't even need to do nothing, sheriff.'"

"I say, I thought it was a consulting gig, commissioner. Don't I even have to consult about something?"

"He's like, sure maybe once in a while we'd have a little talk, like we're doing now. Anyway, he said, you get paid a retainer and the whole team's happy. How does that sound to you, Cheryl?"

"Well, it sounded too good to be true is how it sounded. I asked how much money he wanted to give me for doing nothing. He says, we'll start off with three grand a month. You do a good job of doing nothing, maybe we'll raise it to five in a year."

Keeler said, "And what did you tell him?"

"I finished my chicken sandwich and said I'd think on it. I never brought it up again, and neither did he."

Keeler said, "Doesn't sound too subtle to me."

"No, it wasn't subtle, but then again it wasn't nothing I could pin on him. Up to the commissioner if he wanted to start a side business with some buddies. This is America."

Keeler said, "What about the more direct approaches."

"Yeah, I'll get to that. After that first thing, I began to get a feeling that I was like, missing out on a joke or something like that." She turned to Keeler. "Know what I mean?"

"I guess you mean from inside the force. Your people."

"Yeah. The county Sheriff's office is a small team. We're not town cops, that's a different force. The Trace Junction police.

Sheriff's office handles enforcement out in the county. I found myself increasingly ignored internally. Like I was getting pushed out. That and getting pretty clear messages from my own people. And then, of course, they tried to kill me."

Valdez handed the scope over to Keeler.

He said, "Unsuccessfully, I see."

"Yeah, at least that time. Going into some call out. Domestic situation out in the sticks. It was a setup."

"So, not a domestic violence call."

"No. There was a scene they'd arranged. I didn't know of course. Followed protocol, entered the house and got ambushed. Luckily Carver was there."

"You get hit?"

"Took it on the vest. Guy they'd found to do it wasn't a great shot. Fired two at me, one hit. I got knocked back and shot him. Carver got the other guy."

"Anyone you recognized?"

"Two stone cold gang bangers from down south."

"Hit men."

"I think so, yes. MS-13 tattoos and everything. They bring in hitters for this kind of stuff."

Keeler said nothing.

She said, "There've been a couple more close calls."

"You haven't called in the feds yet?"

Valdez sparked up. "Oh yes, we have. Phone calls, memos. I even took a meeting up in Cleveland. FBI office there made all the right noises. The guy looking at me with his little eyes, nodding and smiling, but so far *nada*. I've got half a mind that the Cleveland office is bought and paid for. Seriously."

Keeler let that lie for a moment, thinking about the sheriff's situation. He had a connection with the feds. Someone in Homeland Security who he had credit with.

Chapter Twenty-Nine

Valdez said, "What?"

"What what?"

"What are you thinking?"

"You don't have a personal connection up there?"

"Up where, Cleveland?"

Keeler said, "With the Feds."

Valdez shook her head. "Nope. I'm just a small-town girl."

Keeler opened up the waitress's phone. "I know someone." He tapped in a phone number he'd memorized a long time ago. A female voice answered.

"Sobell."

"It's Keeler."

A pause. Valdez was watching him. He raised his eyebrows at her.

Dr. Amanda Sobell was the director of National Security Investigations, Homeland Security in Chicago. Keeler had met her a few years earlier. It had been a tricky situation all around. And, Keeler had delivered. For that reason, he figured that Sobell might be helpful. Plus, she'd made promises. But that had been long ago. And, they'd only actually met once, in addition to a few telephone conversations. Sobell said, "Oh yeah, that Keeler. I'm supposed to buy you an ice cream cone or some such."

Keeler said, "Good memory. The ice cream was your idea, if my memory holds."

"Whatever Keeler, I'm busy. What's up?"

"I'm in Ohio. There's a situation."

"What kind of situation?"

"Your kind. I'm helping out the sheriff here, dealing with an MS-13 splinter group calling themselves *Los Quebrados*. Does that ring any bells?"

Sobell said, "No, it doesn't. *Los Quebrados*. What's that mean? Where in Ohio?"

"It means The Broken Ones. Sort of dramatic. Town of Trace Junction. The county sheriff notified the bureau, but says they're doing jack shit."

Sobell said, "That kind of thing takes time Keeler. You don't know, but maybe they're on it and haven't told the locals. You know how the FBI likes to play it. They love to Bigfoot the locals."

Keeler said, "Maybe. But it's about to kick off here in a major way. You're in Chicago, doesn't Ohio fall into your remit?"

"My remit's nationwide my friend. Even global these days." Keeler was hearing the sound of furious typing. Sobell said, "Trace Junction, huh, about an hour south west of Cleveland. What do you want from me?"

Keeler said, "What I want is your tier one combat team. What do you call them over there at Homeland Security?"

She said, "We have SRTs, Special Response Teams. You think that's necessary?"

Keeler said, "Yes."

Sobell paused for a moment and laughed. "Sure, and I'd like

to rewind twenty years and wake up long before I even met my first husband."

Keeler said nothing. He had no interest in her domestic issues.

Sobell said, "For old time's sake I'm going to send you two investigators. You hook up with them and show them what's going on in your little town. Then, we'll decide if the problem requires the mobilization of one of our Special Response Teams. They don't come into town gently, for starters. What do you say?"

Keeler said, "When?"

"Give me 24 hours."

"I appreciate it. Good donuts down here, just saying."

Sobell said, "This is the number to reach you on?"

Keeler said, "Yes, and if that fails they can contact me through the sheriff." Looking at Valdez.

Valdez reeled off the phone number and Keeler repeated it to Sobell.

Sobell said, "We'll be in touch. Might even come down myself. I love a good donut."

She rang off.

Valdez said, "Who was that?"

"That was the director of National Security Investigations, Homeland Security in Chicago. She owes me one." Looking at Valdez, Keeler said, "I've been meaning to ask you about Pete, the Donald's Donuts guy. He mentioned you this morning."

She said, "How do you know Pete?"

"Met him this morning. He seemed to have some faith in you."

She leaned back and took a breath. "Pete's a good guy and cops like donuts, so naturally I'm good with Pete."

Keeler said nothing. She looked at him and sighed. "Pete's onboard with us. He's not the only business owner in town who's decided to try and fight back. We're not all taking this lying down. At this point I'm not really the sheriff since I can't even show up at work. I moved my kids out to California three months ago. They're staying with my sister. Hopefully these sick fucks in *Los Quebrados* don't put their minds to finding out where my kids are. None of us have the training to handle this. Those cartel people aren't screwing around, as you know."

"True." Keeler examined the sheriff in a new light. He said, "You're one of the good ones sheriff, don't ever forget that."

She said, "As if anyone cares."

"It counts."

Valdez said, "Well, I hope so."

Keeler nodded at her. He said, "Now tell me about my sister."

"It wasn't my office that arrested her. That was TJ police."

"Well, I understand that she turned herself in. But the city police would take it even if the shooting was out in the county?"

Keeler said, "What about the shooting?"

Valdez said, "I went to Belleville, following up on the event. Got nothing but stonewalled up there. Anyone involved is now way out of town."

Keeler said, "Probably just moved the girls to a new location. You haven't tried to find them?"

Valdez said, "These people are animals, man. Who knows what we're going to find once this is done. I think we only know the half of it."

"So what's the plan?"

Valdez said, "Maybe we take down some of these hitters here and see what shakes out."

Keeler had been watching the facade through the scope. Nobody had been walking in or out. No vehicles parking out front. Then the door opened. A man stuck his head out and looked around.

Keeler said, "Shit. I think they went in through the back door."

"We didn't think about that."

Keeler said nothing. The guy there was checking to see if all was good. He was glad they had hidden the bodies.

He said, "What's behind that building. Where did they come from?"

Valdez said, "Mercer Avenue. Could have parked up in the Walmart lot. You want to go down there?"

"No."

Two pickup trucks were entering the front parking area now.

He said, "Alright. Coming in now. I guess they plan on moving stuff out."

Keeler had immobilized the second van in the garage bay. They'd need to bring in new vehicles if they wanted to empty out the contents. The trucks parked out front and four men emerged from each vehicle. They'd come in force.

Keeler looked at Valdez. Her eyes were fixed on the building down below. The men were filing in through the front door. The roll up door to the parking bay was coming up. Two more men in there.

Keeler said, "Now's the time."

She said, "Do it."

He watched the last guy come in the door and he put his thumb down on the switch. There was a brief delay of half a second and then all hell broke loose. C4 detonates at supersonic speeds, the crack and boom and the shockwave came later. Initially there was only an abstract violence. The building quivered momentarily, and exploded outward with great speed and force. A sudden jet of dust, stone, flesh, and blood shot out horizontally in every direction.

The collapse occurred at the same time.

An instant later came the first of several secondary explosions, rippling out. First the rest of the DynaLock magazine blew. That was the biggie. Then came the van in the parking bay. Because of the set up, the explosion there was horizontal, fire and dust blowing out into the parking lot.

The place was obscured by an instant dust cloud. Now, no longer a building but a zone of devastation and fire. Nothing moved in there. What Keeler knew, the initial shock wave itself would have killed anyone within fifty yards. Nobody survives a hit like that.

Neighboring buildings had their windows blown out.

Keeler said, "Ba-Boom".

Valdez said, "Holy cow."

He said, "Think that'll send a message?"

"You betcha."

Chapter Thirty

The drone kit was a black backpack sitting in the backseat. Keeler dragged it up front and got the pieces out. One miniature DJI drone, controller, iPad, wires, batteries, SD card adapter for offloading the footage.

Valdez was watching, curious. Keeler got the quadcopter propeller arms out. Looked at her.

He said, "Made in China."

Sirens could be heard. Valdez had her radio on, listening in to the Trace Junction police.

"Cops and fire department incoming."

"ETA?"

"Couple of minutes I guess."

"Alright. I'll be curious to see who shows up. That's another reason to deploy this thing."

Keeler unfolded the propeller arms and powered the drone on. He opened the car door and set the little thing on the ground for takeoff. Once activated, the rotors got to speed in less than a second. The drone was quiet enough, about as loud as an electric toothbrush. Once it was up a hundred feet in the sky, you couldn't hear any sound at all.

Keeler controlled it with a small device, like a video game controller. The iPad was propped up on the dash between them. Right now, they were looking at a bird's-eye view of the area. Which resembled a disaster site.

Keeler said, "You're going to see bad things."

Valdez said, "Understood."

At first, the drone's eye view was of a smoking ruin from far above. The wide-angle camera making everything seem distant, remote even. The roof was mostly gone. Keeler navigated in. Lowering the drone through the center of the erstwhile structure. The closer the drone got, the clearer the picture. Once inside the destroyed building, Keeler flew the drone slowly around in a grid pattern.

It was difficult to make a real assessment, but by his count there were eight or nine bodies in there, presumably cartel foot soldiers. Difficult to tell because these weren't exactly bodies. More like dark stains in the plaster dust. Chunks of flesh, some with hair attached, or limbs. A decapitated head was oddly placed on a fallen beam. Other times, fragments of clothing were the only indication that something had once been human, that and a shoe.

Valdez kept a running commentary composed of four-letter words.

The first emergency responders were pulling up to the site. All Keeler had to do was hit the Return To Home button on the controller and the drone rose immediately up into the air to an altitude of around a hundred and fifty feet and began making its way back to where it had lifted off, just by Keeler's door.

Keeler said, "Nobody noticed us right?"

Valdez had been watching the incoming firetrucks through the scope.

"No."

Keeler packed the drone away in the kit and put it in the

back seat. He sat behind the wheel watching through the medium range finding scope. Valdez had the long range spotting scope up.

She said, "That's the fire chief."

Keeler panned over. A guy with a gut and a baseball cap. Belly leading as he yelled at someone. The fire crews were out. Two vehicles hooking up their hoses and equipment. Men rushing around. The fire chief had his own vehicle of course, a big Chevy Tahoe.

Valdez said, "Cops incoming. I know those guys too."

"Good."

She said, "What are we waiting for?"

Keeler said, "Thing like this, we're waiting for the Wizard of Oz to show up."

Valdez said, "Oh. Right. El-Jefe or whatever."

Keeler grunted an affirmation.

The man arrived after the police had been on site for a half hour. Keeler figured they'd wanted the cops to scout the scene and report back before checking it out themselves. He figured they'd want to know what happened. To what degree would a local team of cops and firemen be capable of evaluating a scene like that?

Keeler's intuitive thought was zero. There's no way they'd be able to make the call that this had been a set up with C4 bricks and detonators. That would take a forensics team from a bigger city, like Cleveland or Cincinnati. Keeler's bet was that the investigation would never happen. Someone here was going to sanitize this scene. The last thing they'd want was outside law enforcement looking in.

When the guy showed up, Keeler liked what he was seeing. The vehicle was perfectly nondescript, Chevy Malibu from at least a decade ago.

Keeler said, "Here we go."

Valdez said, "Yeah, roger that."

The Chevy was stopped by a uniformed cop, who waved the vehicle through after a brief conversation.

Two men came out of the vehicle. One in his late forties, a well-built man with a mane of salt and pepper hair. The other guy was around twenty years younger. Close cropped hair and moving like a panther. Keeler watched that one closely. *El Jefe* and his top soldier. He remembered that the spotting scope had a built-in camera function.

"Valdez, there's a button to take a picture. Get shots of these guys."

"Roger that."

Keeler had a medium shot of the group. New guys coming in and not jumping directly to the action. Standing back a little, taking their time. Discussing stuff. Jefe with a phone in his hand. Looked like he had an open line to someone. Lifting up the phone when he wanted to say something, dropping it to his side otherwise. The younger man was scanning all directions. Alert, functioning like someone with military training.

It's not uncommon south of the border for cartel lieutenants to have backgrounds as members of elite military death squads. This guy in Keeler's scope was turning in a circle, looking around him. Not so much focused upon the detritus of an exploded building, as suspicious of his surroundings. Now, it looked like he was making contact. Nodding at someone out there, head swiveling as he searched for another person. This guy had operatives out in the crowd.

While Valdez kept an eye on the two new arrivals, Keeler busied himself scouting the perimeter for anyone conducting counter surveillance. Sometimes, once you start seeking, you find what you're looking for. He counted three men among the growing crowd of onlookers. These guys weren't looking in.

They weren't gawking at the burning building, their attention was oriented out.

Keeler said, "Shit."

"What?"

"I think there's a team down there monitoring the perimeter. I found three but there may be others."

"Where, what do you mean?" Valdez getting a little confused.

Keeler said, "They put a couple of operatives in the crowd of onlookers. Layered operational security."

Valdez grunted. "I'm telling you, these people don't play."

Keeler said, "Hard to align what I'm seeing here to the dumb harassment I got earlier."

"Who harassed you?"

"Looked like a bunch of good old boys."

Valdez said, "Well, I haven't seen these people either. So, it looks as if you blowing this place to kingdom come has at least given us a little more information than we had earlier."

Keeler said, "The locals would be set up as a first layer. The guys we're looking at here would only come out of the woodwork when absolutely necessary."

"Like we're infected huh? Some kind of human termite colony has dug itself into the soft body of Trace Junction."

"I like the metaphor," Keeler said, "At this point it might even be dangerous if we left. We'd draw attention to ourselves."

The Challenger was dark. Anyone two hundred yards away would just be looking at a parked car in the distance. Unless they had optics. But as far as Keeler could see that wasn't the case.

Valdez said, "Oh, here. We. Go. Check out front of where the roll up garage used to be."

Keeler panned the range finder scope to the right. Locating the two guys who'd come in the Chevy. The older one was yelling at the fire chief, literally screaming in his face. Weird because from their position they couldn't hear anything but the sirens. The fire chief was standing to attention. His eyes down in submission.

Keeler said, "Couple of police officers behind the fire chief. You see them?"

"I do."

"Know them?"

"Mmmm hmmm."

Keeler watched the man screaming in the fire chief's face. That was who he wanted. He said, "Gotcha."

Valdez said, "Now that is the definition of angry. El-Jefe losing his shit."

Keeler said, "We're going to follow them when they leave. See if we can track them back to home base."

The sheriff said, "Sounds risky."

"It is."

Keeler put the car into reverse and backed away from the vantage point. He navigated down and around. Valdez knew the area, and they parked on a side street perpendicular to the route they'd seen the Chevy arrive from. The idea was to wait for the Chevy to come by and then follow.

Keeler said, "How long do you think they'll hang around here?"

Valdez said, "How am I supposed to know?"

"You're supposed to guess, sheriff. Your professional guesstimate is what I'm asking for." Smiling to himself at how ornery she was.

Valdez said, "Why would they hang around? I'm guessing a half hour, max. What would they do here anyway."

Keeler prepped the drone and got it airborne again. The initial buzz dissipated as soon as the thing rose above fifty feet. Valdez leaned into the screen.

"I see their vehicle, but I don't see them. There's still smoke."

"And we haven't seen how the guy's team arrived."

They settled in their seats. Looking into the iPad screen. The battery indicator said eighty percent. Keeler figured that gave the drone a half hour of autonomy. After that he'd need to bring it back to change the battery.

Chapter Thirty-One

Laura Keeler was curled up on her side, facing the wall. The cot began to vibrate, actually the entire cell shaking with a low rumble. The building itself shifting like in an earthquake. She smiled. The earthquake died down.

The image of her brother came to mind.

She said, "My brother is coming for you."

Speaking quietly. She opened her eyes and looked at the wall.

Jail wasn't fun, but it was different. Up in general population things had been a little...social was how she'd put it. She'd had a cell mate, who didn't speak English. But when there's a toilet in the bedroom everything's a little more intimate than you'd otherwise imagine.

Two hours out in the yard walking circles around the cage. Other women there too, everyone sort of...social.

Now, down here in solitary it was different. Dreamy, like an endless space out session with nobody to break you out of it. Laura could understand how people could go bat shit fucking crazy in solitary confinement. Not her though.

She flourished in her own world.

She said, "Introvert."

The mind is your temple, if you allow it to be. Laura didn't see the walls, or the single cot bed and the thin mattress. Didn't feel lonely or isolated, or alienated from herself. She felt good. Warm and cozy, wallowing in the fantasies of past and present.

Ohio wasn't too well known for earthquakes, so what Laura knew was that somehow her brother had managed to create one. He was a man of immense power and range. If it hadn't been for their fuck-up dad, who knows what Tom would have done with his life.

But, Dad happened. Dad couldn't be avoided. Dad was a problem that both Tom and Laura had needed to face, to fix, to solve. Dad required a solution. Her brother had gone to the military and dealt with the anger that way, she'd had to take hers out on their father.

Her brother had been the one to leave first as soon as he could. She didn't blame him for leaving her alone with dad. At that point in time the dad situation was under control, pretty much. The two of them were older anyway and Dad couldn't behave as he used to.

Tom left, one hot and rainy day in September. They'd been in Yazoo City, Mississippi, for the past year and it was raining cats and dogs. Laura sitting on the front steps of the house, protected by the awning. Tom, walking off the porch to the street, instantly soaked, and he didn't give a damn. Turning to her and grinning like the happiest guy on earth.

Laura had put her hands together, saying in gobbledygook, *Be strong brother*.

Tom nodded. Tapping into his own palm. *Stronger together*.

Then he turned his back and made the right onto Maple Ave. towards the Greyhound station. Watching him walk away, Laura knew that this was the end of something and the beginning of another thing. She'd been mature enough back then to know about herself. That, in her life so far it'd been all about being the younger sister.

Well, she'd always be *Tom's sister*, but now she had to take care of herself too. What he'd said to her the night before. Up in her attic room.

He'd said, "It's your time, Laura. I'm getting out of your hair so you can get ready for your own self."

What he meant. Figuring out how to be on her own.

Tom was going to Jackson for the initial tests and stuff at the place the Air Force processed new recruits. They called it a Military Entrance Processing Station. She knew the entire pipeline because she'd been his number one confidante and coach. That's all her brother had talked or dreamed about, the past year and a half.

Laura was able to recite the whole thing. Jackson is where they sucked the new recruits into the system via MEPs. He'd stay in a hotel the first night, before receiving his training orders. He'd be sent to Lackland Air Force Base, San Antonio, Texas for Basic Training. There, the Air Force was going to make a new person out of Tom Keeler. Turn him into another man.

He'd stay in Texas too, for the Pararescue course. The Special Warfare Candidate Course, and all the rest. He'd only get out of Texas for the dive training, but that was months away, at least.

The raindrops were thick and fat, splattering everywhere, positively bouncing off the pavement. Laura's eyes were drawn to the other side of the road. In the verge past the smooth gray concrete curb, she could make out the form of a wounded bird, almost lost from sight in the tall grass. Feathers soaked but moving. Something barely alive there. The way the feathers fluttered wasn't just the rain, it was a living being on the edge of death.

She'd crossed the street in bare feet, the asphalt summer

warm. It was some kind of raptor, a small bird of prey. Its wing was broken and there was blood on the creature's breast. Laura figured the thing had been attacked by a larger predator. For a minute, looking at the wounded bird. Laura visualized the event. The little raptor attacked maybe by crows, or a larger predator, like an owl.

No telling how long it had been out here in the grass. The rain must have saved the bird from falling victim to a house cat, or a scavenging raccoon.

She brought the bird inside, to her mother. They'd fixed a shoe box with cut up old t-shirts. Cleaned the wounds and fed it pieces of chicken. At the library she found a large book about the birds of Mississippi, with hand-drawn illustrations. Her bird was a Sparrow Hawk.

* * *

Laura had fallen asleep. She woke to a noise behind her. In the initial three seconds of consciousness she was disoriented by the idea of time. How long had she been out?

The cell door was opening. Survival instincts kicked in and she turned on the cot. A large guard with a meaty arm was pushing the door open. The guard wore a surgical mask. Which wasn't something that immediately set alarm bells ringing in her head. Then she saw that he had blue latex gloves on.

Two men entered the room behind him. Also wearing masks and gloves.

Laura swung her legs over to sit on the edge of the bed. Looking at them with wide-open eyes. Feet not even touching the floor. She wasn't very tall.

Both men held riot control batons in their gloved hands. That, and the uniforms and face masks made them look a little perverse.

A third guard came behind them. They entered slowly, spreading out so that their approach was from either side. Laura figured it'd be better to take a beating on the bed. Otherwise she ran the risk of knocking her head against the floor.

Laura said, "Uh, you guys look like some kind of medicalized Nazi tag wrestling team."

The man on her right raised his baton to strike. She didn't flinch, watching him to see if he'd do it.

He said, "Oh nice. We got ourselves a brave one."

The other man said, "What I heard."

Both of them now close and imposing. Tall and strong men with weapons against a barefoot prisoner on a single cot.

She said, "How's it going fellas, feeling frisky today?"

The guy on the right said, "It's just orders ma'am, nothing personal. It looks as if someone's unhappy with you. Sent a special request to the warden."

"What kind of request would that be?"

"The kind you don't argue with, I guess. County's in a sorry state these days, but a job is a job is a job."

The guard coming on her left side started cackling with laughter and Laura realized they were high.

The one on her right giggled. "Yeah, let's just do the job and get the fuck out of here. Nobody said we're supposed to enjoy it."

The man on Laura's right said, "Ok, let's do it."

The third guard said, "I might just enjoy it anyway."

By then, Laura was breathing fast and hard.

As the blows came down Laura managed to tuck herself into a fetal position again, facing the wall like she'd done earlier. Except this time sleep was long in coming. And when it came, it did so quickly, all of a sudden, with a thud and the metallic taste of blood.

Chapter Thirty-Two

Keeler was always surprised when the days got shorter and the nights longer. November. It was almost 5pm and the sun had already descended below the tree line. The drone thing had worked out. Giving them a good heads up when the boss man was getting back to his car.

The other guy, his lieutenant, was the driver. Keeler hit the Return To Home command, and they got their drone back a minute later. The boss didn't travel alone. They had a convoy of three vehicles. The lead and tail vehicles maintained a fifty-foot spacing from the Chevy. These were Ford Expedition models. Classic workhorse SUVs.

Keeler had only identified three cartel operatives in the crowd, aside from El-Jefe and his guard. But there were two accompanying vehicles. He decided to revise his assumption to at least four enemy combatants. Two in each car.

The Chevy sedan was sandwiched between the two. There was a pretty decent chance that the rear vehicle would be watching for a tail. No way around that. He slipped the Challenger onto the main road and kept it five car lengths back. They weren't alone out there. Traffic was being funneled into a deviation route around the disaster site, slowing everything down..

It was hard for Keeler to get his head around the idea that a cartel network seemed to have taken control of an American town, or the entire county. Was the civic reality so weak here? He'd been around the country in the last couple of years, since leaving the military but never had he seen anything quite like this.

According to Valdez, she, Kennedy and Carver were the only members of the county sheriff's team who'd resisted capitulation.

There had been a final attempt to kill Valdez using a suicide drone. The device had missed her and taken someone else instead. A random error. The casualty had been an innocent bystander who Valdez referred to as a 'cheerleader', but the signal was clear. The sheriff's expiration date was something on the order of tomorrow, or the next day, or the day after that. Any longer and she ran the danger of actually being killed.

Which is why Valdez and her team had gone into full defensive mode. Basically a retreat from the battlefield. Now they made the odd excursion to sites like the house fire. Keeping their presence felt, while maintaining op-sec and hunkering down in a secure location. Sending the kids to California wasn't the ballsy move—staying in Trace Junction was.

Keeler had only commented briefly on that part of her story. "Cheerleader, for real?"

"What I remember. Blonde, face like a playboy bunny. Before it got blown off. At the Kroger supermarket. Fucking took her head off, plus the cashier got blinded."

"Inside the supermarket?"

"Uh-huh. I don't think you understand."

Keeler said, "Oh, I understand."

They drove in silence for a few minutes.

He said, "So it's over, Valdez, right?"

"What's over?"

"Pretending you're living in the old reality. Like when you showed up to my sister's house. Acting like a cop. You're not a cop anymore, sheriff. You're a combatant. There's no law here anymore. You can take off the uniform. It's just going to be harder for you wearing that."

Valdez looked straight ahead then. At the road rushing at them. Farms and pylons going past.

She said, "Is this what war looks like Keeler? Mundane and normal and fucked up all at the same time."

Keeler said, "That's what it looks like, Valdez. You're in it before you know you're in it. Recognizing that sooner than the other guy is your best chance of getting into his decision loop first. Maybe the enemy thinks it's business as usual. That's our hope."

She said, "I'm wearing the uniform for everyone else. They need to know we're not quitting yet."

Once out of town, things got a little trickier. Dusk, but Keeler had concerns that he'd be easy to spot on those rural roads.

He said, "I think I'll turn off. They're going to make us."

Valdez put a hand on his arm. "Hold on, I think they're going to the Quality Inn." She laughed.

"What's funny?"

"No, it's just that I know the owners. Patel family. Thing about the Quality Inn is that he's got a couple of rooms with mirrored ceilings. You know what I mean. Maybe El-Jefe likes his mirrored ceiling."

Which made a lot of sense to Keeler. Still, it did get him thinking.

"Mirrored ceilings huh? You got native talent here in town or do they import?"

"Most definitely imported. Women around here are surviving on ramen noodles. Doesn't do great things for the skin."

Two miles later the convoy turned into the Quality Inn, a motel set back from the road by a sloping lawn with a large sign and an inactive water fountain. A *No Vacancy* placard hung by the main sign.

Valdez said, "That's the one."

Keeler kept the Challenger on the road, coming by the motel and giving it a good look. Taillights of the convoy in red as they drove up to the parking lot in back.

Main building on the left with offices and maybe a cafe or breakfast room. Next to it was the main motel building that housed the rooms. Most of it was single story, with a small second floor. Above that was some kind of ornamental dome, looked cast out of cement. The spotlights cast the dome in a garish turquoise.

Keeler said, "Second floor's what, some kind of penthouse?"

Valdez said, "No idea. Place has a bar out back with a pool table. Used to be a spot with predictable call outs for trouble every weekend. Everything's been quiet here for a while, actually. Didn't think about it, but I guess that makes sense now."

Keeler said, "No doubt these gangbangers like to play hard. For sure they aren't calling in *Cheryl the sheriff*."

"What's that supposed to mean?"

Keeler grinned. "Nothing. Tell me something. You know the guy from Donald's Donuts?"

"Pete. Sure. Why?"

"No reason."

"Great donuts. I'll tell you that for free."

Keeler nodded. He'd gotten at least one donut for free. About a mile down the road he made a left onto a country lane.

"You know this neighborhood, Valdez? I want to park up

somewhere we can access the motel through the woods. I want to walk in."

"You're on the right track. Keep going a bit. You'll have Chris Whitty's livestock barn on your left. Park up behind it."

"Is that someone's farm? I don't want anyone watching us."

"It's the livestock barn. About a mile from the main house. You'll understand why pretty soon."

The why became clear as soon as Keeler stepped out of the vehicle. The place stank worse than pig shit. The structure was a big old barn, half open to the elements. Keeler pulled up the gravel lane and swung the Challenger around the back.

Chapter Thirty-Three

The woods loomed up ahead, a dark wall of trees.

Valdez pointed. "Park up there as far as you can get. It's going to stink out of the car. But don't worry, they had a cow pandemic here a couple years ago, and Whitty put them all down. Now it's just a bunch of hogs."

"Which is what, better than cow shit?"

When he'd stopped the vehicle, the sheriff looked at him. Valdez waved a hand in front of her nose. "I thought we'd be okay here, wind must be moving the wrong way. So, what do you want to do Keeler? What's the plan here?"

Keeler didn't answer. He got out of the car and took a deep breath through the nose. The stink was terrible. He felt himself growing a little quiet inside. Something he recognized as a kind of softening before action. The trees were denuded of leaves, stark shadow skeletons swaying in a chill wind.

He turned to Valdez, hugging herself in the cold.

Keeler said, "Look, we've just killed eight of their soldiers with a bunch of C4 and bolts and screws. Literally tore them to unrecognizable pieces." He pointed through the woods. "Think about how they're feeling Valdez. They're freaking out about it. The main dude has to be feeling vulnerable. Now, we've tracked them back to their base, in this *Quality Inn* where they feel safe. What do you want to do, let them get all settled and comfortable? You want to let them adapt to the situation?"

Valdez said, "I wasn't thinking about it that way, but no. I don't."

He said, "We want the enemy to completely lose the idea of feeling safe. Ultimately, we want them gone. Are you with me? We want them to leave or die. To quit the battlefield. Right?"

"Ok, I guess."

The sheriff was looking at him strangely.

Keeler looked at her, seeing concern in the eyes. He said, "We'll get them. Don't worry. It's going to happen. I guarantee it."

She grinned, the waffle iron warping slightly. "You guarantee, huh? Ok. We'll see. What do you want to bet?"

"We haven't even started and you're already betting against us. That's confidence, Valdez."

Valdez gave that hearty laugh again. "You need a sense of humor in this game, right? Bet you a diner burger. Cheese and bacon with jalapeños. That's my usual."

That reminded Keeler of the diner. And the fact that he was supposed to return the waitress's phone. She was pulling another night shift. He suddenly pictured this beautiful red-headed woman there at the diner. A mundane alternate reality came to mind, one in which things worked and rolled as normal. Schedules were kept. Money flowed into cartel accounts, siphoned off from the real economy by their entrepreneurial army of thieves.

He said, "Sure. But it's not going to be a bet. You buy me a jalapeño cheese burger at the diner when we run the scumbags out of town. I want bacon on that."

"With your sister, Keeler, right?"

"And Laura, yes. She'll be with us."

He looked back at Valdez, seeing her clearly. A calm sensation began to seep through him. All kinds of chemicals started working on his brain. Dopamine began flooding his system, and he knew it was going to get even better.

He laughed at the sheriff, standing there with a serious expression on her face. "You don't know me Valdez. We've just met. Those guys over there at the Quality Inn are about to get quality time with me. You stay here and hold the fort. Give me an hour to cause a little mayhem. Is there a back way out of here without going past the motel?"

Valdez was quiet. She said, "We can drive past the farmhouse. Pick up Creamery Road back to town. Takes us past the BBQ joint. Maybe we can get some take out for the guys."

"Yeah, maybe." He was thinking about the diner and the waitress now. He pushed that thought into the rear right corner of his mind. A little room called *interesting*. He wasn't getting barbecue after this—he was planning on getting a head start on that jalapeño burger at the diner.

Keeler went to the trunk and got the backpack out. By his count he'd shot off six 9mm rounds back at the drone workshop facility. Which meant he had twenty-four left. Nine in the weapon and another fifteen in the extra magazine. Plus the bow.

Valdez watched him. She said, "A bow and arrow?"

He shrugged. "It's hunting season out there in Ohio, sheriff." He gave a little curt nod to Valdez and threw her the car keys. "Stay safe".

"What, I'm waiting here like a housewife or some shit?"

"Yes." He walked towards the woods.

"Bullshit." Valdez surged forwards after him.

He heard the footsteps. Turning to her, putting a hand on her shoulder.

"No. You hold the fort. I wasn't kidding. I need you here. It's better."

She was pissed off. Keeler didn't care. He pushed her back. "Stay with the vehicle. That's your job, Valdez. Be a good little sheriff."

For a moment she stared at him but ended up with a smile. "Shit. You're an asshole Keeler." Valdez turned back and went to the car. As Keeler entered the woods, he heard her voice behind him.

"I'll be here."

"Good."

He moved up the hill through the trees. He'd known Valdez for a minute or two and already felt right at home with her. Sometimes you just find your people.

* * *

Keeler moved steadily through the woods. He ate up the yards, but didn't rush it. He took his time and stayed nice and quiet. Heel first, rolling down on the balls of his feet. There was no way to be silent, given the dry leaves. Twenty minutes later, the woods up ahead began breaking out into open field.

He stopped moving and started paying close attention to the tree line.

For five long minutes he stayed still, observing. After two minutes of silence, the woods came back to life. A raccoon was up in a tree, watching him. An owl began making its screeching sound again. He didn't see any human beings.

Keeler pressed on.

The motel was set in a large clearing. He was looking at it from an oblique three quarters angle. Behind the Quality Inn, a small wooded area that concealed a lumber yard behind it. At least that's what Keeler saw on the waitress's smart phone, checking it out on Google maps. Keeler put the phone away and sat down, leaned back against a tree. He had a decent observational view from where he was positioned. The motel down below. The broken fountain doing nothing. The sign out front lit up with spotlights. He brought out the range finder scope, steadying it on a knee.

Keeler decided to scan from the outside in. He did a super slow pan from his extreme left, moving to the right and making sure to pause once in a while and just wait for movement.

There were two men sitting in one of the Ford Expedition SUVs, down at the bottom of the driveway. The driveway itself slightly sunken between two mild gradients. Besides that, he couldn't seem to find any security presence outside of the Quality Inn structures themselves. From where Keeler sat, he didn't have a good look into motel windows, the angle was too oblique.

It took a little time to move carefully through the woods for a view of the back. When he settled down to take a good look, Keeler realized that it had been time well spent. To the naked eye, the place looked dark and sleepy. But it wasn't late, and Keeler didn't believe that El-Jefe would be ready for bed. Particularly after his drone workshop had been blown to kingdom come.

Single story main building, with the penthouse up top. The penthouse had a sort of balcony, or walkway on the back side, with an external set of stairs leading down. A light was on in there, but he couldn't detect movement.

Keeler had already seen the office area with breakfast room out front, when they'd done the drive by with Valdez. Looking at the back of it, he was seeing a single story brick building with a solid back door, currently closed. This part of the structure was windowless, although at the front it had large picture windows.

The office and motel buildings were not attached. A narrow alley separated them. The motel side had a low one story extension at the back. A neon martini glass in pink and yellow glowed on the outside. Steps led down to a basement door. The door had a window square in it, dark but on close examination showed some warm and dim light inside. A man in dark clothing leaned against the stair ledge, smoking a cigarette.

Alright. There was a good chance that some of the crew were hanging out at the bar.

Keeler watched the man for a minute. He flicked his butt and descended the short flight of steps to open the bar door. Dim lighting inside. Keeler saw a pool table, and a man stretched over it making a shot. Behind him, others standing. He thought, those are the soldiers, blowing off steam.

So much for an active military posture. These people were very comfortable.

Keeler let his scope caress the remainder of the building. Starting top right and moving in a methodical way, slowly seeking out movement in the dark windows and crevices. Bottom right, pretty close to the bar entrance, second room in. There was a watcher at the window.

Keeler held on it. Steadying the spotting scope against his knee. His eyes adjusted to the luminosity and he knew what he was looking at. The guy was wearing night vision goggles. The smallish lenses gave off a minor reflection.

Alright. That was something.

But Keeler knew how NVGs worked. The guy could easily pick out someone moving across the open space, but he wasn't able to see Keeler at that distance. Still, getting closer to the building was going to be a problem. The waitress's phone buzzed in his pocket. He ignored it and the device stopped after a few rings. It made him feel kind of bad that he had her phone. What if she needed to speak to the babysitter or whatever?

Keeler kicked the waitress out of his mind. Focused on the task at hand. Other side of the motel, on the left. Three rooms in from the end. Keeler spotted another watcher. Same profile. A man on duty with a pair of NVGs.

The question he had was pretty simple. What was the operational goal? What would be the best outcome here? The big goal was to get Laura out. Number one, first thing he cared about. Therefore, killing and maiming was going to bring short-term satisfaction, but it was hard to see how that would get him closer to Laura's freedom.

On the other hand, capturing the boss might bring interesting rewards. Keeler figured that Laura was a captive. He put her in that category. If Keeler could get the boss, he might be able to trade for Laura.

A good outcome here would be to slip through the guards unseen and take the boss. That was going to be high risk, high reward. Keeler felt the beginnings of a plan flower in his brain. Take the boss out using his own vehicle. After all, they'd positioned the SUV out front, facing the way out. If Keeler could neutralize those guards, he'd have a getaway car.

Keeler watched the two men in their motel rooms for a while. One on each end of the place. The errors were multiple, chief among them staying comfortable in a room. He figured there were sentry shifts. Maybe two or three hours each. In between that, what? They probably hang out at the bar and shoot pool. Real question was about their communications. Were they in touch regularly? Was this a professional setup? More observation was going to be necessary. Which meant more time.

Keeler got the phone out. He'd programmed the sheriff's number in there. He sent her a text message.

This is going to take longer than I thought.

The response came back fast. *How long?*

He tapped. *I don't know.*

She wrote back. *Take your time. I'm here listening to a podcast.*

Which made Keeler smile. He doubted it was true, but who could tell these days?

Chapter Thirty-Four

The spotting scope dialed him in to a confined view, like looking through a telescope. Keeler set up with the range finder, getting a medium close up of the place. He had to wait fifteen minutes for anything to actually happen. What happened was unexpected. The penthouse door opened, and a woman stepped out onto the balcony.

Keeler switched to the spotting scope again. He got a close up on her, head and shoulders.

Not exactly a woman. A young female, probably in her teens, all dressed up in heels and a dress. Heavy makeup job. Bright red on the lips and dark eyes. Now that the door was open, Keeler could see that there were others in the place behind her. He focused in on the scope, looked like a group of women, or girls actually, sitting on a sofa at the back of this room.

Keeler focused to the girl on the balcony. She was leaning, arms up on the railing, dragging on a cigarette and kind of swaying in a dreamy way. For a second he thought she was looking directly at him. Which was not possible, given the darkness and the distance. She was just staring into the forest.

The girl pulled on her cigarette, letting the smoke seep lazily out of her mouth and nostrils. Keeler realized she was moving to the rhythm of music. The sounds were now faintly audible, coming from the room behind her. Her features were clearly Hispanic. Maybe an ethnic mix that included elements of indigenous people. Whatever the background, Keeler didn't need to be an anthropologist or demographer to see it.

Of course, it made him think back to Laura's story, and the migrant shelter up by the Amish auction. Was it connected? Only time would tell. The girl flicked her butt and went back inside, leaving the door open. Then, the door was closed by someone else.

Okay. What was he looking at? A room full of migrant girls? Trafficking victims? Dressed up to please and service the guys? All of which seemed possible and even likely.

The back door to the office opened. A man came out mid-conversation. Keeler recognized him immediately, the guy who'd been in charge back at the explosion site. Now, holding a phone to his ear with one hand and a large cigar with the other. That was the target. Keeler couldn't hear what he was saying, and he wasn't a lip reader either. The same guy as before came out after the boss. The man eyeing the surroundings. The bodyguard.

Keeler watched.

The boss was listening on the phone, nodding and mumbling something. He started walking up into the grass behind the Quality Inn. Keeler sat still, watching the presumed cartel man come toward him. Interesting. The bodyguard ducked back into the office, stuck his head in. Maybe he was checking on something or talking to someone. He ducked back out and jogged after the boss. The boss moved up the grassy slope, absorbed in his phone conversa-tion. Now audible. Grunting, saying *si, si*. Keeler caught fragments of Spanish, understood the connective words, but didn't get the content.

The man was halfway across the lawn, heading up the incline to the woods. His pace picked up, like he had a destination in mind. A man with a plan. The bodyguard followed a few yards behind, stopping at the base of the slope. Keeler checked the watchers. Shifted the spotting scope quickly from one window to the other. The two men with night vision goggles. One of them had either taken them off or left. Hard to tell. Either way, that window had gone dark. The other one still watched, ambient light bouncing off the small NVG lenses.

The boss came close, literally entering the woods. Keeler put the scope down and stayed very still. This was bizarre. If the man actually found him, he'd need to act quickly. And do what —kill him? Keeler was sitting perhaps fifteen feet into the trees.

The boss came to the tree line and stopped. Cigar still in his mouth, puffing, he unzipped with his free hand. Keeler stayed calm, steadying his breathing. Watched this cartel chief piss a strong and hot stream into a tree trunk.

A rustling sound came from the woods behind. A cold feeling crept up Keeler's spine. He dared not turn. A branch cracked loudly. The cartel chief stopped puffing and stared into the dark. His gaze seemed to aim at Keeler, but it wasn't. It was directed into the woods. Keeler was so close, he could hear the man's teeth grind into the cigar. That cold feeling moved from his collar up to the small hairs on his back.

Behind him came the sudden sound of an animal rushing away through the woods. Most likely either a white-tailed deer or a coyote.

He breathed. Slow and easy, making sure to fill his lungs with air.

The cartel man said, "*la puta madre!*" He laughed.

And then Keeler had an insane idea. The thought of it, the

whole plan, just came flooding into the front of his brain fully formed. Some back-office work had already been done out of consciousness. But then, that's what the unconscious is for.

The boss would finish pissing, shake it off, and walk back to the motel. True, the lawn was open space and visible to the bodyguard and both watchers. But there was one way Keeler could close the distance and stay unseen.

When men piss, they like to watch it splash. That's why smart urinal manufacturers print a fly on the porcelain. This guy was no different, watching the tree with fascination as his urine splattered.

Keeler eased the pack from one shoulder and unclipped the bow. He shrugged the pack back on and timed his movement with the chief. The man grunted as he finished, shaking off. He zipped his fly and turned.

Keeler rose into a crouch and took four steps to the right. He emerged from the woods fast. Slipped up close to the chief, using the man's body as cover. The guy still on the phone, grunting and listening to someone yap in machine-gun Spanish. That helped—he wouldn't hear sounds behind him. Plus, his thick frame blocked the bodyguard and watchers from seeing Keeler. Keeler timed his steps with the man's.

It wasn't far, maybe thirty steps. Keeler kept the right angle. Drew an arrow from the quiver, smooth and easy. Stayed in step with the big man. Couldn't see the bodyguard yet, the boss's shape still in the way. But the guy would see him soon.

Keeler nocked the arrow and pulled it back. The bow had a tough draw. Keeler pointed it down and pulled steady. The cord eased over the cams, locked in place. He held it. Arrow ready to fly. The grassy slope leveled as they reached the motel. Keeler and the chief moved out of the watcher's view.

Only the bodyguard left to handle.

Keeler took a knee and let the chief move forward, clearing

the shot. Field of fire opened. He drew a bead on the bodyguard, who hadn't noticed yet. The man wore a black varsity jacket, watching his boss. His gaze flicked to Keeler. Realization dawned. He exhaled and reached into his jacket on instinct.

Keeler released. The taut string thwapped. Arrow whooshed and thudded into the notch between neck and chest. Jugular. The bodyguard made a soft screech and dropped.

Keeler had already moved on.

He was up with his knife, hustling the shocked cartel chief against the motel wall. Blade at the man's throat. Took the phone from his hand, ended the call.

Frisked him fast—no weapons. Just a Zippo in the front pocket.

The chief's eyes bugged out. He couldn't stop staring at the bodyguard's twitching body. A rough death, no doubt. Keeler understood the anatomy. He'd been aiming for the chest, but the arrow had taken its own route.

The jugular notch lies between the collar bones. It's the site of several major arteries. Looked like they'd been hit. Jugular vein, carotid, maybe the subclavian. Arterial flow is high pressure—like a hose. In this case, blood aspiration into the trachea had blocked the airway.

Keeler said, "Not a sound, boss. Not one. Nod."

The boss nodded.

Keeler pointed to the body. "Drag him there." He meant the alley between office and motel. The man hesitated. Keeler shoved him toward the guard.

He obeyed. Keeler noticed the man knew how to drag a body—took the ankles and pulled with some skill, but still got winded doing it. When he stood, he looked at Keeler, the shock beginning to fade from his face.

He said, "You're the asshole with the sister. Keeler."

Not a question. The guy looked at him with a touch of

respect. Bobby Kennedy had been right. The cartel had pulled Keeler's military record off a facial match. Not as easy as most people thought. Regular cops couldn't even access that kind of data.

The back door opened. The sound cracked loud in the quiet. That latch click bounced off the hillside. The man in front of Keeler froze.

Someone coughed. A voice called out. "Sergio."

Keeler and Sergio locked eyes.

Again, louder. "Hey, Sergio!"

Keeler switched the knife to his left hand. Drew the pistol from his pocket. Sergio stared at the weapon. The man from the door stepped out. Foot scraped the cement. His breath was heavy.

Keeler chambered a round, controlling the slide. Fed the bullet into the breech. Sergio's eyes moved from gun to Keeler. Keeler nodded and gave a quick grin. Sergio had a decision to make. Behind Keeler, footsteps advanced.

Chapter Thirty-Five

The man from the office crossed the space of the narrow alley in two steps. He passed only three feet away from Keeler, pressed back against the alley wall. The man was in his fifties, with light brown hair and a graying beard. He was dressed in a Japanese kimono and slippers.

Keeler could see that he was preoccupied with the scent of smoke from Sergio's cigar. He walked by, head only slightly turned the other way, toward the woods up the slope. That kept Keeler out of his peripheral vision.

Keeler breathed easier when he saw the guy begin to climb the external set of stairs leading up to the penthouse balcony. He kept still, watching the man's naked heels lift from the slippers with each step. The guy didn't look back. Opened the penthouse door and light flooded out again. He stepped inside and closed the door.

Keeler turned. "Who was that, Sergio?"

Sergio stared at him. Silent. Keeler took a step to the man and jammed a forearm into his throat, pushing him against the wall. He put the buck knife blade point into the hollow below Sergio's chin.

Keeler tilted his head to the dead bodyguard. "Last time. Who was that?"

"That was my brother." The cigar breath was strong.

Keeler said, "Alright. Now who's left in the office?"

"Nobody's there."

"You sure about that?"

Sergio nodded. He said, "You're making an error, Keeler. Your sister is not going to benefit from any arrangement."

Keeler said, "We'll see."

The guy rolled his eyes. Nodded and repeated Keeler's words. "We will see, yes."

Keeler had him go first. They entered the office through the back door. Sergio had been telling the truth. Nobody was there. The back of the office had a kitchen setup, for the motel guests' breakfasts presumably. A large steel-topped food prep island showed signs of a recent improvised meal. Barbecue pork ribs, mostly eaten, plus six empty beer bottles.

Out front the breakfast room was dark. The tables and chairs were silhouetted by a weak glow from the streetlight. Keeler dragged Sergio into the room and sat him in a chair.

Sergio started to say something and Keeler knuckle punched him in the mouth, just a little jab to keep him behaved, knocking his head back. He put his finger to his lips and looked into Sergio's eyes. The guy was dazed but he nodded.

Keeler removed the roll of duct tape from his pack and secured him to the chair, gagging his mouth and making sure he could breathe through his nose.

"Sit tight, Sergio. I don't want you dead yet."

He didn't know how much time he had—probably not much. Keeler figured Sergio's brother had gone up to have some fun with the teenage girls they were keeping as sex slaves. That should keep him busy for a bit, depending on the level of sibling curiosity. Eventually, he'd wonder where Sergio was, but Keeler was hoping by then it'd be too late.

Keeler went out the back way. He stuck close to the wall, edging toward the driveway. Down at the bottom was the Ford Expedition SUV with two men inside, guarding the front.

Sentry duty is boring. Staying alert for hours takes serious training. The vehicle's windows were up. Keeler didn't trust himself to shoot an arrow through glass.

A gunshot would work, but it'd bring the kind of attention he didn't want. So far, the bow had done the job—quiet and deadly. He drew a deep breath of crisp autumn air. Felt good. He needed a quiet way to do this.

The knife came out of its sheath. Keeler hadn't said anything to the saleswoman at Hunt & Hustle Sporting Goods, but he knew this knife. The 119 hunting model of the Buck. The original had been a folder. The latest version was huge and looked scary.

This one had a hollow grind blade. Sharper right out of the sheath. An inch shorter than the Ka-Bar, but that didn't matter. Six inches of steel makes a man six inches dead.

Then, Keeler had another idea.

* * *

It took him five minutes to crawl slowly onto the grassy embankment at the edge of the driveway, then down toward the vehicle. He slithered forward on his belly, inch by inch, eyes alert for movement—but he saw none. Now he crouched behind the Ford.

The problem with commercial drones like the ones he had— can't crash them on purpose. The software didn't allow it. The sensors take over and steer away from any collision.

But landing one? That you can do. Keeler had powered on the drone and left it by the rear office door. Now, crouched behind the vehicle, he used the controller. The drone lifted and rose a hundred feet in the air. Virtually silent. Just the faintest hum, and only if you were listening for it.

He piloted the drone toward his position. When it hovered above, he dropped it down to the vehicle's roof. The buzz would become audible as it neared. He aimed to cut the rotors fast on contact.

Fifty-five decibels—audible inside the SUV, but vague. The drone tapped the roof. A shift inside the car told Keeler someone was alert now.

He figured the passenger would step out first, but no—the driver's door opened. Feet hit gravel. Keeler had the knife in hand, pistol in his pocket. He hit Return to Home. The drone buzzed as the rotors spun up.

He expected the man to grab for it. He was right. The guy stretched over the roof, snagged the drone. Doing so meant he had to stretch out his arm, exposing himself to Keeler. Propellers buzzed like a manic toothbrush. Keeler closed in and drove the knife up through the man's ribs. Five quick stabs, deep.

Not much struggle. The guy's position left him wide open. The drone's hum covered the sound. Two or three seconds total. Keeler struck high, mid, low—hitting something vital, no doubt.

The man didn't scream.

He just slumped and dropped. Brain and body cut off. Keeler let him fall and slipped back behind the vehicle. The man in the passenger seat said something in Spanish. Keeler only caught *cabrón*—asshole.

Nothing moved. Keeler set down the pack and unclipped the bow. Selected an arrow and nocked it to the string. Pulled it back and locked the cams, getting a feel for the weapon.

The drone had hit the ground somewhere in front of the

SUV. The passenger door opened. Keeler peered under the frame. Feet hit pavement—black Nikes with the swoosh. The guy moved to the front, probably checking the drone.

Keeler held the bow steady. Stepped left. Expected the guy to be bent over the drone or checking his buddy. Found him upright, holding the drone, staring at his dying friend. The man probably thought it was a heart attack or something weird from the drone.

Keeler took aim at the chest and let it fly.

The arrow hummed through the air and hit. The broadhead sliced clean and punched through. The shaft rattled onto the street twenty feet away. The bow packed serious force. Must've hit a big artery or something. The guy dropped on top of his buddy and twitched like a dying frog.

Keeler forced himself to look away. He sprinted to grab the arrow and drone. Came back slow, watching the Quality Inn for lights or motion. Nothing. No one noticed. These guys weren't in a war. They were in La La Land. Sergio's brother upstairs with the girls.

Keeler felt no mercy. Just a cold drive to finish the job. Lawfare against his sister, blackmail in town—bad enough. But those girls? That changed the game.

He threw the pack into the SUV. Keys were in the ignition. Went back for Sergio. No time to untie him. He lifted the man, chair and all, balanced the load on his shoulder. The SUV was big. Keeler slid the guy in with the chair intact.

He stepped around the bodies and got into the driver's seat. The sloped driveway gave him enough momentum to coast silently to the road. Engine off, tires soft over the asphalt. No sound.

Hands loose on the wheel, he listened hard. Sergio's nasal breathing wasn't helping.

At the road's edge, Keeler turned, coasted, then finally

keyed the ignition. Engine purred—no revs, no drama. He kept the lights off until he was a good distance out.

On the road, cruising, he used the waitress's phone to call Valdez.

Chapter Thirty-Six

The sheriff was in Keeler's rental car, waiting a quarter mile past the turnoff they'd originally made for the livestock barn. She was parked up to his left, facing the direction he'd come. He pulled the Ford in at a V-up configuration. Driver's side to driver's side, like cops in a parking lot. Valdez rolled down the window.

"What's going on, why'd you want me to meet you here?" Eyeballing the vehicle Keeler was driving. "That's their truck."

He ignored the comment. He said, "Valdez, focus. I need you to lead us somewhere safe. Not the place you and your friends holed up. Somewhere between here and there where we can dump this thing I'm driving. Get that guy Dwight to meet us." He handed Sergio's phone through the window. "He needs to have gear to rip out whatever data's on this thing and make sense of it. Call him on the move."

Valdez eyeballed the vehicle Keeler was driving. "What are we in the car theft business now?"

"No. I've got El-Jefe in the back. Where are we going?"

"Fuck." She looked out the window for a few seconds, looked back up at him. "Follow me."

* * *

They drove for perhaps fifteen minutes, through the back roads. Cutting into a residential area and then back out to a wooded lane. Shortly, Valdez hit the right side indicator and pulled into a rutted dirt track. Keeler followed, bumping slowly. She stopped, and he pulled the Ford in.

Valdez came over, looking in through the window in fascination and horror. Keeler opened the driver's side door and stepped out. Valdez stared at Sergio, taped up in the chair.

"Fuck. Holy shit. That's the guy?"

"His name's Sergio."

"What do you want to do?"

Keeler said, "I want to trade him for my sister."

"Explain."

"Well, it turns out that this guy in the back, Sergio, isn't running things on his own. His brother's one half of the cartel boss crew."

The sheriff was all worked up. Couldn't keep still. She was excited, or nervous, or having a total breakdown. Hard to tell.

She took deep breaths. "Shit. Okay."

"Like I said, I want to make a trade. After Laura's out, we'll see."

"This is crazy."

Keeler said, "The world's a great place Valdez, until suddenly it's not. Once in a while shit happens. Get over it. You want a slap?"

"No." She took a few deep breaths. "Ok, I'm good." She looked around, suddenly wary. "Are we safe here, are they following you?"

Keeler pointed to Sergio's phone. "This is what we need to do. Get information off this phone so we can ditch it. And ditch the vehicle when we ditch the phone. I have to assume this guy's team can track both. We're on a clock here." Looking hard at her now. "You hear me?"

"Yes."

"Good. Where's Dwight?"

Dwight was on the way. Headlights bounced down the track toward them about five minutes later. It was him in the passenger seat with Carver driving. Keeler went straight to the driver's side of the vehicle. The same unmarked car that Keeler had seen him in earlier. Carver stepped out.

"What' up?"

Keeler said, "We're going to ditch that vehicle." Pointing to the Ford Expedition. He beckoned to Valdez. Making a hand gesture for Sergio's phone. He held the phone up for Dwight to see. "This is a hot phone. I want it ripped for data." Looking at Dwight directly. "Do they track phones?"

Dwight said, "Definitely. And vehicles."

"Right. So this phone's going to be tracked. Which means we're on a timer."

Dwight said, "Whose phone is it?"

Keeler said, "I've got the big boss in the back of the truck over there. His name is Sergio, it's his phone."

Both Carver and Dwight swiveled eyes at the vehicle. Carver walked over and looked in. He jumped back when he saw what was inside.

"Damn."

Dwight was less affected. He said. "Give me the phone now." Keeler handed it over. Dwight looked at the phone for a moment. He said, "Facial recognition. You need to get it open."

Keeler went to the back of the SUV and opened the gate. Sergio lay on his side. Blindfolded, gagged, and bound in duct tape. Keeler ripped the tape from his face. The guy gagged and huffed, eyes wide and bugged out.

He said, "You're making a mistake."

Keeler said, "Story of my life."

He held the device so it could read Sergio's face. The phone unlocked.

Keeler tossed it to Dwight. "Do it."

Dwight said, "Roger that."

Keeler reapplied duct tape to his face. He dragged Sergio out of the vehicle and let him drop, chair and all, onto the hard dirt.

It took seven minutes to rip the data from the device. Keeler took it back. He wiped it clean with his shirt and tossed it into the Ford Expedition.

Keeler cut Sergio free from the chair with his knife and let him fall. Sergio landed on his back in the dirt, wrapped in tape, sucking air through his nose.

Valdez held the Zippo. "What am I supposed to do here? Sorry, I'm not an experienced criminal."

Carver snickered.

Keeler looked at him. "What's funny?"

"Nothing."

Keeler said, "Use the fuel line, or maybe oil or transmission fluid. I don't know sheriff, figure it out. You and Carver can pretend you're a team."

He turned and ignored them. Dragged Sergio back to the Challenger. Maneuvered the bound man into the back seat, laying him on his side and shutting the door. The Ford was catching fire. Valdez and Carver stood watching it, clearly impressed.

Keeler said, "Good job."

Dwight was in the front seat of Carver's vehicle. Keeler walked over.

He said, "What did you get Dwight?"

"I have a virtual copy of his phone on my laptop, a mirror. We can access anything."

"Good, you're going to ride with me." He looked at Carver and Valdez. "You two go back to the fort. We'll be along soon."

Valdez said, "What do you mean?"

Keeler turned to her. "I need this guy's technical skills. You did a good job. See you back at the fort."

Valdez nodded. "Alright."

The SUV burned now. The four of them stood and watched. Flames lit up the darkness. The upholstery caught fast. Keeler looked away and studied the others. Valdez, Carver, and Dwight—all hypnotized by the fire.

Chapter Thirty-Seven

eeler drove. Dwight was in the passenger seat with his laptop. The computer was using a hotspot from Dwight's phone to access the internet.

Dwight said, "What are we looking for?"

Keeler said, "I'm not sure. Just go through whatever's on there. We're going to hang this guy upside down from a tree and slowly bleed him."

Which prompted muffled protestations from the back seat.

"So, it would be good to have a few questions, Dwight. Otherwise he'll just die uselessly."

Dwight didn't laugh. He just tapped and scrolled on the computer. Keeler stole a glance. Dwight had some kind of virtual phone simulator on there. It looked exactly like a phone, but it was on a computer screen.

Keeler drove back the way he'd come earlier. He figured that the livestock barn Valdez had taken him to would be as good as any other place for what he had planned. Plus, he didn't know any other place.

What Keeler did with Sergio, was take him into the woods and tie him upside down with the paracord he'd bought at Hunt

& Hustle. The cord was rated at five hundred and fifty pounds. The guy probably weighed around two hundred.

Keeler found a tree with a solid horizontal branch about ten feet up. He jammed the tactical light into the ground to spotlight the trunk. Tying a rock to the cord, he lobbed it over the branch and secured Sergio's ankles with a quick wrap. Anchoring the other end to a nearby tree, he added a friction wrap to make hoisting easier. Sergio was squirming, muttering, starting to panic. Keeler leaned back and hauled him up, slow and steady, keeping the tension right. Once Sergio was hanging upside down, Keeler locked off the line and double-checked everything held.

They were good to go.

He ripped the duct tape away from Sergio's face, taking hair and eyebrows with it. The man had more problems than keeping his eyebrows. He was sucking in air and trying to control involuntary hyperventilation. Blood was now rushing to his head.

Dwight said, "How long until he dies?"

Keeler said, "Like this? Don't know if he'll die, but he'll have problems after hanging there more than a few hours. Maybe irreversible."

Sergio said, "What do you want from me."

Keeler had Sergio's phone out. He said, "Simple. I want you to tell your brother to get my sister out of prison."

Saliva was building up in Sergio's mouth, threatening to choke him. He coughed, spitting out. If it was possible to be laughing upside down, Sergio seemed to be doing it.

He said, "You don't understand anything *Pendejo*."

"What don't I understand?"

"The only reason your sister is alive right now is because she's in the county jail." He coughed out saliva, somehow finding it funny.

Keeler ignored the question. He said, "What's your brother's name Sergio?"

"My brother's name is Arturo."

"Let's just give Arturo a call. See how much he cares about you."

Sergio went very still. It was probably hard to be a serious person upside down, but here he was, looking like he'd gotten all serious.

He said, "I wouldn't do that if I were you."

"Why not?"

Sergio said, "You ever hear of sibling rivalry?"

Keeler ignored him. He turned to Dwight. "Did you get it?"

Dwight was sitting down, back against a tree with the laptop. He said, "Arturo. Yup. Got the contact number."

"Call him and give me the phone."

"Uh.. I'll probably lose the hotspot connection if I do that."

Keeler pulled the waitress's phone out of his pocket and unlocked it. "Go ahead. Just give me the number."

Sergio said, "Don't do it."

"Why not."

"Because if you do, there's no going back." He started laughing to himself. A hyena sound that became an uncontrollable cough.

Keeler hit the call button. The phone rang. The call was answered almost before the first ring had ended. But nobody spoke. The line was static. The only sounds were Sergio struggling to breathe upside down.

Then a voice said, "Who is this?"

Something in the voice made Keeler decide not to mention his sister. It was purely instinctive and contravened the whole plan. Some little voice was telling him, *don't mention Laura.* That was when Keeler began to get a very bad feeling. Like he'd fucked up.

The voice on the line said, "Is this about my brother?"

Keeler said, "Sergio's having some issues at the moment, Arturo. Do you want to have a few words?"

"A few words about what?"

"I don't know. Maybe you have some catching up to do."

This was met with silence. The phone's speaker was giving out just crackle and hiss. Then came the sound of someone speaking to Arturo. A voice further away from the phone saying something in Spanish. Keeler shot a look at Dwight, who was straining to hear. Sergio, upside down, was having a hard time in general. Keeler's bad feeling was getting worse.

The voice on the line said, "Is this not *Madeline's* phone? I'm sorry. I'm just a little confused. You are clearly not Madeline, yet this seems to be a call from her phone. Where is Madeline?"

Keeler looked at Dwight, now alert. What they both understood was that the phone was registered to a person by the name of Madeline. The waitress was Madeline.

The voice said, "What have you done with poor Madeline? I hope that she's *staying safe.*" The guy laughed. "Unlike our sheriff. Dear *Cheryl.*"

Keeler said, "What about the sheriff?"

Arturo ignored the question. "Listen friend, I'm so happy you've finally met my brother. Please, do me a favor and kill him. Bring me his head and you get a bag of gold and a free pass out of my town. I mean that literally. A bag full of gold."

Keeler ended the call. He looked at Sergio, who was looking at him with bulging eyes, upside down.

Keeler said, "Is that what you meant by sibling rivalry?"

Sergio said, "You seem to have misread the situation."

That was when they began to hear the buzzing sound coming from the distance. Except it wasn't in the distance—it was multiple low buzzing sounds from maybe a hundred yards away.

Sergio began humming to himself, almost like he'd checked out suddenly. He was now in a kind of weird trance. The cartel boss accepting his fate perhaps, imitating the buzzing sound like a crazy man. Keeler switched the tactical light off. He recognized the sound. A drone swarm was incoming.

Dwight said, "They zeroed in on the phone already."

Keeler said, "Yes, Dwight. The question is, what to do now?"

"You're asking me that question?"

It was pitch dark without the light on. The drones would navigate through the woods with LIDAR sensors. Light detection and ranging. But in order to identify targets, the machines would use thermal imaging to pick up heat signatures. Human beings would be easy to see through the dark and cold forest.

Sergio hummed louder, dangling and now swaying. Keeler pulled Dwight up from where he sat.

"Move! Livestock barn."

Dwight's face bloomed with instant comprehension. The animals in the barn would be hot-blooded. The humans could hide among the cattle or hogs, and the drones would have a harder time distinguishing the two. Keeler tossed the waitress's phone and sprinted after Dwight to the barn. The cacophony of drones was coming at them now through the trees, maybe twenty yards away.

Chapter Thirty-Eight

Between the woods and the barn was a hundred foot section of muddy grass.

Dwight was sprinting madly in front of Keeler and slipped on his third panicked step. Keeler watched him go down, arriving in time to pull him up by the collar. In the meantime, the buzzing sound intensified. The drones had broken out of the woods and into the clearing. Keeler dropped Dwight and spun to the threat. A blunt object faced him, hovering in the dark, LED lights emanating from the interior circuitry like two blue sparks.

The target was small, hovering and twitching in ways that made it hard to fix through the gun sights. Keeler aimed between the two sources of light. The drone's propellers spun up, revving to a crazy high revolutions per minute.

He fired two shots in quick succession. The second round hit, knocking the drone out of the air. He grabbed Dwight under the arm, pulled him upright and pushed him into a run. "Move."

Another drone was incoming. Keeler glanced back, seeing the twin blue sparks whip in at great speed from the trees. He took a knee and tried to steady the pistol again, firing and missing. A shotgun would be the weapon of choice here. The drone darted five yards laterally in the blink of an eye. Keeler pulled the trigger again and missed. The drone revved up in a fast screech, rising half a yard in the blink of an eye. It re-oriented and shot by Keeler, coming maybe three feet from his head.

Dwight was almost at the barn. The twin sparks of the drone zipped hard in his direction, followed by an explosion when the remote operator detonated the small C4 payload. Keeler's night vision was ruined, just white light in his eyes for something like five seconds. He sprinted to the barn.

Behind him, more buzzing drones were coming out of the forest.

Dwight was alive, squirming on the ground just at the barn's doorstep. The door was half open. Keeler pulled him into the barn, checking Dwight's pulse and finding him alive. He just wasn't moving very much.

The place stank worse than death. Pigs, pig shit, other pig stuff. It was hard to breathe in there. Why would anyone be a farmer, if that's what they needed to go through? Keeler pulled Dwight further in. The guy was mumbling now, alive and sort of helping by using his feet.

Keeler had to drop him to shut the door. A drone buzzed outside, the revs rising and diminishing and then coming hard again. Keeler turned away and tried to dive into the mud. The drone exploded against the door, showering Keeler with fragments. The top part of the door had been blown off. That was a relief, since he'd initially thought the fragments were ball bearings, screws, or other shrapnel.

Keeler got upright. It was too dark to actually see anything in there. But the noise of hogs was loud. The propeller buzz hadn't ended with that last drone's kamikaze run. More were coming, zipping angrily around the barn, seeking entry.

Keeler needed animal heat.

He'd lost Dwight somewhere in the dark stench of the place. He put a foot into the pen area, testing it out. The floor felt spongy—maybe animal feed or hardening manure. It was difficult to tell. Keeler staggered through, looking for the heat of metabolic life. He came to a wood divider and stepped across. The sounds told him animals were close. A large pig stood immediately on the other side of the partition. Keeler crouched by the animal, resting his hand on its warm back, feeling firm fat and flesh through rough hair and skin.

A drone buzzed in, hovering behind Keeler. The hairs on the back of his neck raised. He had no idea if the machine's heat-sensitive eye was seeing him clearly, differentiating him from the pig. It was totally possible that he was easily visible. In which case he'd soon be dead.

He stayed absolutely still for what seemed a long time. The drone whizzed and buzzed, moving. Keeler took that opportunity to maneuver around the pig. He ended in a position where he had his gun arm resting on the animal's back. The evil device hovered in front of him, maybe twenty feet away. A dipping and bobbing target.

Keeler sighted between the blue sparks, waiting for some kind of steady state—some position that he could anticipate. The drone was turning, panning around and looking for targets. He waited until the thing faced him directly. He could tell because of the distance between the lights. Keeler fired once. The recoil made the pig quiver underneath him. The drone fragmented and fell, lights extinguished.

The activity attracted two more drones, buzzing in fast through the broken door. Keeler slid underneath the pig. He had no idea if they'd seen him or not. It definitely seemed as if there were multiple operators communicating between themselves. If this was some kind of intelligent drone swarm, that would be insane.

He couldn't see them, but he heard them. The two drones darted across the intervening space like maddened algorithmic wasps. They came right overhead and then detonated. The pig lost its footing and slammed on top of Keeler, crushing him into the dirt.

He felt a hoof get traction on his leg and push off, as if the animal knew that it was the human who had endangered its life. Keeler was unhurt, except for a stinging sensation at his forehead. He put a finger to it and brought it to his mouth, tasting blood.

No drones remained. Now there was only the sound of frightened animals.

"Dwight." No sound, no response. "Dwight." Louder this time. Still nothing came back.

Keeler brought the tactical light out of his pocket and clicked it on. Pigs were all around, scurrying. One of them had been injured, hobbling and bleeding. Not mortally wounded.

"You'll be alright buddy."

Keeler turned and searched among the animals with the light. Over by the fence, he found Dwight face down in pig shit, body immobile and bloody. He turned him over to find that half of Dwight's face had been blown off by the suicide drone.

Keeler backed off and turned the other way. He thought better of it and came back to the corpse. Dwight had a phone tucked into his front pocket. Keeler had tossed the waitress' phone, and he had burned Sergio's phone, which meant that this slab of technology in Keeler's hand was Dwight's phone. He swiped at the screen and was confronted with a facial recognition demand.

Shit. Dwight had no face to speak of.

Keeler tried it anyway. The corpse had features—a nose, a mouth, two ears, eyes. It wasn't as if the face was exactly gone, it was just very damaged. He could hardly believe it when it worked. The phone made a false snick as it unlocked. Keeler stayed there, crouched in the mire, as he sought out the settings and set up his own face to be recognized next time.

With the light he was able to see a path out of the barn. There were no more drones. Either the operators had given up, which didn't seem likely, or they had shot their load. In that case, they would send men, or another drone fleet, if they had it.

He sprinted back to the Challenger, clicking the fob to unlock the doors. Keeler remembered Sergio, hanging upside down. He moved into the woods and got the light up. The cartel boss was no more. Not in human form anyway. Sergio's brother must have allocated one of the suicide drones for this opportunity. Keeler was beginning to understand now.

Sibling rivalry. Keeler's gambit had backfired big time. He'd just given one of the brothers the excuse to get full reign over the organization. The payload must have exploded at Sergio's chest level. Pieces of the body had been scattered widely. The tree was coated in gore.

Keeler made it to the car on a sort of autopilot. He was ready for more and simply numb when no killer drone buzzed out of the woods. He reversed out of there, spinning the vehicle back to the road and killing the lights. He hit the gas and sent the Challenger careening into the night, watching the darkness out the open window. He stayed alert to incoming sounds. The sparse woods zipped by at the edges of farm fields.

Chapter Thirty-Nine

Laura became conscious when the jail door banged open with a thunk and a thud. The guard removed the key and rattled the chain. He leaned into the cell. She saw him sideways from where she lay curled up. The man was bald, with a clean shaven pink head and a roll of fat around the neck. The rest of him was stuffed into a bulging uniform.

"Yo, Keeler. You're outta here."

"Mmm hmmm."

She came up on the bed to sit on the edge. She watched the man looking at her with total indifference.

The guard said, "Let's go."

She said, "What's the sudden hurry?"

He said, "Not my call, not my *bidness*."

Laura stood and put on the jail house slippers. She stepped out into the corridor as commanded. The guard hooked her up.

"I was supposed to be in the hole five days they said."

The guard clicked the leg chains in. He said, "Time flies when you're having fun."

For a moment she was disoriented, half believing that days

had passed, even though it only felt like hours. The jail had an elevator for moving human freight up and down.

She said, "Where are we going?"

He said, "Canteen."

The elevator arrived, and he made her get in first. Laura didn't know what time it was. There weren't any windows in the hole, or the elevator. Or in most other places inside. The elevator stopped, and the door opened. The guard held the button while she came out. The canteen was down the corridor.

She figured it was nighttime. Her circadian rhythm told her this. It wasn't a classic time to eat, more like middle of the night feelings. When she walked into the canteen, Laura knew immediately that it was out of hours, an off-peak time for some weird midnight snack. Slopes was leaned against a table. Two guards she didn't recognize milled around, looking sullen. Laura made eye contact with Slopes, unreadable.

Slopes said, "Look who crawled out of the hole."

Laura said nothing.

An older man in a suit was standing watching her. He was tall, with light brown hair and a graying beard. Definitely not the warden. She'd seen a photograph of the warden through the window of an office here and the warden was a middle-aged fat man with a red face.

The man said, "Are you hungry Laura?"

The pronunciation was weird, the beginning of her name coming out like he was saying the word *loud*. Lou-ra. The man was not American.

"Sure."

He flicked a hand towards three kitchen staff members standing to attention behind the serving counter.

"Make her whatever she wants." He looked again at Laura, like he was concerned. "What do you want to eat Laura?"

Uncertain what was going on, she said, "What is this, my last meal?"

The man said, "Far from it. We just want to make sure you're treated properly is all."

"Who's we?"

He said, "Myself and my friend the warden. We get along very, very well. In fact, you could say that I have the run of this place." He opened his arms and spread them out.

Laura laughed. Tom must have done something pretty hard core for these people to be so scared of him.

She said, "Your fear of my brother is normal, but nothing will save you."

The man smiled. The expression on his face was both sincere and alarming. Alarming because it seemed a little over the top, as if he were truly happy.

He said, "Oh brother where art thou?" He was going for a theatrical, camp style in the prison canteen. Slopes and the others were impassive, almost submissive. They looked on without participating. Laura was aware of how strange this was.

The man was certainly out of place. The suit was well cut and looked comfortable. Maybe European. He wore suede moccasins with beaded tassels on bare feet, like something out of a Native American gift store.

She said, "Who are you again?"

He stopped playing around. "Again? What's so *again* about this Laura? You're so damned jaded for a woman your age. You have no idea the fun times we're going to be having."

Laura nodded. Whatever the game was, eating wasn't a bad idea. She said, "I'll take bacon and eggs over easy with buttered whole grain toast and a cup of decent coffee. If they've got a side salad, I'll take that as well."

"Important to get your greens in Laura. What my second

wife said before I strangled her and fed the body to a pack of hyenas."

"Very funny," Laura said, "Do you mind telling me who the fuck you are, or I'm supposed to guess?"

He pointed at himself. "Me? I'm Arturo. Very pleased to meet you. As I told you, I happen to be an excellent friend of the prison warden. The warden came to me. He said, here's Laura, a valuable prisoner of ours. Then, he went on and on about you. On and on about how Laura has been so very badly treated by the guards. Once that came to my attention I elected to take steps to repair the situation. To put things back into their proper place, Laura. To *redeem* the situation." He looked at the kitchen staff, already busy catering to her wishes. Glanced back at Laura. "I think your breakfast is on the way."

Laura had a creepy feeling about this man. Nothing but evil vibes came off him. The somewhat European look was clearly a thin veneer over something way more basic and horrible. Arturo, just the first name and nothing else. No honorific, no family name. Just Arturo. Like the name of an evil clown. He was gloating. That was the word. He was gloating at her, as if she were a kind of prize animal.

When the breakfast was ready, he cracked his knuckles. Laura noticed the silver and turquoise rings adorning his fingers. He wore a wooden bead bracelet on his left wrist. What is it called, a Buddhist mala bracelet. There was nothing Buddhist about this guy.

Laura ate carefully and thoroughly, ignoring the fact that she was some kind of center of attention. Arturo was gone by the time she finished. The guards cuffed her and brought her to a freight elevator. They descended to an underground parking lot, where a white van waited with engine running. Three Trace Junction town policemen lingered near the vehicle. They were armed with shotguns. That struck Laura as interesting.

Tom had clearly been a busy big brother. The van's windows were tinted. Slopes pulled the door open on rollers and made eye contact.

Slopes said, "You're fucked. I'm almost feeling sorry for you."

Laura said, "Thanks."

"Don't mention it. Almost. Too much hate in my heart for sorry."

That made Laura simply sad for the bitch. She entered the van because she didn't have any choice. The three cops sidled up to her in a bullying set of gestures. The door slid closed. The latch caught with a thunk and there she was alone. The rear of the van was separated from the front by a solid steel partition.

The van rumbled through the town of Trace Junction. It was definitely night time, but she had no clue what the actual time was. Could have been 10pm or 2 in the morning. The view through the tinted glass was dim, bright headlights appearing as dull orange smudges. The driver navigated through town, and onto the highway heading north. After a fifteen minute drive they turned off, up a series of farm roads until the van stopped at a boom gate. Through the glass Laura could make out a guard house set back from the driveway.

Five minutes later they pulled up to a large building made from corrugated steel with no windows. Laura figured it must be an agricultural facility.

Two men were waiting at the entrance. Neither of them wore uniforms. Both of them looked rough and tumble. They looked very much like the man she'd shot. Bad feelings ran up her spine. This didn't look like a correctional facility, or a judicial facility, or even a law enforcement facility. It looked like a farm.

A man opened the van door for Laura. He was unshaven with a large head and a helmet of black hair. The man wore construction boots and everything about him looked used and beaten down and brutalized. Even his nose was misshapen.

"Let's go." The accented English had a clipped quality.

Laura came down from the van.

She said, "Where are we?"

The man didn't respond. Neither the driver or front passenger made a move. They just sat in the van. Someone grabbed her cuffs from behind. They secured her in place.

She said, "What's going on here?"

Nobody said anything. The van departed in a crunch of tires over sand and dirt and gravel. The man who'd opened the door came around and looked at her.

He said, "Just shut up or I'm a bust your lip."

Laura said nothing.

He said, "You want I bust your lip? I love to do it."

Laura looked away. He stayed there in front of her for a full thirty seconds. The man spit in the dirt and moved around behind her. They removed the cuffs and leg irons. He took her arm and led her to the entrance of the building. The man smelled like fried meat and beer.

The entrance door was a steel slab with what looked like advanced electronics. Some kind of unblinking electric eye stared at her from the locking mechanism. The man kept one hand gripped around her bicep. He put the thumb of his other hand to a sensor and pushed the door open with his foot.

For a long moment she stood there, looking in from the threshold. She saw a large room with beds, like a combination hospital and refugee center. Like photos she'd seen from hurricane Katrina down in New Orleans. Places where people had lived for weeks or months while someone in charge figured out what to do with them.

Except for here in this place, the people were all women. The other thing she was having a hard time coming to terms with was that they were all pregnant. The man with the messed up face was watching her and clearly liking the confusion and fear and doubt he saw on her face.

She said, "What is this place?"

He was giggling to himself half in Spanish and half in English.

Laura said, "I don't speak Spanish."

He said, "We call it the cow shed."

Laura took an involuntary step back. What the fuck was this? The man's stench filled her nostrils as his grip tightened. She tried to pull away and moved directly into the cold tip of a syringe, sinking deep into her neck.

Chapter Forty

Keeler came into town via a rural track. He'd stopped at the side of the road and plotted the trajectory on Dwight's phone before committing to a route. Now, he was slow balling the Challenger through the first sections of town. The sheriff hadn't answered repeated phone calls. He'd memorized her number, but the calls went straight to voicemail.

Valdez and Carver had departed in Carver's beat up looking old American car. A Pontiac or a Buick perhaps. Keeler didn't have Carver's contact. The way things had gone down with the drones had been surprising, to say the least. The fact that this Arturo and his men had access to drone swarms of a battlefield type was alarming. That there was evidently a team of operators with FPV suicide drone expertise was bad news. Back at the drone facility, Dwight had taken one drone van. Keeler had destroyed the second. The attackers must have deployed a third van to attack the barn, where Sergio and Dwight died.

It had been a major error to use the waitress's phone, and there were consequences. Now she was in danger. That psychopath knew her name, Madeline. It wouldn't be long before she received attention. The maniacs could try and use her to get at Keeler. In his defense, he couldn't have imagined that behind the mayhem in Trace Junction were two evil clowns like Sergio and his brother Arturo.

Then again, he'd read enough about cartels to know that brazen outlandishness was par for the course. He had an obligation to warn her of the incoming danger. Further than that, he could get her out of harm's way. Help her get stashed in some safe place until this blew over.

Once he had her out of his mind, he could refocus on the enemy.

Keeler entered the town from the west. The edges of town were simply residential areas with dim streetlights. Nothing was going on there except the occasional errant cat's eyes glowing in the headlights.

Keeler swung the vehicle into a lazy turn, heading toward route 60. Two blocks later, he could already see the main road, the billboards and bright lights of fast-food restaurants and strip malls. The traffic was sparse, but constant. A steady flow of vehicles moved in both directions. Maybe one car every three seconds.

Pulling up to the traffic light, Keeler glanced to the right. It took him a moment to notice the blue and white flashers, among the other points of luminescence, busying up the scene. The police had set up a roadblock at the next intersection. A white SUV cruiser was positioned diagonally across the lane, forcing vehicles into a funnel. There were several cars waiting already. Keeler could make out two uniformed cops waving them through.

The traffic light turned green and Keeler drove straight across. He'd have to come at the diner another way. He had to just hope that they didn't have a read on his vehicle. But, hope is the gambler's whisper—sweet until the dice fall. Hope wasn't going to cut it.

After crossing route 60, Keeler kept going for two blocks before making a right turn. He'd memorized the map and knew that the diner was around a half mile south of his position. He scanned for a similar vehicle to the one he was currently driving. Five blocks down, he found another Dodge, also painted black. It wasn't a Challenger, but a Charger, the four-door version. That was going to do just fine.

Keeler found parking a block further on. He took out the Leatherman from his pack on the passenger seat and hiked back to the Charger. He wasn't worried about pedestrians at that time of night. Any vehicles that passed by wouldn't pick him out, either. Keeler spent a few minutes unscrewing the plates from this new vehicle. It was more than likely that the owner wouldn't spot the missing plates until the morning, if not later.

Plus, Saturday was coming soon, so there was a good chance of the owner sleeping late.

After removing his own plates and affixing the new ones, Keeler got moving again.

He would, as a minimum, conceal his identity to avoid attracting attention from the town's corrupt law enforcement. Valdez had told him there wasn't a single clean cop in Trace Junction. He was going to take her word for that.

Another right turn and he'd be a couple of blocks from the diner. These side streets were completely empty of traffic. The houses here were residential and quiet. Just another Friday night in the town of Trace Junction, Ohio.

A police cruiser had pulled across the road two blocks ahead. The blue and whites weren't active. This was more of a stealth operation than the road block on Route 60 had been. Two uniformed police officers were outside of their vehicle, looking right at his car.

Keeler put his right turn indicator on. He took the first right turn, a block away from the check point. Nothing moved in his peripheral vision. Neither of the uniforms did anything special, no radio up to the mouth. They kept on with whatever they'd been doing before. Keeler felt his shoulders relax. He'd been holding his breath and now exhaled slowly.

A lazy whooping siren rose from behind him. Keeler glanced in the rearview mirror. An unmarked car had its grill lights lit up, nosing close behind him. The cops had set up a trap to catch anyone turning away from the block. Keeler had made the turn and fallen for it. He didn't go too hard on himself. It'd been the right call to make the turn. Sometimes the coin toss goes the wrong way.

He pulled the vehicle over to the curb. The house to his right was dark. A large lawn stretched up to a wooden porch. It reminded him of half a dozen houses they'd lived in as a kid. Each one in a new place. Each one was sort of the same but different. He had the window rolled down. Keeler reached into the glove box for the rental documentation.

The Smith & Wesson rested under his right thigh. He tried to remember how many rounds he had fired from that weapon and figured maybe ten to take down those drones. That left approximately five, if you included the round in the chamber. There wasn't any time to verify, since a plainclothes cop was coming around the side of the vehicle. He was visible in the side mirror. The guy had on a hoody against the autumn chill. Right hand holding a flashlight. Left hand ready at his hip. Weapon was holstered.

In the rear-view mirror Keeler couldn't even see if the cop had a partner. Perhaps the guy was alone. Keeler had taken a right turn after seeing the check point up ahead. He could just as easily have taken a left. It was logical they'd have the other possibility covered as well. Plus, perhaps another car for those who might just pull a U-turn to avoid the check point.

Keeler made the call. Operational assumption was that this cop was alone.

He made another decision. He wouldn't get involved in any kind of drawn-out altercation. Make this fast. He flipped the door latch and kicked it open with his left foot. Keeler's right hand was filled comfortably with the Smith & Wesson's grip. In one smooth set of interlinked movements, he unspooled from the vehicle into a shooting stance and put two rounds directly into the body mass of the oncoming policeman.

Keeler was moving quickly towards him before the guy even knew he'd been shot.

The first thing he looked for was a body cam. After verifying the lack of a wearable camera, Keeler turned to the man himself. The rounds had punched the cop directly into his torso, one at the solar plexus, the other slightly higher and closer to the chest. The policeman was currently in a state of shock and hyperventilation. He was gasping and twitching and trying to figure out how to reach for his holstered weapon. Keeler put a booted foot on the policeman's arm and pushed the pistol into his forehead.

"Stop."

He bent to the man and unzipped the hoody. Keeler had figured on a concealed kevlar vest and had been correct. The bullets had put the man down, but he was in no real danger. He was looking right up at Keeler with fear, uncertainty, and doubt in his eyes. A cropped haircut over a deep frown. The eyes were dark. Mustache and very white teeth.

Keeler ripped open the velcro fastening on the vest.

He said, "Just breathe man. Breathe easy."

Keeler slid a Glock 19 out of the cop's in-waistband-holster and ran a hand over the man's ankles in case there was a backup piece. Satisfied, Keeler stood and tucked the Glock into his jeans.

Keeler said, "Stay right there, buddy."

The vehicle's driver's door was open. Keeler reached in and grabbed the rear-view mirror. The dash-cam was integrated, so it all needed to come out. Doing so took some serious force, but it worked. Keeler identified the locked SIM compartment and decided to save that for later.

He came back to the man with two rounds in his vest. "Don't come after me. You should quit the force. Do it tonight. You'll thank me later."

The cop's eyes shifted and Keeler followed. A small hand held Motorola had fallen out of the man's hand and slid to the curb. Keeler picked it up.

A voice said, "Unit 24, status check."

Keeler pushed the button. He said, "Unit 24, code 4."

Code 4 is a common police code to indicate that everything's under control. Keeler walked back to the Challenger and got in. So far the entire incident had occupied maybe one minute of his time.

The radio squawked as he was pulling out from the curb.

"Unit 24, Roger that."

In the rear view he could see the policeman sitting up and hanging his head over his knees, recovering.

Keeler took his first right turn and then a quick left. Halfway down the block was a large parking lot. He pulled the Challenger into the lot. There was an alley around the back of a small strip of one-story shop buildings. A dry cleaner, Chinese restaurant, and a waffle place. At the back were three dumpsters and a fence, overgrown with bare vines.

Keeler used the multi-tool to pop open the dash-cam SIM compartment. He snapped the little memory card in half and tossed it over the fence. The Glock had precious ammunition, which Keeler ejected from the magazine. That went into his jacket pocket. The gun itself he disassembled.

Keeler fixed the original license plates back on the vehicle.

He hoisted his pack onto his back. The stolen plates and the disassembled Glock went into the dumpster. There was a good chance that the vehicle would be good where it was, at least until mid-morning. Keeler's chronological senses told him it was around ten minutes past midnight.

It was the weekend already.

Chapter Forty-One

SATURDAY

Keeler jumped the fence. The Virginia Creeper vines twisted tightly around the old wire and steel poles. The other side was a muddy patch between parking lots and houses, overgrown with brambles and small trees. He followed a narrow but well-trodden path downhill and into an overgrown corridor between fences.

The path ended at the back of a row of houses. The map in Keeler's mind was showing him that the diner was a block away as the crow flies west. He'd need to go around the set of buildings in front of him and get across the next road. The diner's back side would be through whatever residential or commercial structures he'd find there.

Better to move in this way than to use the streets and sidewalks.

The yard in front of him was pretty deep. Maybe fifty feet before he'd get to the house and the flimsy back door. It looked like an aluminum framed screen door with some kind of cheap wood thing on the other side.

The idea of going through someone's backyard wasn't enormously appealing. You could never know what you'd find. A dog, or an insomniac homeowner with a loaded gun. At least there was a hole in the fence. No doubt the kids used this as a shortcut through to the strip mall where he'd parked. He remembered his childhood shenanigans. There was always the neighborhood as it appeared to adults, and the way it was used by the kids. Like two different realities.

Keeler slipped through the fence into the back yard. There was a trampoline set up with netting around to prevent bouncing children from impaling themselves or worse. The strong stench of dog shit indicated a canine pet who wasn't always taken for long walks to the park. He stood very still and observed what was in front of him. On close examination, the patchy backyard grass showed a very faint trail, connecting his position and the neighboring fence about halfway down.

The way the kids did it.

Keeler moved across, taking the well-trodden line. The second fence had a gap where the mesh met a pole. The other side of that was a dilapidated shed. Keeler moved to the blind side of the shed and took a look at the building in front of him. Just as he'd figured, there was a gap between the buildings here.

He got to the alley, looking down it. Garbage cans and aluminum siding lined the way. Not the best part of town, that was for damned sure. The other side of this was the street, or what little of it Keeler was able to see. Coming through the alley, the aperture of visibility widened, until he was just at the edge near the front.

Keeler stopped moving for two reasons.

Firstly, there was a police car on the other side of the street. As far as he could make out there wasn't anybody in the vehicle. But a cop car isn't nothing. Often, it indicates the presence of police. The second reason was olfactory. He smelled barbecue, a lot of it. A strong stench of burning meat, maybe peppers and onions? He wasn't any kind of expert, but it was Friday night, albeit kind of late for a barbecue.

Keeler was close to the end of the alley. An inner voice spoke to him in a language he could neither understand nor ignore. He moved closer to the edge of the alley and waited, listening and controlling his breathing. Voices came from the left. Two people conversed quietly, about fifteen feet from the alley. He stayed still and quiet. There was a very good chance that these were the cops who'd parked across the street.

Were they waiting there for him?

Keeler moved back into the darkness and leaned against the building on his right side. He got out the range finding scope and steadied it. The opposite side of the street was residential, but this time there were large gaps between the buildings and good amounts of brush for cover. He sighted into the brush.

Mostly, he could see darkness with some variation of texture. As he focused the scope to the middle distance, the darkness began to move. It wasn't simply darkness any longer – which is a lack of light – this was something actually substantial, not just dark, but black or gray. After a few seconds Keeler realized that he was looking at thick smoke. The wind was taking it in the other direction, but the smoke was billowing blackly out of a burning building veiled by the leafless brush and trees behind the houses.

The diner, not a backyard barbecue, was the source of that stench, lingering now in his nostrils. Not just meat, but other things, like paper and plastic, and chemicals, and whatever else was in a burning building. This was a *no go*. He could only hope that the waitress had made it. Keeler turned back and returned to the vehicle. On the way it occurred to him that the fire at the diner accounted for the police roadblocks. Maybe they weren't looking for him specifically after all.

* * *

Back at the car, Keeler sat behind the wheel and dialed Valdez's number. Again it went to voicemail. He used the phone's web browser to find an OSINT site that would locate a phone's location from its last cell tower contact. This kind of service is called an IMSI Lookup. IMSI for International Mobile Subscriber Identity. He put in Valdez's phone number and got back a request for payment. The cost was ninety-nine cents. Dwight's bank card was programmed into the phone and the payment went through without a hitch.

The IMSI Lookup site pinged for a couple of seconds and resolved on a blurry map image that got clearer. The last cell tower that had connected to the sheriff's phone was three miles past the Quality Inn, going towards Trace Junction. Which meant to Keeler, that Valdez and Carver had run into some trouble on the way back to the secure location they claimed to maintain.

It was an open question whether Valdez and Carver had survived, and if their secure location remained safe.

He got the vehicle moving. There was obvious danger of more police, after what he'd done. Keeler was prepared to take that risk. He navigated the side roads, coming out at another intersection with route 60. This time, he crossed north of the diner without incident. He made his first left and drove down a piece until he figured he was parallel the restaurant.

Keeler parked and made his way on foot, emerging behind Donald's Delicious Donuts. The parking lot was empty and the donut restaurant dark. Route 60 was just in front, the two-way avenue blocked by fire trucks and an ambulance. Police cruisers were set up both sides, directing a thin flow of cars through the incident site. The place looked wet and smoldering at that point. Only a shell remained of the building, a skeleton that had just recently supported a little world. The everyday coming and going of regulars, and the employment provided to people like Madeline, the waitress.

The back door of Donald's Donuts opened and Pete the donut man stepped out.

Pete lit a cigarette and stared into space. Keeler kept still, crouched there in the brush. Why was Pete still at work? Maybe he made the donuts at that hour. Perhaps the dough needed to rise or something. The only thing Keeler knew about baking was that it was an arcane process that took dedication and time. He wasn't completely sure that donuts involved baking or frying, or maybe both.

Keeler stayed motionless. He wasn't eager to give Pete a heart attack, so he let him finish the cigarette in peace and go back inside. Keeler walked to the back door, timing it so that he had a hand on the door just as Pete was closing it. But Pete didn't close it all the way. There was a light on in there, and murmurs of conversation.

Keeler stepped into the kitchen. Nobody was proofing donuts, and the place was pretty cold. The waitress was sitting on a steel prep counter. Her red hair was wildly out of place, no longer contained by the perfect twin braids. Her face was soot-stained with a red and sore looking bruise on her forehead. Earl was wrapping a bandage around her arm, talking about something that Keeler failed to hear properly.

The waitress made eye contact as soon as Keeler walked in.

She said, "Well look who showed up to the party."

Keeler shrugged off his backpack and set it on the floor. Earl's head swiveled, and he stared. Pete wasn't in the kitchen.

The waitress said, "We were just talking about you."

Keeler said, "Good things I hope."

Earl said, "Not necessarily."

Pete was in the doorway holding a Glock 17 now.

He said, "Someone here's got a lot of explaining to do."

Keeler noticed that both the waitress and Earl had open beer bottles. The waitress took a slug of hers as she watched his reaction.

Keeler said, "Nice to see you, Pete." He nodded at Earl. "Earl." The waitress was watching him. Eyes shining bright and her mouth tense. He said, "And I guess I should be calling you Madeline."

She blinked. "Might as well."

Keeler said, "Sorry about the phone. It became what you could call a serious liability. Glad to see you made it." Pete took two steps into the kitchen and Keeler put up a hand to stop him. "Do me a favor Pete. Just put that down. Whatever you think I might be, I'm not an enemy. We're on the same side."

Pete said, "I'll be the judge of that."

"Suit yourself."

Pete stood there with his weapon. Keeler decided to ignore him. The donut man wasn't going to be pulling the trigger, at least not on purpose. The concern was mostly with an accidental discharge. Madeline glanced at Keeler and rolled her eyes. Which made him smile.

Earl finished the bandage job. Madeline slid off the counter and stretched. She was wearing her waitressing uniform, and it looked like it had gone a couple of rounds with a side of beef. Blood stains and other stains.

She said, "Pete, get the man a beer. Let's go sit in a booth and talk. I'm too tired for this shit."

She took a slug out of the bottle and held it up to Keeler, wagging it around a little. "You want to know the story? I'll tell you the story."

Chapter Forty-Two

Madeline came on shift at eight pm. Nothing about that evening indicated that it would go lopsided, but that's how it went, to put it mildly.

Friday night was always busy. The first set of customers were families and teenage dates. By ten p.m. the families had cleared out, leaving three tables worth of stragglers. Two families who'd been late to the party, and a group of three middle-aged men. The lull would end by midnight, when the first drunken idiots would be traipsing in for burgers and all-day breakfasts in an attempt to absorb the alcohol content of their evening's endeavors.

At ten fifteen Madeline took advantage of the lull. She sat at the counter eating a bowl of chili. Usually, she ate while swiping and tapping idly on her phone. Looking into the internet and basically spacing out, giving her brain a rest from the incessant chatter of her front-of-house hospitality work. Tonight, she had no phone, only the vague hope that the asshole she'd met that morning was going to come by with her device like he promised.

She didn't really expect that this would happen.

What she expected was that this man would turn up dead in

a ditch at some point and her phone would be lost forever. Clearly this man had a death wish, messing with the gangsters. She cleaned up the chili bowl with a slice of sourdough bread that they sourced from the Weasel Boy Brewery.

Madeline took her bowl and spoon back to the kitchen, pushing through the swinging doors and maneuvering around Jose, the busboy on his way out with a tray of clean white coffee mugs. She got busy at the big sink, not the kind of person to let someone else clean her dishes. That was a prerogative of customers, not employees. She was putting the utensils on the rack to dry when Jose banged back in through the swinging doors, this time carrying a heavy bucket of dirty silverware.

Jose said, "Some guy's out there looking for you Madeline."

She felt a little thrill. Clearly, this was going to be the guy who had her phone.

Madeline started for the door and almost immediately halted. She caught a brief glimpse through the square of glass. Nothing out there but a wide shaped man with a crew cut. Maybe another person behind him. She stopped moving because of the sudden recollection that she'd eaten the equivalent of half a raw onion, which would make her breath stink. Not that she gave a shit what the guy thought.

Whatever, she turned away from the door and detoured for the bathroom.

She opened the door with her left foot. Her right hand used a practiced gesture to flip on the light, while her left hand pulled the door shut and pushed the latch in with her thumb. The bottle of Listerine was in the mirror cabinet. Madeline poured out a cap full and threw it back, gargling and whooshing the astringent liquid around her mouth, in between teeth and sloshing it over and under her tongue.

She spit it out and ran the faucet. Glancing in the mirror at her face, satisfied if not totally thrilled with what she saw. The face was a little sweaty, but the uniform clung nicely, and some guys had a thing for that. Madeline snapped herself out of that unwanted train of thought and rinsed her mouth. This was not how she felt about the asshole who'd she'd witnessed going apeshit earlier in the day. He'd shot one guy with a hunting bow and then jumped on a second guy with his hunting knife. That was all before managing to steal her phone.

Just contemplating that chain of events left her a little breathless and flushed.

There was some kind of ruckus from outside the bathroom. A raised male voice and then the agitation of several people shouting at once.

Madeline put her hand to the doorknob. The latch was embedded in the middle of the knob and popped out when turned. But, when she went to push it open the door refused to budge. She shouldered it open a crack. Which wasn't sufficient to get it more than three inches wider. Looking down she got a real shock. Jose was lying on the floor wedged against the door.

"Jose."

He didn't respond. There was shouting in the restaurant and the pop of gunfire. Three shots exactly. For a second Madeline felt panic rising. Stuck as she was in the bathroom. What she really wanted to do was get the hell out of there and sprint through the door at the back of the kitchen. For that brief moment she felt suffocated, like she couldn't breathe. It was almost the worst thing she'd ever felt.

It took all of her weight and strength to move the door open wide enough to squeeze through in her panic. When she did, she regretted it. She tried to step over the body but slipped and landed a foot onto Jose's soft hip, her shoe squishing into the man's fat. Worse, she tried to avoid hurting him by attempting to take her weight off that foot and sort of leap over. Which made her trip and fall, tumbling against the wall opposite the bathroom. She caught herself in time but managed to bang her forehead in the process.

When she turned around, she saw that Jose was dead. His head was a bloody pulp, limbs akimbo in the most awkward way. Something she'd never seen before. The way that people fall when they're killed in a standing position. She felt nausea rising and turned away from the sight.

That didn't help because doing so caused her to stare agog at two more corpses sprawled dead in the kitchen. One of whom was a friend of hers named Connie Atkinson, a fellow server at the diner. Connie had been shot in the back and had fallen flat on her face, hidden now by a curtain of straight black hair, cast like a wig over a growing puddle of blood.

A volley of gunshots in quick succession ripped Madeline out of her daze. Given the shock of trying to escape the bathroom — and seeing Jose's corpse — she hadn't fully clocked the general situation.

Another shot cracked out from the front of the diner. One of the men from table six came barreling through the swinging doors. He was beefy and middle-aged, and Madeline recognized him as a regular customer. His name was Jim, and he owned a landscaping business. Jim came in mostly after work, sometimes with employees on Friday nights. They'd eat burgers and drink a couple of beers before the weekend.

Now, Jim was red faced with something agitated and wild about him. He held a semi-automatic pistol in his hand, not as large as what Madeline carried, but big enough to make an impression. Which figured, since Jim was the kind of guy to carry something big and dumb like that. He turned to her with eyes bugging, recognition painting itself over his face. Jim blurted three words at Madeline, as if he meant them.

He said, "All hell has..."

Then his head exploded.

Madeline jerked herself into rapid action. Surprised at how calm she suddenly felt. Her purse was right by the bathroom, hung up in the area that employees were allowed to use for their personal affairs. It wasn't exactly advisable to keep a weapon in your purse, in a place that anyone could get into, but that's just what Madeline had done.

Now, she removed the Colt Anaconda her dad had literally forced on her and felt her mood click into another level. Something like relief. Not a hundred percent relief, more like an additional thirty percent confidence. Enough in any case to pull back the heavy hammer, cocking the weapon and making sure that when she did have to pull the trigger it would be a light touch. Clearly there were bad things happening.

At that point, Madeline was behind the wall, maybe six feet away from the swinging kitchen doors. She knew, without a shadow of a doubt, that on the other side of that door was at least one very bad man who intended to kill her. She didn't know why that was the case, but it was a fact that she was convinced of. The other thing was that she had no plans on dying easily or running away. If the guy was after her, he was a danger to her kid.

She took a deep breath and spun through the doors.

Directly in front of Madeline was a big guy with short cropped dark hair and a surly mouth lined with a thin mustache. He noticed her at the same time she noticed him. But unlike him, she had her weapon up and ready in a practiced shooting stance. His was held loose in a hand that casually hung by his side. She sighted on his body mass and pulled without hesitation. The Colt barked. Madeline controlled the recoil, keeping the weapon tamed as it spat fire and lead. A large stain opened up in the man's white sweatshirt, just by the pectoral muscle. A second shot tore through the man's ear and slapped into the back rest of a chair, knocking it over. The man was down before the chair tumbled.

Madeline moved quickly and kicked his weapon away. The air moved in front of her face as a bullet hummed past. The crack from the weapon's report came a split second after. She scurried back into cover behind the counter. Two more shots pulped the wood panel on her right. The pause indicated what, that the guy was reloading?

She shifted out to face the threat. A man bewildered by a malfunctioning handgun. She noticed strange things in that moment. His dumb looking pony tail and a weird grimace exposing badly rotten teeth. She put a round into his face, smashing through his nose and lip and exposing the internal shape of his skull and teeth as he spun weirdly into that unnatural pose the dead can assume.

Before she had even considered doing so, Madeline found herself running back through the kitchen. She leapt over corpses and almost wiped out slipping in Connie Atkinson's blood. Managing to stay upright by jamming her left hand onto the steel countertop, searing her pinky on the hot grill. She sprinted out the back door and down the steps to the rear parking lot.

Two men were out there by a large SUV.

One of them moved to cut her off. Madeline raised her weapon and screamed something at him. What it was, she didn't remember because the diner exploded behind her. The blast wave knocked her to the ground. Next thing she knew, she was just running, hell bent for leather across route 60 to Donald's Delicious Donuts, the Colt Anaconda held in a death grip.

Chapter Forty-Three

The whoop of an ambulance siren started up across the street. The flashers came on and the vehicle got going. Smoke from the burned-out diner was dissipating. No longer billowing clouds, just a kind of hazy fog that coalesced low over route 60. Keeler sat there in the booth. Madeline had just finished recounting her tale. The surreality of the situation came to him. For one thing, they were sitting in the dark.

Four of them were crammed into one of the window booths. Keeler sat next to Madeline, across from Earl and Pete. A sack of barbecue-flavored potato chips was half empty on the table. The booths were not big and Keeler felt the hard muscle of Madeline's thigh against his leg.

During Madeline's telling, Pete had been holding his Glock on Keeler under the table. It wasn't a pleasant feeling. At the same time, he didn't have the impression that Pete would actually use the gun. Maybe he just felt insecure. Still, it took a little resolve to breathe easy.

Every detective knows that eyewitness testimonies are generally ninety to a hundred percent false. People really don't actually see anything in a crazy situation, like what Madeline had described. Still, if she managed to perform half of what she'd just claimed, it'd be an astounding win.

She burped and popped open another beer bottle using a disposable lighter.

Earl said, "God bless."

Keeler said, "Why did the diner explode?"

Earl said, "We figure it was the propane tank they got over there. Idiot kept it in a cabinet. Wouldn't listen to anyone. Told him to put it outside where it belonged. Most likely that tank got hit by gunfire and then blew up once the leaked gas reached the stove."

Pete said, "Gas is heavier than air. Stuff would have sunk down and eventually spread until it hit an open flame."

Keeler said, "So what, you were already here Pete, singing to the donuts or something? Madeline comes running up from a near death experience and you hand her a beer with a pat on the back?"

"Something like that. I called Earl. He just got here."

Pete said, "Now it's your turn." He pointed at Keeler. "You came in here this morning acting all normal and shit. Talking about your sister this, sister that. Sucking up to us basically. Prior to that you were at the diner. According to young Madeline here, a very large breakfast was consumed. I personally served you more than a few donuts. Now, it's sixteen or so hours later and Maddy's narrowly avoided being killed, plus the diner's blown to shit. As far as we can make out, you're the new factor. So, I don't have a question, I have multiple questions, including the ones I don't know that I've got."

Keeler said, "You've been holding that weapon under the table for a while now Pete. I guess it's probably feeling heavy."

Earl glanced down and shifted a few inches away from his friend.

"Jesus Pete."

Pete scowled. He said, "What I'd like sir, is if you could start telling us your story, and then we'll ask the questions. If you prefer, I'll just shoot your dick off right here and now."

Keeler didn't like being called *sir*. It was one of his pet peeves. He hadn't liked it when he was in the military, and part of the benefits from serving in a special tactics unit like Air Force Pararescue was that nobody called anybody sir, excepting unusual moments when you had to address a senior officer on base.

He said, "Don't shoot my dick off, Pete." Keeler turned to look at Madeline and grinned in a meaningful way. He said, "That would be a bad idea, since you'll need my help. These *Los Quebrados* people are sucking the life out of your community. They need to be either made dead, or at least sufficiently diminished to the point that they have no more interest in being here. We need to make it very unprofitable for them."

He glanced around the table at Earl, Pete, and Madeline.

Madeline licked beer foam from her upper lip. "Tell us your story. Is it true you've got a sister here?"

Keeler said, "My sister shot a guy, up near the Amish auction by Hollow Hills. As far as I'm aware, that was back on Tuesday."

Earl said, "Why didn't you tell us about that this morning?"

Keeler said, "I didn't tell you because I didn't know."

"Your sister shoots a guy on Tuesday, and by Friday you still don't know about it?"

"Yeah, I didn't know."

Pete said, "That's hard to believe."

Keeler said, "Suit yourself."

Madeline said, "Is she alright?"

"She's in the county jail. When I arrived in town this morning, I didn't know she was in prison, or what had happened. I learned about it once I got up to her house."

The faces remained impassive. Only the waitress blinked when he made eye contact.

Pete said, "What was it, Windsong Way up in the county."

Keeler said, "My brother-in-law told me when I got there. First thing I did was to come back into town and go see her in jail. She was extremely paranoid about talking. Told me that things were not exactly right here in town. After the visit I started making inquiries. Long story short, the cartel people came at me. Basically told me to get out of town and to convince my sister to shut up and plead guilty." He made eye contact again with Madeline. "When you saw me out by the mall. That wasn't the first shot fired. They came at me from the get go. I guess they wanted to shut down any kind of real investigation into the guy my sister shot."

Madeline said, "Why would they do that?"

"No idea." Keeler sipped his beer. "Like I told you, that shooting seems to be complicated. Anyway, now other stuff has come to light. Maybe related to my sister's case, maybe not. I don't know yet." He pointed across at the diner and raised his eyebrows. "As you can see, someone stirred the hornet's nest." He chin-pointed at Pete. "What you said this morning when Earl was having his issues with the shit heads in the pickup truck. You said something about calling Cheryl."

Pete said, "And?"

"And I've had the pleasure of making Cheryl's acquaintance. Sheriff Valdez is a fine officer, but it's not as simple as all that, is it?"

Earl said, "That's one of them rhetorical questions, Pete."

"Evidently."

Earl said, "Go on buddy. Answer your own damned question. I'm not doing it for you."

Keeler didn't want to say more about Valdez, but this was do or die time. He said, "They torched my sister's house, Pete.

That's where I met Valdez. Suffice it to say, shit happened from there and the sheriff and I have reached an understanding. I guess you know a little about her if you're on a first name basis. She vouched for you, Pete. Anyway, we were operating together and got separated. I've been trying to get in touch, with no success. I've got her last location, at least according to her phone's cell tower pinging." He glanced at Madeline. "I used your phone, and it looks like they tracked it back to you. I only came by here to warn you about that. My mistake. Otherwise I'd be out there checking on the sheriff and her friends."

Madeline's face had a flush to it. Either she was pleased or the beer was working its magic. She said, "Don't tell me you lost my phone."

"It became a liability."

She shrugged. "That isn't a mall up there by the way."

"What?"

"Up where you did your ninja routine. It's the famous Buckeye Factory Outlets." She had a humorous glint in her eye. "We've got civic pride here in Trace Junction."

Keeler said, "No doubt." He indicated the three of them. "So, what's all this? Madeline wipes out a handful of trained cartel killers and here you are at Donald's Delicious Donuts having a good old beer with snacks."

Earl said, "Well, like Maddy said when you walked in. We were discussing you, trying to piece the thing together."

Madeline said, "Unlike you, we live here. And unlike you, we need to deal with the consequences of whatever madness you get up to."

Pete said, "His sister lives here Maddy." He lifted the pistol and set it down on the table between them. He made eye contact. "Sorry man. You can't be too careful these days."

Keeler said, "Let me tell you what I found out so far. Then, you guys decide what you want to do."

He then gave a detailed account of the day. The initial surprise finding out about Laura, then all the stuff up by Hollow Hills and the events at the Buckeye Outlets. By the time he was talking about drone swarms in the woods near the Quality Inn, Keeler could see that he had their attention.

Madeline had gone quiet. She said, "My daughter's safe with her grandmother." She'd turned to fully face Keeler. "What is it you think should be done?"

Keeler said, "I suggest that you three get out of town for a while." He nodded to Madeline. "Anyway, you're unemployed as of tonight. Go to your grandmother's house and stay there for a while. Eventually the FBI or whatnot will be all over this place."

Earl said, "You think it's primed to blow, huh?"

Keeler pointed across the road at the smoldering ruin of the diner. "It's already in the process of blowing, Earl."

Madeline said, "And what are you going to do?"

He said, "You don't know me much. But I'm not the guy who manages the explosion. I'm more like the guy who lights it up in the first place. As far as I can see it's all going very well. I intend to complete the mission."

Madeline said, "What about your sister, isn't she in danger now?"

"She can handle herself."

Earl said, "In that case, you'll need some help."

Keeler said, "Not from you I don't. These are professional killers." They were exposed now and on the defensive. The thing over there at the diner was speculative. They didn't know who you were, if you posed a danger to them. The fact that they came at Madeline guns blazing is actually positive. It means they're confused and paranoid."

Madeline said, "Like they have something to lose. So, what is it they're protecting?"

Keeler took a slug of his beer and grabbed a handful of barbecue-flavored chips. He chewed slowly, letting the beer wash the fried slivers of potato down. He said, "I like barbecue chips, but my favorite is sour cream and onion."

Madeline said, "Answer the damned question."

Keeler said, "I don't know exactly what they're hiding, Madeline. I think they're dealing in trafficked women, but that's par for the course with cartels. Beyond that we'll have to find out."

Pete said, "I probably wouldn't have shot you in the nuts, buddy. What's your name anyway."

"My name's Keeler. I know you wouldn't have pulled the trigger on purpose, Pete, I was worried about the shakes is all."

Madeline and Earl sniggered.

Earl said, "Try going to the range with him. You take your own life in your hands."

"Bullshit." Pete didn't seem to find it funny. He said, "I'm a good shot, Mister Keeler."

Keeler said, "I believe it." He gave Pete an affirmative nod.

Chapter Forty-Four

Laura came to with a bright light shining directly into her face. Consequently, she had to close her eyes again. Her first thought was totally irrational. It occurred to her that she was at the beach. Probably because it was hot and bright. It took a minute for her to actually see anything at all. That minute gave the shocking reality of her circumstances plenty of time to filter up.

The first data point arriving was the fact that she couldn't feel much. Literally no sensation below the waist and very little in her back. It was only her head that could feel the hard surface beneath her, face up. The second piece of sensory information her brain received was that her limbs were locked down. There was sensation in her hands, but not her feet. The problem was that the arms were locked in place. Those hands began to understand their uselessness within ten seconds of regaining consciousness.

"Fuck."

She raised her head and squinted down at herself. Dressed in a hospital gown and strapped onto some kind of gurney. The room was bright white, clearly some kind of medical clinic. By her right side was a largish machine on a trolley with wires running into the hospital gown. Presumably connected to her body. Laura blinked and focused. An intravenous tube was stuck in her arm at the crook of the elbow. She didn't know the terminology, but there was one of those things they put into you where the nurse can simply access your vein by plugging in or unplugging the connective feed.

Her initial thought – that they'd put her here for some benevolent reason – got chased away quickly by the fact that she was immobilized by the straps. Which didn't even account for the lack of sensation in her lower body.

A door opened, and a male walked in. The guy wasn't wearing any kind of doctor or nurse's outfit. He was a goon like the ones who had welcomed her out of the police transport van. All of it came rushing back now.

She said, "Unstrap me from this thing."

The guy just looked at her with the stone cold eyes of someone capable of shooting a woman to death point blank without compunction. He came close to her without even looking directly at her. As if she was nothing more special than the furniture. The man went directly to the machine, examining its display. The screen showed numbers, probably related to her heart rate. Laura was wired up with electrodes. The tube in her arm was hooked to another machine. The man nodded to himself and left the room without a second look at her.

A few minutes later a second man entered. This guy was at least dressed like a doctor.

She said, "What am I doing here?"

The doctor said, "You're here for a couple of tests. That's what you're doing here. Why you're here isn't my business. You got that? I'm just performing the procedure."

He pulled a rolling stool from the corner and Laura began to understand the situation. This was a gynecologist clinic. The panic rose from literally nowhere. She couldn't feel her ass or legs. She began to struggle with the bonds.

"Get me the fuck out of here. I do not consent to whatever crazy shit you're doing."

The man said, "Relax, I already gave you an epidural. Even if I unstrapped you from the gurney you wouldn't be going anywhere, except splat on the floor okay? You're fixed there for your own benefit."

He'd rolled the chair up to her feet and she could hardly see him anymore, needing to strain her neck in order to peek at the guy.

He said, "You're going to hurt yourself, stop it. We're going to start with a quick ultrasound before we begin. I'm sure you know the drill." He began to manipulate her legs and she couldn't feel a thing. "I know you can't scoot down yourself, so I'm just going to be getting you into position with your hips at the edge of the bed there."

Laura felt a pure coldness pass through her, the helplessness of her position. It occurred to her that this would be the worst thing that had ever happened to her. Except for the other things, which flashed through her mind then. She could hardly hear the doctor speaking. Blood rushed around her head at a million miles per hour. His voice was filtering through and echoing.

"I'll insert the probe now—you'll feel a little pressure."

She felt nothing.

"That's perfect. Just try to relax. Deep breath in...and out. Good. I'm taking a few baseline images. Now, I'll place a speculum, just like a Pap smear. You'll feel a little pressure as I open it. Let me know if it's too uncomfortable. Almost done with this part. Normally you'd feel a little pinch now. I'm passing the catheter through. Almost there...and done. You're doing great. I'm going to slowly introduce the saline now. You might feel some cramping—kind of like period cramps. Let me know if it's too intense."

She felt nothing.

He continued, as if caught in the madness of his own deceit. "That's normal. The saline is expanding the uterus so we can get a clear look at everything."

Laura was aware of the man moving around, manipulating equipment. Time was passing in a jumble, all mixed up. What the fuck were they doing to her? Why would they want to get this guy to see her? Maybe it was just a form of torture, an unwanted visit by an unknown gynecologist. Perhaps that was a man's idea of a woman's worst nightmare. Her head spun.

"Okay, I'm seeing the uterine lining now. Everything looks symmetrical...No obvious polyps or fibroids so far. I'll take a few more images." Clicks and whirrs and mechanical sounds. "Almost done. I'm going to remove the catheter and then the speculum. Deep breath in...and out...There we go. All set."

Laura felt the weakness course through her, a deep-set resignation. She knew, at the same time, that this would pass and she would get her strength back. For the moment it was a pure form of anger.

She said, "I'm going to kill you." Easing the words out slowly through gritted teeth. She'd never been more sincere. "I am going to actually kill you."

The gynecologist ignored her. He was by her side, looming over the gurney. Removing the latex gloves and rubbing his hands. A regular guy by the looks of him. Brown hair cut into a side part. Hazel eyes and a regular sized nose. Nothing special about him, except this. How many of these guys were just walking around like normal people? In shopping malls and fast-food outlets, sitting in movie theaters and going to the park with their kids?

The man said, "You may have some mild cramping or spotting for the next several hours, but that's normal. I'll be back to check in on you once we have the test results."

He moved around to the other side of the gurney and made some adjustments to the machine hooked up to the intravenous drip in her arm.

"I'm gonna juice you with the good stuff honey, so say goodnight."

As the bright lights faded away, they transformed into a kaleidoscopic pattern of moving colors, like stained glass. In them, Laura saw fragments of images, like old photographs. In the pictures were the women she had seen earlier in the large dormitory, pregnant women. The other image coming to the fore was the woman whom she had seen being dragged by the hair. The situation that had started the nightmare. The woman was standing in front of her, shaking.

She said, "Laura. Don't let them do it to you. Laura." The voice haunting and accented.

Laura said, "I won't let them."

The woman said, "Stay strong."

And then it was her brother there instead of the pregnant woman. Tom looking relaxed and healthy.

He said, "Stay strong, Laura."

She had enough energy to say one more word and a half. "Stronger together."

Chapter Forty-Five

Pete and Earl both had a lot of gumption. More than they could actually handle, in Keeler's opinion. He managed to persuade them that it'd be worthwhile using the rest of the night for sleep, arguing that without proper rest they'd be more of a hazard than a help.

Now, he was in the waitress's truck with Madeline at the wheel, still in her uniform. Wounded but undeterred. She'd bummed a cigarette from Pete and smoked it unprofessionally. The window was down and her red hair was wild with it.

Keeler asked her how it felt. Running and gunning like that back at the diner.

She said, "At first I didn't feel it." Glancing over to him. "It was a purely energetic thing, you know what I mean?"

He did.

She said, "I think maybe, you know, I got lucky."

Keeler said, "No. You didn't get lucky Madeline, you're good at this."

"How do you know that?"

"Because if what you described is even close to the way it was, you'd have had to get lucky fifty times without any bad luck. See what I'm saying? You made decisions and took chances. That's not luck."

"So you don't believe in luck?"

"I didn't say that. Luck is luck. Nothing you can do about that."

She said, "This is the craziest thing that ever happened to me." Glancing to Keeler. "Probably not the craziest thing that's happened to you, right?"

Keeler said, "Crazy is contextual. Here in Trace Junction? Yeah, it's totally insane."

She took a drag from the cigarette. "Context. That's what all the psychos like to talk about right?"

"Probably."

Madeline coughed violently and threw the cigarette away.

"Disgusting. Why do people smoke this shit?"

It was a rhetorical question. Keeler did an internal shaking of the bones. Letting everything that had tightened up get loose again. It ended with a deep breath and then a loud howl out the window.

Madeline got the vibe and joined in.

He said, "Now look who's getting crazy. How did you get a French name anyway?"

"Cajun mother."

Their plan was provisional. Show up at the location where sheriff Valdez's phone had last pinged the cell phone tower. Hope that there was a good explanation for her being out of touch. Keeler had no preconceptions. The entire thing could go lopsided or might have already tipped that way. What had occurred earlier was already outrageous as it was. Could the whole thing get any crazier?

It was best to avoid using Keeler's car for the moment, since he'd just recently shot a cop while driving in it. Not a regular cop, and not with the correct plates. But still, the

Trace Junction police would certainly have a call out for the vehicle.

Keeler said, "Coming up in a half mile on the left."

They were cruising along a country road. It was late enough that they hadn't seen a single vehicle. Even the cops had coalesced like iron filings to the magnetic draw of the diner explosion site.

Madeline said, "Half mile on the left huh? That's Apple-Bee Farm if I am not mistaken."

Keeler said nothing. Some seconds later Madeline slowed the truck. Nothing was showing up in her headlights.

She said, "Should I turn into the farm?"

"Might as well."

She pulled up the drive, steep and winding into rolling hills. Neither of them spoke. Keeler probed the darkness with his eyes. He saw nothing but the sudden shadows of apple trees and fences. An old oak stood here and there. At the crest of a hill loomed the silhouette of a barn.

Madeline said, "Oh shit."

The headlights picked out a vehicle at the side of the road, turned out obliquely as if it had lost control and run into a rock or something. They were perhaps a hundred yards away. The hills had plateaued. They were now rolling slowly along a straight driveway down the middle of a large orchard. Keeler identified the car up front as the unmarked police vehicle that Carver had been driving.

"It's them."

The rear window was smashed in completely, as was the passenger side window. The trunk and passenger door were open. The roof of the car looked as if it had been carelessly eviscerated by a gigantic can opener.

"Shit." Madeline slowed.

Keeler said, "Drive past it and park up there." He pointed to a natural curve in the driveway. "Kill the engine and the lights."

As they pulled past, Keeler observed the vehicle. The passenger seat was empty. Keeler thought he could make out a dark form in the driver's seat. Madeline stopped the truck and killed the lights.

Keeler said, "Let's move to the trees over there." He pointed into the orchard. "Before we approach again."

She said, "What about you?"

"I'm coming with you."

He wanted to get away from the pickup truck in case it became a target. He was concerned about what he'd just seen. The car's roof was caved in as if something had punched straight through it from above. Keeler didn't want to put the scare into Madeline, but there was something off about this. A vehicle targeted precisely from above. The entry hole reminded him of CIA assassination missiles. A bladed Hellfire variant known as the Ninja missile, sometimes referred to as a Flying Ginsu. But there was no way this was possible, since that particular tool costs somewhere around a hundred thousand dollars apiece and is usually fired from either a Reaper drone or an Apache helicopter.

Therefore, he assumed that he was looking at the impressive, if awful results of a DIY suicide drone modification.

Madeline was breathing hard where they'd stopped by an apple tree. She'd been through a lot already. The orchard was quiet. If it hadn't been for the circumstances, the place would have been idyllic. But there were circumstances. Now, there was only perfect peace. Not even the slightest buzzing of a drone or traffic noise.

He said, "You grab the back of my pack when we move. I want to feel you there so I know where you are. You got me?"

"Got you."

They moved out. A few seconds later, Keeler was shining his flashlight into the wrecked remnants of Carver's vehicle. The man himself was at the wheel, shredded to pieces by whatever it was that had sliced into the roof of his car.

Keeler pushed Madeline away. "You don't want to see this."

He examined the interior. The sheriff's phone was on the floor on the passenger side foot well. He figured she'd dropped it while fleeing the scene. He didn't blame her for that. The place already reeked with the stench of death. A few feet away, embedded in the dirt, he found a scorched, warped circular saw blade. He turned it over in his hand, spotting a fractured drone gimbal attachment still clinging to the blade's center—part of a makeshift mounting system.

Madeline said, "What is that?"

Keeler didn't respond. Someone had built a suicide drone with a high-speed saw, guided it to the driver's seat with surgical precision, and let it do its work. Whoever was behind this had a sick but creative imagination.

He walked back to the trunk and put his light into the cavity. The lockbox was open. That meant if a shotgun had been there, it was now in the hands of someone else. The trunk of an unmarked police vehicle will usually contain a go-bag with tactical supplies. Ammo, first aid kit. Stuff like that. There was no such bag.

He began to build a picture in his mind. The vehicle attacked from above. Valdez coming out in the thick of it and grabbing what she could from the back. He did a quick grid search of the area. Two shotgun shells ejected, around fifteen yards into the trees. He mentally figured it. The extractor claw on a Remington shotgun would expel the used shell when the operator pumped the weapon back. The shell would come out to the right.

Which meant that Valdez had been shooting away from the

vehicle into the orchard. Twenty yards further into the field, Keeler found one of the suicide drones. The pellets had shattered its rotors. The thing lay there on its back, revealing the glistening shape of a C4 charge taped to the underbelly, like a grotesque larval form.

Keeler moved away from the danger zone. Valdez was out there somewhere. Possibly wounded. Certainly armed and dangerous.

* * *

They found her in the barn. The sheriff was collapsed behind the enormous tires of a John Deere tractor. She was unconscious with what looked to be severe wounds to her leg and head. The go-bag was about five yards away. The Remington shotgun still clasped in Valdez's hands. She was breathing and alive but certainly not well. Keeler gave Madeline the light.

"Take this. I need to do a triage of her wounds."

Madeline took the light from him and aimed it where he directed.

Keeler said, "In the bag."

He reached inside, inspecting the contents and grabbing what he could find that might be useful under the circumstances. The sheriff's right calf was shredded, blood pooling around her in a slow seepage. That indicated the artery hadn't been hit. The head wound was a scalp laceration. Relatively minor, but responsible for a terrific amount of blood that had run down the side of her head.

Keeler used the scissors in the first aid kit to cut open the remains of her pant leg. He applied a tourniquet to the leg, stopping the loss of blood. Valdez grunted. He knew that it hurt. Small metal fragments had peppered into Valdez's flesh.

"Put the light on her face again."

The sheriff was still out cold.

Keeler applied a compression bandage to the head wound. He moved his attention back to the leg, examining the shrapnel. He wouldn't want to try removing large or deeply embedded pieces, but it looked as if Valdez had been far enough away from whatever it was that had exploded and sent fragments of metal flying.

Madeline said, "What should we do, call the ambulance?"

Keeler said, "No. I'm taking the shrapnel out of her right now, otherwise it'll poison her and she could lose the leg. We don't have time for an ambulance."

She said, "And other reasons I guess."

He grunted. The fragments were coming out without too much problem. Valdez had been lucky. He did a second pass to make sure he got it all out before cleaning the wounds and then flushed the area with saline solution. The bag had nothing better than a container of Tylenol for the pain. Keeler figured Valdez would need that soon, and more.

They carried her to the truck and bundled her carefully into a sitting position on the bench. She came to for a moment, looking around wildly, snatching for her weapon.

Keeler had relieved her of the sidearm.

He said, "You're all right now, sheriff. We're taking you somewhere safe."

Valdez said, "You."

"Yeah. Me."

She said, "Take me to the house. We got supplies there."

"Where's the house?"

Valdez said, "The house." She sort of raised her hand to point and her head lolled onto her chest.

Keeler slapped her gently on the cheek. "Where's the house Valdez?"

Her head came back up, eyes widening. She said, "Past the barns. Take a left and find the farmhouse behind the feed lot."

Keeler looked at Madeline, making eye contact. She nodded.

"Yeah, I think I know it. I know where there's a feed lot around here."

Madeline started the truck and began to drive through the orchard with the lights off.

The sheriff lost consciousness again. Keeler got the story straight in his mind. He figured that Carver and Valdez had turned on to Apple-Bee farm after spotting the enemy on their tail. Probably the drones. They would have sought cover there, and at the same time wished to avoid letting the enemy know where they were based.

Valdez moaned. "Fuck, this hurts."

He fed her five Tylenol. Figuring it would at least take the edge off.

Keeler said, "How much longer?"

Madeline said, "We're basically there."

She pulled off the main road. They came through farm buildings grouped around the rutted track. The feedlot was a penned-in area tightly packed with cattle. The stench was tough to endure, even passing by it. The house was up the drive, maybe a hundred yards off. Dark and foreboding, like something out of a Halloween story.

Madeline parked the truck and killed the engine.

Chapter Forty-Six

Keeler was pulling the truck's latch, pushing the door open. Valdez gripped his arm hard with her right hand.

"Stop." There was force in her voice. She said, "Three short, three long."

He got it. The code she and her team had used. He'd almost forgotten about the remaining cop on the sheriff's team. Bobby Kennedy. Keeler got out the LED light and hit three short and three long. He was rewarded with the same code twinkling back at him from a second-floor window. Kennedy was up there with a long gun, most likely.

Which is how it turned out.

Kennedy met them on the porch. "What happened?" He saw Valdez and shut up.

Keeler said, "You got a medic kit in here?"

"Yeah."

"Get it."

They laid Valdez out on the kitchen table and Keeler got to work. Kennedy assisted him without question. Taking orders like a pro. Thirty minutes later, Valdez was alright and deemed to be out of danger. Their kit had good painkillers, the prescription kind that kills pain and doesn't turn you into a heroin addict at the same time. They carried the sheriff upstairs and set her in bed with a saline drip to rehydrate. What they didn't have was extra blood, but Keeler didn't think it was a hundred percent necessary.

Keeler closed the door to Valdez's room and found Kennedy leaned against the corridor wall.

Kennedy said, "What about Carver?"

"Didn't make it."

"Where's the body?"

"Out by Apple-Bee farm, except it's not a body, it's a mess. He got hit by a modded drone."

Kennedy took a minute. Head bowed, palm covering his eyes. One big sob and he took a deep breath. Reddened eyes looking right into Keeler's.

"There's going to be payback. What's your name again?"

"Keeler."

"Just tell me you're on board for the reckoning, Keeler."

"I'm on board."

Kennedy went into the bathroom and washed his face. He screamed into the towel and then came out with his game face on. They came downstairs.

Kennedy said, "You want a drink or something? Food?"

Keeler said, "Food. Water."

"Our sheriff made a taco salad yesterday. I'll get you some of that. You can eat and talk at the same time I hope."

"Appreciate it."

While Kennedy fetched a plate of leftovers, Keeler looked at the waitress. She was curled up on the sofa, fast asleep. She looked vulnerable in that uniform. Keeler pulled a blanket over her. That elicited the opening of one eye and a shiver up his spine, before Madeline settled back into dreamland.

Keeler wasn't used to thinking about people on a first name

basis. He even thought of his sister Laura as *Keeler*. That's what more than a decade and a half of military service had pushed into his brain. That and a whole bunch of other things, like situations and weapons and workarounds. He'd retired early, taking advantage of force reduction politics. Now that he'd been in the civilian world for a couple of years he realized that he was enjoying himself outside of the military just as much as he had inside.

In other words, Keeler was the kind of guy who enjoyed himself everywhere. He'd even developed a theory about that. People become themselves in different ways but occupying the same kind of role in different situations. For Keeler it was all about mood. Put a guy like Keeler in prison, he'd end up liking it. Same if he was sent to work down a coal mine. Probably not if you stuck him behind a desk for eight hours a day.

But since that would never happen, he'd never know.

Kennedy returned with a plate of taco salad and a fork. In his other hand he managed to carry two bottles of beer. The labels said Weasel Boy.

"Best beer in Ohio."

Keeler said, "Is that supposed to be a high bar?"

"High enough."

Keeler ate and talked simultaneously, like he'd done a thousand times before, in a thousand operating environments, locations and varied topographies. Eat and talk. Get the stuff in you to perpetuate the fighting power. Talk, because that's what people are good at. Telling stuff. He told Kennedy everything that had happened up until that moment. When he was finished Keeler noticed that Madeline was awake and listening.

She said, "I'm sorry about your sister. Do you know if she's doing ok? I wouldn't want my loved ones to be in their hands."

Keeler said, "I don't have contact with her and I guess it's too late to be reasonable about it."

Kennedy said, "Much too late."

Madeline said, "Any way of finding out if she's ok? This is awful."

Kennedy said, "The jail's under the county authority. Let me take a look."

He pulled a laptop from the coffee table and opened it, getting busy.

Keeler said, "This isn't going to trip any wires, put them onto our location?"

"Nah, I'm running a secure system. Using a satellite connection and running it through Tor. Should be okay."

A few minutes later, after clicking and dragging and swiping, Kennedy looked up at Keeler. "Looks like she's been released. You weren't aware of that?"

"No. When?"

"Earlier, I guess that'd be yesterday evening."

Keeler said, "You got a secure phone I can use Kennedy?"

"Yeah." He brought a phone out of his pocket, used facial recognition to open it, and handed the device to Keeler.

"Thanks." Keeler dialed Laura's number. It went to voicemail. He looked at Kennedy. "They would have given her the phone back, upon release. Correct?"

"If she had her phone with her at the time of arrest, yes. But the battery might have lost its charge."

Keeler said, "Yeah, but she would have charged it since."

Madeline was biting her fingernails.

Keeler dialed Josh's number. Figuring that Laura would have gotten in touch with her husband as soon as she was released. Particularly if she'd gone back home and found the place burned to the ground. Maybe they were together now, up in Cleveland in a hotel. That would be the best outcome.

Josh answered on the fourth ring. "Hello." His voice was equal parts hopeful and fearful, and heavy with sleep.

Keeler said, "It's Keeler. Have you heard from Laura?"

"No, why? What happened?"

Keeler made eye contact with Madeline. He said, "She was released from the county jail last night. She didn't get in touch?"

"No. What's going on. Is it bad?"

The guy was on the verge of panicking. Keeler said, "No, it's probably a false alert. Go back to sleep. Message this number if you hear from her. I'll be in touch tomorrow."

Josh had more questions, anxiety and stress in his voice. Keeler managed to get off the phone with him in under a minute.

"My brother-in-law. He's freaking out." He looked at Madeline. Her eyes had closed involuntarily. "What time is it now, four in the morning?"

Kennedy said, "Four oh six, to be precise."

"Let's get some rest." Keeler said, "We'll reconvene at six thirty. If there aren't enough beds, I'll take the sofa there."

Madeline said, "I'm already on the sofa and it's working out just fine."

Keeler grunted and stood. Looking at Kennedy. "Where am I going?"

"Take Carver's room."

Kennedy went into the kitchen with the dishes and empty beer bottles. Keeler turned to go upstairs.

Madeline said, "What do you think is going on with your sister?"

Keeler turned in the doorway. He said, "I don't know."

Madeline said, "I forgive you for losing my phone."

He said, "Thanks. I was worried."

"Good night, Keeler."

"Good night."

* * *

Keeler lay fully clothed in Carver's bed. The lights were out, but an ambient glow came from the window. Keeler saw the shadow of drones swarming on the ceiling. Dwight had taken that van. Supposedly a drone van, all ready to rock. He'd forgotten to ask Kennedy about it. A potentially interesting development.

Laura came swimming into his mind again, accompanied by galloping horses. Then, he closed his eyes and went into the familiar mental projection of a free fall. A HALO jump over some location. He chose the Arctic. Falling through a bright night sky, speckled with glowing stars and a full moon.

That had actually happened once, a training jump in Alaska. Not exactly Arctic, but as close as you'd get. The objective had been to open the parachutes as low as possible in order to avoid detection by the blue team. He and his crew had come down at the edge of a thick forest. They buried the chutes and geared up for a fast run through the woods. Sleep came before his boots hit the ground.

Chapter Forty-Seven

Laura knew that she was dreaming. She'd opened her eyes and found herself looking at a teenage girl. The girl was indigenous, South American of some kind. Like an angel. She was wearing a white night dress and was severely pregnant. The girl watched her with big open eyes, standing in the middle of the room.

A different room than before. This one was completely bare except for the bed upon which Laura was strapped. There were no windows. A dim luminescence came from a recessed groove in the ceiling. The girl glowed as if some strange inner light emanated from her. She had her hands clasped, one over the other, protectively covering the swelling belly.

Laura said, "Hello there." She felt good. The dream was pleasant.

The girl said, "They will put a baby into you."

"Is that what they do here? Is that what they did to you?"

"Yes. They will put the baby into you and then you will not keep it. You will just grow the baby for them."

Surrogacy. It occurred to Laura that this was no dream, it was real.

She said, "How did you get into the room?"

"My friend got the guard away. I have two more minutes."

The girl wore no watch, or had a phone, or any other time telling device.

Laura said, "Why so little time?"

"Because they finish quickly."

"Oh."

The girl nodded looking at her. The eyes unblinking. She said, "Bad men."

Laura said, "What's your name?"

"My name is Laura."

"That's my name too."

"I know. This is why I come."

The restraints were still there and she couldn't move out of the bed.

Laura said, "Darling. Do me a favor and undo these straps."

The girl sat there looking at her. The wide eyes still hadn't blinked, not even once. It was really weird. Laura was pretty sure the kid was on something, something pretty powerful.

She said, "From one Laura to the other. Undo this for me."

"They will hurt you."

"I'll take my chances."

The girl said, "Laura. Why is your name Laura?"

"What do you mean?"

"My mother called me Laura because of the war. In my country there was a Great War."

Laura said, "Where are you from, honey?"

"El Salvador."

"I've heard about the war. Why did your mother call you Laura then?"

"My uncles were all killed by the bad ones. And my grandparents, and my cousins. Only my mother survive in her family. When I was born she called me Laura because it means victory, honor, glory, and strength in my language. *Victoria, Honor, Gloria, Fuerza.*"

Laura said, "All the more reason to get me out of this now. Do it Laura."

The girl broke from her spell. She came over and undid the straps. Laura sat up and swung her legs over the side of the bed. She put her hands on the girl's shoulders. The kid was so small that her head and Laura's head were now at the same height. She hugged the girl to her, feeling the soft passivity in her body and the hard bump of the baby she carried. Laura pulled back from the embrace, holding the girl at arm's length.

"Do you think the guard is still with your friend? Did they go far from here?"

"They go to the janitor's closet. I tell her to make it last long but the men here not good men."

"Oh god. Okay honey. Let's move. You'll need to get back to bed so that the guards don't find out that you're involved."

The girl nodded. "Yes."

Laura said, "Are there cameras outside of the room?"

The girl shook her head. "I don't think so."

"What are we going to find, when I open that door?"

"Everyone sleeping."

"Sure honey. Just describe it to me. Close your eyes and tell me what you see, walking out that door."

The girl closed her eyes. "Corridor. Go left and there are two rooms."

"What is in those rooms?"

"Machines for testing baby. We go there every day."

"Alright. What else do you see besides those rooms?"

The girl said, "Across the corridor is where we live."

Laura wondered if that would be the large room she saw initially. But the lack of cameras was weird.

"You sure there aren't any cameras?"

"Yes, sure."

The only reason that would be the case was if the people running this scheme were so terrified of any recorded evidence that they simply removed the possibility that could ever happen. It sort of made sense. Things were coming together. The girls in here were surrogate mothers, obviously. Basically Laura had stumbled into a situation where women were being trafficked for use as surrogates. She'd heard about that happening in places like China and El Salvador, but certainly not here in the USA. Not to mention Ohio.

She said, "Let's go."

The girl nodded. Laura put her hands on her shoulders again and turned her around, like a little doll. She slipped off the bed. The floor was cold against her bare feet. The place was strange. Everything perfectly white and clean and brand new. Laura took a deep breath and opened the door.

Nothing but an empty corridor like the girl had said. Two doors on the left side of the corridor. At the end of it was what looked like a secure door. Laura could make out some electronic devices attached to it, maybe biometric locks. She'd figure it out. Beside the door to the room where she'd been kept was a chair. That must have been where the guard had sat. She held the girl by the hand.

"Where is the guard now?"

The girl pointed. "The second door."

"Okay."

The first door would be the room where the girls were tested. There might be useful stuff in there. What Laura had in mind was something very sharp, like a scalpel. The second door was apparently the janitor's closet. Where the guard was enjoying a freebie from one of little Laura's friends. An unimaginably disgusting thought that invited further thoughts with the imaginary scalpel. Across the hall was a set of double doors. Everything opaque. No window into the space beyond.

Laura said, "Okay Laura. Thank you. Now you must go back to sleep and don't ever tell anyone about this. If you do, they will harm you and your family." She hugged the girl, who gripped her tight for a fierce second and then turned on a dime and walked through the double doors.

One guard. Strange.

Laura opened the door to the testing room. The place was pitch dark. She closed the door and ran her hands over the walls. She found a light switch, which made the place suddenly brilliantly lit. This was the room they'd had her in. Where the gynecologist had done his tests. The gurney was centered, with its appendages neatly arranged. A medical lamp extended overhead on an articulated arm. The other limbs held stainless steel trays. Everything clean and orderly now.

A cabinet was off to the side. Laura began rifling through its drawers. The top one contained a neatly laid-out sequence of compresses, sterile speculums sealed in plastic wrappers, lubricating gel packets, cotton swabs, disposable gloves, and alcohol wipes.

She closed it and reached for the drawer beneath. From outside the room a door slammed. A male voice said something loud in Spanish. The soft tones of a female. The sound of boots on the cold clean floor. Laura tensed, aware that the light could be visible underneath the door. She froze in place, literally willing the man to walk by. Evidently, he was concentrating on something else. The voice came again, just outside the door, and continued further to the right.

Laura found the switch for the surgical light, attached to the gurney. She went to the door and turned off the big room light. She heard the sound of the chair scraping on the floor. The man's voice again, this time quieter.

In the second drawer, Laura found a pair of scissors with blunt tips. She tested the blade. Sharp enough, but not easy to use, if it came to that. Beside the scissors was a blister pack with five tools the size of toothbrushes that she couldn't identify. Green plastic handle, and some kind of tip that wasn't pointy, but cylindrical. She carefully opened the package and examined the thing. A steel cylinder with what seemed to be a razor-sharp edge. A tool for taking samples maybe. A biopsy punch.

Well, between those two items, she'd be able to do some damage. Question was, how to get at him? There she was, stuck in a room while the guy lounged just to the right on a chair against the wall. How many steps was that, maybe three or four. The door opened inwards. Would he hear it? She didn't remember any hinge squeak from opening it the first time.

But four steps was a lot. Enough at least for the guy to get his guard up.

And what Laura needed was for the guy to lower his guard.

Chapter Forty-Eight

Keeler checked in on Valdez before heading downstairs. He had no watch but knew the time. 06:23. For some reason that was just how it went. He got it right eight out of ten times. The less he double guessed himself, the better it went. By now, at the advanced age of his mid to late thirties, he had finally stopped second guessing.

Valdez opened her eyes when Keeler came into the room.

Her voice was weak but upbeat. "Still alive in ninety-five."

Keeler took a seat by the bed. "What's that, some bad nineties rap song?"

"Something like that."

He said, "How you doing?"

"Feeling good and sleepy."

"Leg hurts I guess."

Valdez said, "I took a couple more of those pills a minute ago. Why I was awake when you came in."

"Good. Just checking in. Mind if I take a look at it?"

She removed the bedsheet and quilt. Keeler examined the bandaged area visually. No signs that blood was seeping through, which meant that the bleeding had stopped.

"Looks alright."

She said, "Now get on out of here, I need three more hours and I'm good to go."

Which wasn't true. Valdez wouldn't be walking that day, or the day after. Maybe in a week she'd be able to put weight on it. The wounds weren't deep but the blast had been acute. She was most likely concussed.

He said, "Just relax and take it easy. You're out of the game for now, sheriff."

"Screw you too." She said, "Hey, you got my phone?"

"Yeah." The phone was on the dresser by the door. Where he'd put it the night before. He brought it over to Valdez. "Actually, I was wondering if I could use this. I don't have another one at the moment."

"Might as well." Valdez said. "Besides that, I'd recommend that you use the shotgun. It's the only thing that'll work against the drones."

Keeler grunted an affirmation. He was looking out the window. Nothing but a large field out there in the dark. The cattle feed pen beyond it was stinking up the area. He went downstairs, hungry again and craving a good cup of black coffee.

Which is exactly what he found.

* * *

Keeler ate an egg and cheese sandwich with ketchup and a pickled hot pepper. Kennedy was the cook.

He said, "All out of bacon."

Madeline said, "Tastes good just like this. What did you put on here, mustard?"

"That's the secret. Plus you grill it with butter."

"So good. I'd get you a job at the grill if the place hadn't burned down last night."

Keeler couldn't speak with his mouthful. Madeline popped the last corner of crusty cheesy sandwich into her mouth. She pointed a greasy finger at Kennedy.

"So, what's your deal?"

"My deal how?"

Keeler swallowed the last bite and washed it down with coffee.

He said, "We're going to push on, which will involve making decisions. Like, right now. What's your deal Kennedy. Where do you fit into the picture?"

Kennedy said, "Three months ago, I came on to lead an anti-trafficking task force. Moved here from Hawaii, believe it or not. When I got to Trace Junction, seeing what the team was up to. I realized that all this job actually meant..." He took a slug of coffee. "...to the previous guy leading the task force, was a bunch of entrapment schemes."

Madeline said, "What does that mean?"

"Means, you go online with fake social media profiles like you're a hot sixteen-year-old, and get horny middle-aged guys to drool over you. That was the fun part, if I'm honest about it. Seducing those creeps. Then there's the not so fun part. You get them to agree to a meet in some motel and boom. The guy goes away for the rest of his life."

She said, "That's terrible. I can't believe that's how it works. You actually get the John to do it, you trick him?"

Kennedy said, "Welcome to 21st century policing. If they don't ask the girls' age, they're done. Sometimes they're screwed even when they do ask. Only way around it is if the guy insists upon seeing ID."

Keeler said, "Same's true for most anti-terrorism enforcement. It's the FBI who invents the scheme and gets some teenagers from the mosque to sign up. Then the task force comes in and the kids go away for conspiracy."

Madeline said, "Why do they do that?"

Kennedy said, "Sponge theory."

"What's that?"

Keeler said, "You soak up the people who are willing and able to do a bad thing. Think about them like spilled coffee. Put the sponge out there and soak them up. Problem is that the smart guys won't fall for that kind of entrapment, so you only get the small fry, low hanging fruit. You don't get the guys who initiate."

Kennedy said, "Correct. Sponge theory is the best you can say about it. The actual reason law enforcement does this is targets. A department is assigned random targets by the politicals. Like, you need to put away fifty percent more pedophiles than last year. Boom. The wrong asshole gets promoted."

Keeler said, "Story of my life."

Madeline said, "You didn't get promoted?"

Keeler said, "I never asked for promotion. Anyway, I worked in a different context. I did see the guys who went for promotion, mostly the office desk kind. That was never my ballgame."

She said, "But what were you working in, the police?"

"Air Force. I was a PJ for fifteen years or so."

"What's that?"

Kennedy said, "That's some hard core shit is what it is." He gave Keeler a once over with his eyes and offered his coffee cup up for a toast. "Here's to you, pal. I got them green bare feet on my ass once in Iraq. Thanks to guys like you."

Madeline said, "I have no idea what you're talking about."

Keeler said, "We're the guys who go in and save guys like Bobby Kennedy here." He examined Kennedy. "What are we talking about, the corps?"

"Roger that. 1st Marine division, RCT-6."

"Pleased to meet you." Keeler bumped mugs. He said, "What happened with the task force?"

"I'm glad you asked. What happened was I put an end to the bullshit and started turning the project around. In doing so of course, we came up against the elephant in the room. Which, here in Trace Junction means the fact that the town had become incorporated into a foreign cartel business. As hard as that is to get your head around, that's what it is, bud. *Los Quebrados* have taken over. It's that simple."

Madeline said, "That's right."

Keeler said, "How does it work?"

Kennedy said, "Let me draw the picture for you as I've come to see it. *Los Quebrados* aren't so different from other cartel groups, here or back where they come from. They operate in what I think of as rings, like the age rings on a tree or something. Just keep that image in mind. First circle is local business. That's a relatively un-sophisticated situation. The cartels operate without centralized command. Operatives are like freelance managers. So, what they do is, come in here and take over a business. Like a Dominos pizza franchise. It's easy for them to do because they're not afraid of the law. Not even one bit. They use intimidation and violence and get their way one hundred percent of the time."

Keeler said, "For what purpose, just to drain the profits?"

"One, they take a cut. Two, now that they control the business they can sell services to other freelance cartel operatives. Money laundering is one such service. As is transportation. Consider the pizza example, which is a real one. Dominos delivers. So, right there you've got a drug distribution system to rent out."

Madeline said, "Holy cow."

Kennedy said, "Yeah, so the second ring is what they can do with the business."

Madeline nodded. "Got it."

Kennedy said, "Other rings form as opportunities arise. The

increasing wealth of the organization helps them gain inroads with local politicians. Judges, for example, are elected officials who require campaign finance. Boom, you get in there and make them happy. They turn a blind eye."

Keeler said, "I guess something like Dominos pizza is pretty easy. What about other industries? What's a prestige industry here in Trace Junction?"

Madeline said, "We're mostly a service economy, like other places in America. If there's a prestige industry I guess it'd be horses. Remember those two thoroughbreds from this morning?" Looking at Keeler. "Buyers come to get designer horses up in the Amish country."

Keeler said, "Right. Those two from NYC."

Madeline said, "Well, that's what you thought. Doing the Trace Junction thoroughbred guide book tour. Diner and donuts."

Kennedy said, "I'm not aware of that situation."

Madeline said, "My uncle worked up at the animal clinic back in the day. The Amish have been breeding horses for generations. It's a real thing. People come from all over to buy their horses."

Keeler said, "I think Earl or Pete told me that it's not really thoroughbreds they're breeding up there. What did he say?" It came to him. "Warmbloods or Andalusians. That's what Earl said it was."

Madeline said, "I'm no expert."

Kennedy said, "Neither am I."

The horse thing was doing circles around Keeler's mind. If that was a significant source of revenue in the county, it would make sense that the cartel had their hands on it.

He said, "One second. About the horses. Is there a particular company or business that deals in them, or are we talking about a sort of valet service that uses several breeders?"

Madeline said, "I have no idea." Looking at Kennedy. "You?"

Kennedy shrugged. "Nope."

Keeler said, "What about services around that? The NYC people this morning. They had a limo driver, right? You said that there aren't so many of them."

"That's because there aren't crowds of buyers for those horses. You get one or two people come by a month. Maybe it works seasonally. I'm not sure."

Keeler said, "Okay, but what I'm getting at is maybe there's a limo company that they use. Like a valet or concierge service when the buyers show up."

Madeline shrugged. He looked at Kennedy whose eyebrows were peaked in curiosity.

Keeler nodded to Kennedy. "Is that something you can find out?"

"Yup. I can check that out. Sounds good."

"Good."

Madeline looked at Keeler. She said, "So, what's the plan?"

Keeler said, "My guess is that they would have evacuated the Quality Inn by now." He tilted his head to Kennedy. "Do we have access to the van Dwight took from that drone workshop?"

"It's tucked into the barn out back."

"Excellent. We'll take a look at that." He said, "I want to scout the Quality Inn, see if we can get a handle on what's been happening there. The other thing is the thoroughbreds. That's a good angle. My sister ran into trouble up in the Amish country, where you say those horses are bred."

Kennedy said, "Makes sense. I'll run down the limo angle. See if there's anything to find."

Keeler said nothing. He was thinking about Laura. Josh hadn't messaged back on Kennedy's phone. Where was Laura?

Chapter Forty-Nine

Several hours earlier, Laura was still in the examination room holding a biopsy punch in one hand and a pair of surgical scissors in the other. She could hear the guard in the hallway, rocking back and forth on his chair, just a couple of yards away. The only thing separating him from her was the closed door. From the sound of it, the guy was now watching a soccer game on his phone. The announcer's voice was as annoying as always, high pitched, and literally screaming from the phone's speakers.

Laura had often been described as symmetrical. It was a way of accounting for the fact that she was pretty. Given the circumstances, as gruesome as it was, she figured that it would be irresponsible not to use her feminine beauty as a weapon. There was no emotion to it, no ethical issues that needed clarifying. This man on the other side of the door didn't deserve any better than the deceit she planned.

Plus, there wasn't another way out.

She came out of the door naked, shimmying and sashaying across the corridor. In something between a dance and a catwalk. Both of Laura's hands were behind her back, but her tits were certainly out front, and the guy's eyes moved immediately there, rudely torn from the soccer game.

He'd been rocking the chair back and forth, idly shifting the balance from the floor, to banging the backrest against the wall. Now the rear legs came down to rest. Laura was giving it her most winning smile.

She said, "What have you got for me big boy? You ready for another go around?"

He said, "*Qué*"

She was one step away, the sheer fact of her, the physical proximity and smell, operating on this guy so obviously. Hormonal reactions were happening, transference of pheromonal information. Laura was cool, playing it perfectly. She was even aware of the growing bulge in his jeans. She swayed in front of him, twisting to the right in a fake dance. While in fact, she was winding up for the first strike.

Which would have to be perfect.

Laura allowed the natural twist in her waist to begin unwinding. She used natural forces of motion and leverage. In her right hand was the biopsy punch, held in the fist, point down like a dagger. Her arm extended as the movement unfolded, whipping the biopsy punch through at high speed as she guided it flush into the man's left eye. The razor sharp cylinder cut exactly six millimeters into the man's cornea, punching through the hard crust.

A gelatinous material oozed out.

The man's involuntary reaction was a simultaneous howl and instinctive protective measures sending the hands to the injured area. Before he was able to complete this sequence, Laura was already unwinding in the opposite direction. Her left hand contained the surgical scissors with blunt ends and razor-sharp blades. She had wrapped a medical towel around the lower blade, leaving its upper twin as the weapon.

Now, the power generated by the initial strike with the biopsy punch, was unleashed once more. The scissor blade held horizontally as the left arm extended, generating speed. Laura sent the razor sharp weapon into the man's exposed neck, slicing several millimeters deep and nicking the external jugular vein.

The double attack sent the man writhing to the floor, hands up at his neck now trying to stop the bleeding. Laura looked at him impassively, judging and analyzing the efficacy of her efforts. Pretty good. The phone was now skipping across the hard floor. The man had a gun stuck into his waistband.

Laura took the weapon and slid it to the side. She went back in with the scissors to finish the job. She cut deeper into this man's neck so that she was sure of incapacitating him. She was no expert on anatomy but figured that he'd either bleed out and die right there and then or lose consciousness and die slowly. Either way he was out of the game.

She retrieved the phone and the gun and went back to the examination room to get dressed. It occurred to her that there was a room full of pregnant women to deal with. They'd have to wait for the authorities. Right then she had one mission, get the fuck out of there.

The immediate problem was obvious around a minute later. She looked at the biometric door lock. She'd need the guard's fingerprint. The man was currently unconscious, twitching every so often as he bled out. Totally disgusting. Laura was dressed only in that hospital gown, no pockets.

It came to her then, the most important thing to do at that moment was to call Josh. The only hesitation she felt was that in doing so, she would potentially be giving up Josh's information to these people. In case they were tracking everything, which is what she believed.

Didn't matter. She was already over that line.

Laura used the guard's face to unlock his phone. She

stepped into the examination room and called Josh's number. He answered on the first ring.

"Yes."

"It's Laura. I need to tell you something and it's going to be fast cause I have no time. Are you ready?"

Josh said, "Did you get out of jail?"

"Josh, shut up. I have no time. I think I'm being held at a farm facility near the Amish Auction. Get help there."

Josh said, "Farm facility near Amish Auction. That isn't specific enough to get them to you."

Laura said, "I will try and make it to Beachy's farm if I manage to get out of here. Have you got that?"

"Yes."

She said, "I love you honey bunny."

"I'm coming down. I'll be there in an hour and a half."

Not an idea that Laura liked, but she couldn't tell him not to come.

She hung up.

Now, she put the phone and the gun by the door and ran back to the guard. She dragged him by his feet to the door. It took a lot of effort to get him turned around, and even then the hand didn't reach all the way up to the biometric sensor. Laura got the chair over by the door and used it to prop the body up. When she was almost there she took a moment to breathe.

The gun and phone were right by her knees. Laura, kneeling, managed to raise the man's torso up high enough so that his index finger reached the sensor. The thing beeped once and glowed green. She dropped the guard without ceremony and picked up the weapon in her right hand and phone in her left.

She steeled herself for whatever. The only thing she really knew about guns was that real men carry them fully loaded and ready to fire. This shit head would have been LARPING as a real man. She pushed open the door with her shoulder. On the other side was another fake real man, looking at her with a degree of shock on his face.

She said, "Hands in the air."

The guy stood up and reached back behind him. Laura shot him once in the chest. The gun worked. It was easy to use. The man tumbled back and fell against the wall. A second man was just behind the first guard. He was already scrambling for his weapon, just like the first guy.

Laura said, "Don't."

He did. She pulled the trigger. The round went into his shoulder, spinning the man a hundred and eighty degrees. He remained upright, leaning against the wall. His weapon was holstered at the hip and he actually went for it. Laura fired again, hitting him in the back between the shoulder blades. This shot made the man slump forwards and tumble to the ground.

Neither of the two guards looked capable of much.

She had a moment to look around. It was another place, almost. Looking at the door she'd come through, it was clearly hidden from sight. The portal had been set up to look like a decorative panel with a big display showing awards and acclaim apparently garnered for raising very good horses.

A clinic of some kind. Like a veterinarian facility for horses?

Laura didn't stop to find out more. She spotted a door that looked like it led out to the world. It seemed as though there was nobody else in that facility. Just those two guards, lying on the ground. She couldn't tell if they were dying either. How would she know? There was a jacket over the back of the chair where the first man had been. She fetched it and put it on. The guy's feet were bigger than hers, but she was barefoot.

She untied his sneakers and removed them. The socks smelled bad. The shoes fit badly, but at least they were only a little too big. Laura put the phone in the jacket pocket and sprinted to the door. It was locked with a latch that easily snicked open. Then, she was outside. She got her bearings.

Chilly, cold, and dark. Streetlights glowed a dim yellow, casting the surrounding buildings in a warm glow. She'd been there before. It was Belleville. This was exactly where she'd run into those guys in the first place, where the pregnant woman had been dragged by her hair. The thing that had started this nightmare. The phone said 05:21. Beachy's place was maybe twenty minutes uphill through the fields and pitch-black woods.

Laura began to run.

Chapter Fifty

Keeler and Madeline were in the van. With Dwight out of the game, it had been a lucky thing having Bobby Kennedy around. The cop was an ace with computers and tech. Turned out he'd come out of his tours with the Marines and gone straight into a combined bachelors and masters in engineering at Georgia Tech. After that he'd been picked up by a health care information technology company. He'd joined the police after the financial crash. Not out of necessity, but out of the sense that he had to do his part.

The drone system wasn't so very complicated. There were the devices themselves, and a laptop computer that linked them up to the control system. Keeler had used a similar system before, although the technology changed radically every few years.

Bottom line was, it was just easier to use now.

They'd tried it out at the property. Keeler was in the back working the controls. The system was First Person View, which meant the operator wore a pair of goggles that could see from the drone's perspective. A second operator was necessary to keep an objective view. Looking at the satellite map and keeping an eye on the bigger picture. That was Madeline's role.

Kennedy stayed back at the house. His job was to use those computer skills to dig in deeper. Primarily focusing upon the horse trade. Keeler and Madeline parked the van around half a mile from the Quality Inn. Keeler had the small FPV drone zipping over the trees. Madeline was watching on a larger screen.

She said, "Coming up on the tree line. A hundred yards. Why don't you descend into cover."

Keeler said, "Gotcha."

They didn't want to be seen. So, Keeler directed the drone down into the trees. It was a little slower going, but probably worth it. The drone broke through the tree line a few seconds later, exactly across the road from the motel. Three police cars were parked at the verge. Keeler pulled the drone back into the trees.

"Interesting."

He maneuvered the drone laterally, parallel to the road. It came over the road and spun the camera to look at the police vehicles.

Madeline said, "Two cops in each. Wonder what's going on there."

"Me too. They're just sitting there."

"Go back to the building and see what you can get."

Keeler sent the little thing zipping over the driveway and over the Quality Inn's roof.

He said, "Let's take a quick look at the parking lot. See what's left."

Nothing was left at the parking lot. Just empty asphalt and the oil stains left behind.

Keeler sent the drone to the building again. The first thing he did was peer into windows. The top floor penthouse looked empty. Trash was all over the place.

Madeline said, "Someone had a party here and forgot to clean up."

"Yup."

He scanned the two windows over the other side of the roof. Same situation. An empty place.

Keeler said, "Wonder what the cops are doing out front then."

The question was answered ten minutes later, when Keeler found an open window into a ground floor bathroom. The drone barely fit, but the propellers were protected by a circular plastic shroud, making it safe to bump around a little. Keeler got the thing in there and through the door. This was a public bathroom leading out to a corridor. He couldn't get into the rooms, but whizzing along into the reception area, it was clear that the place was empty. A set of stairs went down to a basement area.

Keeler said, "Wonder if this leads to the bar."

Madeline said, "We used to call that the skanky bar. I heard they upgraded in the last few years."

"You don't get out much?"

"Not anymore I don't. And if I do, it's not to a skanky bar like that."

Keeler smiled behind the enclosed goggles. Downstairs it was dark. The drone's camera automatically switched to infrared.

Madeline said, "Boxes over at the back."

The drone was in a kind of lounge area. Wall to wall carpeting and several areas with sofas arranged around coffee tables. Like a chill out room. At the back were cases lined up against the wall. He brought the drone close, but obviously couldn't open the boxes.

Madeline said, "What do you think that is?"

Keeler said, "I'd guess weapons of some kind. That's what it looks like to me. If I had to bet, I'd say that they moved out in a hurry. Took what they could, including the first line soldiers. Takes a hell of a lot of chutzpah to call in the local police to guard your illegal weapons stash."

Madeline said, "These guys are letting it all hang out aren't they?"

The door to the bar was open and Keeler maneuvered the drone in. A few seconds later they were looking at three corpses laid out on the floor. The cartel soldiers that he'd taken out.

He said, "Okay, now it makes sense. Use the cops to keep out any curious neighbors. I guess they're planning on coming back for their stuff."

Madeline said nothing. Which was slightly disturbing to Keeler because he couldn't just take off the goggles.

He said, "You ok?"

"Yeah, I'm ok. Just not a hundred percent used to seeing dead bodies."

Keeler said, "Get used to it."

"I don't think I want to."

He changed the subject. "If our man Arturo felt a threat, where would he go?"

She said, "He might go somewhere else, like another place in town."

"Sure, another hideout. What if he just wanted to get out of town?"

Meantime, Keeler was using the drone to scan the location. The bodies and those weapons cases were all that he found of interest.

Madeline said, "There aren't any hard borders Keeler. He just drives out of town."

"But we're in Ohio. What about the airport? I think it was

Earl or Pete told me that they'd refurbished it for the horse buyers."

"Private airport. He'd have to have a private plane."

Keeler zipped the drone around and back up the stairs.

He said, "How much battery left?"

She said, "Time to head back."

He maneuvered the drone back the way he'd brought it in. Finally, easing the thing out through the bathroom window. Then, all he had to do was hit the command for home. The drone rose rapidly to a hundred yards and began its return journey autonomously.

Keeler took the goggles off and rubbed his eyes. He looked at Madeline. They were close, in the confines of the van's rear.

He said, "We should get eyes on the airport. I hope they haven't left yet."

"You think they're feeling that threatened?"

"If I was this Arturo guy, yeah, I'd be worried." He tilted his head, thinking about that. "But I'm not him, and he doesn't seem very reasonable. I'd say it'd take another big push to get them running."

"What do you want to do?"

Keeler said, "We just need to find the right place to push."

Madeline said, "This is like reverse Jenga."

"The thing where you pile up wooden pieces and see who brings it all down?"

"Yes. You never played that?"

"I have."

Valdez's phone rang. It was Kennedy.

Keeler said, "What do you have Kennedy?"

"Your brother-in-law's phone left me a message without a message."

"What does that mean?"

Kennedy said, "Means he called, I was on the other line. The call went to voicemail, and he left no message."

"You just said he left a message."

"There was no message on the message. Just nothing there."

"Voices or breathing or something, like a pocket call maybe."

Kennedy said, "Could be a pocket call. I called back twice now, and it goes directly to voicemail."

Keeler said, "Can you get a trace on the phone?"

"You need a court order for that. Judge needs to sign off."

"Just do it through one of those cell phone tower pinging sites. It costs a dollar."

Kennedy said, "IMSI Lookup. That's a good idea."

"Do it and call me back." He hung up.

Madeline said, "What's an IMSI Lookup?"

"My brother-in-law called him but there's no message. Josh isn't picking up now. IMSI Lookup is when you locate the last cell tower that connected to the phone. It's how we found Valdez. You don't always get lucky, but here we're out in the country. Tougher in a city."

She said, "Okay, so we go to the airport?"

"Let's do it."

But five minutes later Valdez's phone rang again. It was Kennedy. He'd used the IMSI lookup service. The nearest cell tower to Josh's phone was up in Belleville near the Amish Auction.

He said, "And another thing. Looks like they don't use any special limo company, but they use drivers on a freelance, self-employed basis."

Keeler said, "What does that mean?"

Kennedy said, "The drivers only work once in a while, so they aren't regular employees of the company. They just come on when needed. I got this from my neighbor. He's a truck driver."

"What, the suits and everything are supplied by the company?"

"I don't know. But, they've only got two of those souped-up limos. I've got a name and address. You want it or not?"

"Go ahead."

Kennedy relayed the details. Keeler looked at Madeline.

"1045 Telegraph Road. That mean anything to you?"

"Sure. Out in the sticks."

Keeler said, "You guys have some long roads in this place. Is that really the one thousandth and forty-fifth house on Telegraph Road?"

"I never counted, but that's my assumption yes."

Interesting. "Is it on the way?"

Madeline was driving. She shrugged. Sort of. Looking at him. "So what do you want to do?"

Keeler said, "Let's go to Telegraph Road."

They found the limo driver in his backyard raking leaves.

There was nothing very fancy about the driver's situation. Not the house, or the driver himself. It was a one-story ranch house with two bedrooms, made from brick with a small patch in the back. Keeler went in tooled up but wasn't expecting to use the Smith & Wesson tucked into his waistband beneath his jacket.

He and Madeline had simply walked up to the front of the house. There was no porch to speak of, but a dusty old sofa had been left outside. A small dog barked from inside. The wife came to the door. She had on pink joggers and a sweatshirt with a slogan about horses. *Hoofbeats Make My Heartbeat.*

"Yep. Can I help you?"

Keeler nudged Madeline. She said, "We're legal investigators working on a case. We'd just like to have a word with your husband if that's alright."

The woman said, "Investigators?"

"That's right. Your husband's not in trouble or anything. We just have a couple of questions about one of his clients."

"You mean over at Rays?"

She glanced at Keeler, who didn't know what Rays was.

Madeline said, "Not at Rays, honey. The work he does driving."

The woman looked relieved. "He's out back. You can just go on around."

The guy was happy to take a break. He'd made two good looking piles, and they'd caught him raking dead leaves into a third. He stopped working when they approached. This time Keeler took point.

"Good technique you got there."

The guy said, "Can I help you?"

Keeler was aware of the wife in the house. Probably keeping an eye out from the back window. They had a screened-in porch at the back.

He said, "I'm a legal investigator. My client's a law firm in town. I just wanted to ask you a couple of questions about your driving work."

"Which law firm?"

"Finnegan, Coldfield, and Thompson. They've got an office right in town. You can't miss it."

"Yeah, I've seen that office. What do you need to know?"

"It'd be real helpful if you could tell us about the people you drive for."

The man shrugged. "Just rich people. Come here to get custom designed horses. I pick em up from the airport and take them to their accommodation."

"The local airport?"

"Irville Nashport. Private airport out past the lake."

Keeler glanced at Madeline, who gave him a little nod.

Keeler said, "Where's the accommodation?"

He said, "They stay at the KD ranch."
Madeline said, "Anyone staying there now?"
"I think there's a couple there now, yes ma'am."
Keeler waited until they got back into the van.
He said, "You know where that is?"
"Yes I do."

Chapter Fifty-One

An hour earlier than that, Laura made it to Beachy's farm. She wasn't injured, and the recent events had put the wind at her back, in terms of energy and motivation. She had no idea what those freaks had actually intended to do with her. Make her pregnant? Implant the little creature and set her up so she'd be carrying someone else's baby? The entire sequence of events was insane. She kept turning it over in her mind as she jogged through the woods. Is that what they were doing? Turn her into a surrogate mother, like the other girls?

She alternated between cursing and thinking that thought. It wasn't a very constructive process, but it did mean that before she knew it she was coming up on the little path behind the horse barn. Burning that hell hole to the ground would have to wait.

What she did know about Mennonites, was that they wake up early. They were pretty Benjamin Franklin about things. *Early to bed, early to rise, makes a man healthy, wealthy, and wise.* Although, Franklin hadn't been a Mennonite, as far as Laura was aware. He'd been a puritan or Calvinist.

She came around the barn quietly. There was always a chance that the bad people would know about her connection to the Beachy family. It was public knowledge that she'd been riding one of Beachy's horses when the incident occurred. That had been put out there in the initial hearing, after she'd turned herself in.

She crept around the barn, hearing and smelling the horses in there. Ginny whinnied from inside. That fact instantly warmed Laura's heart. The horse could smell her, was aware of her. She hadn't connected in that way with many horses in her life.

By that time, a dim blue glow had begun to appear at the horizon.

Laura continued past the barns and took the trail through the trees to the main house. She'd never actually been inside Beachy's house but had seen it often enough. Usually she parked at the back side, near the horse stables.

She'd put the gun and phone into the jacket pockets and had it zipped up against the cold. It was freezing out, but Laura was warm from the exertion. The trail was covered in an arc of tree branches dropping just over her head. They made a tunnel. She came out of it and stopped for a moment. There was a noise from up ahead.

Laura got very quiet, very quickly. She removed the pistol from her jacket pocket and took a step to her right, pressing herself into the thick growth. There she stayed, figuring that with the half-light, she would be pretty much invisible.

There was movement ahead, maybe twenty yards away. Laura had the weapon down at her side. She brought it up in a ready position, pistol pointed in a diagonal at the ground a few feet away. If there was an accidental discharge, it would go into dirt.

The thing came closer and Laura could see in a flash that it wasn't human. A doe was moving through the brush. She put the gun away and stepped out into the path.

In a quiet voice she said, "Shoo."

The animal froze for a moment and then dashed away, crashing hell bent through the woods. She'd never hunted, but knew that when a deer is wounded, the first reaction is to get as far away from the source of danger as possible. For that reason, wounding a deer is considered bad form by hunters. You need to be able to take the right shot and put it down humanely.

Otherwise, a hunter has to track it down to where it went to hide. It was terribly common for a wounded deer to die without the hunter ever finding it again. Something would, though. A scavenger like a coyote or bobcat, or even crows.

The deer's headlong flight through the woods lasted for quite a while. It was so quiet out that Laura could hear it moving away for almost thirty seconds. When the silence returned, she started moving again. A few steps later there was a sound from ahead which made her freeze once more.

A voice said, "Stop right there."

Laura stopped. Beachy walked out of the trees with a shotgun aimed right at her.

He said, "Who is that?"

"It's Laura."

"Laura?" Beachy put the weapon down. Coming closer. "What are you doing here? I got the alert from the stables."

Beachy was dressed in jeans and a flannel shirt. He was hatless and bald on top. She'd only ever seen him with a hat.

She said, "What alert?"

Beachy said, "We've had thieves poking around. The system alerts me if someone's approaching at night." He was staring at her wide eyed. "What happened to you? Come inside. You look half froze to death."

Laura felt an involuntary relaxation of her tensed muscles.

Something positive was out there. Someone who cared. A good person. She followed Beachy to the house.

Laura said, "My husband Josh is coming. It's a complicated situation. Do you mind if I tell you all about it when he gets here? I don't want to say it twice."

"Of course."

"Thanks, Beachy."

They came in through the back porch.

Beachy said, "Everyone's asleep. Let's try and be quiet, shall we?" He looked at her carefully. "Have you been in the hospital?" Pointing at her clothing. "That's a hospital gown."

Laura said, "Something like that." She gave him what she hoped was a convincing, imploring look. "Beachy, I'm in serious trouble. I want to call for help, but I don't trust the police. I'm afraid the cops are in on the whole thing. I know it sounds nuts. They're doing horrible things over by the Amish Auction. It's unreal. They've got girls pregnant over there. Surrogate mothers for who knows who."

Beachy was staring at her with wide-open eyes. "Oh my."

He led her into the living room. There weren't any Mennonite quilts to be seen. Just a regular living room with a leather sofa and accompanying armchair and ottoman. The walls were lined with book cases.

Beach said, "You sit yourself down. I'm heating up oatmeal. We'll get some food into you. Coffee?"

"Yes, please."

Beachy disappeared into the other room. She could hear him banging around in there trying his best to be quiet. The stove clicked on and then the sounds of the faucet. Laura took off the horrible man's shoes and swung her legs up onto the sofa. Stretching her legs felt amazing. She propped her head against the pillow and brought out the phone.

It was locked, and she didn't have that guy's face to conveniently use for opening it.

A few minutes later, Beachy came in with a bowl of oatmeal and a mug of coffee.

"Here you go, Laura. Do you want to tell me what's going on?" He was clearly out of his depths.

"Let me eat this first Beachy, then you'll be the first to hear this damned story. Sorry, is that a blasphemous thing to say?"

He said, "Not blasphemous, Laura. I'd say it's mildly profane."

She ate. The oatmeal was good, with raisins and butter and a pinch of salt. It was also very sweet with maple syrup.

"That's really good."

And it was. She literally wolfed it down. Once half of the oatmeal had been consumed, Laura took a break and attacked the coffee. She took a sip of the hot brew and came up for air. There was a sort of bitter aftertaste left in her mouth.

Beachy watched her eagerly. "Good?"

"Yeah. Did you put sweetener in it?"

"No. The coffee's just black."

She went back to the oatmeal. It was very tasty. Maple syrup, nuts, raisins, the salt and butter. Laura finished the bowl off and set it back down on the coffee table. She put her feet back up on the sofa.

Beachy said, "Make yourself comfortable. Do you know when your husband will be getting here?"

"Not exactly. He was in Cleveland. Josh said it'd take an hour and forty-five minutes."

Beachy nodded. "Cleveland's usually a two-hour drive, but it's early morning on a weekend so he very well could be here sooner."

Beachy's face was all red, like he was hot or something.

She said, "Are you all right Beachy? You look sick."

"I am okay, Laura. I'm very concerned for you is all."

She nodded because that made sense. A guy like Beachy was the epitome of a god-fearing man.

She said, "Beachy, I'm just going to take a short nap until Josh gets here." She was watching him under hooded lids. "Can you hold the fort?"

"Sure Laura. I'll hold the fort. Do you want more coffee?"

"I'm good."

Beachy picked up the bowl and went back into the kitchen. Laura closed her eyes. She heard a whispered conversation in there. Probably his wife. There was a female voice and Beachy's low voice. Then the voice of a kid, maybe his son or daughter, she couldn't tell.

The kid's voice stopped and a door was closed. There were a few hushed voices from the kitchen and then Laura faded out. It was like a transition in a movie, one thing transforms into another. She was hearing those hushed voices and seeing the coffee table in her mind. A low, rectangular object with round lacy things on it. What do you call them, doilies?

The transition wasn't visual, it was audio. It felt like she was looking at the same thing in her mind but the unseen things surrounding it were different. It was a heart-thumping shock when she realized where she was, in that dream. Back home with her dad, the last time.

Chapter Fifty-Two

She'd been older, probably seventeen. Tom was gone to the military, and they'd moved yet again. This time to a place outside of Denver. Her dad hadn't gone at her for a couple of years. Mom was out working.

Laura had come home from school, grabbed a donut from an Entenmann's box in the kitchen. She'd kicked off her shoes and dove backwards on to the sofa. The sugar-dusted donut was in hand, and a glass of milk sat on the coffee table. Same kind of coffee table, with dumb white doilies that came with the house, that her mom thought were funny.

The living room ceiling was super high. What they call a vaulted ceiling. The bedrooms were accessed via a weird switchback staircase to the mezzanine. There was even a third floor where Dad had his "office."

Laura finished the donut and the milk. She remembered feeling very, very comfortable, but not quite as comfortable as she'd be in her own bed.

She came up the stairs super lethargic. Head down like the teenager she was, hands gripping the ancient banister, pulling herself up. The banister actually wobbled under her palm. Dad was supposed to fix it. The entire place was half falling apart, but they'd rented it because it was available and kind of great.

The next thing Laura knew, Dad was there on the stairs above the landing, blocking her way. Everything was fragmented into single images in her memory. Her father, the enemy, looking wildly out of sorts. Drunk most likely, startling her and then rushing down to the landing and grabbing at her.

Laura had ducked to the side, under his grabby hand. She darted low and to the right. Really just to escape him. He slipped and crashed into the banister, which made a cracking sound as the rickety joints gave way. Laura turned, looking at him closely. He was maybe three feet away, regaining his balance, back to the banister.

What she remembered most intensely was the great feeling of calm that suddenly settled over her. As if she had power. It's nothing she'd ever felt before. She'd always felt at a disadvantage to others, weaker, less confident. Looking back on it, her brother had been correct. She needed to spend time without him. To become herself. What did he say exactly, *I'm getting out of your hair so you can get ready for your own self.*

Laura took a single step and shoved her degenerate father, putting everything she had into his chest. He was no father to her; he was just a bad guy. The banister gave way and the bad guy fell soundlessly. The fall took maybe, a second. It seemed instantaneous, followed by the crunching thump as he landed. She looked down at him, her not-father, spread-eagled on top of the destroyed coffee table. One of the doilies had fallen to the floor by the sofa. The others lay crushed under him. His face looked happy.

* * *

It seemed as if only minutes had passed, but Laura's eyelids began to tremble and she realized that she'd fallen asleep. The coffee table was still there, and the doilies were different anyway. There was noise from outside. Hard to tell if it was in the kitchen, or the entrance where Beachy had brought her into the house.

The sounds echoed strangely.

Clamorous ones, like banging or something. And then what might have been a gunshot. All of it came through Laura's ears like sound run through a filter. As if the noises were affected electronically. She'd woken up on her side, looking straight at the coffee table. Literally drooling on the couch. Now, she attempted to turn onto her back and get up, but that wasn't working.

She heard a shout and recognized Josh's voice saying an entire sentence worth of words. None of which she was able to understand. It sounded like backwards gibberish. Another crash from out there seemed to reverberate in a delayed echo.

Although she had a hard time moving. Even realizing she'd tried to move came late, like the thought had to travel. Laura found herself partway on her back. Enough to see a person come into the room. This person was not Beachy. It was a woman. Beachy's wife.

Laura opened her mouth to say, *Ma'am*, but that word did not come out. What came out was more like *jam*. The woman was pasty-faced in a denim dress and a plaid shirt. She looked angry. The woman's mouth opened, but no words came out. She turned away and left. Only then did the words she had said reach Laura's addled brain in delayed reverberation.

"You're not going anywhere, you little hussy. We won't have the family ruined because of you."

Then Beachy was there. Everything weirdly blurred and distorted. He was hushing his wife by the door and Laura couldn't understand why she was having trouble perceiving the situation.

Beachy's face came closer to her, all red and weird and puffy.

He said, "Laura, I've given you a high dose of horse tranquilizer. It's all that I had in the house. Everything will be alright, but you will be incapacitated for a little while."

"Incapacitated." She managed to throw herself off the sofa and landed face down on the rug between the coffee table and the sofa. A fuzzy, woolen rug. She couldn't seem to get her face out of it. Laura said, "Josh."

Beachy said, "I had no choice Laura. It's my family." She could see that he was crying, tears rolling down his plump cheeks. "I didn't tell them about the gun."

Then Beachy was seemingly far away. Laura became aware of the door closing and the feeling arose in her that she was completely alone and that something bad had happened to Josh. Laura attempted to crawl but had no ability to do so. There wasn't even the most remote possibility of standing up. Simply getting up on her knees seemed impossible. She couldn't even get a curse word out of her mouth.

So, she lay there like a tranquilized horse. That was the only thing that ran through her mind, on her back finally, but immobile and breathing hard. She said, "Tranquilized horse."

Chapter Fifty-Three

The KD ranch wasn't anyplace that Madeline had been. But it was a place that she'd heard of. The reason for that was the sign they had out on route sixty for the ranch. That sign had been there for as long as anyone could remember. Going on twenty years at least. Not a huge sign, but a discreet one, with just the letters *KD, 2 miles* with an arrow to the left, carved into a thick hunk of wood and stuck on a pole.

She said, "KD ranch. Always figured it was a place with horses right? That's what a ranch is to us folks out here in Ohio."

Keeler said, "I always thought a ranch was about the cattle."

She laughed. "Well, I guess so. But the horses are necessary for wrangling the cattle. Hence the ranch."

Keeler was observing their location with Valdez's phone. The left turn off route sixty went directly to the ranch. A private road. He preferred a more oblique approach.

He said, "Go straight past that left turn with the sign. You'll take the next left."

She said, "That'll take us up to the old cemetery."

Keeler saw it on his map. *Marquand Mills Cemetery.*

"Yes."

Which turned out to be a good staging point for their little surveillance routine. The cemetery was both old and small, with an abandoned chapel in the back that could serve as a good place to park up discreetly. He'd put the previous drone back into its docking station. There were a dozen of the flying devices in the van. A dozen docking stations all lined up on one of the rear walls. Keeler chose one that had a full charge and set it loose. Same drill, him on the controller with the goggles and Madeline running the contextual view.

Five minutes later he had the drone zipping high in the air moving northwest. From up there, it was clear the area was a huge forest in every direction.

He said, "What is this place, a national park or something?"

Madeline said, "I don't know if it's a national park, but it's definitely a place we used to go to in order to get wasted in private. When I was a kid that is."

"You used to get wasted?"

"Still do, once in a while."

Less than half a minute later the ranch was visible from above. It stood out because it was landscaped and groomed, with gardens and organized trees arranged over rolling hills around several sizable buildings.

Keeler said, "That's it I guess. What do you see?"

Madeline said, "Looks like five vehicles in the driveway. Two of them might be limos. They're black SUVs parked together. I guess the others would be staff cars."

Keeler had slowed the drone, creeping it along at a pretty high altitude. He wasn't able to see anyone walking around. Maybe the ranch guests were still sleeping.

Madeline said, "Let's bring it in closer and take a detailed look."

"Roger that."

Keeler brought the drone lower so that he was skimming

over the forest canopy. The drone broke away from the trees, over a tennis court. Beyond that was the landscaped area in front of what he assumed was the main house. A man stepped away from a tree in the middle of that grassy stretch. He had a shotgun up, aimed right at the drone.

Madeline said, "Oh shit."

Keeler sent the drone zipping up into the sky. The image went sideways, and the drone stabilized itself. He backed the drone off over the trees.

Madeline said, "They're going to the limo."

Keeler had been focusing on the man with the shotgun, who was now standing in the middle of the lawn staring at the drone.

She said, "Two people are getting into the limo. I think there's a driver in the vehicle waiting for them. He wasn't outside before."

Keeler said, "Luggage? Maybe they're going to the airport."

"No luggage."

Keeler saw them. Too small in the image to identify. He now backed the drone away, hoping it would be far enough from the property that the guard would think it had gone.

He said, "What are you thinking?"

"I don't know."

Keeler said, "Doesn't matter where they're going. Get the van on the road. We'll intercept them."

"What about the drone?"

"I'll operate until it loses connection."

* * *

Keeler had seen the map. He knew how it was going to play out. To get in front of the limo, Madeline would need to put the pedal to the metal. While she drove, he was in a parallel world.

The goggles gave him a first person view from the drone. She drove them, and he drove the drone.

In Keeler's world, the drone cut over the woods until it was hovering above the long driveway from the KD ranch to route sixty. A minute and a half later the black SUV limo came into sight, rolling over a hill in the direction of route sixty.

Keeler said, "I see them. How long until we're at the turn off?"

She said, "A minute maybe. What do I do when I get there?"

"You block their way. The best would be if you could do that up the road so folks on route sixty don't see it."

"Okay, the problem with that is I'm no race car driver."

Keeler said, "Pull over and I'll drive."

"Gladly."

He ripped the goggles off and killed the drone controller. Madeline pulled over, and they hurriedly switched places. Keeler got the vehicle moving.

She said, "You want me to take over the drone?"

"No. Strap in and hold tight."

The same exact sign for the KD ranch whipped by with an arrow pointing to the right, not the left. Keeler made the right exactly two miles later. He hit the gas. The narrow single track road carved uphill. They were invisible from the main road after fifteen seconds. The SUV hove into sight. The limo driver slowed. Keeler pulled the van in a diagonal across his path, forcing the man to brake hard.

Chapter Fifty-Four

By the time the driver had recovered from that maneuver, Keeler was out of the van with the Smith & Wesson up, moving fast to the driver's side window.

Keeler yelled at him, trying to instill a sense of urgency. "Hands on the wheel."

The two in the back were just figures at that point. The reflection on the windshield was too bright to make them out. The driver had his hands on the wheel when Keeler got to the vehicle. His window was up.

Keeler pulled the door latch. It was locked. He aimed a sharp focused strike at the lower corner of the window, shattering the tempered glass. The driver's eyes bugged, and he started hyperventilating.

Keeler reached in and ripped the keys out of the ignition. "Out of the vehicle."

The two in the back were the same couple from the diner. The New York City people. Keeler didn't aim the pistol at them.

He said, "You two get out."

The driver had some issues with the lock, fumbling. Keeler

helped him by reaching in for the latch. He pulled the driver out by the lapel of his suit jacket. By that time Madeline was behind him.

Keeler said, "Get the phones."

She said, "What?"

"Take their phones." He pushed the driver towards Madeline. "Give her your phone."

The couple slid open the door. The guy came first. A man in his forties, looking healthy and fit. Already had his mouth open, no doubt preparing some convincing words to do with his wealth and power. Keeler knocked him in the side of the head with the gun barrel, immediately silencing him.

His wife gave a sharp cry as if her husband had been shot in the face. Keeler pulled them both out of the vehicle and pushed them into the woods at the side of the road.

He said, "Nobody's getting hurt here unless you're looking to be. I'm going to ask you a couple of simple questions. First, I need your phones."

The woman handed her purse over. "It's in there. Just take whatever you need."

"I don't want to take anything from you."

The man had his palms up as if he were trying to demonstrate how unthreatening he was.

He said, "Man, you don't know what you're doing. We're not just some dumbasses you can rip off."

Keeler said, "Give my friend your phone and shut up. I'll tell you when to talk."

The guy reached into his jacket and handed the phone to Madeline.

The woman said, "What is it you want from us?"

Keeler said, "Stay there."

He backed up to where Madeline was standing. Spoke quietly into her ear.

"Get the woman across the road. Ask her what she's doing here. If she says she's buying a horse, ask her what the horse's name is. The other question to ask is what breed it is."

"Ok."

Keeler pointed to the woman. "You go across the road there. My friend wants a little conversation. Nothing's going to happen to you."

The woman walked across the road.

Keeler waited for her to get there. He looked at the man.

"It's really simple. What are you doing in Trace Junction?"

He said, "We came here to buy a horse."

"And you bought one?"

"Yes."

"What's its name?"

The man looked at him stupidly. "Its name?"

Keeler said, "Yes. The name of the horse. What's its name?"

The man was clearly trying to remember what to say. He said, "It doesn't have a name yet. It's a cloning facility. We came up here to choose the genetic characteristics."

"What did you choose? What are your horse's genetic characteristics?"

The man said, "I'm actually not an expert. Just wanted a decent horse, so I chose some stuff."

"You just wanted a decent horse?"

"That's correct."

Keeler nodded. "Okay."

He waited until Madeline had questioned the woman. They both came back across the road.

Madeline said, "No name. They ordered a cloned horse, and she doesn't know shit about horses."

Keeler said, "In other words they're lying."

"That's what I think, yes."

Keeler turned to the guy, who looked as if he was going to be sick. The driver was pale.

The driver said, "Can I smoke?"

Keeler said, "Go right ahead. This is America." He addressed the man. "What will happen now, is I'll put a bullet into your knee. We don't have time to fuck around. I need to know what you're doing in Trace Junction."

The man gulped, his face now reddened. "I told you. We're here for a horse. It's not our damned fault that we can afford a horse. You can't blame us for having money, we worked hard for everything we've got. I wasn't born rich."

Keeler said, "I'm not blaming you for anything. I'm just asking a question is all. Now that's your last chance to walk straight for the rest of your life. You want to answer my question?"

The man was stubborn. Staring at Keeler hard, seemingly unable to do the right thing.

The woman said, "I'll tell you, goddamn it. There's no need to shoot my husband in the fucking knee." She had broken into tears. Her face was wet with the sudden outburst. Her voice came out shrill and emphatic. "We lost our son. Our son. We lost him and they said we can have him back. That's why we're here. Alright?"

Keeler glanced at Madeline, who was transfixed by the woman's outburst.

He said, "What do you mean, you can have him back?"

The woman said, "It's what they told us. They can bring him back to life and then Danny will be home again. He was only six when he died. It won't be that different."

Madeline said, "What does that mean, bring him back to life?"

The guy had lost the rigidity of his tone. Softening and resigned to what was happening. "Cloning. They're making a clone of our son. That's why we're here. He's supposed to be born this week, so we're waiting to take him home."

Keeler said, "And then what, you take your cloned son back home and give him the same name as your dead son?"

The woman said, "Please. I am begging you. Don't do anything to jeopardize our son. Please. We are not bad people."

Keeler looked at the driver, staring in rapt attention. The driver raised his hand in the air. "I have no idea what is going on. What she said."

Madeline walked closer. A mixture of horror and rage burned in her eyes. She went straight to the man. "What exactly do you mean by cloning? How do you get the DNA out of him for these people to use? How does this work?"

The man said, "Danny was sick for a number of years. I was contacted by someone on social media and directed to a dark-web site." He shrugged. "What can I say? I believe them. It was very convincing. They can really do it."

Keeler said, "What did you do, give them the body?"

He shrugged. "They told me to buy a freezer chest and showed me how to modify it. You don't need to freeze the body. You just need it preserved. The team came up and did their work extracting the DNA, and then we buried Danny."

Madeline said, "But it's illegal, what you're doing. It's not legal to clone human beings."

The man said, "Well, they're doing it all the time, miss. Believe me. You think the North Koreans and Chinese aren't cloning people? You're naïve."

Keeler said, "How much did you pay up front?"

"Ten million."

The woman was sitting down and sobbing in a heaving fit. The man bent to her.

"Come on. Let's go back to the place." He stood and glared

at Keeler. "And now what, you're going to stop them? Call the cops?"

Keeler said, "That's right. We're going to stop them. People are dying and suffering because of the fantasy that you bought. Go back to the ranch and cry me a river, buddy. You're going to face the music."

The woman said, "What do you want us to do?"

Madeline said, "You stay put and wait for the law." She looked at Keeler. "I'm going to keep their phones and take a picture of them, just in case."

Keeler grunted. "Good idea."

Madeline nodded and got busy.

Chapter Fifty-Five

In the van, Madeline put the couple's devices into the glove compartment.

She said, "That's it?"

"No that's not it. My brother-in-law is apparently somewhere near the Amish auction. Where we should have gone before."

Madeline was driving. She took a right on route sixty, back the way they'd come. Keeler was just going to let her drive. Let the new information seep into his brain and fill the spaces where knowledge should live—known or unknown, understood or misunderstood. He glanced at Madeline, her mouth was in a horizontal line. Neither happy, nor sad. A mood of grim determination somehow.

Cloned versions of dead kids, for sale to extremely wealthy people. The babies carried by surrogate mothers forced into this insane labour because they were trafficked migrant women.

Keeler said, "Well, they always said that the cartels are evil. They weren't kidding."

Madeline flashed him a look. "It's not funny."

"I'm not laughing."

"You sound like you are."

Keeler said, "Maybe, but I'm not."

She said, "I don't want my daughter growing up in a world where this kind of thing happens." Looking at him again, like it was his fault.

"I don't want that for her either."

"So what are we going to do about it?"

Valdez's phone rang. Keeler looked at the screen. Josh's phone number.

He answered. "Yeah."

Josh said, "Bro. I've been trying to get in touch with you."

Which sounded very unlike Josh, a man who spoke more formally than that. An almost uncomfortably introverted person. Certainly Josh wouldn't use the term *bro.*

Keeler said, "Okay. Where are you?"

"Beachy's house. He said you know where it is. I'm with Laura."

"Put her on the phone."

Josh said. "Can't do brother. She's sleeping. It's been tough for her but she's okay now. We're waiting for you."

"I'll be there."

Keeler hung up the phone. Madeline looked at him.

"Your brother-in-law?"

"Yeah. He called me bro, and brother. Which means something's very wrong over there." Glancing at her. "The guy doesn't actually like me."

Madeline glanced at him again. "What do you mean? He was speaking in code, trying to tell you something?"

Keeler shrugged. "Might be. It's totally out of character, but someone outside of the family wouldn't know that about us. That we're not close at all. So, he could have used that language to tell me that he's under duress."

"Maybe this will all work out real good for your relationship."

"Maybe."

Madeline said, "Where are we going?"

"I don't know exactly how to tell you. It's in a place called Hollow Hills. I guess you know where that is. Pull over for a minute and I'll look at a map."

Madeline pulled over at a picnic area with a pond. Keeler worked on the map with the sheriff's phone. He found Beachy's farm using the satellite feature and showed it to her.

She nodded. "I know where that is."

"Good. I want to get Kennedy into this. Can you think of a good place to meet up within scouting distance of that farm?"

Madeline thought about it. She tapped and zoomed around the map. "Yeah, that's Hollow Hills, and east of that is Belleville. There's a kind of country-style log cabin place just to the north of there. It's been under construction for years. Kind of thing that ran out of money, or the partners started arguing. We could stage from there."

"Gotcha."

Keeler called Kennedy and made the arrangements. Madeline got the van back on the road.

* * *

While they waited for Kennedy to show up, Keeler did some tests with the drones. They hadn't had much time earlier to play around. So now, he got familiar with the swarm settings. The things were very cool. You could control up to six at a time, switching between them. Keeler understood now, why the drones had attacked one at a time. Because that's how it worked. The controller switched between devices, depending upon where the action was happening.

Each of the drones was autonomous. They weren't going to fall down or hit a tree. While one drone was controlled by Keeler, the five others would follow its lead, setting up in a fixed pattern, or shifting into a variety of patterns that he was never going to have time to learn about.

The other thing to figure out was the C4 charges that had been modded to fit onto the drones. The plastic explosives had been shaped into little packages weighing maybe a hundred and fifty grams. They were fastened to the drones with a small 3D-printed attachment that clipped onto another gizmo fixed to the drone itself.

The part that fastened to the explosives included a detonator housing with wiring that clicked right into a receptor on the drone's underside. These were clever little things. Which reminded Keeler that there was someone out there who'd had a good time with a circular saw blade. That was one person who needed to get payback.

Bobby Kennedy rolled up just as Keeler finished setting up the remaining drones with explosive charges. Kennedy came in very nonchalant.

"What's going on, fellers?"

Madeline was sitting on the tailgate with her legs swinging free.

She said, "Keeler's doing some doctor death shit in there."

But Keeler was done. He came out, squeezing past her and made the short jump to the ground. The place was only partly finished. A half dozen log cabins set in a perimeter around a fire pit area. Someone's idea of a vacation spot project that had run into problems. Three of the cabins were built. The others had fallen into disarray with time.

He clapped Kennedy on the shoulder. "Glad you could make it, pal." Swiveling back to look at Madeline. "I guess you should tell Bobby Kennedy here what we're dealing with."

She told him about the surrogate scheme, and he refused to believe it.

"There is no way that's true."

Keeler and Madeline shared glances.

Keeler said, "Be that as it may, it's not what's important at the moment." Madeline nodded at him, like she approved of the direction he was taking. Keeler gave her a slight tilt of the head in return. "The situation here is ambiguous. My brother-in-law is at a property, just south of our position."

His plan was simple. Keeler would go in by himself. What he didn't want, was a fleet of buzzing drones announcing his presence, and the fact that he expected a hostile reception. What he would do, was carry the drones in his pack. Setting them down at tactical locations. He'd keep the phone line open with Kennedy and Madeline, keeping an audio connection with him as he progressed.

Keeler said, "The drones have a twenty-minute battery life. Less if they're flying. I'm going to leave them on standby, as close to the house as I think is possible without being seen."

That way, Kennedy could operate the swarm on Keeler's command. The controller had hot buttons that could be assigned commands. That was set in the application level. The x button detonated the drone's charge.

Keeler said, "Don't blow me up please."

Kennedy said, "I won't."

"Good."

He got busy with the sheriff's shotgun, a Remington 870 Police model. The weapon held six shells in the magazine tube, plus one in the chamber. Valdez had fired four shells during her escapade. Keeler replenished the magazine tube with ammunition from Valdez's bandolier and put the remaining handful of shells in his jacket pocket.

Kennedy got a look at the hunting bow fixed to his pack. He

was shaking his head and making eye contact with Madeline. She was just looking at Keeler with wide eyes, like she'd never seen anything like it.

Keeler said, "What?"

Madeline said, "Nothing. I guess, be careful."

Which made him smile. "I'll try to be." Looking at Kennedy. "You good to go there, boss?"

"I am." He was still ogling Keeler's gear. Kennedy said, "The hunting bow, the knife, shotgun and a bag full of drones. What else does a man need? You're a bad motherfucker, aren't you?"

Keeler said, "I'm the worst thing that ever hit these people. They're all going to die."

Madeline took a deep breath and shook out her hair. Keeler couldn't keep from staring at her. She'd flushed. He turned away and walked into the woods.

Chapter Fifty-Six

Once out of sight, Keeler was in his element. Solitary, moving towards a target, with a high probability of imminent danger to life and limb. The edge of action. Beachy's house was a half mile away. Not so far. He'd be there within ten minutes. There was no need to walk fast or be in a hurry. Whatever there was to find at Beachy's farm would still be there in ten minutes. The autumn foliage was pretty nice out there.

Keeler hit the command on Valdez's phone to call Kennedy. Kennedy answered.

"Yeah. We're on."

Keeler said, "Good. Going on silent mode."

They were in touch. Keeler put the phone on speaker and then muted his own speaker so that there would be no accidental sonic discharge. He slid the phone into a zipped breast pocket, leaving the zipper open. Kennedy would be able to hear everything that happened around Keeler, but Keeler wouldn't hear them. It was just the way it had to be, and he didn't mind it.

Five minutes later, he slowed into stealth mode. He could feel the wind coming in from open fields, carrying the odor of cow shit to his nostrils. The chicken coops would be on the south-western side of the property, near the road. Keeler was walking in from the north. The horse barns would be south east of the house. He was now close enough to seed the drones. Keeler began placing them in semi-concealed spots. Near enough to trees and rocks that they'd be hard for a casual observer to spot, yet not close enough to prevent the thing from operating freely.

A few minutes later the house came into view. At least, that's what Keeler figured it must be, as he hadn't seen it before. A two-story farmhouse painted blue with white trim and dark shutters framing the windows. It stood alone, surrounded by the woods on the north and east sides. Keeler paused, observing. A truck sat parked beside the house, and a swing moved gently on the porch. Small signs of life, but everything was quiet, calm.

He got busy seeding the drones in the vicinity. He'd depress the button to power the device on and then leave it and move on to another location. Kennedy sent a thumbs up emoji, indicating that he'd received the device connection. Keeler leaned into the phone's microphone.

He said, "If this kicks off you'll want to check out buildings for vehicles and operators. Unless they've got people in the house."

There was no response expected. Keeler stood up and walked to the edge of the woods. He took a knee just inside the tree line and began to pay close attention to the house. Through the medium range finding scope, there was nothing either interesting, or moving, in any of the visible windows.

He moved laterally across the house so that he had a view at a different angle. From that position, he was able to see into one of Beachy's barns. Farm material and a tractor with several tractor attachments lined up against the wall and a hay loft at the back.

The front of the house seemed to be over on the other side. But why go through the front?

He spotted the electrical meter box mounted on the wall. Keeler drew his buck knife and pried at the metal cover until it popped open. Inside was a breaker switch. He used the tip of the knife to push the breaker to the off position. The house went dark.

Keeler went to a window right there beside the meter box. He looked in and saw what seemed to be a sitting room. The buck knife sliced through the mosquito screen. He tested the window and found it locked. It would be possible to get it open, but first he figured on trying the other available options. After slicing the bug screen out of the second window across, he was able to raise it.

Keeler put the pack through first and then the shotgun, leaning over and placing it carefully against the wall. He hauled himself over the sill. He didn't think he had been very loud. But the house was quiet as death. Which didn't tell him much. It was a big house, with carpeted floors. Floors that can suck up sound and muffle noises. He looked around, finding himself crouched there in what must have been Beachy's study. A large oak desk and an ancient computer monitor were prominent. There was nothing particularly Mennonite about the room. A day bed, the desk, an armchair with a little table next to it for the reading lamp.

The door was closed.

Keeler turned the knob slowly, pulling gently towards himself. The door was soundless on oiled hinges. That was the kind of guy that he expected Beachy to be. The type who meticulously maintains his house. A deceiving thought, because it was equally possible that Beachy embraced his inner slob while his wife slapped him upside the head three times a day to keep everything clean and tidy.

He found himself in a corridor. Straight ahead was an open door, through which he could make out a kitchen. He had a view of a range style oven with a gas stove top and a hood. There was a closed door on the right side of the hallway. To his immediate left was a shorter corridor ending in another closed door. Keeler took the left and tested the door. Unlocked. He opened it to find a bathroom.

Keeler tracked back to the corridor and came to a stop a couple of paces away from the door on the right. He could hear voices in there, but was unable to make out what they were saying. He approached and put an ear to the door. One voice now, possibly Beachy.

The voice said, "Yes, I'm starting to wonder about that myself."

A female voice answered. "Well, you can stop that right away."

From down the hallway came a creaking sound. The noise made Keeler's head swivel, the shotgun following. Nothing to be seen. He retraced his steps, one boot at a time. Slowly and surely, each foot coming down heel first, rolling onto the front of the boot's sole. The floor creaked under him and Keeler stopped.

Nothing. No sounds, no movement. No more creaking.

He walked backwards again to the door. Keeler turned the knob and entered, shotgun first.

Josh was strung up in the center of the room with his limbs skewed in all four directions. A ball gag was stuffed in his mouth and he looked like he'd been having a terrible time. The ceiling was vaulted, and ropes were tied to the far wooden beams, keeping Josh's body spreadeagled ten feet in the air.

Beachy and his wife were on the sofa. A coffee pot, three mugs, and a half eaten tray of what looked like homemade chocolate chip cookies occupied space on the coffee table.

Keeler said, "Who's the third coffee drinker?"

Beachy and his wife simply stared agog. Beachy began to stand up and Keeler stabbed the barrel of the shotgun into his chest, knocking the big man back down.

"Who's the third cup for?"

The floor creaked. Beachy stammered, the chest blow clearly painful.

Keeler felt someone's hot breath at the back of his neck.

He had opened the door inwards. His left foot was in contact with it. Now, he swiveled on the ball of that foot and moved behind the door, at the same time as his toe snapped it closed. There was a shot and Keeler felt a burning sensation on his right shoulder, but no force of impact. He got the shotgun level and let go with it single-handed. The recoil put some strain on his wrist. The door grew a jagged hole and something large and heavy went slap against the opposite wall of the corridor.

Keeler took a look. A man wearing a baseball cap, vaguely Hispanic. Now, nursing a very bad wound in his chest. He wasn't going to make it even two more minutes.

Keeler spoke into the phone. "Contact. Send in the drones."

He stepped into the room. "Where's my sister?"

Beachy said, "They have her. It was never my idea." The man looked to be in shock. "They threatened my family."

Josh didn't look good and Keeler wanted to cut him down, but to do so he would need to take his hand off the shotgun. He drew the buck knife and flipped it at the coffee table. The point thudded into the wood, vibrating softly.

"Cut him down Beachy. Nice and easy."

Beachy reached for the knife by leaning forwards from where he sat on the sofa. His wife's left temple received a large caliber bullet clearly meant for her husband. The bullet puckering the shape of her skull and killing her instantly. Her corpse fell against the arm rest, and began a slide into an ungainly position. It was like watching a sludge succumb to a gravitational pull. Beachy jumped up with a squeal. A second bullet nailed him in the throat and he gagged. By that time, Keeler had already taken a big step back into the corridor.

The gunfire had come from the kitchen. Or, some room adjacent to it. He moved to enter through the open door. A shower of bullets whipping across, kicking into the walls and kitchen tiling. Keeler retreated.

Interesting.

He swung around, moving back down the corridor. His sister hadn't been in the room with Josh and the Beachy family. Now it was just Josh, strung up. The man he'd killed was a mound of death right in front of the door, now half open with a large hole in it. Keeler didn't want to simply move past the opening. Maybe the shooter was waiting for him.

The options were two-fold. Either leap over the body or enter through the kitchen for a showdown. It was hard to choose. Keeler figured it would be best to go all gangbusters into the kitchen, figuring that he'd just come in low and fast around the corner. The shotgun had a decent spread, so there was a good chance he'd clear out the shooter. The whizz of a drone stopped him from doing so.

The drone buzz came from the room where Josh was strung up. Perhaps it had entered through an open window. Hopefully it was being piloted by Kennedy, not the enemy. The quad propellers screamed once and a blast quickly followed. The detonation came from the kitchen area. A heavy thud followed by breaking glass and splinters.

Keeler ran into the kitchen. Dust filled the air. He came around the corner, low and fast like he'd planned. On the other side of the kitchen, a man was crumpled into the table. As Keeler approached, he saw that the man's arm had sheared off at the shoulder. The head was missing.

Chapter Fifty-Seven

Keeler leaned forwards and spoke into the phone. "Nice going." He pulled the device and activated the speaker. He said, "Madeline, I want you to guide me. I'm in the kitchen. You guys see anything?"

Madeline's voice came through, strong and clear. "There are quite a few people after you Keeler. I think we should focus on taking some of them down first."

Kennedy's voice came on. "Get into cover somewhere. I've got ten of these things left."

Keeler said, "Roger that."

Madeline said, "Two men in the yard. East side of the house. Otherwise I think there's someone in the top floor."

Kennedy said, "There's definitely someone."

Keeler said, "Got it. Can you buy me a few minutes? I need to cut my brother-in-law loose."

Kennedy said, "Moving on the two in the yard now."

Keeler took the opportunity to go back into the living room. He retrieved the knife from where it had stuck into the coffee table.

"Josh, I'm taking you down now."

Josh didn't even have the energy to mumble. Saliva was dripping around the ball gag and his limbs would probably require months of rehabilitation to work as they had previously. There was definitely a possibility that tendons had snapped.

Keeler cut the legs down first. One at a time. He steadied Josh so his feet touched the coffee table.

He removed the gag.

"Can you put weight on your legs, Josh?"

"I don't know."

"Try."

Keeler had to stand on the table with Josh. He cut down one arm and then had to hold his brother-in-law tight to himself while he released the final limb. Josh flopped into his arms and almost caused them both to fall. Keeler got down first and lifted Josh onto the couch.

Josh slumped there. "I don't think I can move."

Keeler slapped him once, hard in the face. "Get off your ass and move. It's either that or die, *brother*."

Josh glared at him and the slim trace of a smile curled the edges of his mouth upwards. He forced himself to get up. There was an explosion in the yard, just outside the living room window.

Keeler lowered his mouth to the phone. "Talk to me. I've got Josh now. He needs to be extracted."

Kennedy said, "How?"

Keeler said, "I'm sending him out the front door. Just make sure there's nobody in his way." Seeing that Josh was paying attention. "You got this, Josh. Understand what's happening?"

"Yes."

Kennedy said, "Where's Josh going?"

"To the chicken coops." Chin pointing at Josh. "Get behind

the coops and hunker down. That should be far enough away from here."

Madeline said, "Okay. We're there and it's clear. Saw a man out back though, coming in the window."

Keeler said, "Got it thanks."

He pulled Josh up from the couch. The living room opened onto an entrance vestibule in the other direction. Keeler pushed Josh toward the front door. "Go."

Josh hobbled off. A couple of steps in, he was doing much better. Keeler turned away to address the guy who Madeline had said was coming in through the window. She'd also said that they'd seen someone moving around upstairs.

Keeler brought his lips to the phone. "When you can, check out the upstairs. I don't want to go up there if it's a trap."

Kennedy's voice. "Roger that."

A drone zipped around the corner and buzzed right in front of Keeler's face. Hovering there with its camera pointed to Keeler's left. He could see the C4 charge clipped to the thing's belly, insect-like. In a fraction of a second this device could spin and see him. The operator just needed to press a little button on the controller and he was strawberry jelly all over the room. Keeler ducked behind the drone and grabbed it with his left hand. He kept the camera facing away from him and set the shotgun down. With his free right hand he pulled out the wire array connecting the explosive payload to the drone's brain. He crushed the device in his fist and tossed it away.

The guy coming in the window would be close. Keeler crouched behind the sofa and waited. He counted to one entire minute. Which is a very long time to count in a situation like that. Took a lot of patience. Once he'd hit sixty seconds in his head, he popped up with the shotgun.

A guy right there in front of him, already creeping over the carpet, baseball hat set backwards on his head. The man held an

M4 carbine in the ready position, rifle up and tracking only slightly to the left of Keeler.

At precisely the same time as the 12 gauge Remington in Keeler's hands blew both the man's head and his hat against the wall behind him, the phone began to emit the panicked sounds of Kennedy and Madeline coming under fire.

The blast from the shotgun had been so loud that Keeler missed an important part of the shouted conversation coming from the phone.

He said, "What was that? I didn't hear."

Madeline's voice came from very close to the phone they were using. She was breathing hard.

"We're under attack. Retreating to one of the cabins. They've targeted the van. Kennedy took out two drones with his damned pistol."

Kennedy said something in the background. He couldn't make out the words.

"What did he say?"

Madeline said, "He says we're still operating but it might not last. Says to be prepared for that."

Keeler said, "Roger that."

Madeline said, "Are you okay?"

"All good."

Kennedy cursed in the background. A loud sound distorted the digital audio signal.

Keeler said, "What's going on?"

He got silence.

There was nothing Keeler could do for them. They'd have to figure it out. From upstairs he heard glass break. There was a shout and a blast, now quite recognizable as one hundred and fifty grams of C4 exploding into someone's body. The shaped charge had been blunted by the dense solidity of the very flesh it tore to pieces.

Kennedy's voice came over the open phone line. "Got that fucker."

Keeler said, "Good."

He was thinking about Laura. What was the end game? Clearly, Arturo had set a trap for them. Which Keeler had walked into eyes wide open. Now the trap had failed, bodies broken and cartel *sicarios* dead all over the Beachy house.

He spent the next five minutes clearing the house. Nothing was alive in there, except for him. The Beachys must have gotten their children to safety before the mayhem began.

Madeline's voice came over the phone line. "Keeler, do you hear me?"

"I hear you. What's the situation?"

Keeler was in the master bedroom upstairs. He sat on the Beachys' large bed.

She was out of breath still, but more calm than earlier. "They found us and Kennedy got some shrapnel. But he's still operating."

"Can he walk?"

"I don't think he can."

Keeler took the pack off. He had a drone in there and began unpacking it.

"Listen to me. You stay put. I'm putting a drone up. I'll try and see if I can get a look at where they're operating from. It'll be a van like the one you're in, or some other vehicle. How many drones do you have left?"

"He says we have three left."

Keeler said, "Conserve them. Give me five minutes."

Madeline said, "Okay."

He launched the drone from the bedroom window. Keeler quickly had it rise to several hundred feet. From there he had a good view of the property and its periphery. The main structures stood out. The house and chicken coops. Toward the east were the stables. Between the coops and stables was a large cornfield. On the other side of that was a dirt track lined with large trees. Most of the leaves had dropped, making it easy to see a big vehicle, like a Chevy Suburban or similar. He lowered his mouth to the phone and began speaking.

Chapter Fifty-Eight

Ten minutes earlier, Laura had emerged from the disoriented state she'd fallen into after Beachy had spiked her with a horse tranquilizer. The world still seemed wobbly and unstable, but at least she wasn't hearing things backwards, or in a weird delay. Between the time she'd fallen onto the carpet in Beachy's living room, and now, all kinds of things had happened. The problem was, she'd missed out on exactly what those things were.

Now, she found herself in the backseat of a car.

She was able to see things more or less correctly. The car was large, like a big SUV. That was one thing she noticed. Something very spacious. The leather seat felt cool and dry from the climate control. She was in the rear of the vehicle. Another row of passenger seats was just in front.

Piecing it together. She'd been in Beachy's house. Trusting him to help her. He'd tricked her. Bringing her in and then drugging her. Setting her up for the enemy.

A man was hunched over a set of monitors. Laura could see the back of his head. Arturo, that's what he'd said his name was. Another man was beside him, bald, with a spider tattoo on the top of his head. The two of them were discussing something pretty intensely. A low murmur of concentrated verbiage in Spanish. She understood nothing.

Okay, so after Beachy had betrayed her, this guy Arturo had taken her. And, Josh was involved. She'd heard his voice, but that could have been an effect of the horse tranquilizer.

Laura wiped the drool from her face. She'd been out cold. Horse tranquilizer, holy crap that stuff was weird. She'd literally heard things backwards. The man beside Arturo was younger and doing a lot of nodding to the boss. He glanced at Laura. The look sent a shiver down her spine.

Arturo turned. His face was large. The graying beard wild and badly in need of a trim.

He said, "Ah there you are. That idiot Mennonite knocked you out. I would have preferred you conscious and clear for what's going to happen today."

"And what's going to be happening today Arturo?"

He smiled then, beaming actually. "You remember my name. Well, that's really something."

Laura said nothing.

Arturo said, "Well you just go on and sit back. I'll put a movie on for you."

The interior of the SUV was set up as some kind of mobile command center. Controls and switches were mounted everywhere. The man got busy with a dashboard mounted to the back of the chair in front of him.

The screen in front of Laura flickered to life, and she was looking at the woods. Specifically, a drone's eye view flying through the woods.

Arturo turned back to look at her. He said, "They stole one of my vans. Now, we've found it. Your brother's at the house and will be killed soon. Let's watch his friends deal with a *Los Quebrados* drone swarm."

The drone's eye view switched and Laura knew she was looking at a second unmanned aerial vehicle. This one was exiting the woods into a clearing. Log cabins were spread around a construction site. Some unfinished with tarps over the roofs, others complete. The drone was high up and she saw a van parked behind one of the cabins.

Arturo said, "That's it."

The drone hovered up on high. Arturo and the man beside him weren't controlling it. The man was speaking into a radio.

"Ataque."

Clearly the Spanish version of attack. The drone dive-bombed the van in a split second. As it approached, Laura saw the van's front seats were empty. But maybe there were people in the back. The drone tumbled and went straight for the windshield. The image blinked out as, presumably, the thing exploded.

Arturo shouted. "Sí"

The image flicked to another drone's eye view. Coming out of the woods now, just like the previous drone. The thing speeding along at shoulder height, going right to the van. The vehicle's windshield was shattered and caved in. Laura got a sick feeling, knowing what the next move was. They'd fly it through the broken glass and detonate it inside.

If those were Keeler's friends, it meant they were her friends too. On her side.

The drone hovered above the van's hood. The pilot tried to navigate through the hole made by the previous suicide drone. The thing moved closer, probing the size of the hole. A man appeared in front of them, pistol in hand. The gun flashed and the drone tumbled. Its camera caught an oblique view of the grass.

The man beside Arturo said, "*Mierda*."

He quickly switched to a third drone, already descending on the van. It came in fast toward the busted windshield.

Arturo said something in Spanish. The guy repeated it into the radio. The drone hopped up and over the van. Laura could see a woman sprinting, about twenty yards out. The drone hovered for a second. The operator was probably deciding what to do.

The man who'd shot the first drone appeared again. He fired and missed.

Arturo said, "Sucker!"

The drone darted sideways. The man fired again.

Arturo said, "Get him."

The man turned, running now in a desperate sprint for safety. The drone whizzed in and exploded. The camera went dead. Laura's heart sank. She assumed he'd been one of Keeler's allies.

The two men up front burst into a flurry of Spanish. A fast, furious exchange that ended with the bald guy speaking into the radio. Static came through. Then a couple of sentences.

Laura had done a few years of Spanish in high school, and had very little to show for it. But very little isn't nothing. What she caught from the exchange was that they didn't have any more drones ready. Those three had been the attack squad. She figured they'd call in more, but it'd take a little time.

She pulled the door latch. It was locked.

Arturo said, "Don't do that." He nodded at the guy next to him.

The man reached into the footwell and came up with a thick black stick, like a short bat made of some carbon fiber material that sucked in the light. He swiveled over and pushed the stick into Laura's chest. The thing sizzled and clicked, and she was instantly caught in a full-body convulsion.

Laura lost consciousness for several seconds. Her muscles

locked up, the whole body quivering. The pain was immense, centered around her chest. When the spasm eased, she found herself face down in the footwell, gulping air. Her mouth filled with saliva and snot.

The baton got her again. That sadistic man jabbed it into her side. Laura lost consciousness again. When she came to, it felt like the blackout had lasted longer. A hand reached back with a tissue.

Arturo and the other man were watching her impassively. Arturo's mouth was slightly open, revealing the pink end of his tongue.

He said, "Okay, now you behave yourself girl."

Laura sat upright again, her chest still heaving.

The bald guy lit a cigarette. Arturo said something and the man rolled the window down. Laura leaned back against the left door, right behind Arturo. The bald guy with the spider tattoo took two leisurely drags. First, the smoke streamed out in a narrow plume. Then came a slower drag, exhaled through the nose.

There was a whizzing sound from outside.

Both Arturo and the bald guy twitched. The bald guy recoiled from the window. A drone came in fast and hard. Laura ducked and jammed her fingers in her ears. The blast was a dull thud. The vehicle rocked. Debris peppered her. She raised her head to see the bald man slumped in his seat. Part of his head was gone. Arturo was doing something she couldn't quite grasp.

She came upright and looked. He was clawing at his face.

Laura seized her chance. She leapt over the armrest dividing the two seats. She didn't care when she landed on the dead bald guy. She pulled the door latch and kicked it open. The electrocution baton was in the footwell. She grabbed it without thinking. Then, she was running for her life through a large field of drying corn. The plants brown, dry, rustling and crunching underfoot.

Chapter Fifty-Nine

Laura had never been a track star in high school, but she'd played soccer. Her position was mid field, and that's because she could run. But the mid-field soccer kind of running was a hell of a lot different to the way she was now sprinting through the corn field. She was running too desperately, and it wasn't sustainable. Particularly given that she had no idea where she was.

So, Laura slowed down, ducking her head so that nobody would be able to see her in all that tall dry corn. As soon as she stopped, there was nothing but silence.

No terrifying sounds like that incoming drone that'd sheared off a large part of the bald guy's head. Laura didn't know her location, but she figured she was still somewhere near Beachy's house. It also came back to her that she'd heard Josh's voice while under the influence of that horse tranquilizer. The drugs were still in her system and she felt weird. Of course, it was hard to detach that feeling from the situation she was in. That would make anyone feel strange, regardless of drugs.

She was about to set off again when there was a blast from

the direction she'd come in. A muffled explosion. She guessed it was a second drone attack. Another thought came to her mind.

Why run away, when you have no idea where you're going? That shithead Arturo had been wounded in the first attack. Maybe he was dead now, or at least incapacitated. She felt the baton's heft in her hand for the first time. It's uncool being the hunted, and much better to be the hunter. The dry corn was good for hiding in. So, why not go back and get him.

Laura turned and started moving back toward the vehicle, avoiding the path she'd already taken through the corn. The baton in her hand had two buttons. She pressed the first one with her thumb and the tip crackled with electricity. Alright, still some battery life in there.

She moved slowly. Her footsteps were necessarily noisy on the husks and dried debris. Each step had to be deliberate. Heel down, rolling onto the balls of her foot. Toes springing into the transfer of weight to the next foot. Laura found the rhythm, listening carefully, eyes open and constantly moving.

After a minute or so, she could see the vehicle through ten yards of corn. A Chevy Suburban, black, with the rear passenger window now blown out. That must have been a consequence of the second drone attack. She was going to have to break cover to reach the vehicle. She'd be out in the open for five yards.

Laura took a deep breath and committed herself. Three long strides to the edge of the corn, then a hustled crouch to the rear of the Suburban. Looking through the destroyed back window she could see the dead bald guy. No sign of Arturo.

"Shit."

She checked in the back again. Then started around the other side. Nothing in there. Suddenly, she didn't feel like a hunter anymore. She felt exposed. Laura kept low and took a good look around. There was nothing moving. Nothing notice-able except dried-out corn and the SUV.

Laura heard a bang and felt an impact on her left side, like getting hit by a baseball bat. The heavy blow spun her around and laid her flat on her face looking into dirt. She raised her head and glanced around. Nobody there. Who'd hit her with the bat?

Then, she looked down and saw the blood. It wasn't a bat. She'd been shot. There was movement in her peripheral vision and her heart was racing. Arturo came out of the corn. He was dragging his left foot, and his face was a mush of blood and flesh. As he came closer, Laura saw that his eye was missing. Yet there he was, smiling and breathing heavily. His right hand held a pistol.

He said, "You little shit. I blame you. If you hadn't existed, none of this would be happening. You're your own worst enemy, *Laura.*" He said her name with a mocking snarl.

Laura said nothing, waiting for him. She felt a wave of adrenaline coming through her bloodstream. Her face pressed into dirt. She saw the man shuffling toward her in peripheral vision. She waited until he was right in front of her. The electro-cution baton was still gripped in her right hand. Now stuck beneath her where she'd fallen.

Laura rolled over on her side. She brought the baton up and pushed it into Arturo's wounded leg. Her thumb went down on the button. The electric cackle was followed by a sharp high-pitched scream from Arturo. He jumped back.

"Bitch!"

She was now on her back. Looking into the sky and seeing him there, out of reach. The adrenaline faded, leaving her breathless. The fatigue started creeping in.

Arturo said, "*Laura.* That wasn't very nice, but I under-stand your concerns. Really, I do. How do you like it. Bullet in the head, or in the other leg. I could keep you going for a long time."

She didn't respond. The gun in his hand was pointed at her head. So that's how it was going to be.

Laura was a philosophical person. She'd sometimes wondered if it was better to die when you're fit and young, or let yourself slide into old age and ill health. If you let it go, wouldn't your memories of life be worse? Didn't people who allowed themselves to deteriorate end up bitter and angry with the world?

Despite the screwed-up beginning of her life, now she was in a good place. She'd liked Ohio, the horses, school, and eating barbecue with Josh twice a week. Sure, he was from New York City and looked stupid on a ride-along lawnmower. But, then again, everyone looks dumb on a lawnmower.

Arturo said, "Bye bye Laura. I've got to run. It's your time to die."

She was looking directly into his remaining eye, drawing a blank as to what to say, or even think. This was it?

Arturo's glance shifted suddenly. His head turned to the corn field, and she got a good look at his profile—a beaked nose over a stubborn mouth, set into a beard that could use a trim. He looked startled. Laura glanced toward whatever it was Arturo saw.

In that fraction of a second, she saw muzzle flash from the corn. Arturo's head took the shotgun payload and was instantaneously shredded. The shotgun boomed. His skull lost its oval shape and ballooned like a mushroom, the middle pulverized by the shot.

For a brief moment, the cartel boss swayed on his feet. He was certainly brain dead, but his other organs still worked. The body collapsed and crumpled to the ground. It became a simple corpse. Three seconds later, Laura's brother was standing over her with a shotgun. He looked rough, like he'd swum through a pool of blood and guts and come out intact.

She said, "Tom."

He said, "Shhh, don't talk."

He crouched down beside her and put down the shotgun. Her brother's hands moved over her, examining her for wounds. When he found the place she'd been shot, her brother got to work.

Laura said, "Is it bad?"

He said, "Could be worse."

Laura relaxed then for the first time in a long time. Her brother was there, and it was going to be alright.

Chapter Sixty

The entry wound was to Laura's lateral torso—right side, at the 9th rib, one of the *false* ribs. Keeler could feel through the skin the point of impact. The angle had been oblique, suggesting that Arturo had fired from Laura's 10 o'clock. A round had struck the rib and ricocheted along the surface—no full penetration. The false ribs aren't anchored directly to the sternum, which makes them more flexible. No exit wound, no signs of internal bleeding or collapsed lung. Probably cracked the rib, but the injury was not life-threatening.

Keeler was looking at his sister now. Her face flushed with adrenaline. The pain would hit soon.

He said, "How's it feel?"

Laura said, "Kind of stings."

"Yeah, that's going to become something worse."

She said, "I saw your friends getting attacked." Laura pointed at the Suburban. "They were watching it on screens. A woman and a man. Those are your friends right?"

He nodded at Laura. "My friends and yours."

Laura's eyes widened. "Josh! I forget that I heard his voice. Where is he?"

"He's okay. They had him at your friend Beachy's house. We'll pick him up out by the chicken coops." His sister had a big question mark written all over her face. He said, "Beachy got caught up in all of this. He didn't make it Laura."

She looked away. "Shit."

Keeler brought the phone out. The connection to Kennedy and Madeline had been lost. He dialed again.

Madeline answered. "Keeler?"

He said, "Yeah. What's your situation?"

"Same as before but quiet now." He heard her taking a deep breath. "We found their van. Where the drones were coming from. The whole thing exploded. It was insane."

Kennedy's voice was in the background. "Secondary explosions. They had mega shit in there." He sounded weak.

Keeler said, "Good to hear. I'm coming to your position."

Madeline said, "Bring a first aid kit. Kennedy's still bleeding. I thought I stopped it with a tourniquet, but it's seeping through."

"On my way."

There was a body in the Chevy Suburban's passenger seat. Keeler dragged it into the corn. He got Laura up and into a seated position. There would be a first aid kit at the farm.

Laura read his mind. "There's a first aid kit in the tack room, at the stables."

Keeler looked at her, raising his eyebrows. "Fantastic. We'll pick that up and then get your husband." His sister was looking pretty worn out. He said, "You look like shit by the way. Hopefully they have good drugs in the kit."

Laura said, "Thanks." But she smiled.

* * *

Madeline was holed up in one of the half-built cabins with light wounds to the side of her face and hip. Kennedy was slumped against a wall. The wound to his upper left thigh looked bad. He'd wrapped his t-shirt around it and Madeline had used a belt as a tourniquet. Keeler undid the bandaging and found a large steel ball bearing embedded in his quadriceps muscle. He cleaned the wound and packed it with gauze soaked in iodine, then added pressure with a clean bandage. Keeler secured everything tightly with medical tape. The bleeding slowed, but he could still see the muscle twitching under the skin, angry and inflamed.

He said, "You'll walk again, but not tonight," and propped Kennedy's leg up on a rolled jacket to reduce swelling.

Kennedy said, "What I need is a cold beer."

"Coming right up buddy."

He turned away from Kennedy to a window and brought out Valdez's phone. He could see Madeline sitting on the doorstep of an unfinished cabin. Her eyes were closed. She looked like she was meditating. Fatigue—that's what Keeler knew she was experiencing. He tapped in the number he had for Dr. Amanda Sobell, director of National Security Investigations, Homeland Security in Chicago. She picked up on the third ring.

"Keeler."

"Yeah. Where are you?"

Sobell said, "Uh, I'm actually eating a very good and fresh French cruller and looking at the strange remnants of what Pete here says was once the best diner in all of Ohio."

Keeler got a rush of anger. "How long have you been sitting there eating donuts?"

"Maybe five minutes."

He grunted. "Alright. I'll send you my location. Finish your donut and get here. Shit just went ape. You'll need more than your little bunch of investigators. If I were you I'd call in the big guns immediately."

Keeler could hear Sobell sipping, and knew exactly what kind of mug she had at hand. She was a cool customer. Back a couple of years ago he'd run into a situation and they'd cooperated briefly.

She said, "Keep your powder dry Keeler. I'll come by and see what you've got there, and then we'll see. Copy?"

"Roger that." He ended the call and handed the phone to Kennedy. "See if you can send our location to the number I just called. Think you can do that for me buddy? You can give the phone back to Valdez when you see her."

Which would probably be in the hospital.

"No problem." Kennedy got busy.

Keeler walked out of the cabin. Laura and Josh were a unit, sitting side by side on the big Chevy Suburban's tailgate, hugging each other. Madeline was still sitting on the cabin's stoop. Keeler walked over to her.

He said, "How're you doing?"

She said, "What was that order of yours, two eggs over easy with a side of bacon? Hash browns well done, two slices of buttered rye toast?"

Keeler said, "Yeah, wouldn't that be nice. Too bad the diner is burnt toast."

Madeline said, "So, what happens now?"

Keeler said, "I have a contact with Homeland Security. They'll be here soon." He kicked at a stone in the grass. "What happens next is the federal government is going to come in here and clean it up. As soon as they fully understand what a FUGAZI situation you've got here, they'll be swarming like red ants. Believe me."

She said, "Should have happened long ago."

He shrugged. "Yeah, but it didn't."

"Right."

Madeline nodded, like she accepted how things were, as opposed to how they should be. She stood painfully, using the timber as a brace to help herself up. She shook out her hair and pulled it back into a loose bunch at the back.

"You know Keeler, you should let your sister and her husband alone for a while. Get out of their hair. Let them catch up. Since you've got medical training, I've got a more important task for you. Something infinitely more urgent."

Keeler said, "Yeah what's that?"

She showed him a wound on her hip. More of a raw scrape than an actual wound. Still, the denim there was torn away, and her pale skin was clearly visible around the reddened area.

She said, "My daughter's at my mom's. I'll need to go over there later and make it all good. Plus, your friends from Homeland Security are going to show up, which will definitely occupy your time and energy. I know you have to meet and greet them, but after that, I'd like you to come over to my place and perform first aid." Madeline stared straight into his eyes. "You have a responsibility."

Keeler felt a surge of something special.

He said, "I always take my responsibilities seriously."

"As you should."

And he did.

Chapter Sixty-One

It took more than three months before the last vestiges of the cartel known as *Los Quebrados* were cleaned out of town and county. If Trace Junction were a log of dead wood, and *Los Quebrados* were termites, you'd have a hard time telling the wood from the bugs. The problem wasn't just getting rid of the cartel members from out of town. It was the locals who took the money, made the moral compromise, shook hands with the devil.

It got messy.

The first thing that happened, following Arturo and Sergio's deaths, was that the pure cartel members simply disappeared. You don't survive even a week in that business without a sixth sense for detecting power distribution. Once the pendulum had swung, the termites started to depart for another log. And, the forest is full of dead logs.

A dime a dozen, as they say in Ohio.

When Amanda Sobell had a clear picture of what was going on, she got busy. Homeland Security is one serious organization. She called in three Special Response Teams to comb through the county alongside a brigade of HSI investigators, an entire wing of the IRS, and a bunch of other law enforcement officers to provide security. The entire structure of Trace Junction had to be uprooted, tossed, and replanted. In the end, an alphabet soup of federal agencies were required to sort through the catastrophe. By the sixth week of the operation, Muskingum County swarmed with feds.

The entire effort resembled a miniature Marshall plan. Which, for those who are too young to remember, is how the United States of America got Europe back on its feet again after the second world war.

Quite a few families had already moved out, and more followed as the corruption and rot were exposed. Not Laura and Josh—they stayed. Firstly, because they liked it. And second, because Laura flat-out refused to let circumstances like that dictate her behavior. That was one stubborn woman.

Plus, Laura said it was fun watching Josh struggle with DIY. At least that's what she told Keeler. They made a bet on how long it would take Josh to build a chicken coop in the backyard.

One cool autumn afternoon not long after the showdown at Beachy's farm, Madeline held Keeler in her arms. The sun was out, casting warm rays on their upturned faces. She wore a cashmere sweater, and he was more than comfortable. In fact, Keeler felt like a pig in clover, leaned back against this beautiful woman's warm and firm body beneath a willow tree down by the river.

Madeline was no longer a waitress. She'd already started imagining a whole new life for herself and her daughter. Waitressing had been a stopgap gig for a single mom. Now she was thinking about becoming a farm vet—what she'd dreamed of as a kid. She already had a college degree in biology. Vet school would be another four years.

Anyway, under that tree, Madeline's voice purred softly in Keeler's ear. Her breath warm and sweet. They were talking about people who collaborate with evil, and betrayal, and good stuff like that.

She said, "Do you think that the Nazis killed everyone who disagreed with them?"

Keeler said, "I guess so."

Madeline said, "Well, that's the weird thing Keeler. The truth is, that in most cases when people disagreed with them they just went and did their Nazi stuff elsewhere."

"You got a case in point?"

She said, "Bulgaria. The Germans wanted the Bulgarian government to hand over the Jews, just like they did everywhere else. But the Bulgarians said no." Madeline shifted underneath Keeler's weight.

He said, "Want me to move?"

"Not at all." She said, "The Bulgarians refused to cooperate, like refusing was just common sense. They did it politely."

Keeler said, "What happened?"

"Nothing. The Nazis backed off. Fifty thousand Bulgarian Jews didn't have to die, that's what happened. Similar thing in Denmark and Finland."

Keeler said, "So, what you're saying is that evil needs help. Or at least permission?"

"Yeah," Madeline said. "Or indifference. That's the scariest part. Most of the time, they didn't need people to be monsters like them. They just needed people to shrug."

Keeler shrugged. "Makes a lot of sense to me." She clipped him upside the head. She said, "You're not the staying kind are you." He said, "I guess not." Madeline said, "You need to give me fourteen days notice." Keeler said, "I can live with that." And the wind in the willows began to make a whooshing sound, as those long, graceful branches swayed softly in the river breeze. Winter was coming, and there wasn't any time to waste.

The End

Get a Free Tom Keeler Novella

I love communicating with readers, and **I send a free Tom Keeler novella to anyone who joins my monthly Newsletter.**

THERE IS NO OTHER WAY TO GET THIS NOVELLA!

Visit my website and sign up to receive your free copy of Switch Back.

https://jacklively.com/jacklively-books

See you there,

Jack Lively

Hello Friend,

I hope that you have enjoyed this book.

Please consider leaving a review on the book's Amazon page.

I love communicating with readers, and **I send a free Tom Keeler novella to anyone who joins my monthly Newsletter.**

Sign up at jacklively.com

See you there,

Jack Lively

Also by Jack Lively

The Tom Keeler novels can be read in any order.

Straight Shot

Breacher

Impact

Hard Candy

Badlands

Berserker

About the Author

Jack Lively is the author of the Tom Keeler series of thriller novels.

Jack has worked as a fisherman, an ice cream truck driver, underwater cinematographer, gas station attendant, and outboard engine repairman. The other thing about Jack is that since he grew up without a TV, before the internet, he was always reading. And later on, Jack started writing. All through those long years working odd jobs and traveling around, Jack wrote. He'd write in bars and cafes, on boats and trains and even on long haul bus trips.

Eventually Jack finished a book and figured he might as well see if anyone wanted to read it.

Tom Keeler is a veteran combat medic who served in a special tactics unit of United States Air Force. The series begins when Keeler receives his discharge from the military. Keeler just wants to roam free. But stuff happens, and Keeler's not the kind of guy who just walks away.

Jack Lively lives in London with his family.

Follow Jack on BookBub